Larry's Post-Rapture Pet-Sitting Service

ELLEN KING RICE

ALSO BY ELLEN KING RICE

The EvoAngel (2016)

Undergrowth (2018)

Lichenwald (2019)

ON LINE REVIEWS AND AWARDS

Praise for
The EvoAngel

"Compelling characters and plot with a little fungi thrown in! A FINALIST and highly recommended." The Wishing Shelf Book Awards

"Melding together of science and a great thriller . . ."

Praise for
Undergrowth

2019 IPPY Silver Medal Winner:
Best Regional Fiction

"Nothing says Pacific Northwest better than mushrooms, lush forests and gray, rainy days. . . Rice's multi-generational story combines a murder, mushroom research and disturbing backwoods encounters."

"A must-read for Olympia lovers."

"As compelling and hard to set aside as a box of chocolates."

Praise for
Lichenwald

A 2020 IPPY Gold Medal Winner:
Best Regional Fiction ebook

"The writing is clean, witty and engaging. It's a story of the complex layers of people, their predicaments and the botanical world."

Dedicated to the activists in the time of Covid.

"I didn't expect this."
The Book of Larry, All chapters, most verses.

CHAPTER ONE

MARJORIE DINKELMAN'S VOICE boomed like a
Puget Sound ferry on a foggy night. "Your phone's buzz-
ing. Can't you tell?"

Larry groaned. He'd put the cell phone on mute, but his
mother had a sense for action that could compete with any
intelligence service. It was easy to underestimate a three-
hundred-pound woman settled in an extra-large Lazy-Boy
recliner, but Larry's small outfit ran well because Marjorie
kept her keen senses tightly focused on Larry's business.

"Mom," Larry said, "If it's important, they'll leave
a message."

Marjorie scowled. She said, "Someone might be calling
about a dog."

"Nope. You know better. All the dogs are gone. The
dogs are all true believers in the goodness of man." He
shifted on the thin cushions of the sofa. The aches from
his recent cat-catching trips were not subsiding.

The phone kept vibrating.

"Might be a gerbil," Marjorie said. "I like gerbils."

"No gerbils on my list." Larry sniffed. "And we're not
taking rodents. Not unless we get a snake."

ELLEN KING RICE

"Might be a goldfish. We've got room for a goldfish."

Larry sighed. She'd keep this up until he answered the call. If he didn't take the call, his mother would spend the next week speculating on the opportunity he'd missed. He clicked the television remote. *The Treasure of the Sierra Madre* blinked off.

Ever since the Rapture had begun, the organizers of subscription programming had emphasized films in which greed begat disaster. This moralizing pleased authorities and soothed business owners. While most authoritative eyes were currently blind to minor pilfering from now-vacant homes, any looting from businesses would be disruptive and dangerous.

"I was watching that," Marjorie complained.

"It was too loud. Business comes first," Larry said. He tapped his phone icon, accepting the call. "Larry's Post-Rapture Pet Sitting Service. This is Larry."

"My neighbors are gone. Their cat is yowling," a man said.

"A yowler? Well, shit," Larry said.

"Larry!" Marjorie shouted from her recliner. "Watch your fucking tongue!"

"Just a minute." Larry covered the phone with his hand. "Christ, your mouth could strip paint. Why're you harassing me?"

"Sorry?" Marjorie grinned at him. "I just want my baby boy to be professional."

Larry snorted. Her "baby boy" was thirty-four years old with a receding hairline. A small mound of a belly protruded from the bottom of his vintage gaming T-shirt. He uncovered the phone and said, "Sir, where are you located?"

4

"We're out in Holiday Valley."

"Ah. Holiday Valley." Larry waggled his eyebrows at his mother. She sat up in the recliner and smiled.

"Yes, sir," Larry said. "We cover Holiday Valley." He reached for a notepad. "We've been very busy," Larry said, "but I can schedule you for a one p.m. pickup."

"Thank God."

"Yes, indeed. God is responsible," Larry said.

"Just come get the damn cat. He's been yowling for a couple of days. I think his owners got taken up on Monday."

"We're here to help. Anything I need to do to get access to the home?" Larry said.

"Like disarm an alarm system? Jesus. I don't know. It's a huge place on acreage, called the Lucky Seven Ranch. It's not a real ranch. It's just a big place, but this cat's voice carries. We live up the road, and we're hearing that cat all day long."

"Sounds like a Siamese," Larry spoke with assurance, knowing tone mattered more than accuracy.

"You're the expert. The yowling is upsetting my grandson. We're a gated community, so I'll have to let you onto the access road. I'll be down at the gate at one."

"Thank you." Larry tapped the phone off and spoke to his mother. "What do we want from the lovely Holiday Valley neighborhood?"

"The usual." Marjorie smiled. "Booze, jewelry, medications, steaks."

Larry laughed. "Even our scavenging lists are alphabetized."

Marjorie shrugged. "Who knew God had such a sense of humor?"

She had a point. No one anticipated a Rapture that would begin in Afghanistan and then jump to Albania. When Australians went up after the Albanians, the world took note. It was a completely alphabetical Rapture, conveniently in English, making Zambians both envied and pitied as tensions built.

"I hear Vanuatu should be next Tuesday," his mother said. "So Vatican City will be next Thursday."

"That'll be interesting." Larry leaned back into the sofa. "Kinda embarrassing to be a left-behind priest."

"Kinda poetic," his mother retorted, "if the boy buttfuckers all vanish in a poof of ashes."

It had been a bizarre few weeks. As people evaporated from the streets of Kabul and then Albania's capital of Tirana, it had taken some days to understand that the best-hearted people were lifted up in small tornados of whirling feathers. At the same time, mean-spirited and hurtful people exploded into flames, leaving behind small heaps of ashes.

It was surmised the devout winged their way to Heaven while the evil arrived in Hell as burnt offerings. The resulting piles of cinders on sidewalks kept crime to a minimum as a rash of kindnesses broke out worldwide. Even New Yorkers were saying, "After yous guys," at intersections.

There were constant rumors of further rounds of Rapture.

The "Left Behind" weren't stupid. They knew they weren't angels, and they were currently highly motivated not to be jerks. An uneasy global peace reigned.

As an ex-con, Larry's previously meager employment opportunities shifted, then faded and finally expired as the

Rapture moved from the A's through the alphabet to Laos and Latvia.

After Liechtenstein followed Libya, absolutely no one was hiring, although there was a slight thaw in the tightfistedness of some corporate boards. A handful of secretaries and janitors actually received raises.

Despite the worsening job markets, Larry felt sure his mother was no candidate for incineration. She was a good gal. He wasn't a butthole either. A loser, yeah, but not a butthole.

They needed income. With the future uncertain, what would people pay for?

Marjorie came up with the answer of "pets" after watching yet another television interview of a woman weeping over who might feed her parakeet should she depart in a funnel of feathers. "We offer a local registry," Marjorie had said. "We'll provide peace of mind for a price."

"So we arrange for the care of the animals?" Larry had said. "I mean, I can see where I would have to go get a few pets, but most of the time there's gonna be a brother or a sister or a neighbor around. Worse case, I'm a taxi service to the animal shelter."

"I think it could work." Marjorie had nodded, setting all three chins wobbling.

They'd spent a week building a website, with Marjorie doing most of the work. Larry had prowled the parking lots of Thurston County churches during services, tucking flyers under windshield wipers of the parked cars. He was convinced the devout had money to spend on pet insurance.

"I'm grateful for His alphabetizing," Larry had said

when he returned home from a morning of flyer distribution. "And for us being in the good old U. S. of A." He'd been able to express-order a magnetic door sign for his white panel van. The sign said *Larry's Post-Rapture Pet Sitting Service,* written in a classy font.

He'd loaded the van with two coolers, a collapsible hand truck and a large dog carrier.

He knew every dog on the planet had vanished just before Slovenia's Rapture day, some leaving behind a feather on a dog bed or next to a favorite chew toy. Larry had kept the dog carrier anyway. It held a cat well enough. He felt he could also transport twelve-packs of beer in it, although he hadn't yet had that opportunity.

Larry had plowed ahead, nudging local pet owners to register by offering a discount for anyone paying before Turkey followed Tunisia. By the time the Rapture took the first exhausted housewife from Tuvalu, Larry's post-Rapture pet-sitting service was taking clients and making money.

When the Rapture came to the United States, all his registrations were for cats, none of whom seemed to have the least love of God. There were no reports of a cat "Going Up" or "Igniting." He'd had no inquiries about caring for any other species.

Furthermore, many of the cats were too cranky or particular to be adored by family members. The cats registered with Larry came with instructions for pickup. Immediate pickup, some neighbors said.

The county animal shelter shut down the day after all the staff and most of the volunteers whirled up in spectacular tornados of feathers. Larry started bringing the cats on his list home.

Now Larry shifted on the sofa and grinned at his mother. "You're right. I needed to take that call."

Marjorie beamed a wide smile. "Holiday Valley. That's practically resort living out there." She frowned. "Are you going to bring another cat here? The sunporch is gettin' full."

Their sunporch wasn't too bad a place for a kitten to play. One kitten. The faded bungalow's screened porch spanned the south side of the house. Today it did gather a bit of the weak sunshine typical of spring in the Pacific Northwest. The porch could have been a survivable spot for a single feline, but it was no place for a clowder of cats. The narrow floorboards were warped and treacherous, the screens stained and blocked with rust and moss, and the entire porch now stank of cat piss and mold.

Larry said, "We've got fifteen cats on the sun porch. We can't take any more." He shifted his narrow butt, trying to find the remaining soft spot on the sofa. He laughed. "Maybe we should franchise. You know, have a branch location."

"Cathouses R Us?" Marjorie smiled. "That'd be different."

"Yep. Different is my middle name."

"No, it's not!" Marjorie laughed. "Go get the damn cat. We'll think of something."

"I'll do the fetching after a sandwich," Larry said. "I can't be having adventures on an empty stomach."

"When a person is down in the world, an ounce of help is better than a pound of preaching."
Edward G. Bulwer-Lytton (1803-1873)

CHAPTER TWO

LARRY SPEARED THE last dill pickle in the jar. He held the fat, dripping treasure over the open jar and watched as a last few drops of brine plopped away. He didn't want his tuna fish sandwich and corn chips to get soggy.

As soon as he scarfed his sandwich, chips, and pickle, he'd be on his way to Holiday Valley to collect one yowling cat and whatever treasures he could safely purloin from the now tenantless home.

He knew to be careful. There were outright vigilantes in the world. There might also be a neighborhood patrol. These were the worst in upscale neighborhoods. He hadn't told Marjorie much about the nervous and armed men he met when pet collecting. He didn't want his mother to fret.

But the geezers with guns were an issue. Too many of them were jumpy, sad men, left behind as long-suffering wives had evaporated in funnels of feathers. No doubt the ladies had earned some heavenly bliss, but the husbands too often were lost without their partners, and now were subsisting on microwaved dinners and too much grilled meat.

Larry had met roving patrols of men in bifocals and flannel shirts, jaws fiercely thrust forward as they insisted on questioning his *bona fides* while holding shotguns and deer rifles in poses that generally indicated their hunter safety courses were decades ago. Larry wasn't going to suggest refresher training. It didn't seem prudent.

After his first cat-collection call resulted in a hostile conversation with a patrol of grim retirees, he'd stopped at a local logo shop and convinced the store owner to part with several sample work shirts, each with an embroidered name. He'd sprung for one customized shirt that said, "Larry," but he was "Dave" or "Bob" on other occasions. The name wasn't important. Looking official was.

He'd learned to carry a clipboard and a few pages of a printout to show he had accepted an online payment of $240.00 and was authorized to check on or collect the pet in question. The vigilante grandpas didn't need to know that he'd set up his post-Rapture pet sitting website just three weeks ago.

It was, he admitted, a good thing so many engineers were atheists or cynical agnostics. So far, the water services and power grids stayed stable. Internet, cell phone service and television continued, a tribute to the lack of faith imbued in pragmatic capitalists.

Childcare was a problem. In every community, most pre-school and kindergarten teachers were the first to go, lifted up in a whirl of feathers. Bus drivers and janitors soon followed. Some of the kids went and many stayed behind, confusing everyone and generating much discussion.

Regulatory agencies had a high rate of staff loss, both

to feathers and to cinders, reflecting the protective and punitive personalities of government workers.

Switzerland's people-to-feathers ratio was better than most countries, a fact strongly reported in social media, while French authorities tried to suppress the astonishing flame-out rate of Parisian taxi drivers.

Larry's mother followed the news on the television from her oversized recliner. Larry heard her change the station from all-news to a PBS writer's workshop.

Marjorie must have hit the volume button on her remote control. Larry heard a woman's voice thundering out into the living room. "We want to establish the nature of our character with a descriptive word or two."

Larry shivered. Something about the voice raked him wrong. He stuck his head around the doorway, ready to demand a lower volume.

The speaker on the television looked just like Mrs. Carthaven, the teaching terror of Larry's third-grade year. Hell, it *was* Mrs. Carthaven. Older, fatter, grayer, but still a sanctimonious pain-in-the-butt know-it-all.

"We must remember, however," Mrs. Carthaven lectured, "never to describe people as food. A person is not 'chocolate' or 'coffee.'"

"Mom!" Larry yelled. "Turn it down!"

"I was learnin' somethin'," Marjorie said, but she did mute the sound. She said, "That lady looks like old whatzer-name. The bitch teacher you had."

"Yeah. It's her."

"Damn." Marjorie's eyes went soft and sad. "I'll watch somethin' else."

"Yeah, well she's in my head already." He looked at his mother. "She says up, and I gotta go down."

"Sorry, son."

"It's okay. We know about my brain. It's my insta-asshole response. I'll be thinking of food all the time now."

He looked at his mother. Marjorie's round face was the color and texture of pancake batter. She had a dicky heart which kept her pale most of the time. Her large arms puffed out of her floral muumuu like rising loaves of sourdough bread.

Larry swiveled to check out his reflection in the mirror over their non-functioning fireplace. Wispy carrot-salad hair over a cooked cannoli body.

He exhaled. He'd be alright. He had a few issues with authority. This was not news.

"At least she didn't say 'Don't rob a bank'," Marjorie said. "Then we'd be in real trouble."

Larry laughed.

"I'll watch some NASCAR," his mother offered.

Leaving her to it, Larry went back to the kitchen. He set the pickle down next to his sandwich. He bowed his head and said the prayer that had come to him when he first understood the world was changing.

"Lord, this is Larry. So far, so good. Let's keep it that way."

Prayer said, he was ready to eat.

"Come 'ere, Larry," Marjorie called from the living room. "Come quick!"

Larry left his sandwich. He moved through the arched doorway into the bungalow's small front living room. Marjorie had climbed out of her recliner. She was standing at the picture window, peeking out around their fried egg-white vinyl curtain.

"It's that black kid," Marjorie said.

Larry could see the back of a young man in jeans and a faded blue T-shirt, trudging up the sidewalk to a house across the street.

"Probably looking for work," he said.

"But he's a *black* kid, Larry."

Larry registered his mother's tone of voice. Marjorie wasn't scared *of* the kid. She was worried *for* the kid.

"He'll be okay," Larry said. He tried not to think about the armed grandpa vigilantes he'd met when collecting cats. They'd been white men. All of them. With no patience at all. Larry's stomach squeezed, tightening his abdomen with a quick stabbing pain. He tried to ignore it. He was hungry. That was it.

"Don't worry," he said to his mother. "He's not a scary-lookin' black kid. He's kinda cocoa-colored."

Marjorie scowled. "Larry!" she said.

Larry sighed again. He watched the kid across the street knock on the neighbor's door. The teenager was darker than a cream puff or cinnamon bun. Definitely darker than a bagel. He wasn't as dark as an éclair or a brownie. He was, Larry decided, about the shade of a nice rye bread that would go well with pastrami, mustard, and a side of coleslaw.

They watched as the neighbor's door opened for a moment. Pauline, the plump homeowner, made Larry think of a mound of sauerkraut. She shook her head at the teen and closed the door. The teenager's slumped shoulders fell another centimeter. The teen turned, presenting a young face taut with worry behind black-rimmed eyeglasses.

Marjorie looked up at Larry and said, "Did his Momma get taken up?"

Larry shrugged. "I don't know. Maybe. Isn't she, like, a social worker?" He knew the kid and his mother had moved into the faded blue bungalow at the end of the street sometime before Christmas. He remembered seeing a stout, dark woman in the front window of the blue house, stringing lights around an artificial tree. He couldn't recall where he'd heard about her line of work. Her car was gone a lot.

Marjorie was shaking her head. "Nope. Not social work. A pastor. She's a pastor. I'll bet she's gone, and that kid is on his own. I'll bet he's hungry too."

This time Larry groaned out loud. He knew his mother. Amongst her passions of romances, vintage movies, crochet, whiskey and profanity, there loomed three further passions of spectacularly mammoth proportions. His mother adored larceny, drama, and rescue operations.

He had to admit, when he'd started his post-Rapture pet-sitting service, he had shown he was an apple falling close to the tree, combining pilfering with pet care, both anchored by a showy sign on a van door.

He liked animals. They liked him back. He'd always been able to scratch some ears or stroke a furry head, with the occasional exception. One current exception happened to be a formidable tail-lashing gray tomcat who was on the sun porch, intimidating fourteen other cats when he wasn't intimidating Larry.

An imposing tomcat and his kitty cohorts apparently

weren't enough responsibility. Marjorie was going to rescue this kid. Larry could feel it.

Before Larry had a chance to open his mouth with a plea for deeper consideration, Marjorie pulled the front door open. She pushed against the screen door and bellowed with a voice that'd make a bosun proud.

"Hey, there!" she called. "We're about to have sandwiches. Care to join us for some lunch?"

The boy's head swiveled up, then over to focus on Marjorie, with all the hope and enthusiasm of a puppy scenting chickens.

"Damn," Larry muttered. "I'm gonna have to share that pickle."

"The wise adapt themselves,
as water molds to a pitcher."
Chinese Proverb

CHAPTER THREE

HE WAS FIFTEEN years old, and his name was Marcel Westmoreland. The eyeglasses held smudged lenses, but behind the smears and wipe marks, Marcel's eyes were the marvelous green of martini olives. Larry watched in amazement as the broad-chested kid inhaled a third sandwich.

Marjorie beamed a wide smile at Marcel and passed him the small plate holding pickle planks arrayed in an artistic fan. Larry had sliced the pickle thinly to make this offering, and now he was thinking he should be taken up to Heaven in a whirl of feathers for sharing that pickle.

Larry's selfless act wasn't registering with the Almighty however. The kid was helping himself to more pickle and talking around a mouth of tuna fish.

"I'm not surprised I'm left behind," Marcel said. "I saw the PBS Cosmos series when I was eleven. Come on, already. The universe is thirteen point seven nine billion years old, give or take twenty million years. Science is like a toilet bowl flush, you know."

Larry sat back in his chair and watched the pickle planks disappear. "A toilet bowl flush?"

"Absolutely." Marcel nodded his head vigorously as

he swallowed. "You take different models and observations. They don't all agree, but they start whirling around in everybody's minds until they coalesce around a center well of agreement. That's how you know you've figured things out. It all comes together. The predictions of the age of the universe based on measurements of background radiation are in agreement with the predictions based on temperature measurements of the coolest white dwarves."

Marjorie interrupted. "They measure the temperature of the coolest white dwarves? Like that guy on *Game of Thrones*?"

Larry snorted. "Marcel's talking about stars, Mom."

"So am I, smart ass," Marjorie said. "*Game of Thrones* actors were huge stars."

Marcel said, "We are mixing terms. A white dwarf is sometimes called a degenerate dwarf."

Marjorie nodded. "That show definitely had degenerates. My God."

"I am referring to stars in the sky, ma'am," Marcel said. "My mom agrees with you. She doesn't let me watch violent shows." He blinked rapidly. "I think my mom was taken up. Everybody from our congregation too. They are all such good people." He reached under his glasses to wipe an eye. "She went off to the church three days ago. She hasn't returned. I know she'd call or text if she could."

"I'm sorry, honey," Marjorie said. "What're you gonna do?"

Marcel shrugged. "Look for work, I guess."

Marjorie eyed him. "How's your sense of smell?"

"Ah, honestly, not so good. I've got allergies, and that makes me kinda congested."

Marjorie grinned. "Perfect! We've got fifteen cats in the sunroom. They're enjoying our personal pet care services. How would you like a job emptying kitty litter boxes?"

Marcel smiled. "I could do that. I took care of the litter box for a neighbor when she was expecting."

"Trained help!" Marjorie turned to Larry and winked. Larry tried not to groan. His mother had basically just hired the kid. Now it was going to be up to him to figure out how to make that work.

He looked at Marcel's stout build and thick neck. A kid like this could help him hump belongings out of houses. "Play football?" Larry asked.

Marcel shook his head. "My mom said no. She said brains can't be replaced."

"Smart lady," Larry said. "Look, I'm running a pet care business. We put up a website when this Rapture got going and folks signed up for me to check on their animals. Some people are gone, so I brought their cats here. I could use some help. I can't pay you much in dollars, but we can feed you."

"That'd be great. I'm not much of a cook." Marcel hunched his shoulders forward and admitted, "That's an understatement. I just microwave stuff, and I've eaten everything out of the freezer."

Food we've got," Larry said. "I have a run out to Holiday Valley to pick up a cat. I'll, ah, pick up other goods for, ah, the cat's survival. Would you be willing to help me catch the cat and load things?"

"Sure!" Marcel blessed the answer with a wide grin. "Thanks!"

Marjorie shot her son a look. "Larry, he'll need a uniform shirt."

"Yeah. Let me look." Larry stood and gathered two plates and the now empty sandwich tray. He carried these into the kitchen, stacking the dishes on the worn laminate counter- top next to the morning's breakfast dishes. The dishwasher had died some time ago and now, with all the cat-catching and goods collecting, life had been too busy for dishwashing. Marjorie's knees hurt all the time. She couldn't stand for long. She did her best, but it wasn't much.

Maybe Marcel knew how to wash dishes. Or he could learn. Larry liked that line of thinking, almost enough to forgive the kid's pickle-eating ways.

Larry stepped into the hall and rummaged in the hall closet, coming out with a tan uniform shirt on a hanger. The shirt had the name "Dave" embroidered over the left-breast pocket.

"I think this will fit you," he said, taking it to Marcel. "It matches my work shirt, so we'll look like a professional team."

"My name's not Dave."

"Listen, kid," Marjorie said. "It's more important that you don't get shot than we get your name right."

Larry looked at his mother, realizing she knew about the vigilante patrols. Well, duh. She watched television constantly. Larry transferred his gaze to Marcel and said, "She's right."

"So, this adds some verisimilitude to my employment," Marcel said, with a slow nod of his head.

"Versy – who?" Marjorie's eyes narrowed as she studied the teen.

Marcel's face flushed a shade darker. "It's a S-A-T word," he said. "I've been studying. It means to give an appearance of correctness."

Marjorie's face lit up with a smile. "Oh! Like 'truthiness' in political reporting." She reached over and patted Marcel's arm. "You're gonna fit right in. Larry's post-Rapture pet-sitting service is all about appearances." She winked again, this time so weirdly that Marcel blinked in confusion.

Marcel's eyebrows came together in a peak above his smudged glasses. "Are we doing something more than providing pet services?" he asked.

Larry draped the uniform shirt over the back of a dining room chair. He leaned in, putting his hands flat on the table. "We're doing two jobs. We're taking care of some cats, and we're surviving. We're not poofing off in a burst of flames and coal dust, but we are doing what it takes to keep going. When we go collect a cat, we'll see what we can find to help us along. Not breaking into storefronts or any shit like that. Just keepin' an open mind."

"We're not greedy," Marjorie said. "Me and Larry. We got . . . raven eyes. We pick stuff up."

"Raven eyes?" Marcel's forehead creased as he studied Marjorie.

"I'm good with animals," Larry said, "But that job doesn't pay enough."

"Come on, Marcel," Marjorie said. "Jobs haven't paid enough for years. Not to people like us. You think God doesn't know that?"

Marcel blinked and carefully said, "How is this not looting?"

"We're not breaking in," Larry said, omitting in his statement a few exceptions. "And we're taking things that we'll use. That's scavenging, not looting."

"Like cans of tuna fish," Marjorie said. "We're gettin' by, not flyin' high."

"Raven eyes would indicate you collect shiny treasures," Marcel said. "I understand the subtleties of the definitions between looting and scavenging, but I'm not sure my mother would agree with your assessments, even as I understand the needs."

Marcel looked at the shirt and said, "Perhaps it's a good thing I'll be going by Dave."

"Now this was the sin of your sister, Sodom. She and her daughters were arrogant, overfed and unconcerned. They did not help the poor and needy."
Ezekial 16:49

CHAPTER FOUR

THERE WAS A knock on the front door. Marjorie leaned back in her chair at the dining room table and said, "Our cousins, ya think?"

"I hope so," Larry said. "I'd rather you weren't here alone this afternoon." He navigated across the small living room. His mother was stockpiling food, skeins of yarn and whiskey, crowding the front room with boxes.

"Looks like a Costco threw up in here," Larry said.

He opened the front door and smiled at the two women on the front step. Cousin Ilene was an anorexic seventy-year-old dressed in green jeans and a matching pullover. *An asparagus stalk*, Larry thought. Her sister, Odelle, just sixty-two years old, was a woman as round as the O in her name, with a jutting abdomen and short hair dyed burgundy red. *Asparagus and a beet*, Larry amended.

"Did you hear about Congress?" Ilene said as they entered.

"They all poof into cinders?" Marjorie called. "Come on in. This here is our neighbor, Marcel. He'll want to hear too."

Odelle gave Larry a quick peck of a kiss and said, "I

don't know why Ilene thinks this is news. Congress is a swamp, no matter what happens."

Larry grinned. Odelle was smart. Ilene was predictable. He loved them both.

Ilene nodded at Marcel as she navigated the box maze to reach Marjorie and bestow a kiss. Ilene said, "Outta five hundred and thirty-five members of Congress, twenty-five went up in feathers and two hundred flamed out, leaving us with three hundred and ten pragmatists who voted themselves an emergency pay raise."

"Hallelujah," Larry said. "Normalcy prevails."

"Care for a sandwich?" Marjorie asked. "We can make more."

Ilene shook her head. "I don't eat sandwiches." She sat down at the table and reached for the last thin slice of pickle.

"You won't get far on that," Marjorie said. "Me, I'm eating to keep my strength up. I'm ready to hibernate for the upcoming nuclear winter."

"Me too," Odelle said. "But no sandwich for me. We've got real news too."

"From the professors?" Larry asked. He turned to Marcel and said, "Odelle's retired now, but she worked for an insurance actuary. She's got connections."

Odelle pulled out a chair and waved off the bowl of chips proffered by Marjorie.

"There are some new algorithms," she said. "They are coming out of Austria."

"Makes sense. They've been at this a few weeks now," Larry said. "They're on the front end of the process."

"It has to do with stockpiling," Odelle said. "Apparently having a sixty-day supply of something is protective, but having more than a ninety-day supply pushes up the flame-out rate. The early countries are having a second round of disappearances, both the super-nice people and the assholes. The mathematicians are thinking the second round is connected to folks' post-rapture behavior. People can be prudent, but they shouldn't be greedy. This will be on the news soon."

Larry whistled. "Man, does that mean everyone who packed their basements with canned goods is going to be out on the street unloading shit?"

Odelle shrugged. "I suspect a few oenophiles are going to be crying over their wine collections."

Marjorie sat back in her chair and threw a worried look at the living room. "What about craft supplies? What if we've got yarn for good causes? I was going to make afghans to share with homeless veterans."

Larry shook his head with a snort. "Mom, you've been saying that *for years*. When was the last time you finished an afghan?"

"Don't you be snotty with me!" Marjorie's triple-chin wobbled in outrage. "I made a wrap for Charlene's new baby, and I made pot-holders for the Christmas bazaar. Four of them."

"Yes, you did. I shouldn't be picking on you. They were pretty," Larry said, patting her shoulder. "But you have to admit this news is gonna change things." He threw a glance at the living room filled with boxes. "How much whiskey is a sixty-day supply?"

"God only knows," Ilene said, "And I'll bet He is gonna be hearing plenty of prayers of petition for exceptions."

Marjorie's hands flew to cover her mouth as her eyes widened. She dropped her hands and said, "Gun owners! What is a prudent collection of guns?"

"With an American mindset or a European one?" Odelle asked.

"How about nuclear weapons?" Marcel said. "How many is too many, according to God?"

"Sweet Jesus." Larry shook his head, then laughed. "Hell, maybe Sweet Jesus knows what he's doing here."

"People hoard because of anxieties," Marcel said. "My mom helps people all the time who have been traumatized. Their stuff is their protection. It's a safe way to love."

"Marcel's mother is a pastor," Marjorie said to her cousins.

"She's right," Ilene said. "I know a thing or two about trauma and grief. Look at me, a hundred pounds and half my teeth gone, but I'm still trying to be beautiful."

Odelle nodded. "We all have problems. We're about to learn the difference between needs and wants."

"Christ on a crutch," Larry said. "This is going to make people even more nervous."

"Christ has been on a crutch for a while now," his mother said.

"Anything on CNN?" asked Ilene.

Marjorie picked up the television remote and pointed it at the television. "Larry made me turn it off before we ate, so we may have missed something."

"No, we didn't," Larry countered. "They were warming up for an opinionating session. It's gonna be talking heads who don't know diddly squat."

"Shh," Marjorie said as she thumbed up the volume. "Let's listen."

A banner scrolled across the bottom of the screen, announcing a speech from the president to be broadcast later in the day. As the chyron finished, the handsome news anchor smiled with teeth as bright and white as a box of breath mints. He said, "We are fortunate to have with us three of America's top theologians with their views on the Tribulations. Gentlemen, thank you for being with us today during these challenging times."

The screenshot split into quadrants showing four male Caucasian heads, with the perfectly coiffed news anchor on the upper left. The theologian next to him was introduced and easily launched into a confident statement.

"Beyond a shadow of a doubt, we are in the Pre-Tribulation Rapture," the theologian said as his fingers stroked his bright blue tie. "Good Evangelical Christians are meeting The Lord in the air, and soon the second phase will begin. We are in for seven years of suffering, and then Christ, our Lord, will return with his Saints to save us all and lead us into a thousand years of glory."

"Shit," said Ilene. "More eschatology."

"What kinda cat?" Larry asked.

"es-chat means "the end" and 'ology' means 'the study of.' So, it's the study of the end of the world," Odelle said.

"Shh," Marjorie commanded. "Look, the next guy's gonna blow a gasket."

The second theologian's white hair matched his white clerical color. In between the two white zones was a face mottled poppy red. The priest barked, "That is total and utter malarkey, and you should be ashamed of saying such a thing. The book of Revelations is filled with symbolism, I grant you, but the Second Coming of Christ is not on some calendar devised by man."

"As a Catholic, Father Seamus," said the news anchor, "You don't believe in the thousand years reign of Jesus on our Earth? You are an A-millennial?"

"Indeed, I am, sir," confirmed the priest. "That dispensational premillennialism was a cock-eyed dream by a ne'er-do-well Englishman named John Nelson Darby who'd been kicked in the head by a horse. He called himself Anglo-Irish, but there's no such a thing. He put England ahead of Ireland, and his own self-promotion ahead of anything else. He came up with seven dispensations and used them to make seven speaking tours to the U.S. He was, I dare say, a twin to P.T. Barnum in creating circuses."

"I beg to differ!" shouted the blue-tie theologian.

"Gentleman!" The third theologian leaned forward, red bow-tie barely visible underneath his heavy jowls. "No doubt Tribulations are upon us. Clearly the Mid-Tribulation Theories are being proven daily and . . ."

Marjorie thumbed off the volume. "Larry, you're right. We haven't missed a thing."

"That part about the preacher getting kicked in the head by a horse was interesting," Larry said. "It explains a lot of religious theories. Maybe they've all been banged in the head."

"Any news on the Prosperity Gospel pastors?" Ilene asked.

Odelle snorted. "I suspect they all skidded their shorts and became burnt offerings."

Marcel didn't join in the laughter. Larry saw the kid swallow and look down at the table.

It dawned on Larry that he hadn't heard what kind of pastor Marcel's mom was.

"You okay?" he asked Marcel.

Marcel shrugged. "I don't know what good it does for those guys to talk. We're going to know if we just pay attention." He sighed. "Everybody wants rule sets that make sense. I think there will be, but we don't know them yet."

Larry didn't know what to say to that as his mother and her cousins further maligned the pontificating preachers. He did know it was time to leave for the one o'clock cat pick up.

"Come on, Marcel," he said. "Adventure calls."

"How many times shall I forgive my brother?
Up to seven times?"
Matthew 18:22

CHAPTER FIVE

MARCEL SAID, "THE Lucky Seven Ranch is point seven miles off the freeway." He studied the tiny map on his smart phone. "Seven's been a lucky number," he continued, "ever since the time of the Babylonians, which would be about three thousand, eight hundred years ago. The Babylonians created the seven-day week and named the days of the week after the celestial bodies they could see. Monday is really 'Moonday,' and Sunday, well, that's obvious."

Larry steered the van onto the freeway. Roads were now almost completely free of traffic as people were nervous about expending gasoline. He waved at the state trooper sitting in a parked sedan on the median. State troopers remained in abundance, with only a few reported taken up by funnels of feathers or disappearing into flames and ashes. Larry admired the pragmatic nature of the troopers who were intent on maintaining calm as a confusing new reality unfolded.

"What about Tuesday?" Larry said. "That's not a planet."

"Tuesday is associated with Mars," Marcel said easily.

"So, it's *Martes* in Spanish and *Mardi* in French, but northern Europeans connected Mars, the god of war with the Norse god, Twi, who is the God of Dueling."

"And Wednesday?"

"Another Norse substitution. Woden's Day, for Woden, God of wisdom and magic. The Romans decided Woden was the same as Mercury, because both Woden and Mercury guide souls after death." Marcel suddenly straightened in the van's passenger seat and cleared his throat. "My mom left on Wednesday."

"Buddy, I am so sorry," Larry said.

Marcel tried a shrug. "I know she's in Heaven, helping people. You know, people who need her more than me."

"That's bullshit," Larry replied. "We all need all the help we can get. Everybody needs a mom, a dad, a brother, a sister, a friend and a dog. We don't always get what we need, but, man, we need." He snorted. "I left out that we also need sex and a plate of tacos, but to be honest, I'm not making much progress on those fronts."

Marcel laughed.

"Seriously, kid," Larry said. "My Dad died of cancer when I was eight. Agent Orange exposure. He'd been kicked out of the Army for using some hashish when he was just nineteen, which is dumb because tons of guys did hashish in Vietnam. Twenty years later, there's my Dad, dying, no Veteran's benefits, and my mom's working three jobs, ruining her back and knees, and then this neighbor tells me this is all God's will. She said God needs my Dad more than I do."

Larry smoothly moved the van to the right, taking Highway 101 north. "That's such bullshit. It wasn't God that gave my Dad cancer. It was a chemical made by people. It wasn't God that kept my Mom in three part-time jobs with no benefits. Those deals were made by people. She finally got a job as a bookkeeper and that was good for a while, but when there were problems, people threw her away."

He glanced at Marcel. "Which is why you're gonna see I have a certain, well, flexibility, when it comes to rules. I haven't whirled up or flamed out, so God must be okay with me. I'm taking care of my Mom and a herd of cats. That's my life."

"What will you do with the cats?" Marcel asked.

"Keep 'em fed and watered and safe," Larry said instantly. "Find 'em homes, I hope. If things settle down, people are gonna want pets again." He laughed. "I keep digging my own grave. I like dogs. I signed up three hundred and two dogs on the registry and not a one of them is left in the county. All I find are god-damned cats. If I'd stopped to think about it, I shoulda seen that one coming. I shoulda charged twice as much for the cats."

"How many cats are on the registry?" Marcel twisted in his seat to look at Larry.

"Two hundred and fifty-three. My mom has been doing the phone calls to check on them. Most of the cat owners didn't whirl up or poof off. That says something about cat owners. More elastic morals there too, I suspect."

"But you've picked up fifteen so far?"

"Yep. They're the ones stinking up the sun porch at the back of my house. We're kinda beyond capacity. This cat we're going to pick up now wasn't on my registry, but the neighbor sounds worried, and, after three days now of

U.S.A. rapturing, that cat may be real hungry." He smiled. "But I gotta admit, it's nice this one is in Holiday Valley. I'll take things to sustain the pet, and in my mind that means things to sustain Larry and Marjorie and Marcel. Like, maybe, steaks from the freezer."

Marcel snorted. "Actually, your logic is impeccable."

"You let me do the talking. You're the muscle. Anybody complains, don't argue. Just point them to me."

"Got it," Marcel said. "I've been black all my life. It's better if you're the mouthpiece."

"Which," Larry said, "is a tragedy because I suspect you're about two hundred IQ points ahead of me."

"The IQ points only go to 200."

"I rest my case." Larry slowed the van for an S curve. "Look, I don't want to push you into anything that doesn't sit right with you. Are you okay with us liberating a few things to keep the Post-Rapture Pet-Sitting Service in dinners? 'Cause you could wait for me in the van. I'm thinking if 'plausible deniability' works for presidents, it ought to work for pet-sitters."

"I'm okay with surviving," Marcel said. "Taking things to stay alive is logical. It's historical too. Even Biblical."

"What, more Tribulations shit? That stuff makes my head hurt."

Marcel grinned. "More basic than that. The Babylonians stole the Epic of Gilgamesh from the Sumerians. Gilgamesh was a Sumerian king. After he croaks, five hundred years go by, and the Babylonians make him a swashbuckler in their stories to teach moral lessons. Gilgamesh has all these mega-adventures."

He took a breath and went on. "In one of them, Gilgamesh goes looking for Ut-napis-im, a guy who built a big boat and survived a giant flood. The boat was called the *Preserver of Life*. Five hundred years after that, the Yahwists take the story and change 'Napis' to 'Noah.' It's all taking stuff from the folks that were before."

"What's the moral of the flood guy?" Larry asked. "Learn to swim?"

Marcel snorted. "I think the moral on that one is perseverance." He opened the bin between the seats and said, "Got any snacks?"

"You just ate!"

"Sorry! Working makes me hungry. Can I have this?" Marcel held up a dented granola bar of indeterminate age.

"Sure." Larry shook his head. "I was worried about you, kid, but now I'm thinking you're gonna survive just fine." He flipped on the turn signal. "Eat fast. This is our exit."

"Beloved, do not believe every spirit."

1 John 4:1

CHAPTER SIX

"AND SO, I say unto you," the woman said, staring into the camera lens, "these days shall pass. We will be united with our Lord and Savior. We will be washed in blood, saved and in Heaven. Until that moment comes, we need your love. We need your support. And, yes, we need your contributions. We need dollars, and we need them now so that we can continue our outreach to our lost brothers and sisters."

The woman paused. She gracefully reached for the glass of water sitting on the right front corner of her lectern. She knew Clive would bring up the back lighting to give her blonde hair a halo effect. Her hair stylist had worked through half a dozen shades before they had settled on the 'cream-soda blonde' as the right combination of ash and gold to radiate best in the halo lighting.

The golden hair would pick up highlights off the close-fitting bodice of her crimson dress. The dress flared from her small waist into a wide bell of a skirt that dipped to the middle of her well-toned calves.

Sip of water done and glass replaced, the woman looked into the camera and said, "We're all exhausted.

We are all confused. We must do what we have always done. Give. Give to neighbors. Give to family. Give to friends. And give to this ministry. Help us stay on the air, broadcasting the Good News. Operators are standing by. Please give. We need your love, and we need it now."

She kept her eyes soft as the show ended. A decade previously she had made the mistake of returning her features to normal a few moments after her closing words. Her hard-eyed look had only been broadcast for a few seconds, but it impacted donations for weeks. Even now that miserable little clip could be found on YouTube and was regularly used by left-wing reporters to stir up thinking. She wouldn't make that mistake again.

Clive, normally her lighting engineer, was a camera operator today. He was a round-shouldered middle-aged man in baggy pants and suspenders worn over his Ross Hour of Prayer polo shirt. He looked unkept at the best of times, but he was a good-hearted and talented man. She was lucky to have Clive. She could trust Clive to keep the show polished and alive. He raised a hand with a thumbs up and she knew she could relax. She took off her earpiece, shook her hair and stretched her neck and shoulders.

"Nice show, Abigail." A lean young man with wavy brown hair came on stage with a bright smile.

"Thank you, Jared." She kept her eyes soft and smiled back at her personal assistant with a hint of hunger. "Can you bring the early reports to my dressing room in a little bit?"

"Be glad to." Jared turned and strode off the stage, knowing his boss had her eyes on his trim behind. Being called to the dressing room meant Abigail was ready for a little relaxation therapy.

The "therapy" he provided came with a weekly payday bonus. A large one.

Fifteen minutes later he walked down the narrow back stage hallway and stopped in front of the door labeled "Ms. Abigail Ross." Her given name had been Emily, but her husband's nose for donations had led him to do extensive name testing before launching their evangelical television program. "Abigail" performed better than "Emily" as a sympathetic, all-American and trustworthy name, evoking Abigail Adams, gracious wife of Founding Father John Adams. Further testing showed Abigail combined well with "Ross," the surname of flag-maker Betsy Ross, a figure loved by white nationalists.

And thus "Abigail Ross, Tele-evangelist" was conceived, and Emily Beekermann ceased to exist.

Jared tapped on the door.

"Enter."

Abigail sat in her make-up chair, creaming off the heavy foundation so necessary in broadcasting. She smiled as Jared entered the dressing room, his eyes meeting hers in the mirror.

Jared crossed the small space in two strides, setting down a large folder on the cluttered make-up table. "You look so tense," he said.

"I am."

"Let me help you." He stood behind her chair and placed his hands on her shoulders, bringing his thumbs to her neck. He began massaging, circling his thumbs down onto the back of her neck and using his palms and fingers on her shoulders.

She exhaled and leaned back.

Jared nibbled her ear as his hands dropped over her shoulders to caress her breasts. He licked her ear with his tongue as his hands began to circle and squeeze her nipples.

Abigail sighed.

Jared straightened up and said, "You need some release. You should lose your panties."

"What a good idea." Abigail's eyes met his in the mirror again, this time with joy. "First," she said, standing to slip off a pair of ivory silk tap pants. "Tell me how the pledges are doing."

"Fantastic. Phones are ringing like mad. On-line traffic is humming."

"No rumors about Aaron?"

Jared shook his head. "Everyone thinks he went up to Heaven."

"Oh, Jared. You and I are such sinners. Why didn't we flame out when Aaron did?"

Up close it was easy to see Abigail's crow's feet wrinkles and the start of gray roots. She'd need another touch up on the jawline before long. Jared tried not to think about finding a discrete plastic surgeon in the current world situation. Money would help. It always did.

He said, "Don't worry. You are doing good in the world, Abigail. You give people hope."

It was the right thing to say. He was rewarded by a grateful smile. Good. Abigail had been backing up her gratitude with generosity. He found it exhilarating to be in the shadows of luxurious excess. He might get one of Aaron's sports cars out of Abigail if he kept her sweet.

"We need to get out of Atlanta," Abigail said. "We need a rural retreat, and not in the Bible Belt."

"When do you want to go?"

"Soon," Abigail said. "But we don't have a pilot. He's gone."

"I can look into finding another pilot or reserving a jet through another company," Jared said. "But we'll need to know the distance and day to be flown. Are you thinking Colorado?"

"Too cold. Not Montana and not Wyoming."

"West coast?"

"Yes. West coast, but not California." Abigail shuddered. "Too many people in California. Oregon, I think. We could leave tomorrow. Will you find us some options?" Abigail patted Jared's hand. "Janice can help you. She's good at research. Use the Luxembourg account."

There was a tap on the door, and Abigail said, "Enter."

A woman in her late forties opened the door. In a stark contrast to Abigail's high-fashion dress and stilettos, this woman wore a rumpled linen camp shirt, comfortable polyester slacks and crepe-soled shoes. Her soft graying hair graced a sweet face.

"Janice, how can I help you?" Abigail said.

"Ruthie has called again."

"Oh, Lordy. What does my daughter want now?"

"She really wants to leave school. She says she can go home with a friend."

"Tell her, again, that she's safe. That's why we pay a fortune to have her be a boarding student."

"Apparently much of the staff have been . . ." Janice paused. "departing."

"Oh." Abigail frowned. "How inconvenient."

"Ruthie says a friend's family has a vacation home in Washington state. A place called Holiday Valley just west of Olympia. The father is on his way to collect his daughter and says Ruthie can come with them. Private jet."

Abigail threw a look at Jared. "Really. Washington state?" Abigail licked her lips. "Who is the father?"

"Barton Buckley. Construction company owner and producer of conservative documentaries. He lives in Orange County, California, but he keeps a summer home in Holiday Valley. It sounds lovely. Very green and tranquil."

Abigail nodded. "Excellent. Please tell Ruthie she can go with her friend. In fact, I may join Ruthie. She needs her mother at times like this."

Janice's eyebrows rose. She said, "Our pilot is . . ."

"No longer with us. Jared is going to research some options for me. We were just talking about the west coast and possible destinations for a spiritual retreat. I am feeling a calling to speak to our good people of faith in rural areas. It is an urgent calling."

"Oh." Janice put up a bright smile and said, "How exciting. Are you going to start in Alabama and work west?"

"No. With everything going on, it's best to start on the west coast where our Faithful are so lonely. I can be near Ruthie and have some days in prayer." Abigail turned to Jared and said, "Just as soon as we finish with today's reports, I hope you'll work with Janice to learn more about this Holiday Valley. Maybe we can find a retreat near to Ruthie."

Janice's face remained still, even as "near to Ruthie" registered as something very different than "with Ruthie."

Jared looked at Janice. "We could meet at, say three o'clock?"

"Very good. I'll be at my desk." Janice left, pulling the door shut. She waited a moment and then opened the door again.

She wasn't surprised to see Jared kneeling on the floor in front of Abigail. He stood up hastily.

"I dropped a paper clip," he said.

"Need any help?" Janice asked brightly.

"No. I'm sure I can find it."

"I just wanted to confirm that you have a one o'clock session with your trainer," Janice said.

"On the schedule," Abigail said. "Thanks so much."

Janice pulled the door shut and firmed her mouth into a grim line as she waited. Sure enough, the lock clicked.

She wasn't a fool. Not anymore. She'd noticed Abigail's knickers on the make-up counter and the bulge in Jared's trousers. She translated easily what Abigail had said. Abigail was about to leave town, surely with her passwords in hand to unlock her millions. She'd buy some rural enclave and set about surviving. She'd make some local putz her new spokesman and be on her way to a new Queendom.

Janice sniffed. The scales had fallen from her eyes when she'd seen Aaron "Ross" Beekermann burn up in a wall of flames. Abigail hadn't known Janice was there, mixing ice tea in the kitchen. Janice hadn't been alone. Her husband,

Clive, the lighting man and today's cameraman, had been with her.

Clive and Janice had spent twenty years in service to the Abigail Ross Hour of Prayer. Now they had spent three weeks in deep discussion about how to truly serve Christ. Among other things, Janice sent Abigail's four-hundred-dollar, hand-embroidered LaPerla lingerie to be hand-laundered each week, and right now that didn't seem like a very Christian thing to be doing.

Atlanta was growing increasingly restive and resistant to traditional evangelical leadership. It was a city of faith, but it was now also a city of sophistication and immense confusion. Preachers who had been left behind were talking fast, and congregants weren't happy with what they were hearing. The Rapture was Atlanta's only real topic of conversation, replacing even sports and the weather. Many were advocating for the end of televangelist calls for donation.

It made sense for Abigail to leave the rising swell of questions from viewers and skeptics.

But, Janice thought, Abigail counted on her staff for too much. She'd find it impossible to function without help. Jared had weaseled his way in and had been handling the visible details like setting up book signings, but Janice was part of the "Details" squad.

In twenty years of service, Janice hadn't just typed, filed and made phone calls. She'd taken care of Abigail and Aaron's personal details.

In addition to the laundry management, she had stood in line to get license plates renewed. She'd taken Abigail's shoes to be re-soled. She'd taken little Ruthie to the orthodontist dozens of times. She'd even taken the family Shih-Tzu to the groomer for brush outs and to the vet for anal gland expressions. She suspected she and Ruthie were the only ones who mourned the traffic death of the little dog, even as Abigail had made a public plea for prayers of compassion after the incident. Janice recalled that week as a donation blockbuster.

A million dollars went out the door the next week to Luxembourg. There were also accounts in Denmark, Ireland and Sweden. In the past three weeks, Janice had worked to know more about the offshore accounts, using her friendship with Merle in accounting who was nervously filling in after the head accountant had vanished, supposedly in a whirl of feathers.

Now Janice made a decision. When Abigail winged her way west, Janice and Clive would be on the plane as true advocates for Christ. Now was the time to get a bit of insurance to make sure they were invited along. Janice walked down the hall and keyed the number into the security lock on the back office.

"In the midst of chaos, there is also opportunity."
Sun Tzu (544 – 496 B.C.E.)

CHAPTER SEVEN

LARRY TOOK THE van up to the large metal gate barring the entrance to the Holiday Valley neighborhood. He could see through the slats of the gate to a long, green valley dotted with upscale homes.

A tall, lanky man and a small boy in a Seahawks T-shirt stepped around a towering stone gate post. The man had a buzz-cut of gray hair and brown sinewy arms that swung easily as he walked.

Beef jerky, Larry thought. *Tough as a boot.*

The blonde boy looked to be about eight years old, with just a touch of roundness to his face. His bony shoulders held a promise of attaining the angular look of the older man.

Slice of pear, Larry decided. *Pale, but healthy.*

As the two drew near, Larry rolled down the window of the van and called, "Hi. I'm Larry. We're here to pick up a cat."

The lanky man nodded. "Franklin McElroy," he said. "Call me Frank. This is my grandson, who is a Franklin too, but we call him Dobbin."

"Nice to meet you," Larry said. "This is my assistant, Dave." Marcel leaned forward and sketched a wave.

"Whattya gonna do with the cat?" Dobbin asked. His worried blue eyes darted about as he bounced up and down next to his grandfather.

"We'll see if we can just pick him up," Larry answered. "If he'll let me carry him, I'll put him in a pet crate and take him to my place. Then I'll see if I can find a home for him. Any chance you want a cat?"

Dobbin shook his head. "Nah." He rocked up on his toes. "Do you have any dogs that need a home?"

"Man," Larry said, "I would love to find a dog. So far, it's been all cats. Got one call on a big parrot, but before I got there, it shat on a sofa, bit a kid and then went up in cinders."

Frank snorted, then laid a big, comforting hand on Dobbin's shoulders. "Parrots can be rough characters," he explained. "They need to be respected and handled right."

Head nodding, Dobbin swallowed hard.

"Sorry, dude," Larry said. "I have a habit of making jokes and telling stories. You guys lose some family?"

"Yes." Frank's eyes went from cool lake blue to bleak chips of hard sapphire. "My wife, Dobbin's Granny, is gone. She's been ill for a long time, so that we don't mind so much. But Dobbin's parents went too." He sniffed. "My son-in-law went up in feathers first. I never did like the guy, so I've had to revise my thinking. I'm telling Dobbin that old dogs like me can learn new tricks. Maybe what's keeping us here is Dobbin's lack of experience in making choices and my stupidity."

Dobbin looked up at his grandfather with a smile. "We're gonna make good choices."

"Damn straight." Frank smiled with a deep, grooved dimple showing on the side of his face. He looked at Larry. "Which is why Dobbin and I called you to come get this howling cat instead of me fixing the problem with a .22 rifle."

"On the topic of firearms," Larry said, carefully. "Any armed patrols around?"

"Hell, no." Frank shook his head. "We had some so-called 'helpers' show up who wanted to patrol. I suspect one of them knew about the Babcock's wine collection. I told them this valley only needed one mean son-of-a-bitch on guard, and I fill that job position myself."

"Well, sir. I do believe you were persuasive," Larry said. Beside him, Marcel nodded, green eyes wide open.

"Only person we've seen lately is a blonde girl," Frank said. "Slender gal on a turquoise mountain bike."

Marcel leaned forward. "A teenager?"

Frank nodded. "Looks about your age."

With an exhalation, Marcel asked, "Did she say her name?"

"Nope. We haven't had a conversation. I just wave at her. Way things are, she's wise not to stop and talk to strangers. I'm thinking she lives out Oyster Bay road and is taking a trail through the woods. Probably like the rest of us, trying to figure out what the hell is happening."

"Anybody else we might run into?" Larry said.

"I don't think so. There're only seven homes in the valley. There's our place up on the left with the two houses side-by-side. Where you'll be going is at the end of the road there, the Babcock place. The sign over the entrance says "Lucky Seven."

"Some of the homes for sale?" Larry asked, pointing a finger at a pile of real estate signs resting in the grass at the edge of the road.

Frank frowned. "I took those down. I shoulda tossed them behind the gate. Neddles, the real estate guy, is supposed to send someone to pick them up. He said he doesn't expect much home buying right now."

He added, "There're three places for sale. I didn't want folks in town thinking there was, you know, a looting opportunity, out here."

"I'm surprised there's places for sale," Larry said. "Seems like this is prime real estate." His view through the van windshield showed a grassy green valley, rimmed with regal Douglas firs and towering hemlocks.

"It's right nice today." Frank's blue eyes sparkled now, and his deep dimple reappeared. "Late spring is usually nice. We get Californians up every summer who hafta have a northwest home in the woods. They spend one winter here and, about forty-five inches of rain later, they're putting their place back on the market."

Larry snorted. "Okay, then. So, three for sale, two homes that belong to you and Dobbin there, then the Babcock place with the cat. Sounds like there should be one more place. Should we be checking it for pets?"

"Nope. Big construction magnate outta California has what he calls his 'lodge' down there on the right." Frank turned and spat. "He's not exactly my cup of tea. Thinks he's a big deal. But he's not here, and I've never seen anyone at his place with an animal of any sort."

"Did the Babcocks have livestock?" Larry found himself putting up a prayer that the answer was "no." He wasn't sure his animal-charming ways extended to horses or cattle.

"I never have seen livestock there," Frank said. "The Babcocks were vegan. As far as I know, they only had the cat. We've got chickens at my place. In fact, I can give you a dozen eggs to take home."

"Thank you!" Larry smiled. His mother liked omelets.

"But, speaking of taking things home," Frank said. "Anything you're planning to take home today besides a cat?" His speech was careful in tone, but came with a no-nonsense delivery.

"Glad you brought that up," Larry said, easily. "I'm feeding my Momma and her two cousins, all ladies around seventy years old. There's me and Marcel here, whose Mom is gone."

Frank leaned in, frowning. "I thought you said his name is Dave."

Larry leaned back in the van seat as Frank's blue eyes turned to laser beams of subzero ice. Dobbin shifted from foot-to-foot, then tugged anxiously on his grandfather's hand, sending up a worried look.

Marcel started to speak, but Larry waved him off, saying, "I had a uniform shirt with the name 'Dave' on it. I want Marcel to look official. I don't want Marcel getting shot 'cuz he's not fish belly-white like me."

There was a moment as Frank processed Larry's statement. Suddenly, the dimple in the jerky-tough face was back. As Frank smiled, he said, "That makes good sense. I'm glad you are looking after your young associate."

"Which means I have to feed him," Larry said. "We'll corral the cat, then look for cat food. We'll also be looking for fresh produce, canned goods and medicines we can take to town." Larry didn't mention whiskey. There were some things that just didn't need to be discussed publicly. His mother's whiskey habit being one.

"The cat pickup fee hasn't been paid," Larry said. "But we don't want a cat to be miserable. We'll take the cat home with us. And we'll be looking in the refrigerator. What we take won't spoil or be wasted."

Frank looked down at Dobbin and said, "Sounds like Larry is being reasonable to me. What do you think?"

"I think we should let him get the cat," Dobbin said.

"Alright then," Frank said to his grandson. "You go open the gate, and we'll watch Larry and his cat-catching rodeo."

"Nothing ventured, nothing gained."
Chaucer (c1343 – 1400)

CHAPTER EIGHT

LARRY EASED THE van through the gate and said, "Tell me about the girl."

"What girl?" Marcel asked around the last bite of the granola bar.

"The girl on the turquoise mountain bike. Sounds like you know her."

Marcel swallowed and slumped back in the seat. "Ah, . . . it's just gossip."

"Great!" Larry steered the van down the road, taking the gentle curve at a modest speed. "Do tell!"

"Jeez!" Marcel shook his head. "It might not be true."

"Kid," Larry said, "In case you haven't noticed, reality really sucks. I could use a little fantasy involving a pretty girl. So, tell your Uncle Larry."

Marcel laughed. "Uncle? I think that means you're paying for college." He turned his startling green eyes Larry's way with a smile. "But since you're thinking you want a fantasy, I will tell you, just to keep you safe. I think the biker might be Annelise. She's a freshman with me at Capital High."

"Okay," Larry admitted. "A high school freshman is

way too young for me. I'm a lowlife, but not that kind of lowlife."

"Rumor has it she started riding a bike to school from out here because she was banned from the school bus."

"What'd she do to get booted off the bus?" Larry steered the van down the middle of the country road, happy with the complete absence of other traffic.

"That's the part, Uncle Larry, that I do think you should know." Marcel's eyes sparkled. "There's a junior, a big jerk named Willie Neddles, who already lost his driving license with a DUI. Willie was riding the bus, and he was bugging Annelise. You know, looks, words, hands. Rumor says she shanked him."

"Shanked him? Like with a knife?" Larry whistled.

"A nine-inch filleting knife, to be specific," Marcel said. "It was all hush-hush because Willie's dad is Mr. Money. When Frank said those House-For-Sale signs were from Neddles, I think that's Willie's dad. He's a realtor."

"Willie survived the shanking?"

"He did. This was just after winter break. He was back in school by early February. I was in class when someone asked Annelise about what happened. She said she couldn't talk about it." Marcel licked his lips and swallowed. "She said, 'I can only tell you I believe in efficiency in housecleaning,' and then she smiled."

"Damn. I think my nuts just shriveled to raisins."

"Yeah." Marcel grinned.

"The Willie guy," Larry asked. "Did he flame out?"

"I don't know. I haven't heard. It's a hard call, isn't it? When does a jerk become evil?"

"You should ask my cousin Odelle," Larry said. "She's

worked with actuaries. They make tables and charts of everything. Maybe there's a . . . whatdy'a call it? A decision tree."

"You mean like a Yes/No flowchart?" Marcel said. "I guess – or maybe Saint Peter has a bingo board, and you have to get enough markers."

"You fill up a row and, boom, you're upgrading from stupid shit to malignant menace?"

"Nice alliteration, Larry."

"Litter who?"

"Alliteration. You said, 'Stupid Shit.' Both words start with the same sound. There's a name for that."

"And knowing this helps us how?" Larry raised an eyebrow.

"I have not a clue," Marcel grinned. "But I do know that Saint Peter greeting people in heaven isn't in the Bible."

"Wait a minute. Yes, he is. He's got our names on a roster." Larry frowned. "He's at the, ah, pearly gates."

"The pearly gates are mentioned in the book of Revelation, but there's no Saint Peter. No roster either. That part was added in medieval times."

"Shit. Next you're going to tell me there's no Tooth Fairy."

"I actually don't know the history of the Tooth Fairy," Marcel said. "I'll look that up if we can get a wi-fi connection at this house."

"You do that," Larry said. "We gotta keep our priorities straight." He laughed and shook his head. It was nice having Marcel along. Talking Stupid Shit kept his brain from thinking too hard. Alliteration. A nice change of pace from thinking about vigilantes and his mother's anxieties.

Larry took his time driving down the road to the upscale pseudo-farmhouse. His eyes flicked to the rearview mirror where he could see Frank's long-legged form on an ATV, with Dobbin's arms wrapped around his grandfather's middle. Larry said, "Looks like Frank and Dobbin are keeping us company."

Marcel smiled. "I'm interested in seeing a cat-catching rodeo myself. Any tips?"

"Sure," Larry said. "For starters, we are professionals. We walk up to the door and knock or ring the doorbell. We wait. We do that again a couple more times. Then we find the key they have stashed."

"How do you know there's a key?" Marcel asked.

"Most of the time there is one. When I set up my website, I asked about where to find a key, and just about everybody told me their hidey-hole. Most of the time it's under a ceramic turtle or frog. Sometimes it's under a flower pot or the welcome mat. It's almost always within about twenty feet of the front door."

"Okay," Marcel said, "But that's people who contacted you on the behalf of their pet. This cat wasn't signed up, right?"

"True, but let's work it like a regular sign-up. I haven't had to break into a house so far. If we get to that, let me do the window-breaking. I think a judge might go easier on me than you."

"No doubt. Are there still judges?" Marcel pushed his eyeglasses up with a middle finger extended.

"Hell, I don't know." Larry shook his head. "There's

still state troopers on the highway. I'll bet judges are part of the in-between people. Not saints, but not evil. Just proud to a fault."

"I'll disagree," Marcel said. "I'll bet there's plenty of judges who have turned into a humongous pile of soot."

"Humongous being a S-A-T word?" Larry asked as he slowed the van for the turn under a custom-cut arch that proclaimed "Lucky Seven Ranch" in twining wrought iron calligraphy.

"Nope. For that we'd go to cyclopean, colossal or gargantuan," Marcel said. "Or, if we wanted to embrace lyrical euphony, we could say, 'monstrous, mountainous, and monumental which also happens to be another example of alliteration.'"

"Right. What would you call this house?" Larry brought the van to a stop under a large portico in front of the home's towering double doors.

"Expensive." Marcel grinned.

*"Handsome cats and fat dung heaps
are the sign of a good farmer."*
French Proverb

CHAPTER NINE

THEY HEARD THE cat. Even before Larry turned off the vehicle, they heard a loud, insistent yowling that pierced through the van's closed windows.

"G. Rover Cripes," Larry said. "She sounds like she's got her tail in a wringer."

"How do you know it's a she?" Marcel unbuckled his seat belt and opened the passenger door of the van. The yowling sound intensified.

"I think it's a female because she's expressing her opinion with a focused clarity unobtainable by the male mind." He grinned at Marcel. Larry felt it was a pretty upscale answer even if it lacked a S-A-T word.

Marcel waited as Larry walked up the wide steps to the double front doors, each worked with intricate carvings of vines, leaves and flowers. A four-foot bell gong stood in a metal stand to the right. Larry looked around for a doorbell button. Finding none, he shrugged and unclipped the padded drumstick from the gong stand. He struck the gong just as Frank and Dobbin arrived on the ATV.

As the gong reverberated with a deep 'bong', the cat

inside went into overdrive, frantically howling in warbling crescendos.

"Well, sufferin' cats," Frank quipped.

"Are you swearing, Grandpa?" Dobbin asked.

"Huh?" Frank pointed at his ears. He grinned. "Can't hear you!"

Larry motioned to Marcel, pointing at a flowerpot. Marcel moved forward and rocked up the pot. He shook his head. "Nothing,' he shouted.

They rolled up the welcome mat and peered under the bushes flanking the steps. No key. Marcel stuck his fingers in his ears and walked down the steps, looking left and right. He shook his head. No key.

Larry found his head aching as the cat's tempo increased. Dobbin was standing next to his grandfather, hands over his ears and small face scrunched with worry. Seeing Dobbin standing there, innocent and caring, gave Larry an idea. Innocent and kind people didn't always lock doors.

"We haven't tried the obvious," he shouted at Marcel.

Marcel lifted his shoulders in question.

Larry went to the front door and turned the left door knob. It sat, solidly locked. He tried the right knob, which turned smoothly. He pushed the door inward, and a tan streak of a cat bolted out.

"Catch her!" Larry cried.

Marcel dove for the streak and came up with ten pounds of struggle. He pulled the cat into his body and cooed as he held the cat's head with a cupped hand and used a thumb to massage under the cat's chin. The cat struggled for a moment, then went limp. The yowling gave way to a thundering purr.

"Good job, kid!" Larry said. "Outstanding."

"I'm impressed," Frank agreed.

Marcel kept stroking the cat as he used a pinky finger to elevate the tag dangling from a bright pink collar. "It says her name is Bella."

"A girl. Told ya." Larry jerked his head toward the open door. "Let's check out her place."

"Larry?"

"What?"

"What's wrong with her eyes?" Marcel was scratching Bella under the chin. The cat's eyes drooped closed as she purred.

Dobbin and Frank moved close as Larry and Marcel converged. Bella opened her eyes to reveal two bright blue orbs. She stared up at the faces crowded around her.

Frank laughed. "She's cross-eyed."

"Does it hurt?" Dobbin asked.

"Nah. It's just the way she is," Frank said.

"It's seriously weird," Marcel objected. "How could this be normal?"

"I think that's how some cats are," Frank said.

"Let's take her inside," Larry said. "We'll close the door, and you can set her down. We'll see if she moves alright."

The interior of the home matched the grandeur of the outside. A wide, wooden planked foyer led to a gracious, high-ceiling living room with sofas and chairs clustered for intimate conversations. A vast wrap-around row of windows looked out on a territorial view of grass and conifers, with the distant white top of Mount Rainier taking a prime spot in the middle window.

A small mound of white feathers sat on an armchair. A second feather mound, this one pale gray, lay curled on a sofa.

Dobbin walked over to the armchair. His eyes blinked rapidly. His grandfather followed him, reaching for the boy's hand. They stood together, silently looking down at the feathers.

Larry and Marcel, still holding the cat, joined Frank and Dobbin. The quartet stood in silence, all keenly aware of what the feathers represented. Bella's owners had been good people.

"Tell me again who lived here?" Larry asked.

"The Babcocks," Frank answered. "He was a retired engineer. He designed a super-efficient water pump. He built wells in Arizona and then had a nonprofit in South Sudan. Helped a lot of people. His wife did art therapy with autistic kids. Really nice folks."

Frank pointed to a glass door to the left of the living room. "They had some bucks. That's a temperature-controlled wine room. I recognize the door style. That's double-glazed glass, exterior quality, with weather-stripping, with walnut trim."

Dobbin skipped across the living room to look into the wine room. Larry and Marcel followed, with Marcel still holding the cat.

"Whoa," Larry said. "Look at that."

Floor to ceiling racks of wine gleamed under cool lighting. The slate floor complimented the walnut trim, making the space both luxurious and rustic.

Bella gave a small meow and rubbed her head against Marcel's chest.

Larry stepped back from the wine room entrance. He looked around the living room. "There's no food or water out here for Bella. Let's check out the kitchen."

Bella began a low yowl as Larry pushed back an elegant sliding door, admitting the group to a massive kitchen. The cat pushed off of Marcel's arms and jumped lightly to the granite countertop containing a sink. She meowed plaintively and swatted the elegantly arched faucet spout.

Larry turned the tap. Bella leaned in to lap eagerly from the water stream. "She's thirsty, but she seems to be moving alright," Larry said.

"Man, what a kitchen." Marcel's head swiveled left and right, taking in the walnut cabinets with beveled glass fronts and the rest of the enormous granite island set under a chef's rack of copper-bottomed pots. "My mom would go nuts in here."

"Mine too," Larry said, "Would you look at that?"

The kitchen expanse ended in a bartending nook facing a cozy pub space with a picture window. There were ten-foot shelves crowded with bottles of hard liquor that could have graced a deluxe spirit shop. Larry turned to Frank and asked, "Did you know all this booze was here?"

"Nope. I haven't been inside before. My wife came down for a fundraiser one evening. She said it was all done up nice. Dobbin, you've been in here before, right?"

Dobbin nodded. "I sold Mrs. Babcock three canisters of Scout popcorn and two pair of band socks. She said she'd buy wrapping paper from me when I get to middle school."

"Christ, no wonder she went to Heaven," Larry muttered.

Marcel picked up Bella and walked down the long kitchen to a side-door with a large window. A wooden slat below the window proclaimed "Bella's Garden" in violet laden hand-stenciled letters. There was a cat door with a flap at the base of the door. Marcel looked through the window. "What's this?"

"That," Dobbin said, "Is the catio."

*"And straightway he constrained his
disciples to enter the boat,
and go before him to unto the other side."*
Gospel of Mark 6:45

CHAPTER TEN

"JANICE, I DON'T know." Clive shook his head. "Abigail has been so good to us." He pitched his voice low so not to be overheard by the waitress.

They were at their favorite diner on Ponce De Leon Avenue in northeast Atlanta. Despite three cooks and half the wait staff being taken up the first day of the American Rapture, the diner was still open and thriving, serving coffee, grits and pie twenty-four hours a day.

It was a good place for a quick break after the morning rush of making the daily show with Abigail.

Now Clive pushed his fork into a slice of peach pie and left it there. He wasn't hungry.

"We've been over this." Janice closed her eyes and inhaled a calming breath. She exhaled and looked at her husband. "The Devil works when and where he can. It may not be Abigail's fault. She may be beguiled by the Devil. We know what happened to Aaron. He went up in flames. We were there, and we heard it, saw it, smelled it."

Clive swallowed hard and miserably nodded. In a dull voice he said, "And we know she vacuumed up his ashes."

"And I am here to tell you that she is consoling herself with Jared."

"What do you mean, 'consoling'?"

Janice arched an eyebrow and said, "Biblically. Like David consoled Bathsheba."

"Oh, my." Clive slumped back in the dinette seat.

Janice said, "I'm supposed to meet with Jared at three to see about lining up a place for Abigail out west."

"She's leaving Atlanta?"

"Yes. And I think Jared will go with her."

"What about all the staff?" Clive held up a finger to ask for a pause in Janice's reply as the waitress came by with a coffee pot and refilled their cups.

"Thank you," Clive said to the woman, who looked exhausted.

The waitress smiled wearily and moved on.

Janice's heart squeezed. Her husband was such a good man. He thought of others constantly.

Clive slurped on the steaming coffee and repeated his question. "What happens to the Ross Hour of Prayer team?"

"I don't think Abigail is thinking about any of us," Janice said. "And that's one of the things I wanted to tell you. I went into bookkeeping and told Merle to pay everyone six months' worth of salary and to add three months of vacation pay. I also had Merle pay everybody's health insurance for nine months. I authorized money from the Bahamas account for her to do that. I'm a trustee on that one."

"And Merle did it?"

"Her fingers started flying on the keyboard the second

I started talking. You know, we were told that the head of accounting went to meet Jesus, but I'm wondering if he incinerated. The bookkeepers seem so much happier right now." Janice took a bite of peach pie and said, "I just took a breath and told Merle she should pay everyone and she did."

"Abigail doesn't know?" Clive gulped his coffee and gasped at its temperature. "Whew. Hot."

"Abigail will know when people start thanking her," Janice said. "Which ought to be in about half an hour when she gets back from her workout."

"Oh, Janice, what have you done?"

"I've taken care of people who have worked to take care of Abigail," Janice said. "I'm not worried, honey. Everyone will be all smiles, and Abigail likes smiles. There millions of dollars more. It's not such a big deal. Not to her."

Clive shook his head. "It doesn't matter if it's just one dollar, and there's a billion more. You were authorizing the payout with generosity in your heart, but it's not your money."

"Actually, that's my point. It's not Abigail's personal slush fund either. That money was given to support the Ross Hour of Prayer. Well, now some of it – a small piece of it – is out there supporting the Ross workers during the upcoming months of transition." Janice took a sip of her coffee and said, "It's done. If Abigail fires me, then . . ." She stopped. She wasn't sure what she'd do if Abigail actually said to leave.

Clive patted her hand. "It's hard. We've given twenty years of our life to Abigail and Aaron. This Rapture is confusing. It's hard to know what to think."

"We've given twenty years of our life in service to Christ," Janice corrected. She said, "Abigail was our path, and we let her become our lodestar." She sniffed. "My own pride is a sin. I was so excited for her as she moved up. I remember when she started buying perfume from Paris. She threw out her cologne bottles and put out the real deal."

Clive smiled. "Remember when they bought that car? The Rolls?"

"That was a mistake. When she put Aaron in uniform as a chauffeur, he looked so silly."

"They didn't make many mistakes," Clive said.

"No. There's almost two billion dollars in the off shore accounts."

Clive stared at her. "That much? My God!"

"My God is right!" Janice set down her coffee cup with a thump. "It is God's money. Given by God's people."

"I heard Aaron talking about their next campaign," Janice said. "I should have told you then, but, well, I thought it wasn't my business. He was telling Abigail how they could make their last one hundred fifty million and retire with a full two billion dollars in the bank."

Clive stared at her. "Wow."

"Wow is right. They were going to put out a call for donations for septic services."

"Septic services? Praying on the toilet?"

"No!" Janice smiled at her husband. It felt good to smile. There hadn't been anything to smile about for days. "They'd ask for money to install toilets and septic systems in central America and Africa. Aaron had it all worked out. They'd take in two hundred million. They'd spend fifty million on engineers and supplies. Then they'd charge American teens two grand apiece to have an overseas mission trip. The kids would dig a lot of privy holes and ditches, the engineers would put in a few real septic tanks, and Aaron and Abigail would bank a great deal of money."

"When did you hear this?"

Janice blushed. "I was in Abigail's walk-in closet, sewing a button on. I heard them in the bedroom when they came in to freshen up. I think Abigail forgot I was back there."

"Oh, Janice." Clive swallowed hard. "Do you think we should call the authorities?"

"And tell them what? That a televangelist makes a great deal of money? Abigail has top rate fund managers. It'd take a sharp financial forensics team to untangle all the investment layers. And people are kinda busy right now." Janice pointed at a gap in the wall between the restaurant dining area and kitchen which gave a glimpse of a television in the kitchen. The sound was low, but clearly the cooks were keeping up with news and discussion about the Rapture.

"What do we do?" Clive said. "You can't tell bookkeeping to return everyone's money."

"I think you should go home and pack a suitcase. As soon as I can, I'll be there to do the same. If I can't get away, I'll text you the things I want," Janice said. "Abigail's planning to move west and I think we need to be ready to walk onto a plane with her at any minute."

Janet inhaled, then sighed. "She won't call it a vacation. The viewers wouldn't tolerate a vacation right now.

She'll call it a prayer retreat. My guess is that she'll take Jared with her. We have to go with them."

"What about Ruthie?" Clive felt for Abigail's daughter who often faded into the background behind the bright luminescence of her parents. Ruthie was a quiet girl, a dishwater blonde, with a receding chin.

Janice said, "Ruthie is going to Washington State with a school chum, to a place called Holiday Valley. I'm supposed to meet Jared at three to scout for a nearby venue for Abigail."

"Nearby?"

Janice tucked in her chin and gave Clive a direct look. "Do you see Abigail spending time actually living with Ruthie? Given how Ruthie looks?"

Ruthie had entered puberty carrying some extra pounds. Now sixteen, she'd gained an additional twenty pounds at boarding school and recently had acquired a severe case of treatment-resistant acne.

"That poor child," Clive said.

Janice agreed. "But if you and I are with Abigail, then we can look out for Ruthie. Maybe we can find a way to do some good."

"Change Abigail's focus. Engage her heart?" Clive's voice lifted with hope.

"That's not going to be easy," Janice said. "She's so used to luxury now. She thinks her mink mattress topper is a life essential."

"Mink!"

Janice dipped her head in weary acknowledgement. Now that she was speaking about Abigail's private ways, she was finding there were details that had been bothering her for a very long time.

Clive reached across the dinette table and took his wife's hand. "Is there any chance you are wrong about Abigail? Could there be something we're missing?"

"I think we've been missing what has been right in front of us," Janice said. "We so wanted a clear path to salvation that we closed our eyes."

Clive's round face drooped with exhaustion and misery. "I want you to be wrong."

"I'm sure you'd be happier if it turns out your wife is having airy-fairy delusions," Janice snapped. "Instead of believing that Abigail has been acquiring some ugly habits which have grown into fraud."

"That's not it," Clive protested. "It's my own short-comings I have to face. If you're right, then I'm someone who hasn't been brave enough to open my eyes. I could have seen, and I didn't. Was I afraid to make waves?"

"Maybe, but we know One who had the courage to walk on water during stormy times," Janice said, her eyes blazing. She said, "We need to go with Abigail. To save her, to save Ruthie, maybe even to save that handsome toady, Jared."

"What if Abigail doesn't want to change the path she's on?" Clive exhaled and shook his head. "Or what if we're wrong, and she really is channeling God's will?"

"It will become clear in time. Feathers, flames. An angel with a sword. Something will happen to make things clear." Janice squeezed Clive's hand. "Let's have a moment of prayer and make a plan."

"Wisdom begins in wonder."
Socrates (470 - 399 B.C.E.)

CHAPTER ELEVEN

THE CATIO WAS a deluxe screened-in porch spanning the length of the house. Towering potted plants crowded the perimeter. Smaller pots of ferns nestled between sherbet-colored chaise lounges, giving the space the feel of the tropics. Marcel opened the door to the catio and Bella trotted in. She ran along the river pebble walkway, her slender form moving smoothly as her tail floated upright like a small, dark flagpole.

"Damn." Larry walked through the door and gazed down the long porch. "Must be, what, fifty feet long?"

"More like sixty-five," Frank said. His dimple showed as he added, "I was a contractor for many years." He turned to his grandson and said, "Have you been in here before?"

"Yep," Dobbin said. "I didn't see Bella then. Mrs. Babcock said that Bella feels shy sometimes. Look, there's a skywalk for cats."

The boy pointed to 2 X 6 planks installed.close to the ceiling, paralleling the long aspect of the room. Four carpeted cat-climbing towers with resting ledges were spaced along the windows, giving a cat ample opportunity to access the skywalk or to lurk above human visitors.

"It smells . . . great," Larry said. He turned to Frank and said, "I live in an old house with a twenty-foot sun porch on one side. We've got fifteen cats out there, and it's gettin' as rank as a whorehouse on a Sunday."

"What's a whorehouse?" Dobbin stopped his skipping down the walkway and looked up at his grandfather.

"Larry is referring to a greenhouse that grows hore-hound, a member of the mint family," Frank said. His blue eyes were back to icy as he drilled a sour look at Larry.

"I like the smell of mint," Dobbin said. "You don't?"

"Mint is great. My place stinks of cat pee," Larry said. "To be honest, kid, when people started disappearing in Australia, I thought I'd make some money offering post-Rapture pet-care services. It was supposed to be an insurance policy."

"Insurance?" Dobbin looked at him.

Frank said, "You buy insurance to be ready for something bad happening. I've got an insurance policy on the truck. I pay some money to an insurance company every month. If I'm in an accident, then the insurance company helps me get a replacement truck. The company hopes everyone is a good driver, and they take in more money than they have to pay out."

Frank lifted an eyebrow and said, "Some insurance isn't really insurance. It can be a scam if it's not a regulated product."

Larry grinned and nodded his head. "Yep."

He spoke to Dobbin. "I didn't really think it through. I kinda screwed up, which is what I do. I thought Americans would sign up, but not really disappear. I mean, hell, we're the good guys who figure stuff out. I was wrong on that, and my Mom said I had to go get the cats whose owners left. If they stink up our place, well, that's my problem."

Dobbin laughed. "My mom would do the same thing." He fell silent, and looked away.

"Maybe there's some mint out in the garden," Frank said. "We could send Larry home with some fresh mint for his sunporch."

"You said you have fifteen cats," Dobbin said. "Do you have fifteen litter boxes?"

"Ah. No. There's three out."

"Mrs. Babcock said every cat needs their own litterbox. She was thinking about getting a kitten friend for Bella, and she said she'd have to get another litter box."

"They can't share?" Larry stopped in the middle of the pebbled walkway. "I mean, hey, it's a toilet."

"Mrs. Babcock said if they don't have their own litter box, they can start peeing on furniture and walls," Dobbin said.

Larry thought of the big gray tom he'd seen squirting a stream of pee onto the wall of his sun porch. "Yeah," he said. "We've seen that happening."

Marcel stopped in front of a low wall figurine connected to a bubbling water spout and a tray of water. "This is a depiction of the goddess Ishtar. See the eight-pointed star?"

"I'm seeing a hell of a lot more than that," Larry said. In addition to the star, the painted raised plaster showed a buxom woman seductively covered in transparent veils with a few tiny shadows preventing a view of full-frontal nudity.

"She looks cold," Dobbin said. "With her feet in the water. She must feel cold."

"Art interpretation is funny," Larry said. "She looks hot to me."

Bella, the cat, prowled to the edge of the fountain's water rim and lapped up more water.

Larry turned to Marcel and asked, "Ishtar is the goddess of what?"

"Lots of things," Marcel said. "She's based on the Sumerian goddess Inanna, and like her, she's connected to the planet Venus. Let's see. Goddess of the alehouse and fertility. Justice. Contradictions. She's featured in death metal songs as a dominatrix archetype," Marcel said, pushing his glasses up as he spoke.

"Enough of that," Frank growled. "Let's focus here. Forget the goddess. How many more cats are you planning to pick up?"

"I don't know." Larry sighed, his eyes lingering on the portrayal of Ishtar's lush body. He said, "My mom's been calling folks who registered with us to figure out who might be gone. One of mom's cousins, Odelle, says there's new developments. There might be more departures. People who have stockpiled a ton of food and other stuff seem to be flaming out. The sin of greed, I'm guessing."

"So, you might have more business?" Frank said.

"I'm afraid so. We're in early days of disappearances around here. One of the things that worries me is the left-behind cats like Bella who are stuck without access to food or water."

"Soo-Min could do a story," Dobbin offered. "She's a television reporter."

"My niece," Frank said. "She's with Channel Seven. She's working the Capital beat and has been interviewing legislators."

"If you wanted to help the pets, she should be interviewing Larry," Marcel said.

"Hey, hold on," Larry said, "We're not doing a very good job with the cats we've got." He looked at Marcel. "Remember, we're figuring this out as we go. We gotta take care of ourselves too."

"You might find a dog," Dobbin said. "Maybe a puppy!"

"Keep dreaming, kid," Larry said. "I'd love to find a dog. For that I would talk to a reporter." They reached the end of the catio where a narrow door led to the back yard. Larry picked up Bella and stroked her head. "We'll go take a look while you stay here," he said to the cat. "It's a wild world out there."

"No kiddin'," Frank said. "We've got hawks, eagles, owls and coyotes."

Larry held Bella as the others filed through the door, then he gently tossed her toward the catio interior. "Be back in a bit," he said, and eased the door shut.

"Would you look at that!" Frank said. "What a set up!"

A long metal barn sat to their left. The back end of the barn snuggled against an earthen rise populated by conifers and undergrowth. The angle of the berm ran parallel to the road, which obscured the building from passersby. To the right of the barn, a fenced garden stretched back as far as a football field, half in raised beds and the far section in fruit trees.

There were no weeds. There was, however, abundant

evidence of money spent lavishly. Pristine brackets held heavy coils of clean hoses. A tailored watering system linked the raised beds with options, all with gleaming hardware. Ankle-deep cedar mulch lined the walkways.

Frank whistled. "I didn't know this was back here." He pointed to feathery growths in a nearby bed. "That's asparagus."

"Wow," Marcel said. "It's like the garden of Eden."

"Which," Larry said, "did not end well."

A near neighbor is better than a distant cousin.
Italian Proverb

CHAPTER TWELVE

THEY WALKED DOWN to the fenced enclosure with Dobbin skipping ahead and Marcel looking about in wonder as the size of the garden registered.

Frank said, "Looks like beans, squash, and leeks." He pointed a finger at a free-standing greenhouse next to the garden gate. A large solar panel stood outside the building. "Look at that. I'll bet they have tomato starts going."

He was right. Wide tables held plants in gallon pots and seedlings in small divided trays. The tables ran the length of the glass house. The greenhouse was warm. A gentle fan rattled the air, giving the space a feel of freshness and hope.

"You got your lettuce starts, your broccoli, your eggplant and your cauliflower." Frank read the narrow plastic inserts as he moved down the row. "Bell pepper. Red pepper. Cilantro. Basil. Parsley. I'll bet these are supposed to go out soon."

"It's not natural to be this healthy," Larry complained. "This is giving me the sweats. What if the freezer in the house has nothin' but ratatouille?"

Dobbin laughed. "I know! I'm wanting some chicken nuggets!"

"You're a cruel kid," Larry shook his head in mock outrage. "Making an old man like me think of chicken nuggets."

They stepped out of the greenhouse, and Marcel jerked his chin toward the long barn. "How much electricity do you think those solar panels generate?" Elevated panels covered the barn's south-facing roof in neat and expensive-looking rows.

"A lot," Frank said. He turned and looked down the long garden. "Those boxes next to the fruit trees? Bee hives."

"How about that low shed?" Larry asked. "A pumphouse?"

"Maybe," Frank replied. "I was going to say a sheep or goat shed, but you wouldn't keep goats in an orchard. They climb. Maybe they've got some sheep?"

"God, I hope not," Larry said, "I'm not into sheep shearing. Let's take a look in the barn first. There might be a barn cat. Then we can check out the shed."

The barn's big metal doors rolled open with a well-oiled smoothness. "Sure is easy to farm with lots of money," Frank said.

"Blowing my mind," Marcel agreed. "This barn is way bigger and nicer than my house."

Overhead lights sprang to life as they entered, illuminating a pristine floor of brushed concrete. A spacious alcove on the right held garden tools and stacks of bagged organic compost. A tall and shining John Deere tractor with a bucket loader front end sat near the compost.

"This is a thirty-thousand-dollar machine," Frank said, lifting Dobbin into the tractor seat.

Dobbin grinned down at his grandfather. "It's cool. Can I drive it?"

"No. I'm having all the excitement I can stand." Frank didn't smile, but Dobbin did.

Larry grunted. "I just don't want to find any horses. That's an adventure I truly do not want to have."

"What's happened to horses?" Marcel asked. "Has that been on the news?"

"You should ask my momma," Larry said. "She'd know." He shook his head. "I've always been good with animals, but I haven't handled horses. I know they can be skittish and even a dumbass like me knows they're big."

Frank grinned. "Relax. We'd know if the Babcocks had horses. Dobbin would have been all over that." He looked down the center aisle of the barn. "I don't think there's ever been horses here. We'd smell them."

"I'm smelling something," Larry said. "Bit rank. You smell that?"

Frank shook his head. "Not really."

"I'm with Larry. There's something," Marcel said. "Stinks."

They walked past the horse stalls, three to a side, each a roomy box. The first stall held stacked straw bales. Dobbin stayed on the tractor as Frank, Larry and Marcel looked in the next stalls. They were empty.

Dobbin climbed off the tractor and ran to join the men at the far end of the barn where they stopped to study a closed door. Marcel said, "Wow. I'm really smelling something now."

"I would think this would be the tack room. Maybe they made it a compost area?" Frank said. He opened the door.

A large tubular animal on dark legs came blasting out of the gap like a launched missile. The creature shot toward the space occupied by Dobbin.

Larry didn't have a coherent thought beyond, "Oh, no!" as he flung himself on top of the boy. He took Dobbin in a crash to the floor just as the hairy monster planted a pair of cloven hoofs on Larry's kidneys.

"Augh!" Larry shouted, curling over Dobbin. Pain shot through to his abdomen and up his spine.

The creature was away, rocketing through the open barn doors, then veering to the left.

"You okay?" Frank rushed to pull Larry to his feet. Larry nodded, trying to be alright despite the wave of nausea sweeping through his midsection.

Larry inhaled carefully and tried not to throw up.

Dobbin rolled to all fours and stood up, reaching to hug his grandfather. "I'm okay," Dobbin said. "Larry saved me."

Larry hiccupped and waved a hand, pushing away Marcel's offer of support. Larry staggered toward the narrow door that Frank had opened. It led to a small tiled room with a straw-strewn floor. Larry took a whiff of the stench wafting up from the dirty straw and quickly turned to vomit, copiously, onto the barn walkway.

Larry shook his head, trying to clear his system as he croaked, "We should stick to cats. Really small, nice cats."

"Marcel, can you go take a careful look outside?" Frank asked while keeping a hand on a very pale Dobbin.

Marcel jogged to the big doors and peeked out. He pulled out his cell phone and started videotaping. After a moment he stopped, and stood in the open doorway, tapping at his phone.

Larry made his way to a hose bib and turned on the water, rinsing his face and mouth. "I'm getting a bit long in the tooth for surprises," he said as Frank escorted Dobbin to a nearby straw bale and had the boy sit down.

Frank lifted an eyebrow and said, "Thanks for protecting Dobbin."

Larry slumped down on the straw bale next to Dobbin and weakly reflected on the past few minutes. He had shielded Dobbin. It surprised him. He liked the kid. He liked Marcel too. He liked rescuing Bella. He'd better be careful with all this. No one was going to take care of Larry but Larry.

"It's a pig," Marcel said, rejoining them. "My iNaturalist app suggests it's a Vietnamese pot-bellied pig. It's out there on the grass, rooting around. It's a rare species. It's considered small as pigs go, but it sure doesn't look small to me."

Larry stood up slowly. He leaned against a stall door as the muscles of his back complained. "I agree," he croaked. "That is not a small pig."

"I'll be right back," Frank said. He stepped around the pool of Larry's recent vomit and carefully eased into the small, stinking room at the end of the barn.

He reappeared a few minutes later.

"Our pig has a name," Frank said. He brought over a tube of ointment, labeled with a folded tag from a vet clinic. "Gentlemen," he said, "We have just met Miss Violet Babcock who is recovering from a case of ringworm."

"You're calling her *our* pig?" Larry laughed weakly. "That's not my pig until she's bacon."

The pig under discussion appeared in the open doorway. She let out a squeal and trotted up to the group, causing Dobbin to take refuge behind his grandfather. The pig skidded to a stop close to Larry. She wrinkled her forehead and peered at him.

Larry swallowed hard.

The pig extended her neck and carefully snuffled at Larry's knee cap. She grunted softly and stepped closer.

"Whoa, pig. Easy there." Larry tried to step back, but he was against the stall door. "Easy there, Violet. I was just kidding about the bacon."

Violet gave another deep snuffle and looked up at Larry with adoring eyes.

"A friend is, as it were, a second self."
Cicero (106 - 43 B.C.E.)

CHAPTER THIRTEEN

"WHAT WAS SHE doing in that room?" Larry asked. He was still leaning against the door of a stall, with some color returning to his face as he gently scratched Violet behind her velvety and very piggy ears.

"You should see the inside," Frank said. "It's like some sort of tiled spa."

Marcel was scrolling through a webpage on his smartphone. "Which makes sense. Porcine ringworm is a fungus that can live on wood. Maybe they didn't want the stall wood to get infected."

"Let's take a look," Larry said. He pushed off the stall door and gingerly made his way across the barn aisle, Violet at his heels.

The group reached Violet's recent bedroom and took turns peering inside.

"I think it's a dog-grooming station," Marcel said. "There's one of these on the west side of Olympia. See the raised tub? You can stand next to the dog and wash without straining your back."

Larry took in the tiled floor and walls. The floor was mostly covered with loose, wet straw stinking of pig feces, but the quality of the tile was evident. He whistled. "All this to wash a dog? If you mucked this out, it'd be nicer than my place."

"Mine too," Marcel said as he scrolled on his phone.

"Just my luck," Larry said. "A glorified dog spa . . . with a pig in it."

Marcel read off his phone, "Pot-bellied pigs are social animals and do best when kept with a companion."

"There's another Violet?" Larry gasped. "Holy mackerel, cheese and crackers."

Dobbin laughed. "You're getting better, Larry."

"Watch it, kid," Larry said. "Christ on a crutch, we do not need another Violet."

"I'll bet the other Violet is down in the orchard in that shed," Frank said.

They watched Violet root in the wet straw. She unearthed a plastic dog dish and pushed it around.

"She's hungry," Larry said. "Which reminds me. We didn't feed Bella." He checked his watch. "Time is getting on. I guess we'd better go see the shed and find out what more disasters our day contains."

"This is fun!" Dobbin said. "Rescuing animals is a good thing!"

"You have a point," Larry said. "The rescue is nice. The maintenance, however, is a problem."

"My Mom talks about that to her congregation," Marcel said. "We can take on more than we can maintain. Then we go blind to the mess we're creating."

Larry rubbed his eyes. "Yep. But it makes me nuts to think about the animals around here who are thirsty right now. I don't see how keeping more cats on my sun porch is the answer, but being thirsty sucks wide."

"I don't think you're supposed to say 'sucks wide' around me," Dobbin said.

"Let's cut Larry some slack," his grandfather said. "This tube of ointment was issued on April 28th. That's ten days ago. I'm not seeing any skin problems on Violet. Maybe she's ready to go back to her shed."

"One way to find out." Larry led the way to the fenced garden. Violet trotted alongside. She stopped to root in the grass for a moment, then snorted and galloped to catch up to Larry as he opened the gate to the enclosure. She picked up speed and ran the length of the garden, stopping outside a gate to the orchard area.

She squealed and an answering squeal came from the low shed.

"Hang on, Dobbin," Frank said, "That may be a bigger, faster pig."

Dobbin slowed, and reached for his grandfather's hand. The group cautiously approached the gate, breaking into smiles when it was clear the shed and a nearby wallow were encircled by a stout fence of hog wire. Two blue barrels sat outside the fence, labeled "Violet" and "Nigel."

Violet nuzzled a near twin of herself through the box wire of the fence. Nigel had the same dark, bristly exterior and the same clear, piggy eyes.

"I'll bet he's hungry," Larry said. He moved to the barrels and pried one open, finding it filled with a brown kibble. "Huh. Pig food?" he asked Frank.

Frank nodded confidently. "I'll bet there's a dispenser hung on the fence."

There was. Marcel and Larry used nearby buckets to fill the two dispensers, which immediately caught Nigel's interest. He abandoned Violet at the fence and rushed to the slot now releasing pellets of pig food into a metal tray.

Frank opened the gate to the pen, and Violet raced to join Nigel at a companion tray. "We're in luck," Frank said, studying Nigel's rear end. "Nigel's a barrow."

"A burro?" Larry scratched his head. "You sure on that?"

Frank's dimple emerged. "A barrow. A neutered male pig. That's a good thing. Should make him easier to manage." He lifted Dobbin to the top of the feed barrel so the boy could see the pigs eat. Larry and Marcel stood with Frank at the gate.

"I can't take these guys home," Larry said. "Can you and Dobbin come feed them?"

"Nope." Frank shook his head. "Not doing that."

Dobbin's head whipped around. "We can't?"

"Larry and Marcel are the pet-sitting professionals," Frank said. "You and I should be the support personnel." Frank pointed at the blue barrels. "Those are full of food today, but that's not going to last." He turned to Larry and said, "You've seen that house. There's got to be four or five bedrooms. There's probably a hot tub and a gym and maybe even a home movie theater. I think you should move your Momma and her cousins out here. Bring the cats. You can put some of them in the catio and some in horse stalls."

Whoa. Move in?"

"Why not?" Frank said. "We could use some neighbors."

"Meanwhile, you'll be doing what, exactly?" Larry said. "Besides gate opening?"

Frank laughed. "Dobbin and me need a job. We've been kinda at sea the past couple of days. We'll reach out to Soo-Min and let her know what you've been finding. People need to be looking around for animals that are locked up and thirsty."

"I got no argument with that," Larry said. "I'm not so sure about the moving. My mom would take some convincing." He rubbed the small of his back. "It's been a long day already," he said. "Violet weighs a ton."

"More like a hundred-fifty pounds," Frank said, cheerfully. "And you've got Marcel here to help with the moving." He motioned to his grandson. "Dobbin and I will help. Tomorrow we can make a run to the feed store. We'll see if we can pick up some pig food and some cat kibble. I've got a truck."

"You can't be greedy," Larry said. "Taking too much stuff could be dangerous."

"Hey, I'll pay for it if they're open," Frank said. "Maybe we can use sawdust for the litter boxes," he added. "Less monetary value."

Larry exhaled. Frank was making some sense.

"And there's that wine collection," Frank pointed out. "You could unwind at the end of the day."

"I'm more of a Budweiser guy," Larry said. He added, "My mom always wants me to move up in the world, but I'm not sure "King of Cats" was what she had in mind."

Larry wiped his face then dropped his hands to his sides with an exhale of breath. "I'm just trying to get my head around this idea. Marcel and me. Three old women. Then we'll have sixteen cats, two pot-bellied pigs and a deluxe wine cellar."

Larry looked at Marcel. "What do you think?"

"Life's a balancing act," Marcel said. "My mom says there's evil in having people believe they don't deserve nice things. And there's an evil in thinking *only* about nice things."

"Sounds like you're okay with us doing some cat care and having a view of Rainer?" Larry asked. "Hell, don't answer that. Who wouldn't be?" He turned back to Frank and said, "I'm kinda feeling like there's got to be a pile of shit that comes with this theoretical pony, but I agree with you. We should move out here."

"Look." Marcel pointed across the valley to the trees. A cyclist in a black helmet on a bright blue bike flashed across an opening in the woods. A few moments later the biker reappeared on a trail that led down to the far end of Holiday Valley.

"That's Annelise," Marcel said. "The girl from my class."

"Well, now" Larry said. "That's exactly what's been missing from my day. A psychopath with a filleting knife."

"Better safe than sorry."
Samuel Lover (1797-1868)

CHAPTER FOURTEEN

MARCEL SEMAPHORED A hello with waving arms. The bicyclist bumped down the hillside trail and reached the pavement at the end of the road. She gave a small wave and kept peddling, slowly moving nearer.

Larry refilled the pigs' watering pan from a hose coming off a watering extension pipe while Frank tightened the clamps on the blue feed barrel.

The group trooped back through the garden of raised beds, and Marcel again waved vigorously at the biker.

"Let's go around to the front of the house," Marcel said. "Maybe she'll come up the drive."

"Oh, goody," Larry replied, but he did do as Marcel suggested, taking the time to study the Babcock house from the exterior. It was a massive home with more solar panels collecting the sun on the back half of the peaked roof. "Know anything about solar panels?" he asked Frank.

"A bit," Frank said. "Those panels are another good reason to move your mother out here. They may keep you in hot water."

"Oh, yeah. Let's keep Larry in hot water," Larry muttered.

They reached the front of the house just as the bicyclist

was reaching the turn off to the long driveway. Marcel made another wave with his arms.

The bicyclist turned down the driveway and pedaled almost to the parking area. She stopped, putting a leg out to balance the bike while leaving her other foot on the pedal as she turned the front wheel to the left.

Larry appreciated her use of physical distance. She was stopping far enough from them that she could sprint away on the bike if she became uncomfortable.

The long-legged girl wore black cycling pants and a neon pink T-shirt which stretched snuggly over high, well-shaped breasts. She had the sleeves of a black fleece sweater tied around her waist, the body of the sweater fanning out behind the bike seat.

It was a smart outfit for the current unsettled times. She'd be seen by drivers while wearing the neon pink, but she could also hide quickly with the help of the black pullover. Bright blonde hair puffed out from under the black bike helmet and cascaded down her back.

Artisanal chocolate truffle with coconut, Larry thought. He noted the long knife sheath strapped to her thigh and decided to keep his labeling to himself. He wasn't entirely sure his brain was using the word "artisanal" correctly. Best not to be wrong and be shanked for being stupid.

"Marcel?" she called.

"Hey! Annelise!" Marcel said. "Good to see you. We're here seeing to some pets."

Annelise dispensed a slow, regal nod.

"This is my neighbor, Larry," Marcel said. "He runs Larry's Pet-Sitting Services."

"I've heard about you," Annelise said. "My friend Penn

said you took her grandmother's cat in. She was really glad, because it's a cat who pees on walls."

"A big gray tom?" Larry asked.

"I think it's a white Persian," Annelise said.

"Oh. That guy." Larry rolled his eyes. "That one's a stealth pisser. He squirts and then pretends it wasn't him that soaked the wall."

Annelise lips curved into a half-smile. "That's what Penn said."

Marcel continued the introductions. "This is Frank and his grandson, Dobbin."

"Nice to meet you," Frank used a warm tone, but Larry noticed Frank stayed back, hand on Dobbin's shoulder. Larry suspected that Frank had noted the sheathed knife and was being respectful of boundaries.

Smart man, Frank.

"How's your family?" Annelise asked Marcel.

"My mom's gone up," Marcel said.

"I'm so sorry." Annelise swallowed. "Or should I say congratulations? I keep muddling this up. Sorry."

"Nah. It's okay. She's a really good lady," Marcel said. "My dad's around, I think. As usual, he hasn't stopped by. I'm sure he's too busy."

Now that's interesting, thought Larry. *I didn't think to ask about Marcel's father.*

Annelise nodded, as if Marcel's update was not news.

"How's your family?" Marcel asked.

"I'm good," Annelise said. "So, did you find any pets here?"

She didn't give any information about her parents, Larry thought.

"We found a cat," Marcel said, "A huge house, a garden and two pot-bellied pigs."

"Oh! Are the pigs cute?" Annelise's face lit up with a smile.

A birthday cake with a thousand candles, Larry thought. *She's radiant.* He kept his thoughts to himself, seeing no need to sound like a creepy-assed old fart. It was best to just pretend he didn't think words like 'radiant.'

Marcel turned to Larry. "Do you think they're cute pigs?"

"When Violet isn't using my kidneys as a launching pad to freedom, she's cute," Larry said. He turned to Annelise and said, "I got in front of Violet when she was in a hurry. I won't make that mistake again."

Dobbin laughed. "I think they're cool pigs," he said. "Want to see them?"

"Not right now, thank you," Annelise said. "I'm out for some exercise, and I don't want to be gone too long." She looked at Larry. "Are you taking the cat and the pigs?"

"Actually, this is a better place to keep all the cats we've picked up. Frank just suggested we move out here," Larry said. "If I do that, I'd be bringing my mom and her two cousins, Marcel and the cats we've collected so far. Would you be okay with that?"

Annelise blinked as if surprised Larry would ask her opinion. She came up with a slow nod of agreement. "Sure. Makes sense. It's a nice place."

"See anything we should know about?" Larry asked.

"No. It's been quiet." Annelise looked up the valley. "I live, I mean, we live, on a road that comes in from the east on the other side of that ridge. There's been traffic up and down the road, but it's getting quieter. Over here I've only seen you guys." She nodded at Frank. "I feel safer riding over here."

"Good call," Frank said. "Dobbin and I are up at the double houses. Give us a shout if you need anything. We'd be glad to help out."

"Thank you," Annelise said. "When will you move in?"

Larry checked his watch. "Man, the day's getting on," he said. "I'm thinking the sooner the better, but it's going to depend on how good I am at herding cats."

"Character is fate."
Heraclitus (c. 535 - 475 B.C.E.)

CHAPTER FIFTEEN

A VOICE HEAVY with the lilt of Georgia said, "M-ah-y great-great-great-grandmotha came to us from London," the caller said. "It's just brakin' my hart. All those sweet, sweet dawgs."

Abigail clicked the remote, increasing the volume on the talk show and the latest interviews of Atlantans responding to details of the Rapture.

A news anchor came on with global updates.

The news out of the United Kingdom was particularly bleak. Beefy tradesmen were bawling in their beers over missing terriers, bulldogs and whippets. Gaunt farmers and shepherds were suicidal over vanished collies. The upper classes were distraught over disappeared spaniels and poodles. Even the royal corgis were gone, and the famous stiff upper lip of The Empire had given way to tears and waves of despondency.

"We can't lie," one British mental health expert said when interviewed by an Atlantan reporter. "We don't know where the dogs have gone or why. The resulting combination of grief and uncertainty are shredding the fabric of British society."

Abigail turned off the show. She mulled the crisis as she strode into her spacious spa bathroom. "Grief and uncertainty" were topics worth considering. They might be pools of feeling to be tapped for dollar donations.

She turned the spigots to fill the whirlpool tub. As steam rose, she poured in a generous glop of a perfumed bubble bath and watched as a foamy layer began to build. Sighing, she stripped off her workout clothes and kicked them in the direction of the door. A maid would deal with them later.

Naked, Abigail walked over to the bedroom wall and touched a recessed mahogany panel. There was a smooth click and the panel slid to the right, revealing a small wine bar with a row of refrigerated bottles.

Abigail selected a chardonnay and opened it. She poured the wine into a glass, filling it to the rim. Smiling at this small social crassness, Abigail slurped greedily, gulping the wine down.

She drained the glass, then refilled it. This time she sipped daintily as she carried the wine glass back to the tub. She stepped into the water, holding the wine glass high, then sank down into the bubbles with a sigh.

Abigail soaked in the warm water, sipping her wine and thinking of the things she needed to do. There were so many details, only some of which she could delegate. At moments like this, she missed her husband. Aaron had been a man of laser focus, able to visualize and prioritize what needed to be done so others felt their needs would be met.

"You don't actually have to *meet* their needs, Abs," he'd said. "But they do need to feel you are *going* to meet their needs. Just as soon as they donate." Then he'd add a quick grin and say, "And buy the T-shirt." He'd chuckle and say, "Nothing says you're on the team like having the team's T-shirt."

He was right, Abigail thought. Their first several million came from a $25 price tag on a $3 T-shirt with a small "Ross Hour of Prayer" silk-screened in an arc over a red heart and a gold cross. The navy-blue shirt was classy, as T-shirts went, suitable for church wear if it was a casual church or a Wednesday evening service. They sold thousands of the shirts every year.

Abigail shifted in the soap suds. The merchandizing profits were in Luxembourg. She hadn't heard of flameouts in the banking industry, but that didn't mean they weren't occurring. The banks Aaron chose were famous for their layers of hush-hush.

She emptied the wine glass and set it on the tub rim, thinking of Jared. Did she want his lithe, hard body in the bath with her? No, she decided. She wanted him in the swimming pool out back where she could be wet and free of constraints.

Technically she and Jared weren't adulterers. She hadn't touched him until after she'd hoovered up all of Aaron's ashes. She was now a widow. Jared was a single man of twenty-eight. He was no infant.

She had, she acknowledged, lunged at him a bit when he'd come in to offer his condolences. She'd been surprised when his hand ran up her back, but it had felt so good that she'd smiled. She'd leaned into him, and when his hand tentatively cupped her breast, she'd abandoned any pretense of mourning and smothered his mouth with kisses.

With all the breaking news and constant coupling, it had been an intense few days. Abigail rubbed some bubbly foam into her abdomen and up under her breasts, washing away the sweat of her workout. Her trainer had been surprised at her lack of complaints, not knowing her keenness to be trim for Jared.

Of all the secrets she carried, one important one was the pink dipilator hidden in her lingerie cabinet. Not even her makeup artist knew how religiously she was running the tiny vibrating razor over her chin and upper lip. She wouldn't admit to granny chin hairs. Not to herself and certainly not to Jared.

Had Janice figured out something was going on? Was that return to the dressing room some sort of warning?

Abigail shook her head. Janice and Clive were beasts of burden – sweet, docile, and very necessary. They owed their jobs and their futures to the Ross Hour of Prayer.

Still, she should take Janice's near interruption of a lusty interlude with Jared as a reminder to be careful. The Ross Hour of Prayer had ten thousand Prime Prayer Partners who were the "boots on the ground" in the mission of spreading the Good News. Each Prime Prayer Partner paid a monthly fee of eighty dollars and received not only a specialized e-Newsletter every quarter, but also a photo Christmas card from Abigail and Aaron with their auto-penned best wishes for a Holy New Year. The Prayer Partners were unlikely to approve of her romps with Jared.

Which led back to making plans. She and Jared would go west. She'd call it a retreat into prayer, but it would be the start of a new phase in her life.

Abigail licked her lips. The U.S. president was to

address the nation soon with the latest interpretations and prognostications from religious and scientific scholars. Whatever the news was, it was best to be prepared to speak.

What did people crave? As always, this would be the thing to monetize.

No surprises there, Abigail decided as she turned the lever to drain the bath. She toweled dry, thoughts circling and descending to a conclusion. Her people always craved the certainty of a soda pop machine. They wanted to hear if they would only do "A", then "B" would surely follow, just as a pop can clunked out of a vending machine after inserting enough coins.

The news of the Rapture upended decades of teaching. Some of those who went up in feathers hadn't been "Saved." Several million hadn't even been Christians. Then there were the millions left behind who were in confusion because they believed ardently in Jesus. Lastly, many churchgoers had, like Aaron, been incinerated.

A photo on the dressing table stirred Abigail's thinking. In it, Ruthie was holding her little tea-cup Shih-tzu, Snowflake. How Ruthie had loved that dog.

"Man's best friend," Abigail murmured. Maybe she could do something about dogs going on before *to prepare the way.*

She frowned. The concept seemed a bit of a reach.

There was a tap on the door to the master suite. "Abigail?"

It was Jared.

Abigail called, "Come in. I just finished my bath."

Her handsome assistant opened the door and put his

head inside. He smiled as Abigail wrapped a towel around her middle and beckoned him to come closer.

"I booked a jet. It will be standing by," he said. "I'm supposed to meet Janice soon." Jaret put a hand on her waist. "To hear what she's found out."

"Text her and say you'll be a little late," Abigail said, reaching down to run a palm over the zipper of his pants.

Jared nuzzled her neck and said, "I'll tell her something came up."

"The rainbow is a sign from Him who is in all things."
Hopi proverb

CHAPTER SIXTEEN

ANNELISE DIDN'T STAY long. She promised to bring them news of any pets or livestock in need.

She took Marcel's phone number and said, "Should I be keeping my eyes out for books on ancient Sumer?"

He smiled and shrugged. "You think you're gonna find one?"

"Maybe. There's a professor who lives off Oyster Bay road," she said. "And I think his wife's a librarian. I know there was a whole neighborhood of Unitarians in the affordable housing bungalows. Those people musta gone up to Heaven. They were always protesting stuff – and they were always having vegan bean bakes and used book sales."

"I heard about that. There was a book sale supporting gay rights for clams and free-range shellfish," Marcel said.

Annelise laughed, her face again luminescent with joy. "I think it was plastic-free oceans, plagiarism-free politics, persecution-free love and perfume-free meetings." She shrugged her shoulders. "I can go take a look."

"Thanks." Marcel tilted his head toward the big house. "Stop by anytime. We're making this our headquarters."

"You vegan or vegetarian?" Frank asked.

Annelise shrugged. "Sometimes."

"Come back by this evening if you're hungry," he suggested. "Dobbin and I are going to barbeque up a storm to welcome Larry's family. We'll have all kinds of stuff. We'll eat about six or so."

Annelise tipped her head back and studied Frank. "I might be able to make it," she said. "Don't wait on me." She turned her bike and launched off smoothly.

"You're making dinner?" Larry said to Frank as they watched Annelise cycle off.

"Might as well," Frank said. "I've got a freezer full of meat at my place. No telling how long the power will last. And you've got your family to move, plus the cats."

"There is that." Larry thought about his mother and her two cousins. "I should give my mom a call. This could get interesting. She doesn't go out much."

"Tell her I make a terrific plate of ribs." Frank's eyes twinkled. "Did you see the size of the grill on that side patio?"

"I thought the Babcocks were vegan," Marcel said.

"Maybe they grilled veggies," Frank shrugged. "The grill is a beauty." He looked down at Dobbin. "Feeding people will keep us out of trouble."

Dobbin grinned and nodded.

"Okay, then," Larry said. "Let's get Bella some food and see if they had a cat carrier for her. I've got a couple carriers in the van and another at the house, but we've got fifteen cats to move."

Twenty minutes later Frank was opening the main gate for Larry and Marcel. They had Bella's cat carrier, and

Larry had survived the Round One phone call of convincing his mother to move.

He tapped off the cell phone and drove the van through the open gate as Frank and Dobbin waved.

"My mom's afraid," Larry said to Marcel. "She's had a rough time, and she's afraid."

"Makes sense," Marcel said. "It's scary times. There are no guarantees."

"Tell me about your dad," Larry said, turning the van onto the highway. The four lanes of pavement were empty for as far as he could see. It was unnerving.

Marcel looked out the window as towering Douglas firs flashed by. He sighed, pushed his glasses up and said, "Not much to tell. He's a pastor at a mega-church. My mom was the assistant pastor. My dad had an affair with an attorney he met at a criminal justice conference. It caused a big stink. My parents split, and my dad kept the big church. He has a new wife and two little girls. I don't think the new wife is working. She got fired, my mom said, and the church ladies don't like her. I don't hear from them much."

"Have you talked to your dad since your mother went up?" Larry asked.

Marcel's shoulders hunched forward. "He's left some messages. Don't worry about him. He looks after himself real well."

"Alrighty then," Larry said. "Tell me about the ancient Sumerians. Why the hell did you pick them? Aren't most kids your age into heavy metal bands?"

Marcel smiled. "It was an act of rebellion. I was supposed to write about Europeans for a history class."

He shifted in the van's seat and leaned forward. "But when I started reading, it was just so amazing. The Sumerians were . . . like magic."

Larry took his eyes off the road to look at Marcel. The kid's face was lit with the joy that Larry suspected most people had only for Christmas morning on years when the bills were paid.

Marcel said, "The Sumerians showed up in the Euphrates Valley about five thousand B.C., or maybe earlier. The big cradles of civilization are the Euphrates Valley with the Sumerians, the Nile River Valley with the Egyptians and the Indus Valley in India. The Sumerians may be the first, and, get this, nobody's certain where they came from. Some think they were from Asia, but the language doesn't align. They called themselves 'sang-gigga,' which means 'black-headed,' and they may have been from Saharan Africa."

"They were getting out of the sand dunes?" Larry put on his blinker to exit the freeway. He took the van up Mud Bay road to west Olympia.

Marcel said, "There was desertification. The Sahara once was green with rivers. Then there was a climate change."

"Were oil companies making money hand over fist?" Larry pulled the van into a parking lot in front of a strip mall. "Don't answer that. I want to check in at the vet clinic here and see if they have any extra cat carriers."

The clinic door stood propped open, which Larry took as a good sign. A stout young woman with pink, purple and blue-streaked hair sat at the counter. She wore cantaloupe-orange scrubs and a sad, round face.

"Our vet's not in," she said.

Larry looked at her. Her eyes were pink-rimmed and

tired under blue-mascaraed lashes. "The vet got taken up?" Larry asked.

The young woman sniffed and nodded. "Both the vets. My parents too. What am I supposed to do? I can't go home. It's too lonely. Besides, we've got two cats here recovering from spay jobs, but no one has come to get them."

"Any dogs?"

She shook her head and started weeping in earnest, smearing the royal blue mascara. "We have three kennel runs with feathers. One of them was the sweetest little spaniel. And we were holding a pug." She sniffed. "Pugs are just so adorable. I'm not surprised she was taken up, but what do I do now? Her owners are gone too. I just got a phone call from their neighbor." Her tears came fast now and plopped down onto the counter.

"We can take the cats," Marcel said.

Larry stared at him. "We can?"

"Sure. We could hold them in the catio." Marcel turned to the young woman. "I'm Marcel. This is Larry, of Larry's Pet-Sitting Services. We're starting a cat repository out at Holiday Valley. We came in to find some cat carriers. We could take your cats with us."

"That's awesome! Oh, it would be so great to have a place for these cats."

"Wait, wait," Larry said. "Let's begin from the beginning here. What's your name?"

"Me? Oh! My name is Cosmos."

Larry realized he hadn't yet applied his food-to-person liner-note formula. He looked at Cosmos and thought, *Tutti-Frutti. Totally.*

"A half-truth is a whole lie."
Yiddish proverb

CHAPTER SEVENTEEN

COSMOS'S COLORFUL EXTERIOR came with a competent skill set. With cat care promised, she regrouped to a professional state and asked what was needed. She soon disappeared into the rear of the clinic and returned with two bundles of collapsed cardboard boxes. "Two dozen disposable cat carriers," she said. "Under the circumstances, no charge."

Larry exhaled with relief. "That is going to really help my day. Thanks."

"You're welcome. Can you take the two cats from here?" Cosmos leaned forward, with hope written on her face.

"Ah," Larry paused. "You said they've been spayed. Do they need special care?"

"They should be fine. I checked them this morning. No swelling, no heat. I'd keep them separated from other cats for a few days."

"What are you going to be doing after we take the cats?" Larry asked.

"I hadn't thought that far. I could leave more messages at the phone numbers for the people who had dogs with us," Cosmos said. "Then lock up?" Her voice rose and trembled.

"Look, my afternoon is about to be nuts," Larry said.

Cosmos eyes filled with tears.

Larry swallowed hard. "So," he said, thinking rapidly, "What if you did your phone calls, and then you could transport these two post-surgery cats out to Holiday Valley for us. You got a car?"

Cosmos nodded with vigor. "The red Honda Civic around back is mine. It's kinda vintage, but I definitely could bring the cats out in it." She sniffed. "I was supposed to be paid today." She gulped back another round of tears. "Holiday Valley's about, what? Five miles? I think I have enough gas to get out there."

Larry found himself pulling his wallet out to hand Cosmos a twenty.

"Oh! Thanks! I'll pay you back!"

Larry waved that offer away. "We don't want you stranded on the side of the highway. Just bring the cats. We're going to set up some horse stalls to hold cats and you could make sure these cats are set up right."

"Of course!" Cosmos beamed a sigh of relief. "That makes total sense."

"You'll have to get past the entry gate. Let me give our friend Frank a call."

Larry jerked a thumb at the stack of cardboard. Marcel took the hint and hustled the stack to the van while Larry called Frank.

Frank liked the idea of help from a cat-experienced vet tech. "Maybe she could look at Violet's ringworm too," he said.

"Good idea," Larry said. "She's got some calls to make. Can I just give her your number so you can meet her at the main gate?"

"I've got a better idea," Frank said. "I'll go reset the keypad number to something everybody can remember. How does 666 sound?"

Larry laughed out loud. "Perfect. I'll tell her." He tapped the phone off and turned to tell Cosmos, but she was already onto another topic.

"We sell organic cat food," she said, pointing at a display board. "Do you want me to bring some?"

"Oh, man," Larry said, "That would be fantastic. How much have you got?"

"Gosh. Bags and bags. Cans too. By the case."

Larry stared at her. When her face wasn't strained with worry and grief, Ms. Tutti-frutti was pretty. She was vibrant and generous and very pretty. Larry swallowed. Hard.

He said, "Cosmos, I can't tell you how much that would help."

She shrugged. "I'm glad to help. I'll mark the food down as a donation in the books. You could take it all, I think, but I couldn't get it all in the Civic. Not in one trip."

Larry thought for a moment. "Let me call Frank back. Maybe he can bring his truck and load up, which would help us a ton."

"Alright."

Later Larry wondered at what came out of his mouth, but, in the moment, it was logical and right. He said, "Why don't you stop at your place and grab a suit case of clothes and stuff? It's a big house out there. We're, ah, kinda making a community of folks. My mom, her cousins, Marcel here. Me."

Cosmos blinked, then smiled. "I'd like that. I don't want to go home. There's nothing to do except miss my parents and worry."

A few minutes later the details were settled. Frank and Dobbin would bring the truck for a load of cat food. Cosmos would assemble a box of common medicines and crate the cats before stopping at home for extra clothes and her phone charger. Frank cemented Larry's offer with, "We'll find you a place to bunk. We could use your help."

Larry headed out the door as Cosmos called, "See you out there later." Her face produced deep dimples as she smiled and said, "Thanks so much! You saved my life!"

As Larry backed the van out of the parking slot, he said, "Hey, Marcel. Don't go offering more homes to cats."

"I thought that's what we're doing. Keeping cats."

"Let's just ease into this. It's my name on the van, so let me make some of these decisions."

"Sorry, Larry." Marcel looked down and exhaled. "I guess I blew it."

"Not too badly. Cosmos knows cat care, and she has a fucking ton of cat food. We scored here, buddy."

Marcel's face brightened. "I like her," he said. "Cosmos is cool. When she smiles, she's really pretty."

Larry did not want to discuss the loveliness of Cosmos.

"You were telling me about the Sumerians," Larry said.

Marcel chuckled. "Thanks, Larry."

"For what?"

"For being a good guy."

Larry shook his head. "I don't know about that."

"I do." Marcel took a breath and said, "The Sumerians. They were most likely from Africa. They invented so many things. In the space of a thousand years, they came up with the wheel, the sailboat, and the first written language. They created the first day off, the first major cities, the first school, even the first aquarium. They were amazing."

"What else do you study? Just so I know what channels I can choose from." Larry automatically checked the rear-view mirror and the side mirror as he took the van down Harrison Avenue. No one was out driving. He should check in with his mother on what the news stations were saying about gas supplies. Odelle might know the real news.

Marcel was oblivious to Larry's wandering thoughts. "I studied the Bible," Marcel said. "A lot. Every preacher's kid knows the Bible. And then I learned about alpine lake snails," he said.

"Do what?" Larry turned his head to stare at Marcel. "What kind of snails?"

"Alpine lake snails. There used to be a regular kind of snail," Marcel said patiently. "When a mountain range uplifts, like the Rockies, you get all these little lakes made at high altitudes."

"Gotcha. Alpine lakes."

"Right." Marcel pushed his glasses up. "And the snails in each lake start to diverge. Over millennia, they become different species."

"Yippee?"

Marcel snorted. "I got to thinking. When Noah had his ark, did he have all the different kinds of alpine lake snails on his boat? How did he collect them?"

"Two by two?"

"There are 43,000 species of snails," Marcel said. "That'd be 86,000 specimens for Noah to collect and maintain. Although many snails are hermaphrodites, so partner optional."

"Whoa, whoa," Larry said. "They're *what?*"

"Hermaphrodites. An individual snail can have both male and female reproductive capabilities."

"They can diddle themselves?"

"Right. Or they can double mate – bringing either part of their sexuality on-line."

"Well, that's got to be handy." Larry whistled. He shook his head. "Okay, then."

"So," Marcel continued, "I started wondering about the whole Noah and the animals-on-the-ark story. I did a lot of reading, and that's when I found out that the Yahwists stole the story of Noah from the Babylonians, who got it from the Sumerians. My anti-European paper came later."

"And your studies led to your acceptance of my . . . flexible . . . morals?"

Marcel shrugged. "If the church community is going to tell children this fiction as the truth, why should I care if you liberate a Rolex watch from a side table at the Babcock's house?"

"Ouch. You saw that?" Larry's sparse orange hair looked especially odd above the dark rose of a blush now rising on his cheeks. "I thought no one was looking."

"Frank didn't see you. Dobbin did. He didn't tell Frank, but he mentioned it to me."

"I knew I liked that kid." Larry turned the van blinker

on for a right turn despite being the only vehicle on Division Street. He sighed. "I have some trouble resisting temptation. Not big stuff. Little shit. My mom calls it our Raven Eyes. We see something nice, and we go for it."

"My mom calls that stealing."

"She has a point," Larry admitted. "I'm hoping God is keeping score and a few good deeds like cat rescuing will tip the scale. I think it's working. We're not cinders so far."

"We know some looters have flamed out! What's the difference?" Marcel stared at him.

Larry thought for a moment and said, "When a looter starts out, they have intention. They know they are going to take something. Me, I take something because it showed up in my face. Or I go take something 'cause we really need it. Not like "need a bigger television," but more like "Wow, that's cool! And it's right here for me!""

"That's splitting hairs," Marcel said.

Larry sneezed. "This van is full of cat hair, so there's lots of hairs to split. We're doing fine."

"I think you should put the Rolex back."

Larry looked at the long shadows the trees cast on the sidewalks as they drove north on Division. He didn't need a fancy watch to know the day was moving on.

"Okay," he said. "I'll put it back."

Overhead a cloud moved east and a bright sunbeam lit up the van. Larry swallowed. Maybe he'd best put the watch back real soon.

"Now the works of the flesh are evident . . ."
Galatians 5:19

CHAPTER EIGHTEEN

"LOOK," LARRY SAID, as he turned the van off Division street and onto a side street that led to his house. "We told Cosmos to pick up some clothes and gear. If we're setting up out at Holiday Valley, we might not be back in town for a few days. Do you want to stop at your house and pick up some stuff of yours?"

"That'd be good," Marcel said. "I'd like to water the plants and leave my mom a note." His shoulders came hunching forward. "That's what we do."

"Not a problem." A few minutes later, Larry rolled the van to stop in front of Marcel's blue-stucco home. "Take your time, kid. I'm gonna have a smoke."

Marcel left the van, walked down the sidewalk, then up the steps to the front door of the blue bungalow and unlocked it, leaving his key chain dangling when he went inside.

Larry climbed out of the van and stretched. His back ached. He suspected he had a good-sized bruise from Violet's run for freedom. His knees hurt. His neck was stiff. The pet-sitting business was harder on his body than he'd thought it would be.

He opened the van door and rummaged in the front seat side pocket until he found the crumbled remains of a pack of cigarettes and a lighter. He wasn't a big smoker, but today the nicotine was calling him.

Larry shut the van door and leaned against it. He lit up the cigarette and inhaled, savoring the sweet moment when a burst of nicotine coursed through his system. He could see Marcel through the bungalow's picture window as the teen crisscrossed the living room.

A sleek black Lincoln Navigator came down the quiet street. To Larry's surprise, the driver drove up and parked behind Larry's van. A black woman sat in the passenger seat of the big car. The driver, a lean black man in a white shirt and bright tie, nodded at Larry before turning off the Navigator.

The couple conversed for a moment. Larry watched them as he took another drag on the cigarette.

The driver emerged from the car, taking a moment to pull on a well-tailored close-fitting suit jacket.

Long drink of cool scotch, Larry thought.

The man moved with athletic ease. He walked up the sidewalk toward the blue bungalow.

Marcel stepped out of the house, stuffed rucksack in hand. He frowned at the man in the suit, then turned his back on the visitor and focused on locking the front door.

"Marcel!" The tall man stopped in the middle of the walkway.

"What?" Marcel stuffed the keys into his rucksack.

"Are you okay?" the man asked.

"Since when did you want to know?" Marcel's voice

came loaded with all the rage and snideness a fifteen-year-old could muster.

Which was, Larry, reflected, a very large truckload of rage and snide.

"Don't be this way," the tall man said. "I'm your father, and I love you."

Ah, thought Larry. *This is his missing dad.* Larry took another quiet puff on the cigarette. *This could get interesting.*

The woman in the Navigator opened the car door. As she emerged, Larry noted two details that he would classify as *Bog Standard Male Basic Note Taking.* The woman had a face of breathtaking beauty, and she was heavily pregnant. She shook her head and stretched, causing a profusion of beads and braids to fan out over her slender shoulders. She turned to look at Larry, her dark eyes firing rays of disapproval at his cigarette.

This had to be the new wife Marcel had described. An attorney. Not liked by the church ladies.

Lawyers had never been a friend to Larry. He hoisted the smoking cancer stick in her direction in a mock salute.

Her frown intensified, and her eyes sparked at Larry with intense dislike.

Not a food, Larry thought. *A poisoned chalice.* He blinked. Where had that thought come from? He'd been listening to too much Marcel. "Chalice" had to be an S-A-T word.

The woman slammed the car door and swung her bulging front toward the back of the car. She opened the rear car door and reached in, emerging a moment later with a small girl in a pink dress. Dark fluffy twists of hair held in place by ball clasps crowned the girl's head in neat rows.

The woman carried the girl around the vehicle and set the child down on the lawn in front of Marcel's house. The woman opened the car from the sidewalk side and extracted a second girl, this one in a dress a darker shade of pink, but with the same carefully curated hair.

Twins. Larry took a last puff on his cigarette before dropping the butt to the sidewalk and giving the end a grind with his shoe.

"You're going to pick that up," the woman said to Larry.

He shrugged and left the butt, just for the hell of it.

The woman whirled away and joined the man on the walkway, facing Marcel as the two little girls raced around the small lawn in a game of ineffectual tag.

"Hi Marcel," the woman said. Her voice was soft and tentative.

Marcel ignored her.

"Speak to your step-mother," his father insisted.

For a moment Larry thought Marcel would refuse. Then Marcel's nose quivered and he said, "Hi, Aisha. I'm surprised you're still here."

Larry felt his eyebrows reaching skyward. Marcel wasn't suggesting this gal was Heaven-bound, that was for sure.

"Pregnant again?" Marcel said. "Wow."

"These things happen," his father said, wearily.

"No. Dad. They don't. These things are choices." Marcel said flatly. "Choices you have been happy to make."

The two little girls squealed and dashed to hug their

father's knees. He rested a hand on each well-baubled head. "We could use your help, Marcel," he said.

"My help?"

"You can see Aisha. Her blood pressure is sky-high. With all that's happening, the community needs me."

"You aren't here to see to my welfare." Marcel said. "You're here to get services."

"I've been calling you for days," his father said. "I checked my contacts. They said your mother has been taken up, God rest her soul. We're here now to bring you home. You can be an important part of our team."

"Oh, hell no." Marcel shook his head. "I am not going to be a live-in baby sitter for your adulterous offspring."

"They're your sisters!" Aisha said. "I have wronged you, but they have not."

"They share, at best, fifty per cent of my heritage. Or it might be zero, depending on where else you took yourself," Marcel said.

"Marcel!" His father roared. "Apologize for that!" One of the little girls burst into tears. Her sister looked confused and on the brink of joining in.

Larry stood up from his lounging against the van.

Aisha inhaled. Her voice shook as she said, "Don't bother apologizing. You won't mean it. Just open the door. I need the bathroom."

"Find a bush," Marcel said. "You're not going in my mother's home."

"Stop this hatred!" his father shouted.

"I am so sorry that I hurt you," Aisha said, "but I need to pee."

"You already stole my mother's husband and the father

I once loved," Marcel said. "And that father used to say that a person's past behavior telegraphs future behavior. I can't trust you in my mother's home."

"Let her in!" his father roared. "She's a pregnant woman!"

"Hey folks," Larry called. "I live just down the street. The missus can use the bathroom at my house. Just go down to the yellow house and knock on the door. My mom is there, and she'll let you in."

"Does it stink of cigarettes?" Aisha said, tilting her head back so Larry had a good look up her nose.

"No, ma'am." He said. "It does not." He chose not to mention the sun porch's fierce stench of cat piss.

"Watch the girls," Aisha directed her husband. "I'll be right back."

"Oh, goody," Marcel said.

"A house divided cannot stand."
Matthew 12:25

CHAPTER NINETEEN

ONE OF THE little girls let go of her father's knees and made a bee-line for the street. Larry took a step toward blocking her, calling out, "Hey!"

Marcel's dad whipped around. He scooped up the twin at his feet and came running as the escapee twin halted in front of Larry.

"I think that's a sandbox," Larry said, pointing at a green plastic turtle lying like a large flat tortilla in the next yard. "If we take the lid off, there might be toys."

The little girl registered the word "toys" and followed Larry's pointing finger. She made a sharp turn and ran for the turtle, ignoring her father's calls to stop.

Larry ambulated after the kid, saying, "It's okay. No one's going to care."

Marcel's father capitulated. He carried the second girl over to the turtle and helped Larry lift off the lid. The two girls dove in, jabbering, as they dug small buckets and play shovels out of the sand.

Marcel came down the walk, crossed the lawn and stopped nearby with his rucksack over his shoulder and a frown on his face.

"Thank you, sir," Marcel's father said to Larry. "I'm Charles Westmoreland."

"Larry. Of Larry's Pet-Sitting Services. Marcel is my partner in rescuing left-behind pets. Cats mostly, although today we did have two exotic pets and Marcel's assistance was of pivotal importance." Larry was surprising himself. He didn't know he knew words like 'pivotal.' He knew the word 'exotic,' but that was a topic for another time and place. Still, it was all in a good cause. If he were in Marcel's shoes, he'd choose pig-shit smells over toddler wrangling too.

"Blessings upon you," Charles said, squatting down to hand one of the girls a plastic shark. She beamed a giant smile and grabbed the shark. She rammed the piece, face down, into a hill of sand and chortled.

"Naomi has her mother's vibrancy," Charles said.

Her twin took a shovel and beat it against the rim of the plastic sandbox until the rim dented. Charles redirected her to moving sand, which the girl did with enthusiasm, flinging sand into her sister's hair as she went.

"Vibrancy," Larry said. "I can see that."

"Marcel," Charles said, "I cannot express how sad I am for the hurts I have caused you and your mother."

"Try," Marcel grunted.

Charles sighed. "I am not surprised your mother has flown to Heaven. She deserves all the good that Heaven can offer. I only hope that you can see that Aisha and I are still here. We are imperfect souls, but we are not evil."

"I understand there's a second round of flame-outs happening soon," Marcel said. "Maybe you're on the second string."

Charles barked a laugh even as he intervened with his daughters, who were now digging to the bottom of the sand box and flinging sand with enthusiasm. "We need to be together now, Marcel," he said. "We don't know what will unfold next. The authorities remaining have done a remarkable job of keeping the peace, but there could yet be riots and looting and pogroms. I've told you all your life about the special challenges facing a young black man. It won't get any easier."

"I've got a job. I'm doing fine," Marcel said.

"And what are you paying Marcel as a salary?" Charles asked Larry.

"Food," Larry said. "Which is a hell of a lot when you eat like he does." He grinned at Marcel, who didn't smile back.

"And it's not just food," Larry said. He spoke fast, as if it might reinforce his support of Marcel. "We're about to re-locate to a big place out in Holiday Valley. Marcel's part of a team. There's, ah," Larry quickly counted in his head, his mother, two cousins, Frank, Dobbin. Hell, he might as well add in Annelise and Cosmos. Himself. Marcel. "There's nine of us. A dedicated band of volunteers in the service of left-behind pets."

Aisha came striding back down the sidewalk like a rotund ocean liner. She stopped twenty feet away, horror filling her face. "Oh, my God!" she cried. "Look at their hair!"

Larry, Charles and Marcel all looked down at the two little girls in the sandbox. The girls had invented a new game: shovel sand onto your sister's head. Their dark hair was now dust-frosted with a great deal of sand.

"I was gone three minutes!" Aisha shouted. "Three minutes!"

"Sorry, baby," Charles stood up, brushing sand off his slacks. "It's just sand. It'll brush off."

Aisha looked at him with stunned amazement. "Brush off? You think all that sand is going to just fall off?"

Even Larry was figuring out now that sand adhered well to hair. Sand also adhered to cotton dresses and polyester socks.

One of the little girls looked up at the angry words. Her face crumpled with a look of agony, and she began to cry. Fat tears ran down her cheeks, and her twin's face rapidly followed suit, making them bookends of innocence and unhappiness.

"It's okay," Marcel said, setting down his rucksack to kneel next to the girls. "We can fix this. We dealt with sandy clothes at VBS last year."

"VBS?" Larry said.

"Vacation Bible School," Marcel said. "I was a junior counselor, and we spent a day at the beach" He was dusting off one of the girls, who stopped her tears to look up hopefully. Marcel said, "Larry, do you have a shop vac at your place?"

"Yeah, I do."

"Any chance you've got a compressed air machine?" Marcel asked.

"Like you'd use with a nail gun?" Larry said.

"Right."

"The neighbor's got one. He was a framer. He flamed out, but I bet we can get the unit from his garage." Larry said

Aisha looked at them with horror. "You are *not* using a nail gun on these babies!"

Marcel shook his head. "Of course not. We can do a shake-off dance, then play some 'blowing in the wind' games with the air and then a 'I'm in a tornado' game with the vacuum. It may not get all the sand, but it should be a lot better."

"Come on, babe," Charles said. "We wanted help from Marcel. Let's accept some help."

Aisha whirled on her husband. "We have another issue here, Charles. The woman in the yellow house? I recognized her. That's Medicare Marjorie. She's a thief."

Charles' eyes darted to Larry, who shrugged his shoulders.

"Yep," Larry said. "That's my mother."

"Gratitude is the most exquisite form of courtesy."
Jacques Maritain (1882 – 1973)

CHAPTER TWENTY

AISHA KNELT DOWN next to her daughters and took their shovels. One girl started to fuss. Aisha silenced her with a look.

"Marjorie Medicare stole *millions*," Aisha said.

"No, ma'am," Larry said. "The medical office where she was working as a bookkeeper had a team of people who stole millions."

"She spent tens of thousands of dollars at casinos," Aisha said. "That was well documented." She stood one girl up and began brushing off sand.

More like hundreds of thousands of dollars, Larry thought. He said, "Our casinos are run by tribes, so you could say she was giving back to communities that have long been underserved by America." He shifted on his feet and added, "She also bought a walk-in freezer for the food bank and paid for a new roof and a new van for Animal Services." He didn't clarify that the van he was driving had also been purchased and declared as a donation but never delivered to a nonprofit.

"She ripped off the government," Aisha said. "Horribly."

"She was trained to do so by an office manager," Larry

countered. "The doctors who made millions prescribing unneeded scooters and back braces got off with a lecture from the AMA. The office manager got six months' probation. Only my mom went to jail."

"Perhaps now is not the time," murmured Charles as he helped his wife brush off the second little girl.

"I beg to differ," Larry said. "Now is the time. We're in the middle of people's worthiness being judged. Or so we think. My mother went to prison for three years. She gained eighty pounds from the stress of it all. She lost just about everything. Marcel said you worked in criminal justice reform. Well, could you please put fat old ladies on your list of people who need a break?"

Aisha blinked, then stood up slowly, some of her inner fires banked. "Your mother's choices are not comparable to the situations of the people I served," she said slowly, "Although I can see some of your points."

"One point being," Larry said, "Is that my mom surely made you welcome in your moment of need."

Aisha froze. She inhaled, and a small smile of acknowledgement emerged. She said, "That she did. She offered me a sandwich too."

Larry smiled back at her. "You shoulda taken it. She makes a great tuna fish." He looked down at the two little girls, still coated with sand. "Marcel and me have fifteen cats and three ladies to move. We need to get on it. Do you want these girls blown off?"

Aisha looked at her sand-encrusted daughters. "I don't see that I have an alternative."

"That's the spirit," Larry said. "Total surrender in

the face of disaster. I do that all the time. Okay, Marcel. What'da we do first?"

"Some dancing to shake the sand off. It's best if everyone joins in. It gets the action really going. We can do the Hokey-Pokey," Marcel said.

"Oh, hell no. Not me. You go ahead." Larry said. "I'll go liberate the air compressor and get the shop vac set up down at my house." He checked his phone. Three messages from Marjorie wanting an update. "It's getting late, and we've got a date with a plate of bar-be-que this evening."

He left just as Marcel belted out in a big baritone voice, "You put your right arm in!" to the delight of his little sisters. Aisha stripped off two sand-loaded diapers as Charles joined in with some serious long-legged wiggling. The girls were out of the sandbox and dancing by the time Larry was a few feet down the sidewalk.

It didn't take long for Larry to crowbar open his neighbor's garage side door. He helped himself to a cold beer from the garage refrigerator, gulping so fast he had to pause to belch. "Hoo—eee. That's better. Hokey-pokey, my ass." Larry found he was smiling. Marcel was a good guy.

Larry opened a second beer and thought about Marcel's family. Aisha was an adulterous attorney. That was interesting. He visualized a match-up between Aisha and the tight-assed judge his mother had faced. If his mother had Aisha as her attorney instead of the soggy-toast lawyer her employer had provided, things might have turned out differently.

"The problem with a soggy-toast ass is that it's too wet to burn," he decided. "Too bad." He tossed the empty beer cans into a recycling bin and borrowed a moving dolly to move the air compressor out of the garage and down the sidewalk to his place.

Two beers helped with ache management. Larry left the air compressor on the driveway and opened his garage. He pulled out a shop vac and a pair of orange, industrial extension cords. He started to plug things in and realized he hadn't yet told his mother he was home. She might react poorly if she heard unexpected noises from the garage. It would also be a good idea to get her moving along with moving out.

He bounded up the steps to the house. "Hey, Mom!" he called as he opened the door. "You packed?"

"Hell, No!" Marjorie shouted. "I'm not going!"

"Okay," Larry said. "Odelle, how about you? Ready to live in a swanky house with a hot tub and a wine cellar?"

"I do believe so," Odelle came to the door and motioned Larry back outside. She followed him down the steps, closing the door behind her. "She's afraid, Larry," she said.

"I know. But I think we'd all be safer out behind a locked gate," Larry said.

"She's afraid she'll break the nice furniture."

"What?"

"She's big. She knows it. She's fretting that she'll sit on an antique chair, and it'll break."

"The place isn't like that. It's got sofas. Big ones."

"Doesn't matter."

"Would it help," Larry said slowly, "If we took her recliner?"

"I think it might."

Larry exhaled. His mother's recliner was sizeable. He'd

have to take the large dog crate out of the van. He hated that idea. Somehow, he'd been hanging onto the notion that somewhere, sometime, there would be a dog for him to collect.

"Alrighty, then," he said. "We're now moving three old ladies, fifteen cats and a very large recliner."

Odelle leaned in and gave him a kiss on the cheek. "I don't know why you're still with us. You're one hell of an angel."

"Tell that to my probation officer." Larry grinned. "Don't bother. I heard he went up in a blaze – only he didn't leave ashes – he left an oily smear."

Odelle pulled her chin in and she produced a pseudo bass voice. "Justice is mine, saith the Lord," she intoned.

Larry snickered. He swung his arms to loosen his muscles. If he was moving his mother's massive recliner, he might as well have another beer.

"Doubt grows with knowledge."
Johann Wolfgang von Goethe (1749-1832)

CHAPTER TWENTY-ONE

"ABIGAIL IS NOT available," Janice said for the fourth time in five minutes as the private number for Abigail's special friends had been ringing non-stop.

The Ross Hour of Prayer 800 number only took donations and recorded prayer requests. There was a separate, private line of access for their biggest donors.

And those donors were wanting a piece of Abigail now. They had been calling for days.

The student intern who had been taking the calls quit after lunch in a cloudburst of tears. The intern explained, over a profoundly running nose, that she was ready to be a foot soldier for Christ, but she wanted to go teach prayer in some foreign land, like, maybe India. She didn't want to work as a call center operator, being abused by hostile, elitist Yankees.

Janice handed the intern a box of tissues and wished her well.

The research into housing options for Abigail took precedence over the donors. Janice had switched off the phone line and concentrated on learning about Holiday Valley. Now, close to three-thirty in the afternoon, she was finished with that task and waiting for Jared to finally arrive from whatever task he was doing at Abigail's house. She'd started answering the phone, which was like fighting a Biblical number of locusts.

Janice tried not to dwell on Jared's closeness to Abigail. She answered the phone again, withstanding yet another barrage of instructions as she furiously typed in the caller's message and multiple cell phone numbers. She assured the donor Abigail would be returning calls soon.

She hung up, and the phone rang again. This time she could see the caller's ID. It was Trevor Templeton, a toothy-smiling televangelist from the Fort Worth area known for his wide smile, hand-tooled cowboy boots and his back list of two dozen bestselling self-help books. Trevor was a favorite friend and frequent guest speaker on the Ross Hour of Prayer.

Janice took his call as Abigail and Jared walked into the office. Janice covered the microphone and whispered, "It's Trevor T."

Abigail leaned over the desk to put Trevor on speaker. "Hi, Dear. It's Abigail!"

"Abby! God Bless My Soul! It does my heart good to hear your darlin' voice." Trevor's twang typically came and went, depending on the audience. Today the twang was strong and edged.

"Good to talk to you, Trevor. How are things in Texas?"

"Rapidly changing."

Abigail's eyebrows flew up. Trevor was signaling something. She said, "You're on speakerphone with me and my dear assistants, Janice and Jared, who have my full confidence. What are you seeing that's changing?"

"There's going to be more rounds of take ups and flame outs," Trevor said. "Way beyond all that's happened so far."

"How do you know this?" Abigail asked, leaning in closer to the speaker.

"My abuelita. That's my grandmomma. On the Mexican side." Trevor spoke rapidly. "There will be seven Raptures."

"Seven?"

"Seven! The number seven is throughout the Bible. Joshua won at Jericho by having the walls circled seven times." Trevor took a breath and rattled on. "There are seven men of God in the old testament. There are seven appearances of angels. The world was completed in seven days. The candlestick of the Holy of Holies had seven branches. There are seven holes in a man's head, and Abraham's blessing has seven parts."

Abigail interrupted Trevor's rising litany. "You're talking about Numerology, Trevor. That's hokum. It's not a faith-based set of beliefs."

"I'm telling you the blessings of the Lord are promised seven times in Revelations and the angels are preparing to pour out seven vials of God's wrath."

"Trevor, if that is correct, people would be breaking out in sores."

"Only those bearing the mark of the beast, and those who worship the beast. People could be covering their sores with clothing too."

"Thank you for calling," Abigail said. "Let's have a word of prayer together."

"Wait! Abigail, do you own any property? Like,

maybe a ranch or a lake house here in Texas? Something in your name?"

The mania in his voice was gone, replaced by a tone of pragmatic urgency. Abigail straightened to a full stand and stared at the speaker. "No," she said. "We have our house here in Atlanta. Aaron never was keen on real estate. Too much maintenance, he said."

"Is the house in *your* name?"

"I . . . don't think so. Aaron's gone up, you know."

"I heard. I am so sorry for your loss." Trevor barely paused before adding, "You need to be on some property that *you* own." He sniffed and said, "I am going to be paying for my sins. Save yourself."

"Help me understand. What are you talking about?" Abigail said.

"My granny says a future round of the Rapture will be big and ugly. People living in a house owned by a female will be passed over. It's not the blood of a lamb that will protect the inhabitants, it's the female ownership of the abode."

Trevor sounded like he was weeping. He said, "Everything we've got is in my damned name. I've got three ranches in the Hill country, a lake house near Austin, a condo in Aspen, and a beachfront place on Oahu, and none of it does me any good."

"Can't you just transfer the title to your wife or daughters?"

"I'm working on it, but I think the Lord will see through that sleight of hand," Trevor said. "I've been selfish, building a worldly empire. I am suddenly aware of how male-centric Texas can be."

Abigail opened her mouth to speak, but Trevor went on with a soupy hiccup. "God is gonna smite me de-ad," he wailed. "Mary Lauren has left me and taken muh girls."

"I'm so sorry," Abigail said.

"It's my own fault. I was hound-dogging, and she knew it. And now my publisher is sayin' it's no time to put out a book on Faith in the modern marriage." The sound of nose blowing came through the speaker. "Abigail, my bank account is flatter than the road to Lubbock. I owe taxes on everything. I am one hell of a sinner. I've been enjoying the ladies. And horses. And boats. And gambling. I've been a bad, bad boy."

Abigail rolled her eyes and said, "Trevor, we've known each other a very long time."

"Yes ma'm, we have."

"You've been tempted before. You've strayed before."

There was a sniff of confirmation that came drippily over the airwaves.

"This might be," Abigail said, "An opportunity to preach on being a redeemed sinner."

"Oh, honey. I'd like to think so. But my granny is right on this new Passover. I can feel it in my bones. If I don't get to a household owned by a female, I'm going to burn for eternity."

"Could you stay with your grandmother?"

There was a further hiccup and sniff before Trevor said, "She lives in a mobile home in McAllen with three cats."

"A modest home for your retreat into prayer."

"Ah hate cats," Trevor said.

"But you believe your grandmother's prophecy?"

The sound of a sigh came across the phone connection.

"Yes'm. I do. My abuela has a different kind of faith. She sees things. She's a *curandera*, a healer."

Trevor's voice deepened and he said, "We don't believe in other paths to God. It's Christ only for us Christians. But my abuela has a path to God through herbs and certain mushrooms. Everything she's ever told me about has come to pass."

Jared spoke for the first time. "Are you talking about psilocybin mushrooms?"

"Yes, sir. The mushrooms are sainted children to her, and they speak profound messages. They are saying that a Shepherdess will come with the Shepherd. Honestly, Abigail, I was thinking you might be our next Leader. Not that dried up prune of a President we've got." He sighed. "Sorry, Abigail. I've had half a bottle of Jim Beam. I am out of my mind and seriously drunk here."

Abigail checked her watch and nodded to Janice, who accepted the cue and loudly cleared her throat. Abigail said, "Trevor, my staff is waiting for me. I've got to go, but go to God in prayer. I will keep you in my thoughts and prayers with great diligence."

"Bless you, Sister."

Janice turned off the phone.

"Whew." Abigail shook her head. "Dear misguided man. What a mess."

"Do you think he's right?" Janice asked. "About there being a next Passover? Where female-owned houses will be the safe ones?"

"The Lord only knows." Abigail looked at Janice and asked, "Is your home in your name or Clive's?"

"Clive's, I think. I'm not sure."

Abigail frowned. "Most homes in Atlanta are owned by men, I suspect."

"And you said your house is the same?" Jared asked.

"Yes. Aaron's name. I suppose it's all mine once Aaron's will is probated, but that could take weeks." Abigail shook her head. "I'm sure this is just one more cockamamie theory. We'll be fine. Anything on places to stay near where Ruthie is going?"

Janice nodded. "I spoke with a real estate agent named Bill Neddles. He says there are three homes for sale in Holiday Valley that are summer homes. He can contact the owners and see if they are interested in renting. There may also be a big place available which has lovely territorial views. He's heard that the owners are gone." She paged through her notes and read, "It's called the Lucky Seven Ranch, only it's more a country home than a real ranch. Six bedrooms. No livestock."

"Lucky Seven." Abigail smiled. "Let's not tell Trevor. I don't want him on my doorstep."

"If you go out there, will you be broadcasting?" Janice said.

"Eventually, I suppose." Abigail looked at Jared. "There is so much to figure out."

"You'll need some technical help. Clive and I could come with you." Janice said this in a rush, then fell silent, watching Abigail carefully.

Abigail ran her tongue over her lips, thinking. Janice was right. She'd need day-to-day grunt work done. There might be someone locally who would do laundry, fetch groceries and interface with Ruthie, but Janice already knew Abigail's preferences.

And Clive was a master of sound and lighting. If she was going to do any broadcasting, Clive would be an asset.

Abigail smiled and said, "Janice, that's a marvelous idea. Please call Mr. Neddles back and set up an appointment for us to see Holiday Valley in the morning. Then call the airport. We'll leave as soon as I'm packed."

"We need the storm, the whirlwind, and the earthquake."
Frederick Douglas (1817- 1895)

CHAPTER TWENTY-TWO

LARRY DIDN'T HAVE time to raid his neighbor's refrigerator for thirds on beer. Marcel and his family arrived at his garage just as soon as he had the shop vac set up. The twins were diaper-less and brushed off, but their hair remained coated with sand.

Larry had to hand it to Marcel. The teen had a talent for combining silliness with effectiveness. Marcel swooped around the driveway with his arms flat out, calling, "I'm an airplane! Come fly with me!"

The little girls charged after him, plump little arms out and tiny legs at a gallop. After two circles around Larry's small front lawn, Marcel led the girls to the air compressor. He flipped it on and had the girls mesmerized as he used the air to make his cheeks flap and his hair dance.

"Who gets the first turn?" Marcel called.

The girls elbowed each other in a race to be first to have their hair blown.

Charles stood nearby, beaming. Aisha's elegant face held a more reflective look. *Not at peace*, Larry thought. *But not breathing fire for now.*

With a mock salute, Larry left them to it. He went inside his scruffy bungalow to charm his mother into moving.

"Mom, I've been thinking," Larry said.

"Now there's a change of pace." Marjorie sat in her recliner with her feet up. She V'ed her toes apart and directed a remote control at the television, turning up the volume.

Larry walked over to his mother and looked down at her. A smile touched cousin Odelle's lips as she walked down the hallway, leaving Larry alone with his parent. Larry pouted his lips and did his best to look sad.

"Don't do that!" his mother said. "Don't you go giving me the puppy-dog eyes!"

"Mom," Larry said. "Turn down the TV."

Marjorie threw her son a sour look, but complied. "What?" she said.

"I think we should take your recliner."

"What?" Marjorie leaned forward, bringing the recliner to upright. "Take my recliner where?"

"To Holiday Valley. To the gigantic, spiffy house with a barn and a garden that's all behind a big-ass locked gate."

"I don't want to go. I'm fine here," Marjorie said.

Larry noted the lack of heat in the words. "Mom," he said. "We can't keep fifteen cats on the sun porch. We're supposed to have fifteen litter boxes. Maybe that's the reason the big gray tom is spraying on the walls. He needs his own litter box." Larry didn't bother to add that he thought the gray tom and the white Persian were a perverted pair of felines with a general hatred of others.

He pressed the point of caring with his mother. "We've rescued these animals. We have to see to their needs. There's space to do it right in Holiday Valley, but I can't be out there worrying about you."

"I'll be fine," Marjorie argued.

"There's a wall of whiskey out there. First class."

Marjorie grunted. "Nice try," she said. "Whiskey I've got. Don't worry about me, I'll be fine. We know all the nasty folks are burnt up."

"Not true." This came from skinny cousin Ilene, who was sitting at the dining room table, drinking coffee and scrolling on a computer tablet. "We know *some* of the nasty people have been burnt up."

Odelle walked by, carrying a stack of washcloths. "Let me take these out to Marcel's family," she said. "They may want to wipe down those kids." She turned to Marjorie and said, "Aisha has the cutest little girls. They've been in a sand box. Do you mind if she brings them in to clean up in the tub?"

Marjorie sat up and looked at Odelle. "Of course, she can wash off her kids. Put out the good shampoo. She's not going to want to use my cheap stuff." To Larry, Marjorie said, "How is Marcel related to Aisha?"

"Well," Larry said. "That beautiful pregnant woman is the reason Marcel's mother is divorced. And, get this, Marcel's dad is a minister."

Odelle stopped in the living room, her eyes wide. She said, "He must be pretty persuasive. I can't imagine a deacon's assembly being real welcoming of all that."

"Oh." Marjorie leaned back in the recliner. "Makes me feel better though. *Thou shalt not commit adultery* is on the same list as *thou shalt not steal*, so I can't see where Aisha'd be snooty about using our ugly old tub."

"She wasn't snooty at all about using your toilet," Odelle pointed out. "And it's stained and disgusting. She was really nice."

"Odelle, if you think my toilet is disgusting," Marjorie said, "you could lend a hand and clean the thing. My knees are bad, and Larry has a poor sense of smell." Marjorie groaned. "Now I am really embarrassed. Pregnant ladies can have sensitive noses. God only knows what she thinks of me now."

"She knows you're Medicare Marjorie," Larry said.

"Oh, fuck." Marjorie's face crumbled. "I guess everyone on the planet knows and will never forget."

"You don't have to worry, Mom. With everything that's going on, no one cares about ancient history." He snorted. "Strike that. Marcel's interested in ancient history. He's into the Babylonians."

"No, you Nimrod," Marjorie scolded. "Marcel's interested in the ancient Sumerians. They were *before* the Babylonians."

"When did you talk to Marcel?" Larry said. "He's been with me the whole time."

"We talked when you were finding him a uniform shirt," Marjorie sniffed. "I don't only talk about sandwiches."

"Marjorie and Larry, I love you dearly," Ilene said, "But could you please put a sock in it right now? If Marcel's dad is a two-timing pastor, there's something important they need to hear."

"Something you read on-line?" Odelle asked.

"Yes," Ilene said. "Religious stuff. Coming out of Mexico. It's blowing up big."

Larry looked at Ilene's determined face. Something was up. Something bad.

"Better late than never."
Anonymous

CHAPTER TWENTY-THREE

AS LARRY WALKED to the door to invite Marcel's family in, he fished the Rolex watch out of his pocket and snuck a look at the time. The handsome timepiece confirmed his suspicions. The day was getting on. He didn't want to contemplate how long it was going to take to load Marjorie's recliner and install fifteen cats into cardboard boxes.

Ilene said her finds were important. One thing at a time then.

He hustled down the front steps. Larry saw Aisha smiling and laughing as she blew air onto one little girl. Marcel had the shop vac's narrow attachment on, and he was making a dramatic production of hoovering his own head as the second twin watched closely. Charles stood to one side, looking down at a smart phone with a troubled face.

Larry waved with both hands. Marcel and Aisha clicked off their machines.

"Ilene's found some things on line about religious leaders she thinks you need to know," Larry said. "And Odelle wants to know if you'd like to rinse and shampoo the girls in the tub."

"I hate to trouble you," Aisha said.

"No trouble," Larry said. He hesitated. "I'm hoping Marcel can stick around long enough to help me load a recliner."

Marcel's face went still. "I'm not going anywhere, Larry. I'm staying with you."

His father stepped in to pick up one of the girls. "Aisha, I think we should wash the girls, and perhaps we can hear your concerns at the same time. But we need to do this quickly. I am needed."

Larry noted that Charles hadn't argued with Marcel's idea of staying.

They trooped into the house and found Odelle had already filled the tub. As Aisha set a toddler into the warm water, Marjorie waddled in. She offered Aisha a tray loaded with a plastic pitcher, two plastic cups, a tea strainer, a small pot and a colander.

"They should enjoy themselves," Marjorie said.

Aisha nodded a thanks and knelt down next to the tub as Charles set the second girl into the water. Charles closed the toilet seat and sat down. "This is an odd spot for a news update," he said, shrugging out of his suit jacket. He tucked the jacket into a towel rack and rolled up his shirt sleeves before picking up a pot to ladle water over a child.

It was a small bathroom. Odelle squeezed in next to the sink. Skinny Ilene took up a position in front of the linen closet. Marjorie's bulk filled the doorway as Larry and Marcel looked in over her shoulders.

Ilene spoke rapidly. "I've been following up on what Odelle was saying this morning. She's been in touch with the actuaries, who are trying to make sense of a second round of flame outs and takings up. Tell them, Odelle."

"Two things," Odelle said, "First is that the second round of flame outs may be related to greed."

"That's been on the news all day," Marjorie said, mostly for Larry's benefit. "The authorities have been making a ton of hay about how looting has been minimal, and it had better stay that way."

"Right." Odelle continued. "What they didn't talk about was the language associated with the second round of Rapture."

"Language?" Marcel asked.

"Yes." Odelle said. "We know the first round of Rapture has been alphabetical, by country, using the English alphabet. That's odd because there's more people who speak Mandarin Chinese than English. Or you might think that the Rapture would be associated with a Biblical language like Hebrew or Aramaic."

Charles looked at Aisha, who was rinsing one girl's head. "And what are they concluding?" he asked as he accepted the shampoo bottle from her.

"They haven't," Odelle said. "There's a belief there is a pattern but it's not English or Chinese or Hindi or Arabic or Russian."

"It's not about a language," Ilene said. "It's about goddesses."

Charles frowned.

"Seriously," Ilene said. "Hear me out. I like to read woo-woo astrology stuff. I was adopted, and I think my birthdate was changed."

"That's right," Marjorie nodded. "I'd forgotten about that."

"Ahh, we're burning daylight here," Larry said. "There's a lot to get done."

"The reason she's reading the horoscopes," Marjorie said, "Is because she's trying to figure out her birthday. Reverse correlation, right?"

"Right." Ilene said. "I've correlated enough good days and bad days with horoscopes to think I'm a Capricorn."

Larry made eye contact with Marcel and gave a head shake. Marcel shrugged but stayed silent.

"The history of Capricorn," Ilene said, "Goes way back. To before the Babylonians."

That got Marcel's attention.

"The goat-fish," Ilene said, "Was the sacred animal of the God Enki."

"A Sumerian God," Marcel said. He blew out a big breath. "Wow."

"Yes." Ilene went on, "Anyway, I've spent years reading about Capricorn. I found where the god Enki had a fight with the King of Gods, a guy name Enlil. This bigger dude gets tired of people noises and he's going annihilate all mankind. He's going to send a big flood. But Enki blabs about it to a guy who builds a boat, and mankind survives."

Marcel smiled. "The Epic of Gilgamesh! The man with the boat is Ut-napish-tim, who becomes Na'ish, who becomes Noah."

Charles finished washing his daughter's head and said, "This is all very interesting, but I'm with Larry. I'm not understanding the urgency here. I'm sitting here feeling my phone buzz with messages. My congregation needs me, Ilene."

To Aisha he said, "I'm getting requests to participate in an ecumenical council in Medina to write guidelines for northwestern communities."

"Medina? Marcel said. "In Saudi Arabia?"

"No," Charles smiled. "Our Medina is on Lake Washington, and is home to Bill Gates and Jeff Bezos, among others."

"I saw that on television," Marjorie said. "There's a buncha empty waterfront mansions, and the ones that aren't empty have really nervous owners. I'm not surprised they're throwing a pow-wow for big wigs."

Charles winced. "Let's be respectful of our indigenous cultures."

"What?" Marjorie stared at him.

"Let's not call it a 'pow-wow'," Charles said.

"Okay. It's a mega-potluck then. With caviar, I suppose." Marjorie nodded firmly, her triple chins jiggling.

Ilene interrupted. "Enki had two servants. One was the goat-fish and the other was a two-faced minister. Dark days are coming because there's about to be *a Council of Two-faced ministers*. You're gonna be in danger. I can feel it."

"Oh, Ilene, we are in an extraordinarily confusing time," Charles said. "The internet and radio are filled with theories."

"Dad, don't talk down to her!" Marcel said. "The Sumerians had the first Holy Trinity. They were the Heavens, the Winds and The Earth. An, Enlil and Enki."

"And a goddess," Ilene said, firmly.

"Ninhursag," Marcel confirmed. "Mother of all creation. Her symbol was later taken up by the Greeks as their letter Omega."

"But the Gods were too busy for everyday people's troubles," Ilene said. "So, the big God, An, sent along the ah, ah . . ."

"Annunakis," supplied Marcel.

"Yeah. Them. The Extra-terrestrials." Ilene smiled. "Thank you, Marcel. I get this all mixed up at times. The important thing is, the Goddess got disrespected, and She's returning to kick some butt."

"Huh?" Larry shook his head. "Not following you there, Ilene."

Charles cleared his throat as he carefully draped a towel around his little girl and lifted her from the bathwater.

Marcel spoke first. "Dad, you can't say Ilene's material is any weirder than the seven-headed dragon in the Book of Revelations."

"There's a *dragon* in the Bible?" Larry blinked. "Really?"

Aisha said, "Yes, there's a seven-headed red dragon who faces down a woman, dressed in white, with stars in her crown. She's pregnant with a male child. But is this historic or allegorical or futuristic?"

Larry looked at his mother to see if she was as confused as he was. Marjorie was watching the little girls. Larry shifted from foot-to-foot and tried not to think about dragons or extra-terrestrials. It was hard enough to manage some cats and a few relatives.

Charles cleared his throat. "Which is exactly why the teachings of Christ are so relevant today," he said. "Jesus upended the system of powerful people telling others what was meant by the prophets. We are all imperfect, and all worthy of love. His teachings are far more important than stars in crowns or the color of dragons."

Charles smiled at Ilene and added, "The Romans had a two-faced God named Janus. He may have been based on the Sumerian minister. I don't know. Janus looks to the past and to the future. He represents open doors and thus is the root of the English word, janitor."

He dried the toes of his little girl and said, "We can do this all day. There're many ways to find connections between the past and the present. We don't have the luxury of time for these discussions at the moment."

Ilene's face fell. "You don't believe me," she said. "Disaster is about to descend in its next configuration, and you guys don't believe me."

"Beautiful person, thin life."
Japanese proverb

CHAPTER TWENTY-FOUR

"I APPRECIATE YOUR concern," Charles said. "I truly do. But we can't live in fear of every individual with an active imagination." He shifted the little girl in his arms and said, "People have been scouring gospel and historic texts like crazy, and they do come up with some odd allegories."

"Al Gore -ees?" Marjorie said. "The climate change guy?"

"No, ma'm," Charles said pleasantly. "An allegory is a story that has a message, like the Tortoise and the Hare. You can make up an allegory to broadcast just about anything." He finished rinsing Naomi and nodded to Aisha. "I think she's as clean as she can be."

Aisha opened the tub drain as Odelle handed her a towel.

"I *am* highly interested," Charles said, "in hearing if your sources articulated any particular action against the two-faced ministers."

Ilene's scrawny shoulders came forward in a hunch. "All sorts of stupid stuff," she said miserably.

"Of course." Charles nodded. "The usual we expect from narrow minds and inflamed psyches." He enfolded his daughter in the towel and rubbed her gently. She looked up at him with beautiful wide eyes that suddenly drooped closed as she put her head against his chest.

"I should be fine," Charles said. "I am a small fish in the ocean." He smiled. "And not as interesting as a goat-fish."

"That's not true," Aisha said. She looked up at Marcel and said, "Your father's ministry has been growing. He is revered by many, which means some feel threatened by his message of prosperity for all."

Charles stood up, holding his small daughter to his chest. "Marcel, I know you think I've been preaching the standard prosperity gospel," he said. "And I'll admit that I started there. But I'm not preaching that message now. I truly believe that God's creations of beauty and bounty are meant for all people to enjoy. We cannot continue as a planet and a nation of vast income disparity."

"A message that some see as a threat," Aisha said.

"But he'll be okay at this . . . ukulele-council," said Marjorie. "That's just religious folks, right?"

Aisha frowned. "It's wrong to think religious people are reasonable. Charles and I attended a class on early ecumenical councils. There was a strong-willed man named Dioscorus who ran the Second Council at Ephesus. He was incredibly manipulative. He disenfranchised some participants, saying they were unqualified to be judges. He installed his own rule set for the proceeding. He refused to include material sent in by the Pope, and he had a mob organized. The mob killed one poor man who was clinging to the altar. That intimidated everyone else to voting a certain way. It was an ugly fight over whether Christ had a beginning."

"A beginning?" Marjorie said. "Isn't that what Christmas is all about? Babe in the manger?"

"There were those who argued, with intensity, that Christ is and was eternal," Aisha replied.

"That had to be a collection of butt-headed men," Marjorie said. "No woman would go around erasing childbirth."

"Amen,' Aisha said. "My point is that religious councils are made of people and can be manipulated and even dangerous." She paused in drying her daughter's shoulders. "I just realized something. If the Buddhists are right and there is reincarnation, perhaps the highly manipulative Dioscorus returned as a senator from Kentucky."

"I think in Buddhism, rebirth is immediate," Charles said. "Meanwhile, I'm sure we're over-stating things. I'll attend the council to make contacts to improve regional care."

"Medina," Aisha said. "Some real movers and shakers live in that neighborhood."

Charles smiled. "Marjorie's right in that there should be fine food. Please don't think I won't enjoy it." His face sobered, "But the well-being of everyday people will be at the forefront of my thinking. Aisha, I know your values and cherish them. I won't let you down."

To Ilene, he said, "I thank you for sharing your findings. I do have many concerns, and I speak about them. I hope you will continue to hold me in your prayers."

He leaned over to the diaper bag that Aisha had opened and extracted a diaper and a purple-footed blanket sleeper. As he maneuvered his daughter into the diaper and pajamas, he said, "Marcel, we're all called to service in different ways. You would be an immense help to me if you came with us.

I'm not worried about traveling to the ecumenical council. It may be days of dull meetings. But I am worried about your sisters and Aisha. Her blood pressure is too high."

"Your kids, your wife, your problems, Dad." Marcel looked over Marjorie's shoulder to speak to Aisha. "He'll always be gone," Marcel said. "It'll always be something. A meeting, a need, a conference. And pretty soon he won't even take your calls." Marcel's voice deepened with scorn. "Last fall, I needed a new winter coat and shoes. He wouldn't even answer the damn phone."

Charles closed his eyes, a look of pain on his face.

"I called a dozen times," Marcel said. "I finally rode my bike over to the Goodwill and got a jacket and some shoes. I told Mom I was running for president of the Recycling Club, which was bullshit, but I got her to be okay with me wearing old shoes. She bought a new pair for me this spring after she got her tax refund. You've been nowhere in the picture."

Aisha swallowed hard and stood up. "This was my fault. I told Charles not to take your calls." She looked down at the little girl she was holding and said, "I have been half crazy. For a long time, the girls weren't sleeping on a schedule. One was always awake. I had mastitis. You were so horrible the few times I'd seen you, I just thought if you didn't have a Dad for a bit, maybe you'd miss him."

"Oh, Lordy," Marjorie said. "And I thought I was a fuck-up."

Aisha managed a wince of a smile. "Marcel, I can't rewind time. I can tell you that I am filled with regrets, and I am paying for my mistakes." She shook her head. "I'm not your mother, and people let me know that every day.

With their looks and words and frowns. I had no idea what a pastor's wife puts up with. It's hell on Earth."

She reached to the diaper bag and pulled out a second purple sleeper. As she guided her daughter's limbs into the sleeper, she said, "I was valedictorian of my high school class. Top ten at Brown university. Then I was at the top of my law school class at Gonzaga, and one of the youngest public defenders in the history of the state."

Aisha zipped close the diaper bag. "Now I am losing my mind changing diapers." She looked up at Marcel and said, "This next baby is a boy. When Charles heard that, he put his hands on my tummy and cried. He said he was happy, but I know he was missing you."

Marcel stared at her. Charles gave a weary shrug.

Aisha said, "Charles, I don't think you should force Marcel to come with us. Don't shame him or intimidate him. I don't want him to hate me any more than he already does."

She looked at Marcel. "I think helping Larry rescue pets is a great idea. That sun porch is really full of cats. I hope you'll find some fresh cat litter. If your father or I can help you in anyway in the future, then please call."

She looked down and said, "Oh, Marjorie, I am so sorry. Look at all this sand in the tub!"

"Don't worry about it, honey," Marjorie said. "I'm moving."

Larry stared at his mother.

"Don't look surprised," Marjorie said. "Somebody needs to be supervising you and Marcel." She inhaled and looked around the crowded bathroom. "This meeting's adjourned. Let's get on with it."

There are seven colors in a rainbow.
Red, orange, yellow, green,
blue, indigo and violet.

CHAPTER TWENTY-FIVE

"YOU SPOKE OF other languages being assessed to predict the next round of Rapture," Aisha said to Odelle as
the group moved through the tiny living room. "Who is
the assessor?"

Odelle smiled. "A friend of mine is an insurance actuary." She paused. "I worked for him for three years and
loved it. Then my plantar fasciitis acted up, and I retired."

"That's a lie, and God is going to smite you into ashes,"
Ilene said. To Aisha, she said, "Odelle's boss is the nicest
man who was married to the world's nastiest woman. She
flamed out, no surprise, on Day One of the USA rapture. I keep telling Odelle she doesn't have time to waste.
She needs to talk to Harold, face-to-face. Not this online
chat shit."

Larry moaned in disbelief. He loved Ilene. He truly
did. But he had a recliner to load and fifteen cats to catch.
He did not need more of his family's penchant for drama
at this particular moment.

Odelle turned on her sister. "You be quiet! You don't
know what you're talking about! Harold and I respect

each other as friends. He's nice enough to treat me as a colleague, and you can just put a cork in it!"

Burgundy-dyed hair swishing, Odelle pivoted her round tummy toward Aisha's protruding stomach and said, "I am fortunate to be in discussion with an actuary who is in touch with other actuaries. Do you have a suggestion for our evaluations?"

"I do," Aisha said, balancing her now sleeping daughter on her chest and threading her way around Marjorie's giant recliner. "It has to do with the Book of Jubilees. It's an ancient religious work that's been called the Lesser Genesis."

She stopped as Odelle opened the front door. The two round-fronted women descended the front steps together and began the walk back to the black Navigator and Larry's van, still parked in front of Marcel's home.

Larry and Marcel followed as Charles brought up the rear with the second toddler. Marcel carried the diaper bag, and Larry slouched along, his mind skittering through the logistics of moving. He had a feeling that moving Marjorie was going to be harder than moving the fifteen cats. It was not a good feeling. No doubt Marcel would have a S-A-T word to describe what Larry was feeling. "Ominous" came to Larry's mind. For now, 'ominous' could serve as a placeholder. Larry longed for another cigarette.

"No sense borrowing trouble," he muttered as he picked up his pace. He wanted to hear what Aisha had to say.

"The Book of Jubilees," he heard Aisha say to Odelle as they walked up the sidewalk to Marcel's house, "Is not part of the Catholic or Protestant or Eastern Orthodox bibles. It is, however, part of the canon of an Ethiopian church. I'm mentioning it to you in part because it included numerical rule sets, most revolving around the number seven."

"Seven" Marcel interrupted. "I was telling Larry about the Sumerian history of seven."

"A jubilee is based on seven," Aisha said. "A jubilee is forty-nine years, or seven 'year-weeks'. The book has information on Genesis and describes classes of angels. Archeologists have found the Book of Jubilee in Hebrew, but it's also in Ge'ez, a nearly extinct language from Ethiopia."

"I've never heard of it," Odelle said.

"The Ethiopian Orthodox church says they have the Ark of the Covenant in a chapel where no outsiders are allowed," Aisha said.

"Like Indiana Jones and the Ark?" Marcel asked.

"Yes." Aisha's braids swung as she walked. "The Ark of the Covenant may be in Ethiopia."

"Aren't there, like language specialists looking into this Rapture-language correlation?" Marcel argued. "You know, Ph.Ds and professors and all? Why would you be right about Ethiopian Ge'ez?"

"I don't know that I am," Aisha said with a polite calmness. "Remember I was talking about the awful manipulator, Dioscorus? He was shit-canned at a following meeting, called the Council of Chalcedon. The Ethiopians, who were at both councils, finally had enough of the politics. They went home in disgust, refusing to accept the voted changes."

She stopped on the sidewalk next to the Navigator and

looked at Marcel. "That a black delegation's concerns and contributions were not heard is typical. We know white men in power consistently ignore black contributions. This is a centuries-old habit. I want you to know that the Ethiopian Orthodox Church kept the Book of Jubilees in the language of Ge'ez. It might be worth going back to original text if Odelle's friends are striking out with modern languages."

Charles opened the big vehicle. They loaded the sleeping girls into car seats. Marcel set the diaper bag in the footwell of the back bench. Aisha gave him a nod of farewell as she climbed into the front passenger seat with an effort.

Larry amended his classification of Aisha. He no longer pegged her as *a poisoned chalice*. This time he went with *hard-frozen ice cream*. It was an adjustment he kept to himself.

After shutting the passenger door for his wife, Charles turned and stood in front of Marcel, saying, "We have done you injury, and I am so very sorry. Please call me whenever you see fit, and I will pick up." With that Charles hugged a rigid Marcel while pressing a fold of cash into Marcel's waistband.

Odelle waved as the big vehicle pulled away from the curb. She started to say something cheerful, but fell silent as she turned to Marcel.

Larry looked over and noticed Marcel's rigid face. Larry could see a clenched jawline and a vein in Marcel's neck pulsating rapidly.

Odelle said, "I'm going to go tell Ilene about the

Jubilee book. Reading about angels might keep her outta my life."

She clumped away, down the sidewalk, leaving Larry next to the teen.

Neither spoke.

Marcel clenched his fists

Larry spat on the sidewalk and said, "We need to move the van down to my house. It's only fifty yards or so, but you want to drive?

Marcel's head pivoted and his green eyes came to a sharp focus. "I'm fifteen. I don't have a driver's license."

Larry shrugged.

"It's probably a really bad idea," Marcel said.

"One way to find out."

"It's illegal," Marcel said.

"I'm kinda flexible on legal issues." Larry pulled his car keys out of his pocket and held them up. The keys sparkled bright silver in the late afternoon light.

"Up to you," Larry said.

Marcel reached for the keys. "You know this could end with a wreck, right?"

"We're only going a little way down an empty road," Larry said. "How bad a driver can you be?"

"One way to find out!" Marcel was already opening the driver's side door.

Larry climbed into the passenger seat and said, "You know where the brake is?"

"Sure." Marcel inserted the ignition key and turned it. Too far. The starter whined like an early morning coffee grinder.

"Easy!" Larry shouted.

Marcel let go of the key. "Sorry!" he shouted back.

"Alright then," Larry said, trying for an easy tone. "Let me put on my seat belt. Then you put your foot on the brake and shift into drive."

The next horrible discovery came quickly. Once the van was in drive, Marcel eased his foot onto the gas pedal. He pressed down on the gas, and the van rocketed forward. Marcel tried to brake, but his seat was too far forward for his height. His knee hit the steering column as he stabbed for the brake.

By the time Marcel's size twelve foot came close to the brake pedal, the van had overshot Larry's driveway. When Marcel did find the brake pedal, he stomped on it, bringing the van to a squealing halt and slamming Larry into the seatbelt.

"Put it in park," Larry said, "And find the seat adjustment under the seat."

Marcel did so. He listened carefully as Larry coached him to back up the van.

The van came to a stop in front of the driveway. It was about three feet from the curb.

Larry realized one of the positive aspects of no longer having neighbors was there was no one to complain about parking details.

"Good job," he said.

"Good job? That was horrible!" Marcel turned off the ignition with shaking fingers.

"You're too hard on yourself," Larry said. "No broken bones, no tickets, no night in jail. We're good."

Larry emerged from the van with a set of aches coming

from a diagonal line across his chest. "Good to know the seat belts work. Think positive."

The muscles didn't listen.

Marcel came around the front of the van and handed the keys back to Larry.

Larry took a deep breath. "You can do this, buddy," he said softly.

"Do what?" Marcel said.

"Be positive in the face of certain doom."

Moving Marjorie was next.

"Who can find a virtuous woman?
For her price is far above rubies."
Proverbs 31:10

CHAPTER TWENTY-SIX

"JANICE," ABIGAIL CALLED. "I'll need the mattress topper. I think it'll fit in a duffle bag."

"I'll see to it." Janice blinked back tears. She was exhausted by Abigail's whirl of demands. She vaguely remembered sitting down with Clive for pie, but that had been hours ago.

Clive came up the back steps and let himself into the glorious expanse that was Abigail's kitchen. He was carrying a Subway sandwich bag. Janice's verge of tears exploded into weeping as he came close.

He hugged her and guided her to the kitchenette dining nook. This was their private spot in the Ross empire. Abigail rarely ate at home. She never cooked. The small table with its vinyl benches at the back of her vast kitchen was not her habitat. Years ago, Clive and Janice discovered they could find a moment of peace at the simple table overlooking a garden of blooming perennials.

Now Clive opened the bag and pulled out a wrapped sandwich. Janice knew it would be her favorite, a meatball sub with extra pickles.

"I figured you'd be hungry," he said.

Janice picked up a napkin and wiped away her tears. "You figured right."

"I followed the list in your text." Clive handed her the sandwich. "Go ahead. Eat. I'll talk. Then we'll figure out what to do next."

With a damp sniffle, Janice unwrapped the sandwich. She paused and murmured a brief prayer of thanks. Clive closed his eyes and folded his hands, sitting still until she said, "Amen."

"Amen," he repeated. "I've been busy too. I went by the house and packed our suitcases. They're in the car. I put in your peach flannel pajamas and the little hair dryer."

"Thank you." Janice spoke around a mouth full of meatball.

Clive smiled and reached out to pat her arm. "We're going to get through this," he said. "God will direct us." He hunched over the table and his voice dropped. "I called our Claudia."

Janice stilled, mid-chew. Claudia was Clive's niece by way of his older brother. An Atlanta beauty, Claudia had combined her looks with smarts, religion and her father's political connections to land a job in the White House. Janice didn't really know Claudia. She'd seen the young woman at family reunions, of course, but Claudia's upscale luster was too much for Janice to feel comfortable striking up casual conversations.

Clive said, "Claudia confirms what you heard from Pastor Trevor. The brain-iacs of the C.I.A. and National Security agencies have been working non-stop. There seems to be another Rapture coming. There may be a protective benefit to being in a home or building owned by a female."

He paused to reach into the sandwich bag. He pulled out a bottle of Dr. Pepper. He opened the bottle and passed it to Janice.

Clive continued, "Claudia said the President will be making an announcement tonight. They anticipate a tremendous rush to county clerks across the country. I called the courthouse. The lady who answered said they were understaffed. Half their clerks are gone."

"Feathers or flames?" Janice asked.

"She didn't say. I didn't ask." Clive shrugged. "But clerks working customer service on their feet all day? I'll bet it was feathers. Maybe one or two flame-outs, but it had to be mostly feathers."

"Did you ask about putting our house in my name?"

Clive nodded. "I could download a quitclaim form and fill it out. Then I'd have to find a notary to witness the signature. That part's easy."

Janice handed him the Dr. Pepper, and he took a sip. "The challenge," Clive said, "is getting the property transfer paperwork finalized at the County Recorder's office. They're backed up. It could take two weeks. Or more."

"Which is too long," Janice said.

"That's what I thought," Clive said it slowly, watching her process the finality of their decisions. "And that's when I packed the suitcases."

"I researched this Holiday Valley," Janice said. "There're seven homes out there. Two are owned by the McElroy family. Then there's the big home owned by Ruthie's friend's family, and there are three summer cabin-style places that are for sale. One of those is owned by a woman."

"That's the one Abigail wants?"

"Probably not. It's a modest summer cabin. There's one more place, the Lucky Seven Ranch. Six bedrooms. Large barn, garden and orchard. It's owned by Ms. Julie Marian Babcock. The real estate agent, a man named Neddles, says the Babcocks have gone up."

"We're flying across the country to live in someone's house who can't say *No, thank you* to our being there?"

"You think that will hold Abigail back one second?" Janice snapped.

Clive sighed. "My life was easier when I was blind and didn't see."

Janice felt for her husband. He liked sleeping in his own bed. At the same time, a squiggle of disquiet wiggled into her stomach to accompany the three meatballs she'd consumed.

"Clive, we can't ignore what we know." Janice took back the Dr. Pepper and swallowed a large slurp of soda.

He grinned at her. "Christians ignore things we know all the time. Look at our voting patterns."

She snorted, bringing the Dr. Pepper up in a carbonated bubble of laughter. "Oh, Clive," she hiccupped. "Thank you for that."

"What do we do next?" he asked.

"Well, if you have a strong stomach, you can help me get the mink mattress topper off Abigail's king-sized bed and wrestled into a duffel bag."

"We're traveling with a mink mattress topper?"

"Abigail is. And it smells of sex. Recent sex."

"Oh, Lord."

"That's exactly who I think we should be calling into this situation," Janice agreed. She folded up the sandwich wrapper and slid it into the Subway bag. "Let's have a moment of prayer before we get back to the grindstone." Janice reached across the table and took Clive's hands.

Clive obediently bowed his head.

"Lord," Janice prayed. "There is a house in Holiday Valley that is owned by Ms. Julie Babcock. Bless that house. Bless our journey. Show us Your will. Show us our path."

"Jannnicceee" Abigail called from upstairs. "I need you. We need to get a move on!"

"Forgive us our trespasses as we forgive those who trespass against us," Janice finished.

"Amen," said Clive.

"Enoch walked faithfully with God; then was no more because God took him away."
Genesis 5:24

CHAPTER TWENTY-SEVEN

THE RECLINER WAS a massive bitch to move. Larry would have pissed and moaned and procrastinated, but his brain was locked on the vision of Frank serving up a plate of steaming ribs. The bar-be-que would be his just as soon as he could get Marjorie, her cousins, and a sun porch full of cats moved.

Larry heard Odelle telling Ilene about the Book of Jubilees and the apparent need to research angels. Ilene, he knew, would take this direction to heart. Sure enough, the ladies were already clustered around Ilene's laptop as Larry began studying the path from recliner to van.

"Let's lean the chair back," Larry said to Marcel. "You take the head, and I'll take the foot."

Two minutes later Larry realized he'd made a terrible tactical error. Taking the foot of the recliner and backing across the living room went well enough, but going down the steps brought gravity into the equation.

He should have had Marcel take the lower load. What the hell had he been thinking? What good was a young assistant if the management was too stupid to employ the perks of management?

Larry didn't have time to dwell on these questions. As soon as his feet went down the step to the lawn, he had another problem. The damp grass sloped down to the curb. Gravity remained in existence as Larry rapidly shuffled down the slope, recliner weight concentrated in hands now searing with sharp spikes of pain.

They reached the sidewalk and Larry dropped his end with an "OOFFT."

"That went well," Marcel said.

Larry swung his arms and flexed his hands in a vain attempt to stave off the pins and needles coursing up his limbs. "Do me a favor," Larry said, moving into management mode. "Can you unload the coolers out of the van?"

"Sure!" Marcel made short work of emptying the van, although he needed Larry's help to walk the giant dog carrier up the driveway to Larry's garage. Odelle's Subaru station wagon sat in the middle of the driveway. Larry eyed it as they shuffled past, carrying the dog kennel. The station wagon didn't have the height to take the extra-large crate.

"I hate being without this," Larry said as they set the plastic crate down on the garage floor. "I keep hoping we'll get a call for a dog."

"Can't we just put it back in the van after we do the trip with the recliner?"

Larry shook his head. "I don't know. Fifteen cats in carriers will take a lot of room. Which reminds me, we've got another problem. We need litter boxes." He walked back down the driveway with Marcel. They coordinated a lift and slide to load the recliner into the van. Larry sagged against the bumper after the final shove. "Damn, that's heavy."

"Thinking about the litter boxes," Marcel said. "Can we use the cardboard transport boxes?"

"Nah. Think about it. You've got wet pee and damp poop. The cardboard won't hold up." Larry inhaled. "Let's go inside. I've got an idea, but my mother isn't going to like it."

He was correct.

"My casserole collection?" Marjorie yelled. "As PISS POTS?"

Larry flinched but regrouped. "Just the big ones, Mom."

"They're collectibles!"

"Which should have been declared as ill-gotten gains," Larry said. "We weren't supposed to keep stuff you bought with the Medicare money."

Marjorie's chins wobbled as her lips worked furiously. Larry knew she was vacillating between indignation and tears.

"It's okay, Mom," he said. "Maybe we can use the cardboard kitty carriers as litter boxes."

"That won't work," Marjorie said. "You're gonna have wet pee and damp poop."

"I said exactly that, to Marcel," Larry agreed. "I'm just trying to do something right for a change." He grinned at his mother. "King of the Proper Piss Pots, that's me."

"Oh, you rascal." Marjorie's eyes softened as she broke into a smile. "I never could tell you 'no.' Take the damn casseroles."

"Love you, Mom."

"Could you leave me the cast iron Nieman Marcus pasta pot?" Marjorie said. "That sucker's heavy. It's my back-up weapon if we ever have a burglar."

"Sure, Mom. I can just picture the bad guy standing around the kitchen while you grab a chair, climb up and yank down the right dish to bash him. No problem. That'll work."

"You hush!"

Larry set up a chair in the kitchen so Marcel could reach the casserole dishes adorning the cabinet tops. Marjorie's colorful collection spanned the perimeter of the small kitchen. Marcel handed down dish after dish, which Larry stacked on the crowded countertop and then on the floor.

When Marcel sneezed, Larry laughed. "These are dusty because we eat a lot of sandwiches," he said. "Mom's got fantasies of being a cook, but that's as far as we've gotten."

"I heard that Larry!" Marjorie called from the living room. "Hustle your butt out here. Ilene has found something."

Ilene was at the dining table, peering at her laptop, saying, "You won't believe this!" as Larry and Marcel came in from the kitchen.

Odelle was on her own laptop, looking unimpressed. "I just messaged Harold, and he's not worried."

"You told me to research what they said on angels, and I'm doing that," protested Ilene. "And don't go giving me guff from Harold. I get enough from you."

"Easy," Larry said. "Mom, can you turn down the TV?"

His arms ached. He tried not to think about hauling

the dozen large casseroles to the van. He could delegate, he realized with a start. He could delegate moving the casseroles to his assistant and take a moment to grab another beer from the neighbor's garage fridge.

Hell, he could pick up a six-pack and let Marcel drive.

Cheered by that possibility, Larry leaned over Ilene's shoulder. "What's up?" he asked.

"There are different kinds of angels in the book of Jubilee," Ilene said.

Marcel leaned against the wall and brought out his smart phone. He started rapid-fire thumbing as Ilene spoke.

"What's scary," Ilene said, "is that some of the fallen angels got it on with naughty women. Their babies were called Nephilim. Really bad, underworld guys. The Flood almost wiped them out. Only God decided," she gulped. "That ten percent of them could come back as *ghosts to lead men astray*."

Marcel said, "You know, what's even more interesting is the Book of Jubilees says that the angels brought Enoch the gift of writing. We know that the first written language was cuneiform Sumerian. Maybe Enoch was Sumerian?"

As much as Larry liked Marcel, he wasn't so sure everyone of merit in history had been Sumerian. Then again, what did he know about history?

A more important wonder was if there might be more beer inside his neighbor's house. He should look. There might be some pickles. If he could find a large jar of dills, he could survive his family and a few more lectures on Sumerians. He wouldn't mind hearing more about the self-diddling alpine lake snails. But angels, even ghost angels, not so much.

He should look for some more cigarettes.

Larry's drifting mind didn't have time to wander far.

"And who the hell was Enoch?" Odelle barked. She had her arms crossed and was frowning down at Ilene.

"There are several Enochs mentioned in the Bible," Marcel said. "One of them was the grandfather of Noah. Genesis says Enoch didn't die. He was taken up."

"We've got bigger problems," Marjorie said, picking up the television remote. "Look at the screen scroll. The president is about to speak."

"I'd rather hear from the ghosts," Ilene said.

"Nearly all men can stand adversity, but if you want to test a man's character, give him power."
Abraham Lincoln (1809 – 1865)

CHAPTER TWENTY-EIGHT

THE PRESIDENT WALKING to a podium to speak to the nation was not a person elected by the American people. The people's choice was gone, as was his Vice-President and a cluster of aides who had been in the Oval Office on the first day of the American Rapture. A Secret Service Agent had heard the crackle of flames and had bravely barged in, ready to sacrifice his life for the leader of the free world.

Instead the agent found an array of piles. There were four mounds of feathers and four heaps of ashes. In the three days since, the internet exploded with opinions on whether one of the feather piles had a tint that matched the dyed hair of the controversial late President. One of the ash piles was clearly bright white, which also triggered much commentary.

Conspiracy buffs had a field day analyzing the placement of the piles. Spiritual leaders bent the details to serve their message.

Even Ilene was impressed by the depth and breadth of the pseudo-analysis, finally commenting that Bigfoot could not be responsible as everyone knew that Sasquatch was a forest creature too shy and too smart to be in the White House.

Now the wizened Speaker of the House had been sworn into the Presidency. Bookmakers were giving fifty-fifty odds on whether her next destination had halos or flames.

Marjorie unmuted the television as Madam President stopped at the podium and began to speak.

"My fellow Americans, we are at a moment of tremendous challenge," the President said. "While we are confused and grief-stricken at the loss of loved ones, our social order is holding. Deliveries of food and medicine are being supported by our brave members of the military. Furthermore, our power grid and internet services remain intact, robust and fully functional."

"Members of Congress, our Governors and our Mayors are to be commended for their selfless hours of service."

Marjorie buzzed her lips to produce the sound of an extended fart. "I know they're working hard," she said. "That's kinda their job."

"Shh," Larry said. He didn't really care about the next several paragraphs of praise for fellow world leaders and members of the military-industrial complex, but he knew it was best to treat Marjorie like a rude parrot, curtailing crude sounds early when visitors were present.

"Many scientists, theologians and linguists have been hard at work," the President said. "Their analysis is still in the early stages. However, there is evidence that a second round of Rapture may soon be unfolding. It is important not to panic."

This time it was Odelle who hooted in disbelief. "Keep calm and Rapture up?" she said.

Larry's eyes stayed on the television screen. His brain provided a food association for the President. *Dried apple with cinnamon.*

"The first round of Rapture," said the President, "has traveled around the world, by nation, in an alphabetical fashion, based on the English alphabet. There are indications that the second round of Rapture may be associated with an ancient Ethiopian alphabet called Ge'ez."

"Oh, My God," Marcel said. "Aisha was right!"

"This ancient language," the President said, "has masculine and feminine forms of many, but not all, nouns. I must stress we do not have complete clarity on what comes next, but there is some indication that property owned by a female head of household may be 'passed over' during the second phase of Rapture."

"Holy Shit," Marjorie breathed. This time Larry did not correct her.

The President continued. "It is important to recognize the uncertainties in this analysis of scripture and history. Out of an abundance of caution, I encourage Americans to use the next twenty-four hours to identify female-owned residences and buildings. Citizens should move to these locations as further information is gathered and analyzed."

"It is," the President said, "important to undertake these actions with dignity and respect. There is no need to panic."

Larry thought rapidly. When his mother had been prosecuted and convicted of Medicare fraud, almost all of her assets had gone to court fines and restitution. The one bit of good her wet-toast of a lawyer had succeeded in doing was moving the house to Larry's name.

It had taken some fast sleight of hand and a close relationship between the attorney and a particularly naive and sweet-natured county courthouse employee to shield the home. The judge had grumped, but reporters were already posting the news that the physicians and office manager of the fraud operation had skipped away with few consequences.

Now his name on the title and mortgage was a problem. He doubted he'd go up in a funnel of feathers. A spurt of flame was a distinct possibility, no matter how many cats he rescued.

His mother would not do well without him.

Larry's phone chimed. He looked down and saw Frank was calling. Swiping quickly, he said, "Hey, Frank. See the news?"

"Yes," Frank said. "When the authorities say "Not to panic," the first thing that happens is panic. I know my place is in my name. I own my daughter's place too. But I just checked the county website. The Babcock place has Julie Marian Babcock as the owner. I think you should get your family and Marcel out here and take up residence before anyone else does."

"Working on it," Larry said. "We've got the recliner loaded. I'm about to bring out some big casseroles for litter boxes. Did Cosmos get to you?"

"She sure did!" Frank's voice lilted up. "She's a dynamo. She checked out Violet for ringworm, and she's been stringing some bird netting over the stall bars. We'll have three cat-proof stalls by the time you get here. We'll have that plus the catio. There are some bags of wood shavings that were probably for the pigs, but Cosmos says it'll work for kitty litter."

"Good," Larry grunted. "It'll take two trips, but we'll get on our way quick-like." He tapped off the phone and said, "We need to get our show on the road. The big house is registered to a gal."

Ilene said, "You've got your hands full, Larry. You don't want me and Odelle constipating the system." Her face was somber, brave and more than a little sick-looking.

"Oh, yes I do!" Larry shook his head. "Well, that came out wrong." He crossed the small living room to put a hand on Ilene's shoulder. "Please come. Momma will do better with you out there. I'll do better." He grinned at her. "And sooner or later one of your whack-a-doodle theories is going to be right."

She sniffed in mock outrage before a smile crept onto her face. "You're sure?"

"Absolutely." He turned to his mother and said, "Mom, we should get some clothes together. We need to get this show on the road."

"I won't fit in the van!" Marjorie said. "You don't have a seat belt extender! I told you to get one!"

"We loaded your recliner. You can sit in that."

"Without a seatbelt?"

"I don't think the state troopers are doing seat belt checks. We'll drive real careful." Larry sighed and gave up the idea of having a few beers while Marcel drove.

He rubbed the small of his back. It hurt. So did his arms. And his ribs. His shoulders didn't feel so great either.

Larry tilted his head and felt his neck muscles pull in protest.

He needed to get his mother loaded and out to the Babcock house. Then he and Marcel had to speed back and catch fifteen cats. A cold beer sounded so good.

"How can Ilene and I help?" Odelle asked. "We've got some room in the station wagon."

"Start loading casseroles," Larry said. "I'll be right back."

"Where are you going?" Marjorie called.

"I'm going to run next door to check the inside refrigerator. There's some beer in the garage we can take out for this evening, but right now I am really hoping to find a jar of pickles."

"Pickles!" Marjorie shook her head. "We're about to be zapped to Hell and gone, and you want pickles?"

Larry shrugged. "When you want a pickle, you gotta hunt for pickles. I'll be right back."

"The nail that sticks out gets hammered."
Japanese proverb

CHAPTER TWENTY-NINE

IT WASN'T EASY for Marjorie to leave her home. With help from Ilene, she managed to stuff a bag with clothes and a pillow case with toiletries. Larry promised he'd be returning quickly for the cats and could retrieve anything she felt needed fetching.

As Marjorie climbed into the van and made her way to the recliner in the back, Larry left Marcel loading casseroles into Odelle's station wagon while he made a rabbit-footed dash to the neighbor's house.

He entered through the pried-open side door of the garage. With rapid efficiency he emptied the garage refrigerator, stacking three cases of beer on a moving dolly. He then took the steps up to the house, grateful when the garage-connected door swung open easily.

Larry had a few years of experience helping himself to things he wanted, but it was a new experience to be pilfering in a post-Rapture and now pre-Second-Rapture time frame. This was no time for raven eyes to be lighting on shiny small collectibles. Larry stopped in the small den and eyed the gun cabinet. His neighbor had been a manly idiot, with an unsecured shotgun proudly displayed on hooks above a grimy fireplace. Two boxes of shells sat on the mantel.

"Never occurred to the butthead that he might forget to open the damper and have a flameout from a fire," Larry muttered. "Much less some intruder breaking in and picking up that thing."

The irony of thinking dark thoughts about intruders was lost on Larry. He was busy calculating whether or not to take the shotgun.

He decided not to. There were too many gunslingers running around already. He didn't need his incompetent-to-nonexistent firearm skills in the mix. Besides, he suspected Frank would have some opinions on who was providing security. Plus, there was no point in scaring Marjorie and Dobbin by showing up with a shotgun that he didn't know how to handle.

The Bible on the end table was in a different category. It might be useful. It was old, with a once-black cover now faded to a rusty brown. Larry had never owned a Bible. He didn't particularly want one now, but it might keep Ilene's busy mind on a track that could provide some useful nugget.

Larry picked up the Bible and moved on, collecting a box of matches from the mantel. He detoured to the kitchen where he found a paper bag folded flat on the counter. He opened the bag, put in the Bible and the matches, then rapidly filled the bag with groceries from the refrigerator, including a large jar of dill pickles. After a moment he paused and swore. He unpacked the bag and started over, this time placing the pickle jar in the bottom of the bag and ending with the Bible on top. He had no idea if the Good Lord cared about pickle juice leaking onto a Bible, but now was no time to find out about celestial objections to foodstuffs being packed on top of holy guidance.

He found two more grocery bags in the pantry and filled them as well. His arms protested as he hustled down the steps to the garage, clutching three full bags of goods to his chest. He was able to stack the grocery bags on top of the beer cases. It took some care to wheel the load out of the garage side door. Now the long muscles of his lower back were complaining.

He persevered, inching the dolly over a ratty span of grass to his own driveway. Marjorie sat ensconced in her recliner in the van. Larry was glad she hadn't climbed out to follow him with chastisements.

"You're taking all day!" she yelled. "Let's get this show on the road."

"Right." Larry couldn't summon the energy to point out that she liked pickles and beer as much as he did. He tucked the boxes of beer into the van behind the recliner as Marcel took the grocery bags and loaded them in the front of the van.

A few minutes later they were on the way to Holiday Valley. Marcel lifted the old Bible off the top of the grocery bag stuffed in at his feet. He flipped through the pages and carefully asked, "You prefer the Scofield Bible?"

Larry was thinking about beer and barbeque. He said, "Do what?"

"This is an old Scofield annotated Bible."

Larry smoothly accelerated onto Highway 101. "I

picked up the Bible in the neighbor's house. I was thinking Ilene might find something in it."

Marcel said, "She'll find some hateful stuff in the annotations of this version. Scofield was a Confederate who ended up as a minister in Texas. He interpreted a verse from Genesis to say that blacks are cursed by God and are an inferior race destined to be only servants."

Marjorie leaned forward in her recliner. "Wait a minute. He got the Bible to say that?"

"No." Marcel shook his head. "What the Bible says is that Noah was drunk and naked in his tent. His son, Ham, came and made fun of him. When Noah sobered up, he was mad about it. He cursed Ham, saying he would never amount to much."

Marcel pushed his glasses up on his nose and said, "That ugly bit of family life isn't very nice, but Scofield made Ham into the ancestors of blacks and said blacks could *only* be servants. He called it the Curse of Ham."

"Is that why Jewish folks won't eat a ham sandwich?" Marjorie asked.

"No, that's from Leviticus," Marcel said. He exhaled. "Sorry, Larry. I shouldn't have said anything."

"Nah, you should of and you did," Larry said.

"Let me get this straight," Marjorie said from her recliner. "This minister preached that blacks were only good to be servants. And he did this after the Civil War?"

"Yes, ma'm." Marcel said. "He wasn't the only one, but his went the furthest. Early 1900's. Part of Jim Crow. And he's the one that started all the Rapture stories. He said there would be a thousand years of a millennial kingdom of Christ, beginning in Jerusalem. None of that is in the Bible."

"Then what the hell is happening now?" Marjorie said. "Aren't we in the Rapture?"

"Honestly, I don't know." Marcel twisted in the van seat to look at Marjorie. "I just know Scofield made up a lot of stuff about the teachings of Jesus. Scofield had a history of whoppers. He lied about his war service, and he forged checks. He never went to a seminary. He was a shyster." Marcel shook his head. "And he sold a lot of annotated Bibles. The margin notes are his ideas, not Christ's."

"So maybe we're *not* in the Rapture?" Marjorie pressed.

"I don't know. From a physical science aspect, all of this doesn't make sense," Marcel said. "Not with what we know. Not yet at any rate." He turned back to look down the freeway which was empty of traffic.

"You think something else is going on?" Larry asked.

Marcel inhaled and said, "I'm fifteen years old, and I don't know squat, but, yeah, somehow there are always physical laws to the universe. Always. Like gravity."

Larry nodded. "Gravity I get. Next time you get the end of the recliner that's on the downhill side."

Marcel laughed. "That's my point entirely. You know that next time we move something big, the gravity issue will be the same. The person on the downhill side has more to handle."

"Sorry, son," Marjorie said.

"Nah, it's okay. You're worth a few minutes sweat, Mom." Larry looked in the rearview mirror to catch her eyes. He grinned and said, "But watch yourself. After ten minutes of furniture moving, I charge by the hour. Big bucks."

"Oh, hush!" Marjorie grinned back at him.

Larry said, "Alright then. What laws of the universe do we think are at work?"

"Flames are easy," Marcel said. "Heat, air, fuel. Lots of situations where that can happen. Combustion we understand. The feathers? I don't know. Feathers are made of proteins. Some sort of immediate amino acid reassortment? Punctuated evolution?"

"Punctuated?"

"Instead of gradual changes as a species reproduces, with punctuated evolution, you get a fast rate of change," Marcel said. "But going from no feathers to producing a whirl of feathers is a heck of a lot of change."

"Unless the feathers are made elsewhere and delivered at the time of take up," Larry said. "Like confetti showing up at a parade. The athletes get covered with the stuff, but their bodies didn't make any glitter."

"That's brilliant!" Marcel said. "Wow. I'm liking that theory."

Larry smiled. "Anytime. Wild-assed guesses are a specialty of mine."

Marjorie snorted.

"I think," Marcel said, slowly, "There might be elements of biochemistry in the process."

"Whatdya' mean?" Marjorie asked. Her voice was almost at a shout because her recliner was well back of the van's front seats.

Marcel turned in the seat to respond. He said, "We know that bodies respond to living conditions. If you're under stress, there's more cortisol. People under stress have more health problems, like heart disease and diabetes."

"Tell me about it," Marjorie said. "My jail time just about destroyed me. Got me fibromyalgia so bad. I just about want to die some days."

Marcel nodded. "Exactly. People with freedom and lots of resources tend to be much healthier. So," he said, "What if people who are doing good in the world have some chemical going around in them?"

"And people with a mean streak have a different bio-chemistry?" Larry said. "Something highly flammable?"

"Maybe," Marcel said. "If that's the case, then a mechanism starts to make sense. It's not the Hand of God."

"What about this business of safety in a female-owned home?" Marjorie said. "How does that work?"

"I have no idea," Marcel said.

"Maybe it's a happiness thing," Larry said. "In a house where power isn't all in some dude's hands."

"Harmony, tranquility or maybe empowerment," Marcel said. "More endorphins. Bottom line, this is going to make sense eventually."

He opened the console top and poked around. "No more granola bars?"

"Look in the sack at your feet," Larry said. "There's a bag of pretzels I got from next door."

Marcel began rummaging in the grocery sack. He pulled out the bag of pretzels and ripped into it, saying, "Noah and the ark makes sense, you know. There probably was a big bunch of clouds raining on a mountain top and some smart guy figured out a flood was coming. He gets his sons to help him build a raft and load the family's livestock on it. Boom, we get a legend."

"What about the cubits part?" Marjorie asked. "I don't know a lot of Bible, but don't they give a floor plan on the Ark? You know, so many cubits this-a-way and that-a-way."

Marcel shrugged. "Salesmen add in details all the time. Doesn't mean they're right."

"More of that 'details give ver-si-mili-tude'?" Marjorie said.

Marcel turned in the front seat and looked at Marjorie in astonishment.

She grinned at him. "Just 'cuz I'm not studying for the S-A-T doesn't mean I can't expand my vocabulary."

Marcel smiled back at her. "Touché," he said. "Nicely done."

"Enough already," Larry said. "What's going on with the Rapture stuff?"

"I think the preachers have it wrong," Marcel said. "I just don't know how."

Larry shrugged, his neck muscles twinging as he brought his shoulders up. "Hey, my money is on you."

Marjorie pulled a flip phone out of the front pocket of her extra-large muumuu. She thumbed the keys and bellowed, "Hey, it's me, Marjorie!" There was a moment of silence and she said, "This you, Aisha?"

Marcel whipped his head back around to look at Marjorie.

She spoke into the phone. "We're on our way out to that big house in Holiday Valley. You okay?"

Marjorie held up a finger in warning to Marcel as she listened to Aisha's answer. Marjorie said, "We're headed to a female owned a-bode. We'll be safe out there. You know how to find us? Because I want you to bring the girls out. We'll help you."

She nodded her head, as if Aisha could see her. "Right. I hope you'll change your mind. You'd be so welcome to be with us. Bye-bye."

"Why did you call Aisha?" Marcel said. "I don't want her around!"

"I called her because we don't exactly know what's going on," Marjorie said. "And those two babies have done nothing wrong." Her triple chins were wobbling with righteousness. "She called me a bit ago to say thank you for using the tub, so why shouldn't I call her back and tell her that's she's welcome to come visit?"

Marcel shot a look of rage at Larry, who hunkered down over the steering wheel.

"Don't look at me," Larry said. "I'm just the cat-collecting guy."

"Marcel," Marjorie said, in her near shout. "I do know something about Noah, Ham and God. It doesn't matter which one of them did right or wrong. It's not about what they said or did. Some folks decided they needed a hammer to do some 'smiting' down on black folks, and they picked a Bible verse to do it with. If it wasn't the Ham guy, it would have been somebody else. Probably a woman." She snorted. "We should look into that woman at the well with the butt-load of husbands. I'll bet she was a regular gal."

Marjorie leaned forward in the recliner, oblivious to Larry's slowing for the Holiday Valley exit.

Her voice was still at a near shout despite the van's

reduction in wind noise. She said, "I can't do anything about Ham. But I know what it's like to be the one who has done something unforgiveable. You don't have to forgive Aisha. You're in control of that, and you may not ever. She knows it. What I can do is let her know I understand *being unforgiveable*. I really do."

She twisted in the massive recliner and reached into one of the boxes Larry had packed behind the chair. She said, "Now, be a sweet kid and hand me some pretzels to go with this beer."

"The more you know, the more you don't know."
Aristotle (384-322 B.C.E.)

CHAPTER THIRTY

FRANK MADE LEMONADE. Larry sat at the giant granite counter in the Babcock's kitchen and poured himself a second glass. The sweet, tart drink went down like liquid sunshine.

"Thanks, Frank." Larry smacked his lips. "This is really good."

'We all need to re-hydrate,' Frank said, refilling a glass for Dobbin. "Particularly after moving that recliner. It's a monster."

"Appreciate your help,' Larry said. "The chair's important to my mom."

Cosmos came in, her rainbow-hued hair now framing a smiling face. "The stalls are awesome!" she told Larry. "I added some netting to the bars and put in some straw bales for cats to climb. We just need litter boxes. Frank said you brought some?"

"We've got large ceramic casseroles coming in my cousins' car. Odelle and Ilene are picking up some clothes, but they should be here soon." Larry set down his lemonade glass. "Now we move the cats." He shook his head. "I'm not looking forward to this."

"Can I help?" Cosmos said. "I handle cats every day."

"Hell, yes, you can come!" Larry sat up straighter. "If you can get the cats into the carriers, then Marcel and I could load the boxes. I'm likin' that idea!"

She frowned. "They may do better with you because they know you."

"Nope. They don't know me well, and the ones that do hate me. At least the gray tom does."

Marcel walked into the kitchen and said, "That's a fib. Larry's superpower is animal magnetism. They like him. I saw him refilling water bowls earlier, and those cats love him." He paused, "Well, maybe not the gray cat."

"Fifteen cats," Cosmos said as Marcel poured a glass of lemonade. "Are any of them feral?"

"Nah," Larry said. "There's a couple little, sweet cats. We've got, I don't know, four or five striped tabbies."

Marjorie shuffled into the kitchen from the catio, carrying Bella on her shoulder. "You doing a cat inventory?" she asked.

"Yeah. I'm trying to remember who all we've got," Larry said.

"I can tell ya." Marjorie began reciting. "Three gray-striped tabbies. One spotted tabby. Two tortoise-shells. Two rag doll kittens with blue eyes. Such sweethearts! The orange-striped cat with the big yellow eyes. Three all black cats, and then the black-and-white cutie who looks like he's wearing a tuxedo." She ended with, "And then the two really pissy toms. The big fluffy white guy, and the nasty-tempered gray."

"Your memory is impressive," Frank said to Marjorie.

She smiled. "That's how I was so good at keeping

double books." She tapped her head. "I remember shit." She looked around the grand kitchen and whistled. "This place is really something."

"We've got six spaces we can use as bedrooms," Frank said. "Can we show you around?"

"I'd like that," Marjorie said, eyeing the wall of whiskey as she went past.

Larry stood up with a groan. "Come on," he said to Marcel and Cosmos. "Let's get this done."

"Can I drive?" Marcel said.

"Let me think about that." As Larry spoke, the front door gong sounded. "Betcha that's Odelle and Ilene."

It was. Cosmos and Marcel made short work of ferrying casserole dishes to the catio and barn. Larry took the time to speak to Ilene. "There's some stuff I'd like you to look up," he said. "Can you read about a Reverend Scofield who wrote an annotated Bible?"

"Okay." Ilene looked at him, curiosity written on her lean face by the arch of her eyebrows.

"Apparently he's a guy who pushed off the big 'there will be a Rapture,' idea," Larry said. "Marcel says there's no Rapture in the Bible. Not even in, ah, Revelations."

"Oh, I knew that," Ilene said. "Didn't you read *The Sacred Mushroom and the Cross*?"

"Nope," Larry said. "Missed that one."

"Dr. John Allegro, 1970," Ilene said. "He was a specialist in ancient languages and the Dead Sea Scrolls. He said much of the Bible comes from visions from consuming psychoactive mushrooms. Particularly Revelations."

"Okay." Larry thought about that a moment. "I'm kinda

seein' that." He sighed. "Don't go putting magic mush-rooms in my head, Ilene. I haven't got the brain space."

"How can I help, then?"

"We need to know more about the Rapture part. Aisha said something about Revelations might be historic instead of futuristic. I'm not sure I followed that, but maybe the guy writing stuff down was recording a bunch of bad experiences."

Ilene's eyebrows came down to the dubious setting. "But you do think there's some aspect of Christian eschatology?"

"Hell, there's that word again. Es-cat, but it has noth-ing to do with furry friends, right?"

"It's the study of the end of the world," Ilene said. "How Christ is coming back. A thousand years of har-mony plus or minus seven years of tribulation." Ilene looked at Larry's uncomprehending face, and she sighed. "Haven't you been paying attention? People disappearing means we may be in a pre-tribulation phase. The presi-dent's speech indicates there may be multiple Raptures, signaling a discordance in established premillennialism views. What do you think I've been looking at for the past six weeks?"

"Ah, Reddit?"

"Well, among other things, yes. Give me some more clues here, Larry."

"I dunno! Marcel has this itch that it's not all Biblical."

"I suppose I could check the bird flu forums and see if there is discussion on viruses." Ilene's voice was filled with doubt. A moment later she was warming to the assignment. "The mycology forums are always interesting. Maybe there's someone who has had some recent mushroom dreams." Ilene smiled, "And I haven't been on an earthing forum in a while."

To Larry's blank look, she said, "You know! Grounding your feet. It's important." She nodded her head vigorously. "Don't worry. If it's out there, I'll find it!"

"I'm sure it'll be way out there," Larry muttered as he turned to acknowledge the return of Frank. Dobbin came skipping down the hallway after his grandfather and then did two frog jumps to enter the kitchen.

"Your mom likes the green bedroom," Frank said. "Me and Dobbin are in the guest room with the twin beds. Ilene and Odelle are in the craft room with the Murphy bed. Marcel gets the sleeper sofa in the office. Cosmos wants a chaise lounge in the catio, and we're putting you in the Master bedroom. King-sized bed."

"That sounds awesome," Larry said.

"There's still a frilly twin bed in what looks like a maid's room."

"If Annelise shows up, we should offer her a spot," Larry said. "I have a suspicion she's on her own."

"I'll be sure to tell her she's got her own space then if she wants it. I hope she'll be here for dinner. You headed back for the cats?"

"Yeah." Larry checked his watch and swore. "Getting late. We still on for barbeque?"

"Yep. I'll get the grill going soon," Frank said. "You hungry?"

"Gettin' there." Larry's stomach squeezed a reminder that it'd been a while since the tuna fish sandwiches.

"I've already made some potato salad," Frank said. "My niece, Soo Lin, may come out and eat with us. She's a television reporter who's been covering the capital. She might want to ask you some questions about cat-saving. You know. A television interview."

"Ah, I don't know about that," Larry said.

"Viewers will like you. It'd be a nice change of pace from the politicians and the preachers."

"Yeah . . ." Larry lost his train of thought as Marcel approached with a bag of jalapeno potato chips. "Marcel!" he said, "Gimme the chips!"

"Why?"

Larry pulled out the keys to the van and jingled them. "I'll be handling the chips because you're driving."

"A firm tree does not fear a storm."
Dayak proverb

CHAPTER THIRTY-ONE

COSMOS DIDN'T HAVE a seat belt. That didn't register with Larry until they were all in the van and Marcel was inching the vehicle down the long drive. Larry's focus had been on opening the chips and feeding his inner cat-catcher.

Once he gulped down half the bag of chips and swilled a bottle of water, the senses beyond his stomach began to check in. He was in the passenger side seat, belted in and feeling slightly nauseous from the after-effects of faux jalapeno spices.

Cosmos was sitting on the van floor where Marjorie's recliner had been. The space behind Cosmos held the stack of cardboard boxes and a trio of plastic cat carriers.

Somehow this suddenly seemed really, really dangerous. Why was it okay for his mother to travel in a massive recliner in the back of the van, but he was seriously weirded out by Cosmos being unsecured?

Larry exhaled and looked around further.

The van was fine. It was going to stay fine because Marcel was driving down the center of the road at three miles per hour.

Marcel wasn't so fine. He had a death grip on the steering wheel and looked like he might pass out at any minute. Larry looked in the back of the van again.

Cosmos, sitting cross-legged on the floor of the van, smiled up at Larry and oscillated her fingers in a cheery waggle. Larry offered her the bag of chips. She waved the offer away with a smile.

Her cheerful nature made Larry feel worse about her lack of a safe seat. If they were in an accident, she could be badly hurt.

"Well, then," Larry muttered. "We'd better not get in an accident." He thought for a moment. Then he spoke to Marcel. "So, tell me again. Why the Sumerians?"

"Huh?" Marcel stayed hunched over the steering wheel. He spoke while keeping his eyes riveted on the road in front of the van.

"Relax," Larry said. "There's nobody else out on the road. You've got this. Go ahead and take a deep breath."

For a moment he thought Marcel hadn't heard him. Then Larry saw the teen take in some air.

"Go ahead and bring us to a stop," Larry said.

The van lurched to a standstill. Cosmos only slid a few inches forward, thanks to the low speed.

"Not bad," Larry said. "Let's take it up to five miles per hour and stop again. Try for some smoothness."

Marcel took them down the long driveway and through a wide turn onto the access road with a series of accelerations and halts. When they neared the electronic main gate, Larry gauged Marcel as done. "Stop before the gate," Larry said.

"Before the gate" ended up being a little more hair-raising than Larry would have liked, but Marcel got it done. With Larry's coaching, he put the van in park and turned off the ignition.

"Good job, kid," Larry said. "Why don't I take it from here?"

Marcel made no objection. He quickly hopped out of the van, punched the gate code and made his way to the passenger side of the van as Larry crawled over the console and dropped his scrawny ass into the driver's seat.

He was congratulating himself on being a pretty decent driving instructor when he realized he was still holding the bag of chips. He took a look inside and realized he'd crushed the remaining chips to crumbs.

He looked over his shoulder at Cosmos who grinned at him. He smiled back at her, appreciating her diplomatic silence.

Larry handed the chip remainders to Marcel and took the van through the gate. The van rolling past the gate-posts activated a sensor and the gate rolled closed behind them.

Marcel dug out a handful of the leftover chip grit and began to eat.

"Why the Sumerians?" Larry repeated as he eased the van onto Highway 101. "Sounds like you've been studying them a while if Annelise knew to look for books for you."

There was a moment of chewing and Marcel said, "Last fall, we're doing reports on ancient history of the world. We had a teacher who went on and on about the Bronze Age. I chose Sumerians" Marcel shrugged and pulled out another handful of chip grit.

"Well, bullshit," Larry said. "That's the polite society

version. You said it was an act of rebellion. Tell Uncle Larry the truth. Was it naked ladies? Swords? Chariots?"

Marcel blinked. Then he said, "It was the teacher being an ass."

Cosmos wriggled closer. "This sounds good."

Marcel laughed. "It's funny now, but it wasn't when it started." Marcel chewed a few more chip crumbs and said, "To make bronze you need copper and an annealing metal like tin. That happened throughout Europe about two thousand years before the birth of Christ."

He swallowed and said, "But bronze metallurgy didn't happen in the New World or much in sub-Saharan Africa. If you use metallurgy as a marker for civilization, you get skewed results."

"I think I'm following you," Larry said. "It's like you can't win a beauty contest if your talent is speed hot dog eating."

"Right," Marcel grinned. "Although we all have to admire the guy who can eat seventy hot dogs in ten minutes."

"And the Sumerians?" Larry asked. "How did you use them to de-ass-ify the teacher?"

"We're all looking stuff up, and the teacher keeps talking about civilization and bronze, in a way that, just, I don't know. It was brutal. It left out the Guatemalan kids in the class. I'm used to being an outlier, but these kids were getting kicked in the slats with that guy's slant. One kid tried to say if you define civilization as urban centers, the Mayan empires were really impressive."

"But Mayans didn't do bronze?" Cosmos asked, leaning forward.

"Nope. They did gold."

"Gold?"

"Yep. Didn't count. The teacher said we were doing the Bronze age, so no Mayan stuff. Pissed me off. I dug around and found the Sumerians were working bronze a thousand years before the Europeans. And they invented writing. And the wheel. And they didn't just have bronze axe heads, they had *surgical instruments*." Marcel grinned. "And there's a strong case that the Sumerians were out of Africa. Made my day."

"What'd the teacher do?"

"Not much he could do. Half the class went with me on non-European Bronze age exceptionalism. China, Russia, Mongolia, India, Korea, Thailand. It was fun. I did a ten-page report and a Power point presentation, emphasizing the many aspects of civilization beyond the making of bronze. The Sumerians gave me lots to work with. They had epic storytelling, bookkeeping, and a base-60 math construct that gave us the sixty-second minute and the sixty-minute hour."

Marcel funneled the last few chip bits into his mouth. "I earned an A and a reputation for being counter-suggestive. Kids in my class have been bringing up the Sumerians ever since."

"Is 'counter-suggestive' an S-A-T word for *difficult?*" Larry said.

Marcel shrugged, a smile lighting his green eyes. "I like to think of it as not easily steam-rolled."

"Good." Larry pulled the van into the driveway of his home. He said, "Keep that quality in mind as we start stuffing cats into boxes."

"A cat is an example of sophistication minus civilization"

Anonymous

CHAPTER THIRTY-TWO

THE FIRST CAT was easy. Larry walked into the sun porch. A small ragdoll kitty raced to twine between his legs. He picked up the cat, stroked her head and carried her to the living room. Marcel and Cosmos sat on the floor in the space usually occupied by Marjorie's big recliner. They were rapidly constructing a row of cardboard cat carriers. Larry simply walked to the first open box and dropped the kitten in.

She gave a tiny meow when she landed, but she stayed put, looking up at Larry with big, unblinking eyes.

"Stay!" Larry commanded as he folded the top down. He slid the slot ends over the long cardboard handle, and Cat One was done.

"Good job," Cosmos said. "I've always struggled with getting a cat into one of these."

"We'll have some struggles shortly," Larry said. "I've always been good with animals, but we got some characters coming." He went back to the sun porch, and looked over the feline crowd. He chucked a tabby under the chin and picked her up, holding her firmly against his chest. She broke into a deep, rumbling purr.

"You are a sweetheart," Larry said. "No wonder some-body paid me to put you on the list." He carried the tabby into the living room and opted for a different technique. He knelt down next to an open carrier and placed the tabby in the box with careful, confident moves. The tabby made no objection until the cardboard lid began to close. Even then she settled after a few soothing words from Larry.

"You're amazing!" Cosmos said.

Larry didn't take the compliment seriously. He was able to bring out two more cats before he met the Buzz Saw. This cat, a lanky orange tiger, went from purring in Larry's arms to mountaineer-with-crampons the moment she saw the line of cardboard carriers. She dug claws into Larry's chest and did her best to turn him into an escape route. Larry plucked the cat off his head as she rear-footed his forehead, raking in two deep gouges. She flailed and shrieked as Larry held her at arm's length. He mashed the cat down into the carrier box and yelled, "Hurry!" as Marcel and Cosmos converged to close the top.

"Holy Mother of God," Larry said once the lid was tabbed shut. "We should duct-tape this one in. If she gets out, we're never getting a second chance."

"She freaked out when she saw the boxes," Cosmos said. "Maybe you could use a towel and drape it over the head of the next one."

"Good idea." Larry looked at her. "You want a turn?"

"Sure!" Cosmos got to her feet as the orange tiger sent a siren's worth of complaints through the cardboard. "But maybe we should move these others to the van first?" She pointed at the carrier holding Ms. Buzz Saw. It was now thump-walking across the floor. "Seeing or hearing her could weird out the next cat."

"On it." Marcel picked up the first carrier and started for the van. Cosmos followed, carrying another, leaving Larry with the orange siren, who was now doing her best to claw an enlargement through the small vent holes in the cardboard.

"I got help," he muttered as he picked up the wobbling box. "Just not with you."

He carried the cat and carrier out to the garage where he sealed the box with multiple wraps of duct tape. The orange Buzz Saw caught him once with a claw through a vent hole. "Come on, behave," he said. The cat ignored him and tried another claw.

Larry looked at the large dog carrier sitting empty on the garage floor with a pang of longing. He wanted a dog. A good dog. A dog without claws that eviscerated like a cat's claws. A dog to play fetch and hang out with. Well, that ship had sailed. No Golden Retrievers left. Not even a Shit-zoo.

"Ah, hell, I think it's Shih Tzu," Larry muttered as he trudged to the garage door. He hit a button and the garage door rumbled up. He called to Marcel, "Let's take this crate in. I've got an idea."

They carried the giant dog crate into the sun porch and set it down. Cats scattered to hide under the ratty wicker chairs or behind Marjorie's collection of pots, most containing long-withered tomatoes and herbs. Larry swung the wire gate to the crate to an open position, a development the remaining cats eyed with suspicion.

The big gray tom took a position high on a carpeted cat tower and looked down on Larry with unfriendly green eyes and a tail that lashed a steady beat of disapproval and hatred.

"Yeah," Larry said, looking up at the gray tom. "We'll get to you in a minute."

Larry went into the house and came back with Cosmos, a can of tuna and a piece of aluminum tubing.

"Okay," he said to Marcel and Cosmos. "This is a telescoping rod with a magnet. My mom uses it to pick up a dropped needle or pin. We're going to use it to bring the wire door shut once we've got some cats inside."

"That's brilliant!" Cosmos said.

"Thanks," Larry said. "Can you get on top of the crate?"

"Sure!" Cosmos climbed up on the crate and sat, cross-legged. Larry handed her the extendable tube and connected the magnet end to the wire door.

"The trick," Larry said as he handed the tuna can to Marcel, "Is to be boring after you to get in there and bait the crate. You and me will back off. We'll go to the other side of the porch, and be doing nothin'. If Cosmos sits real still and there's tuna in the crate, we might get a couple cats to go in."

Marcel crawled into the crate and placed the opened tuna can at the back. A slender black cat with amber eyes peeked out from under a wicker chair and watched as Marcel backed out of the crate and crossed the sun porch to stand next to Larry.

"Let's turn our backs," Larry said. "We should just talk like we don't care about cats."

"Okay," Marcel said, rotating with Larry to look away from Cosmos and the crate. "Nice weather we're having?"

"Christ, kid. That all you got? Tell me something Sumerian."

"It's interesting that our second round of Rapture has a female lead component."

"That's Sumerian?"

"In epic tales the Sumerians told, there would often be a moralizing message that would be delivered twice. First it would come from a male character, like a king. Then the same message would be delivered by a female character. When the female spoke, the audience is really supposed to pay attention."

"Not bad advice for any era," Larry conceded.

There was a twang of metal and a glad cry from Cosmos. "Got four!" she said as she jumped down and fastened the gate shut on the crate.

The slender black cat meowed a complaint as it milled inside with a calico and two more tabbies.

"Nine down, six to go," Larry said.

"Five to go," Cosmos said as she plucked a cat off the cat tree. She held the fluffy white cat in a football carry and moved to the living room, confidently draping the cat with a towel and sliding the towel bundle into a cardboard carrier.

"Good job, Cosmos!" Larry was relieved. The white guy had been more than a little pissy in the past. He must have been on empty because Cosmos returned with no evidence of kitty incontinence on her bright scrubs.

The gray tom looked down at Larry from the cat tower, tail still jerking with distain.

"How do we get him?" Marcel asked.

"That," Larry said, "Is a good question."

"Tricks and treachery are the practice of fools that don't have the brains to be honest."
Benjamin Franklin (1706 – 1790)

CHAPTER THIRTY-THREE

"THE BIG GRAY? We could stone him," Cosmos said.

"Stone him?" Larry winced. "We're kinda in the rescue business, aren't we?"

"Not that kind of stone!" Cosmos laughed. She pulled a small baggie from the front pocket of her vet tech scrubs. "This has catnip in it. I meant to leave it with the cats I brought out, but I forgot."

"We sprinkle some out and he's happy?" Marcel asked.

"No. Rolling in catnip would make him livelier," Cosmos said. "But if we mix the catnip with some food and he eats it, we might get five minutes where he's stoned, and we can pick him up."

"Worth a try," Larry said. "We should put him into one of the plastic cat carriers. I don't think cardboard is going to hold him. Do we try some more tuna?"

"Chicken livers work best," Cosmos said. "Or pâté."

"We're not exactly a pâté household," Larry said. "Let me look in the pantry. Maybe there's something good and smelly."

He found an ancient tin of anchovies. Cosmos ripped

open her baggie of catnip and doctored the oily fish. She divided the fish into three cereal bowls.

"Three bowls?" Marcel asked.

"He'll turn up his nose if we deliver his own serving," Cosmos said with an easy confidence. "We'll have better luck if he thinks he's a hot shot, chasing off a lesser cat."

It took less than a minute for her prediction to be proven correct A tubby black cat pounced on the first bowl Cosmos set down. He immediately began to eat as the gray cat watched from his ledge.

The three other remaining cats converged as Cosmos walked close to the cat tower. She set the second bowl down and walked away. The gray tom leapt down to land in the cat trio before Cosmos could set down the third bowl.

The gray tom scattered the trio, who quickly regrouped around the last bowl.

Cosmos stepped off the porch and back into the house.

"How long does it take?" Larry asked.

"We should give it a few minutes."

The television remote was on the floor of the living room, near where Marjorie's recliner normally sat. Larry picked it up and turned on the television. An ad began.

"Rapture got you worried? Try our all-organic God's Blessings soda, filled with the goodness of green kale and pomegranate juice. Just $6.99 at your nearest convenience store."

"Jesus!" Larry said. "Somebody's making money."

"Given that the stuff is probably all water and sugar, I think you're right," Cosmos said.

"Did you get some lunch?" Larry asked her.

"I'm good."

"That's not what I asked. If you don't eat regularly, you won't stay healthy."

Cosmos blushed a bit pink and said, "I'm on a diet. I know I could stand to lose a few pounds."

"Oh, no! You're perfect." Larry's attention returned to the television screen, so he missed Cosmos's eye blink and happy, quick smile.

Two television anchors at a desk were on screen. One said, "In Olympia, reporter Soo Min Carlevaro is standing by at the county courthouse."

"This is Frank's niece," Larry said. "The television reporter."

A dark-haired woman with an abdomen swollen with pregnancy appeared on the screen, saying, "The lines are growing at the county courthouse as people arrive to complete paperwork for property transfers. The two remaining clerks are providing forms, but there is no notary public to witness signatures, and most people we spoke to were unaware that Thurston County has a septic system inspection requirement. Normal processing time for a property title transfer has been two weeks. Let's hear from Mr. Joseph Henty on how his application was received."

The reporter turned to her right and held the microphone out to a burly man in a plaid flannel shirt worn with jeans and a thundering scowl. He said, "The president of the United States has told us to shelter in female-owned property and now the imbeciles at the county courthouse are telling us it is a two-week process to transfer property. I own my house, free and clear. Don't owe a dime on it. Why the hell do I have to put it in my wife's name? And why can't the authorities gin up a temporary hall pass for the situation?"

"Temporary hall pass?" Soo Min asked, carefully.

"Right. There should be some paperwork that puts my place in my wife's name for a week or two until this latest Rapture passes. Then it'd revert back to me, and we'd go on like we always have. Completely do-able. Makes total sense. It's these idiots in government who have no brains that are mucking up the system."

"As you can see," Soo Min said, pulling the microphone back and turning to face the cameraman, "tempers are high in Thurston County. Back to you, Amber."

"Christ on a crutch, what an A-hole," Larry said.

"Amen," Marcel said.

Larry looked at Cosmos. "Think enough time has passed?"

"One way to find out," she said.

"What do you want me to do?" Marcel said.

Larry thought a moment, then said, "We can all go out on the porch together. If you two can pick up a cat, great. Leave the gray guy to me. I'll take in a towel. If he's going to be a monster, maybe I can toss the towel on him."

Plan made, they moved back to the sun porch where five cats lay sprawled on the stained flooring. Cosmos picked up a big black cat, and Marcel easily hoisted a striped tabby. They quietly moved their purring cats to the living room, leaving the gray for Larry.

The big gray tom lay sprawled out with his back legs wide apart.

"Oh, no," Larry said, "You're really stoned." He knelt down beside the cat and said, "How ya' doin', buddy?"

The cat didn't move.

Larry reached out and fondled the gray's ears. There was no response.

"Damn. I hope we didn't kill him."

Cosmos and Marcel returned. Larry motioned for them to come closer. He said, "This guy is totally out."

"Great!" Marcel said.

"Is it?" Larry shook his head. "Look at him. He's totally gone."

"Cat nip hits cats differently," Cosmos said. "He must be one of the susceptible ones. He should come around soon."

"He's going to be so pissed. That's not a very dignified look." Larry looked at Marcel. "You said Noah was pissed off when someone saw him drunk and naked?"

"Yeah?" Marcel cocked his head and said, "You worried this is a Noah?"

"I'm thinking he's going to hate me when he wakes up."

Marcel laughed. "Maybe you're doomed to be his servant."

Larry snorted. "That sounds about right. Larry gently scooped up the cat. "Crikey, you're a big fellow." He draped the cat over his shoulder like a sleeping baby and followed Cosmos and Marcel back to the living room. Larry slid the gray tom into a plastic cat carrier and wished for a padlock.

They made short work loading the last of the cats into the van. Larry exhaled as they slid in the last carrier – the one holding the big gray tom – who was beginning to flop and move.

"He's gonna be so mad at me," Larry said.

"Hopefully, he won't remember anything," Marcel said.

"Nah," Larry said. "He won't forget. Not ever."

"Maybe you can appease him with some of Frank's bar-be-que," Cosmos said.

"Now you're talking." Larry peered through a ventilation hole in the gray's cat carrier. "Hear that, buddy? We're going to get some great food."

The gray cat sat up in the box. A moment later a bright green eye appeared at the ventilation hole, accompanied by a deep rumbling yowl.

Larry said, "Let's go. We've got to get a move on before this guy really sobers up."

"Are you afraid of a cat, Larry?" Cosmos laughed.

"Yep. That cat about makes me skid my shorts."

"He's just a cat," Cosmos said, scrambling in to take a seat among all the cat carriers.

Larry hoisted himself up to the front seat. He started the van as soon as Marcel climbed in.

"That's not just a cat," Larry said. "That guy is a force of Nature."

"Does he have a name?" Marcel asked.

"He most certainly does." Larry shook his head as he pulled the van out into the street. "His name is Lucifer."

"Revenge is a kind of wild justice."
Francis Bacon (1561 – 1626)

CHAPTER THIRTY-FOUR

LARRY PULLED THE van into the Lucky Seven Ranch at a quarter to six, driving through a brisk rain shower. The slanting light of the late spring evening caught the raindrops on the gravel, turning the front drive into a sparkling entrance.

"This is the prettiest place," Cosmos said from her spot between cat carriers in the back of the van. "Just look at it."

"We've got company," Larry said.

A blue and white KBRN News truck sat parked in the circular drive.

"Frank's niece?" Marcel said.

"Probably."

"She may want footage of you unloading the cats," Marcel said.

"Me? Oh, hell no. She can film you."

"She should film both of you," Cosmos said. "You're a great team."

"Hey, you're on the team too," Larry said. "And you're the prettiest one."

Cosmos smiled and shook her head. "Maybe she's only here for Franks bar-be-que."

The dark-haired reporter came out of the house as Larry took the van down the side path to the barn. Frank and a tall, wide-shouldered man came down the walk after the reporter.

Frank did introductions. "My niece, Soo Min Carlevaro. This is her husband and cameraman, Vico."

Larry shook their hands, keenly aware of Soo Min's rounded belly and the glowing beauty of her mid-pregnancy face. He was also keenly aware of Vico's looming size and friendly, but hawk-eyed, study of Larry.

"Larry," Larry managed to say. "Of Larry's Post-Rapture Pet-sitting Services and my colleagues, historian Marcel Westmoreland and Animal Technician Cosmos." Larry paused. He realized he didn't know Cosmos's last name. "Ah, Cosmos . . ."

"Cosmos Ponomarenko," Cosmos said.

"Glad to meet you!" Soo Min waved at the van. "I understand you have *fifteen* cats?"

"Fifteen in the van," Larry said. "Eighteen on our care roster, if you count Bella and the two cats Cosmos brought out."

"May we film the unloading?" Soo Min's eyes were alive with interest.

Larry was as susceptible as any man to a beautiful woman finding him interesting. He came up with "No problem" before his brain stuttered to a stop.

Soo Min was a professional at interviewing. She kept up a steady stream of open-ended questions as her hands signaled to her husband. A few minutes later Larry found himself talking easily. Soo Min held a microphone while big Vico filmed the conversation with a large camera set on an industrial-strength tripod base.

"Cosmos has fitted three of the barn stalls with netting and bales of straw for climbing and resting," Larry said. "One of those stalls contains two cats recovering from recent surgery."

"You have cats with different needs?" Soo Min asked.

"Ah. Right. We need to think for a moment about which cats we want to go where, so we don't set up troubles." Larry opened the back of the van.

Vico brought the camera and tripod closer and filmed the interior as Larry said, "See that vibrating box? That has a lady ginger cat." He turned to Soo Min and said, "Most orange cats are male, but this one is female, and she's very unhappy."

"Where will you put her?" Soo Min spoke into the microphone, then tilted the microphone to catch Larry's answer.

"We'll put her in a barn stall, along with two of the striped tabbies who are pretty mellow."

Soo Min watched and Vico filmed as Larry and his team moved the first three cat boxes to the barn. Vico caught the orange eruption of the angry ginger tiger as Larry used his pocket knife to slit the reinforcing duct tape on the cat carrier.

The orange tiger streaked to the top of a hay bale before turning to hiss at the camera.

"Wow," Soo Min said. "That is a challenging cat to handle."

"Larry has the most amazing talent," Cosmos said. "The animals just love him."

"Is that how you got into the pet-sitting business?" Soo Min asked.

"Ah, yeah." Larry didn't see a need to speak to the money-making focus of his original thinking.

The two striped tabbies spilled out of their open boxes and looked about the big stall before starting a game of kitten tag. Vico filmed them for several minutes.

"The rag doll kittens might make a good shot," Marcel said.

"They should go in the catio," Larry said. To Soo Min, he said, "They're young, and maybe can't handle a cold night in the barn."

The big-eyed fluffy midget of a cat that Larry pulled out of the next cat carrier evoked a lengthy "Awwwww" from Soo-Min. Cosmos brought out the second rag doll kitten and handed it to Larry.

Vico gave a quick dip of the chin, signaling to his wife that this was a money shot. Vico zoomed in, capturing skinny, scruffy, scratched Larry cradling the two kittens. Neither of them knew it, but it would take less than an hour for the video of Larry to be seen around the globe. In unsettling times, the world needs kitten footage.

Cosmos and Marcel picked up the large dog carrier filled with four more cats and carried it in behind Larry into the catio. Vico filmed the kittens lapping water from the fountain of Ishtar, then he filmed the black and tuxedo cats exploring the indoor garden.

Larry relegated the pissy white Persian to a second barn stall along with the two tortoise-shells.

Soon only a spotted tabby and Lucifer remained in the van.

Dobbin appeared, skipping down the side of the house. "You're here! Grandpa and me have been bar-be-queing. Ready to eat?"

"Big time," Larry said. He handed the cardboard carrier with the spotted cat to Marcel. "Can you stick him in the barn?" Larry said.

"Sure." Marcel said. "And Lucifer? Where does he go?"

Cosmos turned and looked at Larry, tilting her head and arching an eyebrow. Soo Min winced and rubbed the small of her back. Vico turned to his wife, and missed Cosmos's look of concern.

Larry understood. Liberating Lucifer was going to be dicey.

"You guys go ahead to dinner," Larry said. "Give me a minute with this guy. I'll take him inside quiet-like."

The crowd left. Larry climbed into the back of the van. He sat his skinny butt down next to the plastic cat carrier and listened as a rumbling warning came from the big gray tomcat.

"I know," Larry said. "I apologize. I really do. Giving you a kitty-roofie was a bad deal, but I was out of options there. I'm about to take you into a first-class catio. It'll beat the hell out of that stinking sun porch. You'll be King of the catio jungle, and, just so you know, we put the white pisser kitty out in the barn."

Lucifer twitched an ear and fell silent.

Taking that as a sign of acceptance, Larry picked up the cat carrier and walked to the catio's back door. He wanted the release done before Lucifer changed his mind about being agreeable.

Inside the house, Cosmos signaled to Marcel and Soo Min. "Come look," Cosmos said, moving to the door between the kitchen and the catio. "Larry's going to let out Lucifer."

They crowded around, looking through the window in the upper half of the door. Marjorie and Dobbin came into the kitchen from the backyard, followed by Frank, bearing a large platter of bar-be-qued ribs and wings. Frank set the platter down on the granite-topped kitchen island.

Marjorie and Frank saw the trio at the kitchen door and moved to see what was of interest. Vico came out of the kitchen-side bathroom and joined them. He was so tall that he didn't need to crowd in to have a good view into the catio. Dobbin snuck in front of the group and managed to stand on tiptoes to see through the window in the door.

Blissfully ignorant of his audience, Larry sized up the various cat-climbing structures rising up from the potted plants. He decided on an apparatus about a dozen feet from the kitchen door. He placed the cat carrier on a mid-level platform and leaned in, talking to Lucifer.

He opened the door.

The crowd at the kitchen window leaned in, waiting for a feline eruption.

Lucifer sat in the carrier.

Larry nodded at the cat. He propped the door open and stepped back.

Lucifer emerged, ears twitching. He turned his lime-green eyes to the crowd at the window and lowered his chin, beaming rays of disdain so intense that Marjorie squealed, "Yikes! He hates us!"

Turning his back on Larry, Lucifer swarmed up the cat-climbing tower and disappeared into the upper greenery.

Larry sketched a salute, then turned to see the faces watching him.

He smiled and started to wave.

A twenty-pound bomb of gray came hurtling off the upper catwalk, hitting Larry in the back of the head. Lucifer smacked Larry's right ear, raking it with fish-hook sharp claws.

"Oow! Jesus!" Larry swung around. Lucifer was already on the ground and racing for cover.

Cosmos pulled the kitchen door open. "Come on, quick!"

Larry didn't need a second invitation. Cosmos, and the heavenly smell of grilled chicken, beat the hell out of another round with the gray cat.

"Opportunities multiply as they are seized."
Sun-tzu (c. 544 – 496 B.C.E.)

CHAPTER THIRTY-FIVE

THE PILOT AND the co-pilot of the Gulfstream jet were much too professional to check the time. Flying the rich and powerful required constant flexibility. If Abigail Ross wanted to take one more phone call, then she would take one more phone call. The pilot sat in the cockpit, scrolling through a tablet while the co-pilot stood at the fold-down staircase to the jet and waited as Abigail stalked the perimeter of the airplane hangar, smart phone held to her ear.

Janice sat inside the jet, looking out a side window. She studied the patient co-pilot and then closed her eyes to make a prayer to be blessed with a pilot's level of composure. The jet was packed and ready. It was loaded with all of Abigail's "necessities" because Janice had worked like a demon for the past two hours.

She now spoke quietly. "Lord, Thank You for Clive," Janice prayed. Clive had insisted she take a few minutes to rest while he loaded Abigail's things into the back of Abigail's Cadillac Escalade. When Abigail decided to stop at the main office for documents and a flurry of phone calls, Clive pressed Janice to use the bathroom suite in

Abigail's professional dressing area to shower and change clothes to be fresh for the trip.

Abigail would not have approved, but she had left with Jared to collect things from a safe deposit box.

Janice used Abigail's dressing room bathroom, noting the marble tile was far finer than the old linoleum at the house she shared with Clive. She changed into clothes from the suitcase Clive had packed and was ready to go by the time Abigail and Jared returned.

Now, waiting for Abigail to be ready for departure, Janice reflected on the day. It was hard to be Abigail's sole support staff member. Jared was of little help. He had promoted himself to semi-supervisor, only adding to Janice's tasks.

The meatball sandwich seemed an eon ago. Janice inhaled and tried to be positive. There was food on the jet, back in a slick walnut-paneled galley. The positive thought about dinner arrived with a sour tail. No doubt it would be up to her to unwrap the food, microwave it and transfer it to Abigail's preferred porcelain plates. It would be her job to clean up too.

Funny how the thought of these very familiar tasks now had Janice's stomach curling with acid. "I was blind, but now I see," Janice muttered, imbuing the lyrics to "Amazing Grace" with a strand of fury.

Clive took the seat beside her with a weary smile. "We're good to go. Everything's secure."

"You could do a broadcast?" Janice asked.

"If she wants to. I've got two cameras. Lights. Microphones. Field mixer. To do a really good job we need someone to manage the lights and sound separately from me on the camera."

"I can do some of that," Janice said. "I've done it before."

"I know. You're doing everything else though."

"No kidding." Janice sighed.

Clive patted her hand.

Jared was seated at the front of the jet. He had been studying a laptop. Now he stood up and walked back to Janice and Clive with a smile on his face.

"I told my friend we were headed west," Jared said. "

Janice wondered if "Ashley" was a far more age-appropriate love interest. She didn't say anything to Jared who was now thumbing a remote.

He brought up a YouTube clip on the big screen television bolted to a bulkhead. "Ashley sent me this clip. It's very cute."

The video began with an advertisement for a sporty convertible. The tag line read *When you are taken up, don't go through a roof! Buy your heart's desire now! Don't wait!* Then the feed switched to show a skinny guy with a small potbelly, cradling a pair of ragdoll kittens. *Larry* was stitched over the left front pocket of his uniform shirt. The man's hands were large, with pronounced knuckles that made his stroking of the kittens seem all the more tender.

"Ohh, That's so sweet!" Janice smiled. "And it says he's from Olympia! Look there's another clip of him."

Jared started the next video clip, this one fronted by a church advertisement. *Repent! Drunkards, Democrats, Liberals, Pagans, Fornicators, and Women in Yoga Pants! The time for change is now!*

A fast tap on the remote took them past the advertising to footage of Soo Min interviewing Larry. The camera view widened and a black teenager in glasses and a shirt marked *Dave* came into view, along with a young woman in bright scrubs and rainbow-tinted hair, each holding cats inside a long sunroom lush with greenery.

"From the Lucky Seven Ranch in Holiday Valley, this is Soo-Min Carlevaro reporting on Larry's Post-Rapture Pet-Sitting Services."

"Abigail is going to want to see this," Jared said.

"Larry is one of the neighbors?" Clive said.

"I guess." Janice frowned. "The realtor said there were three houses for sale. Those all looked rather modest. Like summer cabins. There are two big properties. The one where Ruthie will be staying, and another place where the people have gone up. I think that was the Lucky Seven Ranch. Maybe someone else has already moved in?"

"This Larry guy has two hundred million views," Jared said. "He's a YouTube star."

Abigail stalked across the tarmac, headed for the plane. Janice watched her through the airplane's window and said, "Abigail doesn't look happy."

She wasn't.

Abigail stormed up the steps. Entering the jet, she said, "Let's go!" to the pilot and then pivoted to march down the aisle of the jet. She flung herself into a leather-covered seat. Her cheeks were flushed, and her eyes flashed as she extended an index finger and pointed at the seat across from her. Jared was being summoned.

Jared ambled up the aisle and took the seat indicated. Moments later the jet was turning onto the runway.

Clive and Janice exchanged looks before linking hands in prayer. Neither was an eager flyer.

Twenty minutes later the jet flew high above Tennessee, and Janice felt confident enough to unsnap her seat belt and stand up. "I'll see about some dinner," she told Clive.

She walked forward and was relieved to see Abigail looking meditative instead of angry.

"Abigail, would you like something to eat?" she asked.

"Yes. I would. In fact, I think we should all eat together. Could you put some things out on the back table?"

It was easy to lay out a gourmet spread from the items in the well-stocked pantry. Janice put out melon wrapped with prosciutto and a tray of cold cuts and fruit. She sliced a loaf of crusty, olive-studded bread and heated a tray of chicken cordon bleu. Clive helped set up the food onto a slide-out table top with an elegant veneer.

Abigail and Jared joined them. Abigail reached her hands out. The quartet joined hands, and Abigail began a prayer.

"Lord, let us be mindful of our blessings," she concluded a few minutes later. "Let us work together to open hearts to You. Amen."

"Amen," her employees chorused.

Abigail said, "I was on the phone with David Johnson."

Janice and Clive exchanged looks. There were hundreds, if not thousands, of men named David Johnson, but the one that Abigail meant was surely the head of one of the biggest Christian organizations on the planet.

"There's an ecumenical conference in Medina," Abigail said.

"In Saudi Arabia?" Clive said.

Abigail's mouth went into a near smirk. "Medina, Washington. Home to many highly important people."

She said, "There are some two hundred religious leaders participating. Keebler is there. Hoyt is there. Hudson. Pletzel is arriving tonight. There's an emissary from the Pope named Taralli. They are concerned enough about the female-protection aspect of the next round of the Rapture to be staying at Frenelle Featherstone's compound."

"Frenelle Featherstone?" Jared said.

"A woman billionaire. Cosmetics," Abigail said. "They'll be designing 'God's Way Forward,' according to David. I told him we'd be in the area. I said I was meeting my daughter for some family time, and we'd be close by."

She picked up a fork and stabbed a melon bite. "He said he'd be glad to include me on the newsletter list."

"He didn't invite you to join them?" Janice said.

"No. He did not." Abigail's eyes flashed as she said, "He said it was a gathering of the nation's *important* church leaders. When I reminded him of the Ross Hour of Prayer's audience, he had the gall to say I was one lucky gal to have had Aaron's leadership, and he was truly sorry to hear that Aaron had gone up. Then he said he'd heard I was taking a sabbatical. He expressed sincere best wishes for my next career *as an anchorite*."

Clive and Janice sat in stunned silence.

Jared said, "What's an anchorite?"

"A religious recluse," Abigail snapped. "A hermit locked in a hole. A nobody."

Janice finally spoke. "We have a mole. Someone from

our office must have called him today to say you were closing the show."

"I think you're right," Abigail said. "That drippy little intern who was taking calls. I'll bet it was her."

"What are you going to do?" Jared said.

"Pray for guidance," Abigail said, reaching for the chicken. "I miss Aaron. The Lord knows I do. But I have found I can take quick action on my own."

Clive reached under the table and took Janice's hand. She knew her husband. He was thinking of how fast Abigail had vacuumed up Aaron's ashes. Janice squeezed Clive's hand, and they exchanged a worried look.

Abigail said, "We'll find a female-owned place, and we'll stay there until I can get it purchased. Then I believe I'll build a nice little God-based empire."

Janice gazed at the prosciutto bites. She'd lost her appetite.

"Enjoy yourself. It's later than you think."
Chinese proverb

CHAPTER THIRTY-SIX

THE SWEET AND sour bar-be-que sauce hit Larry's taste buds with the wham and wow of a Las Vegas show girl.

Larry sagged against the back of the breakfast nook booth and closed his eyes as he chewed.

Cosmos giggled. Larry's eyes flew open, and he saw her smiling at him. Marjorie stood nearby, grinning.

"You look like you died and went to Heaven," Marjorie said.

"Feels like it." Larry took another bite of chicken. "Christ. This is amazing."

Frank had put an impressive spread of food on the island top in the Babcock's kitchen. Marcel went galloping through the buffet of chicken, salads and sides before disappearing into the formal dining room with a plate holding a tower of food.

Dobbin and Ilene were already at the dining table, Dobbin's face smeared with bar-be-que sauce. Ilene had her laptop open and was chatting away as she ate and scrolled through internet sites. Soo Min and Vico sat nearby, eating and talking with Ilene.

Larry had taken a look at the crowded dining room

table and had opted for the peace of the kitchen breakfast nook. He didn't need Ilene's updates on angels, ghosts and general mayhem as he ate.

Now Cosmos slid into the opposite booth seat, bringing a plate of food with her. "It smells fantastic," she said. She bit into a drumstick and said, "Wow!" She swallowed and said, "I wish we had some pickles."

Larry stared at her. "What kind of pickle?" he asked.

Cosmos took a bite of coleslaw and seriously pondered his question. "Normally my favorite is a bread and butter pickle," she said. "But with this bar-be-que? Hmm. You definitely wouldn't want a sweet gherkin. And I don't think I'd want the garlic that comes with a kosher dill."

She took another bite of chicken, chewed and swallowed. She said, "I think this calls for a traditional dill pickle. A crisp one. Not mushy."

Cosmos tilted her head and studied her plate. "I could also see where the crunch of a half-sour pickle would fit."

"You're a pickle savant!" Larry's voice held a tone of awe. He said, "Cosmos, this is some talent you've got there. In my experience, true pickle appreciation is scarce."

Her cheeks went pink, which set off her blue eyes.

Larry ate more chicken, trying not to smear his face with bar-be-que sauce. He refrained from licking his fingers, an act of gentlemanly demeanor that should, he thought, make up for lifting the Rolex from the Babcock's master bedroom.

Frank came into the kitchen carrying another tray of steaming foods. "Ribs and grilled pineapple. Some asparagus too," he called. "And Odelle's found some fresh brains."

"Bar-be-qued *brains*?" Dobbin said.

"He's teasing," Ilene told him. "Odelle's friend is here."

Odelle came into the kitchen, followed by a tall man with large ears, a bald pate and an easy smile.

Cosmos looked at him and waved. "I know him," she said to Larry. "He had a Labrador that came to our clinic for years. Sweet dog."

Larry said, "Is that Harold? Odelle is always going on about her conversations with her old boss."

Cosmos nodded. "His name is Harold." She leaned in and whispered, "His wife was horrible. She brought the dog in when Harold was at a conference and had our vet put the dog down. It was an old dog with some issues, but Harold had been diligent with the medications. The wife said she couldn't be bothered."

"Wow. She flamed out," Larry said. "Ilene told us that."

"She likes him."

"Huh?"

Cosmos said, "Watch Odelle. She likes him."

Larry looked over to see Odelle hand Harold a plate. It didn't seem especially romantic to him, but, then again, sharing some rather fabulous food was a nice thing to be doing.

Cosmos said, "Look at how she's listening to him."

Larry cut his eyes back to Odelle. It was true that she was usually a bossy old hen who had plenty to say. Between Ilene, Odelle and Marjorie, he rarely got a word in.

Harold was talking, and Odelle was smiling.

"Huh." Larry snorted and shook his head. "Okay, then."

"It's sweet!" Cosmos said.

Larry filed "listening" away as a possible activity he could manage.

Marcel came into the kitchen from the dining room, smeared plate in hand. He scraped some detritus into a trash can and fell into line behind Odelle and Harold, ready for Round Two of dinner.

Marjorie followed him and motioned Marcel to come closer to Larry and Cosmos.

"I called Aisha," Marjorie said. "I just watched some of the news, and that ecumenical conference in Medina is making a big splash." To Larry, she said, "I told Aisha she should come out and be with us. I can help her with the girls. We can give them the master bedroom."

Before Larry could think to say anything, Cosmos said, "There's another chaise lounge on the catio. You could bunk out there with me."

Larry processed that suggestion and found it went down fine.

Marcel's face wasn't signaling any sort of joy. His jaw worked as Marjorie folded her arms over her ample bosom and said, "You're going to be out caring for cats and what all. No one's asking you to do diaper duty."

"That miserable bitch!" Ilene shouted from the dining room.

"Hey, that's not fair," Marjorie said. "You barely know Aisha."

"Not her." Ilene called. "Our president - that dried up prune of a political hack! You won't be believing this!"

They all moved to the dining room, Larry nodding a greeting to Harold, as they took up positions behind Ilene to see her computer screen.

She turned up the volume, and they saw the cut from the President at a podium to a television anchor, who said, "A stunning development out of the White House where the President has announced an all-female leadership team, titled the *Disciples of Discipline*, to implement a transfer of all U.S. properties to females. The President says this is to protect citizens from further flame outs as analysts have found the next round of Rapture will incinerate anyone not in residence in a female-owned property."

"That's not correct," Harold murmured.

The television anchor said, "The President described the chaos unfolding in Highland Park, Texas where affluent homeowners have been dumping clothing, furniture and even jewelry and firearms onto the streets in an effort to show piety."

His statement was supported by film footage showing a well-coiffed man wheeling a golf bag down a driveway as a stick-thin woman followed, her arms full of mink coats.

"Wow," Soo Min said. "That's crazy."

"Great footage," Vico said.

"The President stated," the television anchor continued, "She will call on Congress to immediately pass legislation which will mandate all American property as woman-owned. The mission of the *Disciples of Discipline* will be to ensure each Congressperson understands the immediacy of the situation."

"Good luck with that," Frank said. "Even the ones who are dumb as a box of rocks are going to know there's a vote for political suicide."

Ilene muted the news as the screen filled with talking heads, each showing some variation of dismay or disbelief.

"I can't believe this," Ilene raged. "First taste of power, and she's as bad as a man ever was."

"Maybe she's saving everyone," Odelle protested.

"Oh, come on. It's not as dire as she's saying," Ilene said. "I will admit that Venus is in retrograde, which is hard on relationships. It is important to talk about feelings of self-worth, and it is high time to renegotiate relationships. Odelle and Harold, I hope you are listening!"

Odelle turned crimson, but Ilene plowed on before her sister could say anything. Ilene said, "Look how wrong that whole "world ends in 2012 because of the Mayan calendar" thing was."

"Do what?" Larry said.

"In 2012," Ilene said. "A lot of people thought the Mayan calendar said the world was going to end. Same thing in 2000 with the ending of the millennium, and then there's the Kali Yuga, a bad patch that ended in 1900."

"At the very least," Harold said, "Our President is misrepresenting what analysts have found. From my contacts, it looks like all a person has to do is take shelter in a woman-owned structure, and they will be "passed over" during the next phase of the Rapture, which may last only a few minutes."

"It's that Curse of Ham again," Marjorie said.

Harold looked at her and said, "Excuse me?"

"Marcel was saying a preacher guy put in cheater notes to the Bible."

"Annotations," Marcel corrected.

"Whatever. It made Noah's kid into a reason to bash blacks." Marjorie raised an eyebrow and said to Marcel, "I got that right?"

"Uh. Essentially."

"I'll take 'essentially' as a 'yes'," Marjorie said. "Now we have a President doing a power grab for women using Rapture predictions. Let me guess. Next she's gonna say you might get extra protection if you donate her way."

Frank said, "Something else may be brewing. Marcel, isn't that your friend?" Frank pointed out the window. The entire group turned to look.

A bike rider in pink and black was rapidly bumping a blue mountain bike down the back hillside of the valley. When she hit the tarmac of the road, she picked up speed and came barreling towards the Lucky Seven Ranch, legs pumping like pistons.

"Remember, upon the conduct of each depends the fate of all."
Alexander the Great (356 – 323 B.C.E.)

CHAPTER THIRTY-SEVEN

LARRY WATCHED ANNELISE for just a moment before deciding something had to be up. Nobody rode a bike that hard for fun.

"Come on, Marcel," he said. "Let's meet her out front." He went to the kitchen and rinsed his hands. Marcel followed his lead, as did everyone else.

By the time Annelise skidded to a stop at the double front doors, Larry was on the steps, along with Marcel, Frank, Dobbin, Marjorie, Ilene, Odelle, Harold and Cosmos. Vico and Soo Min were already on the driveway. Vico shouldered his video camera and began to record as Annelise swung a long leg off the bike. She wobbled slightly before gaining her balance. She looked up, her face streaked with sweat.

She said, "Larry. You've got to come. There's a dog."

"A dog!" Larry was already moving down the steps, believing her. "Where?"

"I'll have to take you there," she said. "There's an outbuilding up a creepy sideroad."

"What kind of dog?" Cosmos asked.

"Big. Loud." Annelise unsnapped a water bottle off the

frame of the bike and took a drink. "I think maybe a pit bull. I looked through a window, but it was hard to see."

Cosmos exchanged a look with Larry. She said, "We need to be careful."

Larry swallowed, hard. A pit bull was not his favorite dog. A left-behind pit bull might have some issues.

Frank said, "There's a catch pole in the room where Violet was staying."

"What's a catch pole?" Soo Min asked, extending her microphone.

"A long pole with a loop at the end," Larry said. "You can slip the loop over the head of a dog and walk the dog to a crate. The pole keeps the dog a few feet away from you."

"Have you used one before?" Soo Min asked.

Larry nodded. "I did some work at the animal shelter." He left out the part about it being community service hours in restitution for shop-lifting charges. He said, "For a big dog, it can be helpful to have two poles going."

"This sounds like specialty equipment. Were they keeping an aggressive dog here?" Soo Min asked.

"There's a pair of pot-bellied pigs here," Larry said. "You might use a catch pole to guide a pig along."

"Larry has a talent with animals," Marjorie said, leaning over to speak into Soo Min's microphone. "You watch. He's a wonder."

Larry tried to keep some version of confident professionalism on his face as he contemplated the high likelihood of being bitten while being filmed for a television audience.

He looked at Vico and Soo Min. No way would Soo

Min give this story a pass. This was a dog. In a world bereft of canines, this was news. Big news.

"Alright, then," Larry said, nodding. "Cosmos, will you get that catch pole? Marcel, will you load the big dog crate back in the van? I'll go get some treats."

"I wanna help!" Dobbin said.

"Ah, get us some water bottles," Larry said. "And a water dish."

Dobbin raced away.

Larry jogged back up the steps of the house and out to the catio. He opened the door to the catio carefully and took a peek.

Lucifer beamed hatred with his green eyes from a perch at the end of the catio. Larry nodded at Lucifer and said, "Gonna be gone in just a sec." Larry dashed into the porch, snagged a small container of cat treats and leapt back into the kitchen, pulling the catio door shut until it caught with a click.

"Lucifer versus pit bull," Larry mused. "My money would be on Lucifer."

He moved to the pantry and pulled out a box of plastic bags, then hustled to the granite island to fill two bags with grilled chicken parts. "At least we've got first-class bait," he murmured.

Hustling out to the van, he found Dobbin facing down Frank. "I wanna go!" Dobbin said. "I'll just watch!"

"No way," Frank thundered. "A pit bull? You have no idea how fast and mean that kind of dog can be! We're leaving this to the experts!"

"Grandpa, that's Larry! You said he was nice enough for a low-life!"

Frank's mouth went open and shut as he fumbled for a response.

"Ah, Dobbin," Larry said, "I, ah, actually need you to be doing a thing for me here."

Dobbin turned a tear-streaked face towards Larry with a sniff. "What?"

"Ah, let's go around back." Larry put a hand on Dobbin's shoulder and steered him away from his grandfather. As they passed Annelise, Larry told her, "Go grab something to eat. There's lots inside. We'll be ready to go in a few minutes."

Larry guided Dobbin out to the front of the barn and then let go of the kid's shoulder. "Listen, kid. I need some help here on the home front."

"I want to see the dog!"

"Me too." Larry looked down at Dobbin. "We have to take Annelise. She knows where the dog is. I should take Cosmos because she's a trained vet tech. I want Marcel along because he's smart and strong. I only have one passenger seatbelt, and your granddad will just plain flat kill me if something happened to you."

Dobbin looked down and kicked the dirt. "I could ride with the television people."

"Who have jobs to do. If this really is a dog, they've got to get the news out. And Soo Min is pregnant. I know diddly-squat about pregnant ladies, but I do know they get tired. Must be like toting around a sack of potatoes all day."

Dobbin sniffed, but smiled a bit.

"And the dog isn't our only responsibility," Larry said. "We ate our dinner. But the cats need to be fed. Nigel and

Violet need to be fed. Watered too. You and your grandpa could help out with that."

Dobbin drug a hand under his nose, kicked the dirt, then nodded again.

"And there's more." Larry pulled the Rolex watch out from his jeans pocket. "A friend named Aisha is coming out with her two little girls. They'll be staying in the big master bedroom. And that's a problem."

Dobbin looked up.

Larry rolled his eyes and said, "Your granddad is right. I'm sorta a low-life. You saw me. I took this watch. Now we might have some more Rapturing coming, and I need somebody to put it back in the dresser drawer in the big bedroom. I'd do it, but I'm kinda busy. I could use somebody smart and quiet-like. And, well, without telling your granddad."

"Like, duh." Dobbin smiled. "I could do it."

"Aisha's real sharp. Don't underestimate her."

"Got it." Dobbin took the watch and slid it into his front jeans pocket where it made a noticeable bulge.

Larry looked at the boy's bumped-out pocket. "Soon would be good."

"*I can calculate the motion of heavenly bodies,
but not the madness of people.*
Isaac Newton (1643 – 1727)

CHAPTER THIRTY-EIGHT

COSMOS CAME OUT of the barn carrying the catch pole. She showed it to Larry and Dobbin, saying "This is first rate. It works a treat. We put this loop of coated cable around the head of the animal, snug the loop, and the pole keeps the animal from getting close to us." She showed them a button half-way up the pole. "Here's the release." She thumbed the button and the loop dropped away into a single strand.

"Have you used one?" Larry asked as he took the pole and experimented with it.

"No," Cosmos answered. "I've seen a dog brought into the clinic by an animal control officer. We got the dog calmed down and didn't have any troubles."

"How'd you calm it down?" Dobbin asked.

"I did a play bow," Cosmos said. "You lean over like this," she said, bending at the waist. "And you use a high, happy voice. It signals to the dog that you want to play."

"Play bow," Larry murmured. "Sounds good."

A rumble of thunder came from up the valley and a scattering of raindrops descended.

"We'd better get this show on the road," Larry said.

Marjorie had other ideas. When Larry, Cosmos and Dobbin made it back to the front of the house, Marjorie was waiting. "Before you take off, we need a master plan here. Come on. We'll do this in the dining room."

Larry shrugged. They followed Marjorie's fast-moving wide body as she shouted, "Hey, everyone. Gather round."

Annelise was shoveling in a mound of potato salad as Marjorie bellowed, "You first. Where's the dog?"

Caught mid-swallow, Annelise coughed, spewing out potato chunks.

Marjorie ignored the spray and said, "We need to know, now."

"It's off Oyster Bay road. There's a gravel road that used to go to an old ashram." Annelise took a drink of water and said, "There's some grimy yurts and an old RV. Then there's a mobile home and a big concrete building with garage doors. It's kinda gross."

"What were you doing back there?" Marjorie asked.

The girl shrugged. "Just checking out the neighborhood."

"Looking in windows?"

"I heard a howl. That's when I rode in to the place and looked through the window in the building. It's dark inside, and it's hard to see, but there's a dog. Chained up."

"Where are your parents?" Marjorie said.

Annelise's shoulders came forward. "Working."

"On this continent?"

Annelise's mouth opened, then shut. She rallied with, "My family is my business. I'm here to get help for a dog."

"Well, bullshit," Marjorie said. "We can't care for a dog if we don't care for you. We're burning daylight. Tell us what's going on with you, and then we'll make a plan that will work."

Annelise shot a look of anger at Marjorie, who crossed her arms across her ample bosom and stared back. Annelise sighed. Larry knew the feeling. His mother could cut down to the basics like a trauma surgeon.

"My Dad is overseas," Annelise said. "I can't say anything more than that. Government stuff. My mom is at a research station in Antarctica." Annelise shrugged. "They think I'm with friends."

"And you are," Marjorie said. "Here's the deal. You show these guys where the dog is. Then they take you to your place to grab some clothes, and you come back here. We know this is a female-owned property. You stay the nights here until we know more about this next round of Rapture."

She turned to Vico and Soo Min and said, "You next. What's up with you?"

Soo Min said, "I've been getting messages from my producer. People are loving the footage we shot of Larry and the kittens. He's a YouTube star. Anything he does, is worth filming." She took a breath. "Larry aside, if this is a dog, it is a global story."

"It's a dog!" Annelise said.

Soo Min shook her head. "It's your opinion it's a dog. We could get there and find out it's a big robot. Or a mountain lion caught in a garage. Or a hoax. We should keep an open mind and check it out."

"You feeling okay?" Marjorie asked.

Soo Min ran a hand over her large abdomen. "I'm fine. Dinner helped." She turned to smile at Vico. "Don't worry. Vico's got my back. And we'll stay the night in Olympia at his mother's place."

Vico nodded. "My momma has owned her house for years. Female-owned. No question."

"Alright." Marjorie turned to her cousins, "Now you."

"Mommm!" Larry objected. "There's a storm moving in. What we need to do should be done in daylight."

"Alright." Marjorie said. "Harold and Ilene are going to get us up to date on the multiverse theories and cosmetology. We'll tell you about it later. I'll make sure we get our priorities sorted."

"That's cosmo-*gony*," Harold said. "I've got quite a theory under development."

"Won't that be fun," Larry whispered. It occurred to him this was no time to mess with cosmic evaluations where sarcasm might not score well. He leaned in, gave Marjorie a kiss on the cheek and said, "You ride herd on all of us. We'll get back as quick as we can."

In the end, Annelise rode in the broadcast vehicle with Soo Min and Vico. Larry took the wheel of the pet-sitting van with Cosmos in the passenger seat and Marcel sitting, cross-legged, on the floor behind the front seats, wedged in front of the large dog carrier.

"Harold sounds interesting," Marcel said.

"Odelle says he's smart," Larry agreed. He turned to Cosmos and said, "This may sound sexist, but I'm glad Harold came out. He's big and smart. Frank is . . . well, Frank. Makes me feel better about leaving the ladies there."

Cosmos laughed. "I think your mother is the most terrifying one."

"Yeah," Larry smiled. "If bad guys show up, she

might just cook them an omelet and then hit them with the skillet."

A black Navigator turned into the Lucky Seven drive just as Larry was turning onto the main road. Aisha was at the wheel of the big SUV. Larry waved, and she gave a curt nod of recognition.

"And now we're all set in our protection plan," Larry said. "Our own personal dragon showed up."

Marcel snorted.

Larry followed the broadcast truck out of Holiday Valley and down the freeway. He knew it'd be a convoluted trip, exiting at Steamboat Island road and then doubling back after the fire department to reach Oyster Bay Road.

"Be about a mile if we were crows," Larry said.

"There really was an ashram out here?" Marcel asked.

"Oh, hell, there's probably been a dozen ashrams and communes out here," Larry said. "This is, ah, a rural-urban interface, and we're on the west coast. There's blueberry farms, dairy farms, dance halls, Christmas tree farms, whore houses, boat builders, sail-makers, oyster growers, kung-fu classes, organic everything, and yoga with and without goats."

He guided the van off the freeway and up Steamboat Island road. "This area was also a hotbed for methamphetamine makers a few years ago. Some buddies of mine got into that, and it is some super-nasty shit."

"You ever try it?" Cosmos asked.

"Nah. Weed, booze, cigarettes for sure." He looked over at Cosmos and said, "Frank calls me a low-life. He's right, but I'm a chicken around things that go 'Boom.' Meth labs go 'Boom' all the time."

Larry turned the van down the road winding west to Oyster Bay Road. He said, "It's not a good idea for Annelise to go poking her head around like she is. I don't know if anyone is making meth out here these days, but I'm damn sure paranoia is around, big time."

"Marjorie told me that you've met some armed patrols," Cosmos said.

"Yep." Larry nodded. "You guys do me a favor. Stay in the van until I get a quick look at this garage building."

"I'm faster than you," Marcel said.

"Yeah, and I'm about sixteen shades whiter," Larry said.

"I could go," Cosmos argued. "I'm the vet tech."

The idea of Cosmos coming up against an angry git with a gun made Larry's stomach roil.

"Just let me take a look," Larry said. "Among other things, if it goes south, you guys can be the get-away drivers."

Vico was driving the broadcasting rig. He signaled a turn onto Oyster Bay road. Larry followed suit. There was no other traffic.

They passed dark country houses set back from the road and screened by swaths of towering Douglas fir. They went by a field of black Angus cows and an organic farm with an empty wheelbarrow out front with a taped-on sign stating, "No eggs for sale. Don't Ask."

A few more raindrops hit the windshield, scattering dust without enough force to wash the grime away.

Vico turned down a pitted gravel side road, and Larry followed with the van, waiting a moment for some of the road dust to settle. He eased the van forward but even at a low speed, the van joggled with tooth-rattling force as he navigated the corrugated road.

Annelise was right. This road led to a distinctly dodgy set up. They passed two faded and torn yurts with broken steps. A piss-yellow mobile home sat back in the trees, stained with green algae stripes. Half of a jeep with the hood up emerged out of a bed of sword ferns like a cartoon version of a movie prop metal shark.

Vico stopped the broadcast van twenty yards from a concrete building with rolled-down garage doors. Larry pulled up next to the broadcast van and signaled to Cosmos to roll down the passenger side window. Vico rolled down his window and called, "She says this is it."

"Okay." Larry leaned forward and said, "I'm not likin' this place. I'm going to turn the van around — in case we need a fast exit."

Vico blinked, then nodded. He followed the van and turned the broadcast truck to point outward.

A rumble of thunder promised to deliver rain shortly.

Larry turned off the van and said, "Cosmos, I'll leave the keys in the ignition. Could you slide over to this seat in a minute and be ready to go?"

Her usually merry eyes went solemn. She nodded.

"I'm just supposed to sit here?" Marcel said.

"Yep." Larry said, "But you could pass me the catch pole." He turned and looked at Marcel. "Just give me a chance to do a quicky peek in the window."

As Larry climbed out of the van, he could hear Vico having the same discussion with Soo Min. "Baby first!" seemed to be the deciding comment before Vico was able to leave his wife at the wheel of the broadcast van.

Vico went to the back of the rig and emerged with a big video camera. He hoisted it with ease and joined Larry.

Together they walked up to the building, gravel crunching underfoot. Larry went to the side door where he could see some smears on the window, which was probably Annelise's work.

Vico began filming.

Cupping his hands against the window, Larry peered into the dark garage, his foot touching the door with a tap.

An unearthly howl went up. Larry could make out a pair of cocked ears above a forehead that looked as wide as a dinner plate.

"It's a dog," Larry said. "A really big dog. I think it's chained up."

Soo Min must have been monitoring the broadcast feed, because moments later she was descending from the broadcast van. She was quickly followed by Cosmos and Marcel.

Larry gave up on crowd control as everyone came to the window for a look. Soo Min had a microphone up and plugged in within seconds and began to narrate. "We're here, outside of Olympia, with breaking news. Student Annelise Schmidt discovered a dog. We are here with Larry Dinkelman of Larry's Post-Rapture Pet Sitting Service as Larry and his team begin their rescue operation."

"Rescue operation," Larry muttered. "More like sausage-making debacle. She hasn't really seen the size of this thing."

Cosmos heard him and offered a weak smile. "Some big dogs are really sweet," she said.

"We're about to find out. Hang on a sec." Larry spoke

to Marcel, "Go get us some water and doggie treats." Marcel gave a quick nod and jogged off to the van.

Larry twisted the door knob and had mixed feelings as it turned easily. He eased the door open a few inches as the dog began a barrage of barking. Larry slid his hand in and found the light switch.

A row of grimy and insect-spotted fluorescent lights went on, casting dark shadows from a jumble of toolboxes and lumber.

At the far wall, a massive black pit bull with a spike-studded collar strained against a thick chain, barking wildly. Dog turds surrounded a tattered dog bed.

Marcel returned from the van, water bottle and bag of bar-be-que chicken in hand.

"Thanks." Larry handed the catch pole to Marcel and took the food. Larry opened the door a few inches and slid through the slot. Vico stepped up to the door opening and kept filming.

"We're live," Soo Min said.

Her words had no meaning to Larry, whose attention was fully on the dog. Larry stopped a few feet away as the dog lunged against the chain. Larry bent over, doing his best to remember what Cosmos had said about the play bow.

The dog kept barking.

Larry straightened up and dug into the bag of chicken. He tossed a big thigh piece to the dog, who snatched it out of the air.

Four chicken thighs later and the dog was wagging its tail.

Larry took a few steps forward and bowed again.

He moved closer. Larry could see the dog's collar was too tight. The stench of urine and the volume of turds around the dog bed suggested this dog had been here a very long time.

Taking a deep breath, Larry stepped up to the dog and offered the back of his hand for a sniff.

The dog licked his hand.

Larry poured some water into the palm of his hand and offered it to the dog. "I'm not seeing a ding-dong," he said. "Your preferred pronoun might be 'she'?"

The dog lapped water and wagged her tail.

"Can we get this chain off you?" Larry spoke gently. "It looks heavy as hell."

He moved slowly, watching the dog carefully. He stroked her ears and she leaned into his hand.

Vico kept filming.

Larry reached down to the chain clip under the dog's chin. The dog licked Larry's arm.

He unsnapped the chain just as a boom of thunder shattered the quiet.

The big dog leapt at Larry, taking him to the floor.

"Experience is one thing you can't get for nothing."

Oscar Wilde (1854 – 1900)

CHAPTER THIRTY-NINE

PEOPLE FROM AROUND the world were watching. They tuned in by the thousands after Soo Min reported that a dog had been found. In minutes, the numbers of people watching the live footage exploded into the millions.

Work stopped around the globe as messages went out to friends and family. "A dog. A guy found a dog." This was followed by, "It's a rescue operation."

People gathered around computer monitors and television sets. Children were shushed. Buses stopped. In Switzerland, trains stayed in the station past their departure time. In major medical centers, patients headed into surgery begged for a small delay to watch the news, and anesthesiologists and surgeons agreed.

A dog.

In a world without dogs, Larry had a dog.

Millions held their breath as Vico filmed Larry trying a play bow. Several million swore when Larry tossed out chicken thighs, the viewers screaming, "That's a choking hazard!"

Millions applauded when Larry approached the big

dog, and millions wept abundantly as he patted her head and scratched her throat.

Now millions were watching, bug-eyed, as Larry sprawled on the floor under the dog, and a young black man came charging into the garage with a pole in his hand. Right behind him came a plump young woman with hair bouncing in a rainbow of curls.

Larry was shouting.

"It's okay!" He pushed the dog's big face away from his nose and tried again. "It's okay. She's scared of thunder."

Millions sighed in relief and wept more tears as they realized that Larry now had ninety pounds of trembling lap dog who was going nowhere until the storm passed.

Larry worked his hand up to the dog's ears and started scratching. He gave great ear, he had to admit.

"Poor thing," Cosmos said. "She needs a thunder shirt."

"A what?" Larry said from his squashed spot on the floor.

"There's a zip-on compression jacket for dogs," Cosmos said. "It's like being hugged. It can help a dog deal with storms or fireworks."

"Oh. There's a good dog. We'll get you a shirt," Larry crooned. "XXXL." He kept scratching and talking to the dog.

She liked what he was saying. The dog laid down on his lap, cutting off circulation.

Larry shifted a little, but kept up with the baby talk and ear scratching.

"Is there a name on her tag?" Cosmos asked. "She might like to hear her name."

Larry shifted the collar and mumbled.

Marcel and Cosmos came closer, and Larry repeated the name. "Jezebel," he said. "Isn't that, ah, Biblical?"

"Yes, but these days it's used by white supremacists to label a black woman as a harlot," Marcel whispered.

"Do what?" Larry said.

"Names they use," Marcel said with a deep frown. "Mammy or Jezebel. Docile, smiling servant or fuckable twat." His low voice was covered by a rumble of thunder.

"Christ." Larry shook his head. "No wonder nobody's left here. Those guys musta fried to a crisp." He scratched the dog's ears. "Who the hell gives a dog a name like that?"

"A jerk," Cosmos said. "But maybe that's why she got left behind." Her voice was quiet, almost covered by a rain shower beating down on the metal roof.

"Whaddaya mean?" Larry said.

"Maybe she thinks she's a bad dog," Cosmos said. "That happens. You believe what you're told. People do. Dogs too."

"Oh, man! That stinks!" Larry gave the dog an even finer ear rub. "You are beauty. You are SUCH a good girl."

Soo Min called from the doorway. "Larry, we have many people tuning in. Can you repeat what you just said? What is the dog's name?"

Larry looked up and saw the strain on Cosmos' face. He winked at her and called, "The dog's name is Dottie."

Cosmos broke into a smile that had Larry think of the sun. And the stars. And maybe the moon as well.

"Dottie" scooted closer to Larry as another rumble of thunder arrived.

"Easy," Larry said, "I ate dinner. There's no room for you in my innards."

*

The jet flew west as the lights of Midwest cities began to sparkle in the evening light. Abigail Ross and her staff were following the speeches and proposals coming out of the ecumenical council in Medina, Washington. C-Span2 was broadcasting, and the council was in its ninth hour. To a man – and they were all men – the speakers were well-dressed and well-spoken.

When Charles Westmoreland strode to the podium and addressed the crowd and the cameras, he made a powerful case for policies to lift all people out of poverty by redistributing the wealth of those who were gone.

Abigail said, "Who is he?"

Jared's fingers flew across a laptop keyboard. "Olympia native. Church of four thousand. Church of the Evergreen Life."

"He has charisma," Abigail said. "But, at best, he'll get a small plank in." She shook her head. "Just listen to them! They're carving up the bird."

"The bird?" Clive said.

"Money, power and position," Abigail said. "The stuff of the future – sitting out there like a big Christmas goose. Those guys are setting up the next system of governance." She smiled. "That is, they are *trying* to."

"What about the President?" Janice said. "Isn't her 'females own everything' idea a power grab too?"

"The *Disciples of Discipline*?" Abigail's nostrils twitched as she said the phrase with a tone of dismissal. "Yes. It's her power grab. Nothing Biblical about it, except for the flavor of the name."

Abigail's cell phone chimed. Abigail muted the television broadcast and answered. "Hello, Darling. We were just watching the news," she said.

"It's Ruthie," she said to the group.

Abigail fell silent as her daughter spoke. Then Abigail said, "Of course. That makes perfect sense. We can meet you there. Love you. Say your prayers! Bye-bye."

She clicked off the phone and said, "Ruthie's friend's family has changed their plans. They are going to Palm Springs to stay with a grandmother, who owns a ranch in the area."

"Are we going to California then?" Janice asked.

"Yes. Could you start looking for housing options for us? I'll let the pilots know." Abigail stood up. She said, "Don't worry, Janice. Palm Springs is beautiful. There's lots of amenities."

Janice didn't point out that she and Clive couldn't afford "amenities."

Jared was scrolling through a news feed. "Abigail, listen to this! There's a dog – in Olympia!"

"A dog!" Abigail sat back down.

"Can you put that up on the big screen?" Abigail said.

The four watched in silence. They saw a skinny, balding man with a potbelly come out of a garage, leading a big black dog with a wide head. The dog was marked with a white chest stripe and two white front feet. A second leash on the dog was held by a woman in medical scrubs with a head of rainbow-hued corkscrew curls.

The dog's toenails dug into the gravel as she surged forward, dragging her guides with her.

The two people moved the dog towards a white van

with a sign on the door which read *Larry's Post-Rapture Pet-Sitting Service* and gave a phone number.

On screen, a young black man in a shirt labeled *Dave*, came out of the garage's side door, carrying a catch pole. He pulled the door closed.

The reporter, a dark-haired and pregnant woman put a microphone into 'Dave's' face and asked, "Will you take the dog to the Lucky Seven Ranch?"

"Yes," the young man said. "We'll take good care of her."

In the jet, Abigail said, "Oh, my Lord! That's *our* place!"

"Our place?" Clive whispered to Janice.

Janice whispered back, "It's the female-owned large facility down the road from where Ruthie was going to go. In Holiday Valley."

As the television camera shifted back to the white van, the pet-sitting service phone number came back into focus.

On the jet, Abigail snapped, "Get that number!"

Jared typed the number into his laptop.

Near the garage, Soo Min said, "That's a very big dog. What breed is this?"

"Best ask Larry. Or Cosmos," Marcel-'Dave' said.

Larry and Cosmos pulled Dottie to a stop to release some of the strain on their arms and on Dottie's neck. Larry knelt down and rubbed Dottie, who licked his face with enthusiasm.

Cosmos turned and spoke to the reporter with cheerful confidence. "Dottie clearly is some part of a Bully breed. We can tell that by her big head. She has the sweet nature of an American Staffordshire terrier, but, being so big, she almost certainly has some other breeds in the family tree. She may be part Great Dane or mastiff."

"This is Soo Min Carlevaro, reporting from west of Olympia. There is a dog. She is being moved by professionals to a place of safe-keeping. We'll keep you updated."

In the jet, Jared turned down the volume on the television screen and said, "The whole world has to be watching this." He muted the sound completely as a barrage of talking heads popped up on the news feed, all with an opinion on the meaning of the appearance of a dog.

Abigail sat back in the fine leather of the jet's executive seating. She said, "That dog is the key to our future."

She said, "Aaron always told me the best way to build an empire was to give people what they want."

She smiled at Jared. "Americans don't want all the property in the United States owned by women. They don't want all the property owned by men either. They want a dog and hope for the future. We can capitalize on that. We'll give people another path. Not the president's way, not the council's way, but a third way. The Abigail Ross way." She grinned. "Memberships available. This could be absolutely fabulous."

Clive reached under the walnut-veneered flight table and took his wife's hand.

Janice quietly squeezed his fingers in acknowledgement. They now could see Abigail's motivations. But what did God want of His servants?

Clive said, "What's your thinking, Abigail?"

"We'll need to get out to the Lucky Seven Ranch as quick as we can," Abigail said. "And then we need to find a chink in the operation." She smiled. "We'll look for a way in. You'll need to help me find an opening."

"There is only a finger's worth of difference between a wise man and a fool."
Diogenes (412 - 323 B.C.E.)

CHAPTER FORTY

ABIGAIL SAID, "WE'LL need to get the world's attention. We'll do that by connecting with the world's first Post-Rapture dog. Did you see her? Powerful and beautiful!"

She sipped her specially blended tea and said, "We should be ready to quickly expand with prayer and programming." She smiled. "You know how it goes. If a viewer buys into one piece of the Ross program, most of the time we can translate that into a full supporting membership. Hope carries our viewers forward."

"Isn't this manipulative?" Janice managed.

"What are the public's alternatives?" Abigail snapped. "A prune of a President making a power grab for XX chromosome activists? Or stodgy old men using Scripture to stay in power?

Clive said, "Aren't you planning to use scripture to guide people? Or is it guide people to you?" For the first time in twenty years of working for Abigail, Clive's tone of voice had a tone of disapproval.

"I am *inspired by Christ*," Abigail said, eyes flashing. "Surely you, of all people, know this. I work so hard! I have been a good and faithful servant! And the Lord has blessed me abundantly." She swept a hand around, indicating the plush interior of the jet. "I wouldn't have this without the Lord's grace."

"And the Lord will bless you more," Jared said, smiling. "Lead us and we will grow in strength."

"Those who trust in the Lord will renew their strength," Abigail recited. "They will soar on wings like eagles. They will run and not grow weary. They will walk and not be faint."

She smiled at Janice and Clive. "Let us pray," she said.

Clive held Janice's hand as Abigail spoke in prayer. After several minutes she closed with an "Amen."

Jared boomed an echoing "Amen" while Clive and Janice had an "Amen" more subdued.

Abigail ignored their lack of enthusiasm. She opened her laptop and said, "My brain is just humming with ideas. Jared, look and see what scripture says about dogs."

She looked at Janice and said, "Would you be a dear and phone Ruthie? Tell her we're being delayed. We have been called to a mission in Washington State."

Janice did the deed, connecting almost immediately with Ruthie. She didn't know which was more upsetting – that Abigail so easily jettisoned her trip to see her daughter, or that Ruthie was so completely unsurprised.

*

"I smell like dog shit," Larry said.

"It's on the back of your jeans," Cosmos said. "There are some big smears."

"Great." Larry heaved on the dog leash. "Dottie! Slow down!"

The big dog gasped for air as she flung herself forward.

"Do you want me to use the catch pole?" Marcel asked. "It might slow her down."

"Nah," Larry said. "She's just pent up. You get a little crazy when you get out of jail." He laughed. "Ask me how I know."

Soo Min and Vico followed, filming as Larry and Cosmos wrestled with Dottie, giving her praises and doing their best to keep her under control as they encouraged her to stretch her legs.

As they neared the back of the Pet-Sitting Service van, Larry said, "Do you think we can get her into the dog crate?"

"No," Cosmos said. "A dog like this isn't crate-trained, and she's too excited to learn right now."

"When we get her to the house, we should take her down to the orchard," Larry said. "It's fenced. She can run around and get her sillies out."

"That'd be good." Cosmos's pink-and-tan sweating face clashed with her rainbow-hued corkscrew hair as she worked the second leash to keep Dottie under control.

Marcel opened the back doors. Dottie seemed to realize the van was her chance to leave the property. The dog surged, leaping into the van with the grace of an Olympic hurdler.

Dottie eagerly sniffed around the large dog crate. She turned around and licked Larry, who was standing at the van's bumper, giving her ease on the leash.

Vico kept filming as Larry caressed the big dog's ears.

Annelise and Soo Min came closer, with Annelise smiling. "See," she said. "I told you it was a dog!"

Larry turned to the teenager and said, "Super find. Absolutely fantastic." Then he lowered his chin and said, "Super find. Stupid process."

Annelise's face clouded with anger as Soo Min angled her microphone toward Larry. Vico kept filming.

"You can't keep doing this," Larry said. "Biking around by yourself. I don't know who was keeping this dog here, but this place has bad, bad mojo."

Annelise started to speak, but Larry held up a hand. "I kited some checks," he said. "Back when check writing was a thing." He grinned. "And I helped myself to some stuff from a warehouse. Stuff that wasn't mine."

Larry frowned. "I spent over a year in the county lock up. Most of the guys were like me – not too bright. No impulse control."

His eyes went flat and hard. "But there were some nasty dudes in there, Annelise. Predators. *They are built different.*"

Larry stared at Annelise as he added, "They *don't hesitate.* You think you're gonna have time to outsmart them, but you may not even get a second."

Vico kept filming. Soo Min was silent. Larry didn't register the presence of the reporters or comprehend that his lecture was being broadcast around the globe. He was focused on Annelise.

"You can pick out the predator," he said, "and think you're okay because you're paying attention and keeping an eye on him. That works for a while – but you're totally screwed if there is a second predator – somebody ready to jump you from behind, or someone *who studies you and builds a trap.* That barking dog sound could have been a lure."

Annelise's eyes went big.

"Yeah," Larry said. "Someone can notice where you ride your bike and when. They study your habits and figure out how to get an advantage. One guy to get your attention and another to attack."

He moistened his lips and said, "I'm not telling you to quit living. I'm saying take Marcel with you, or somebody else, so you double your chance of not being surprised." He looked hard at Annelise and said, "You got lucky."

Annelise give a miniscule head nod of agreement. Vico captured her chastened face on his camera and the footage went, live, out to the millions watching. While Larry was busy checking on Dottie and closing the van doors, the Twitter-verse exploded with stories of lures, traps and deceptions.

"I'll tell you what," Larry said to the group. "I already stink. I'll sit in back with Dottie."

"I could drive," Marcel offered.

"Thanks, buddy," Larry grinned. "But my day has already been exciting. Why don't you ride shotgun, and let Cosmos drive?"

A few minutes later Cosmos was at the wheel of the van. Marcel sat in the passenger seat, and Larry sat behind the seats with a lap full of Dottie.

Vico leaned in and filmed Dottie washing Larry's face with a giant pink tongue.

"Let's take you home," Larry said to the dog. "It's kinda a zoo, but you'll like it."

"Unite to move forward."
Hawaiian proverb

CHAPTER FORTY-ONE

A BEAUTIFUL, ATHLETIC girl found a dog. The news ricocheted around the globe including to the McMurdo Station in Antarctica where Dr. Gordon-Schmidt emerged from a snow tractor after a week-long excursion collecting ice core samples and documenting local populations of midges, rotifers and nematodes.

It didn't take Dr. Gordon-Schmidt long to figure out: a) the beautiful, athletic girl in the news was her daughter; and b) her daughter had omitted some significant details about the neighbors who were supposedly housing her – specifically that said neighbors were on the "gone-up" list posted on the county website, and Annelise had been alone and unsupervised for several days.

Back in Olympia, Vico was pulling the broadcast van past the security gate of Holiday Valley when Annelise's phone lit up with a call from her mother.

Dr. Gordon-Schmidt left no room for discussion or alternatives. By the time Vico parked the broadcast van in front of the big house, it was clear Annelise's rambling days were done. She was to stay with the Pet-sitting Service team until Dr. Gordon-Schmidt returned, a matter of at least several days as even in times of The Rapture, Antarctica was Antarctica. Flights were infrequent and often delayed or canceled.

Vico smiled in sympathy as Annelise rolled her eyes and shut off her smart phone.

"Is your Mom Italian?" Vico asked. "She sure sounds Italian."

Soo Min laughed. "All moms sound the same when they are worried."

Annelise managed a wry smile. "She's not usually a yeller. Larry's lecture got to her." She exhaled. "It's worth it. Grounded for a thousand years, but we found *a dog*."

They watched as Marcel came around to the back of the Pet-Sitting Service van and opened the van doors. Larry had both hands on Dottie's now loosened collar and was leaning back, using his weight to control her exit from the van. She strained forward, like ninety pounds of canine rocket, ready for lift off.

Vico said, "They're going to take Dottie down to the orchard so she can run around. I should get some footage of that." He turned to his wife and said, "How are you holding up?"

"I'm tired," Soo Min admitted. "But this is the story of a lifetime." She hesitated, then said, "I think we should stay here tonight."

Vico nodded. "I'll call my mom and let her know. Frank said he has some air mattresses at his place. We can collect them after filming Dottie."

He leaned over and kissed his wife on the forehead. "We'll stay the night, and tomorrow you'll earn some prizes."

The door to the big house opened and people streamed out, all eager to see the dog. Marjorie came, huffing with effort as she navigated the deep, loose gravel. Harold came, carrying one of Aisha's twins while listening to a cheerful Odelle who was pointing things out to the toddler.

Aisha came, balancing her second daughter on her hip. Frank, Dobbin and Ilene followed, all smiles at the sight of the big dog dancing and straining at the end of a leash as Marcel clipped on a second lead.

Dottie crashed to the end of the leash in an effort to gallop away, but this time Marcel's two hundred pounds was on one end of the second leash. Cosmos had the first leash. She had experience, and Marcel had brawn. Sandwiched between the two, Dottie slowed down long enough to have a long pee. Larry ambled along with them, moving easily and opening the gate to the orchard.

Marcel and Cosmos took Dottie into the orchard, and Larry stepped inside with them before swinging the gate closed. Cosmos and Marcel unhooked the leads from Dottie's collar.

The dog stood still for a heartbeat, every muscle quivering.

Vico caught this handsome moment of grace, and then the twilight gloaming of the spring evening was invaded by the spirit of a giant hare as Dottie bounded away. She bounced, careened, scrambled, righted herself and ran. Her claws dug into the dirt as she neared the fence and was forced into a wide turn.

She lapped the orchard twice. Vico knew the streaking dog wasn't in focus, but it didn't matter. Her joy and physicality came through as she went zipping around a third time.

Larry and the crowd of watchers lined up at the orchard fence all cheered Dottie on.

"You Go, Girl!" Aisha shouted.

"Yippee! Look at that!" Ilene yelled.

Dottie made another two laps of the orchard. Finally, she slowed, made another lightning turn and came bounding up and into Larry.

"Oooffff." Larry cleared his throat and tried again. "Off! Down, Dammit! Dottie, get down!"

Dottie dropped and did her best to sit on Larry's feet.

He caressed her ears. "Good girl. You're a really good girl."

Dottie licked his hand and got up for another round of wiggling. Larry knelt down and gave Dottie a strong chest rub.

Around the world, people watched Dottie kiss Larry with a broad wet tongue. Some people cheered. Many wept.

In a world gone crazy, an imprisoned dog had been liberated.

Inside the Babcock's house, Lucifer twitched an ear as the phone began to ring.

*

ABIGAIL WATCHED THE Dottie footage as it went viral. As soon as the jet set down at Boeing field, Abigail was ready for action. She drummed her fingers on the leather armrest as the jet rolled to a stop.

Jared read her mood and unclasped his seat belt. "Be ready to really move," he whispered to Janice. "She's got a limo ordered, and she won't wait for anyone."

Janice nodded. She'd seen Abigail in this mood before. When the door to the jet opened, Abigail descended immediately with no word of thanks to the pilots.

Long accustomed to serving the wealthy, they didn't expect acknowledgements. One pilot did sketch a small salute to Janice as she struggled down the stairs, computer bags in hand.

Abigail stalked across the tarmac to a waiting limousine. Janice hustled to keep up until Clive called to her.

"No need to run," Clive said. "Abigail may be in a rush, but she's not leaving me and the video equipment behind." He smiled at his wife. "That'd be stupid, and we know our Abigail isn't stupid."

The jet's co-pilot helped Jared load a stack of suitcases and gear bags onto a luggage wagon. The two men pushed the wagon over to the chauffeur, who made quick work of stowing the collection.

Clive double-checked the bags to make sure all the gear had been transferred.

He was right. Abigail waited.

Jared was breathing hard as he slid into the limousine, next to Janice. A moment later Clive climbed in to sit on Janice's left. Abigail had the forward-facing bench to herself. She ignored her employees. She placed a call, saying, "We've landed. We'll be in Olympia in about an hour. I want to go out to the Lucky Seven tonight."

What followed wasn't pretty. Clive and Janice did their

best to fade into the upholstery as Abigail shouted, "I said tonight. I do not CARE if it's dark!"

Jared motioned to the driver, and the big car picked up speed on the interstate as Abigail continued to harangue and complain.

Near the Tacoma exits, Abigail finally began to listen to her local contact.

"I see," she said.

Janice relaxed her fingers, which had been frozen in a claw grab around a brief case handle. Clive exhaled.

Abigail wiggled her hand in a "come here" way. Jared and Janice interpreted this as a demand for the laptop computer to be brought out.

A moment later Jared had the computer open on his knees.

Abigail said, "Hang on a minute, Bill." To Jared, she said, "Our realtor is Bill Neddles. Note the name, please."

Jared typed rapidly. Abigail said, "Bill recognizes some of the people out at the Lucky Seven. His staff has been doing some background checking. I'm going to repeat what he says. Take notes, please."

Clive and Janice eyed each other. The "please" meant Abigail was moving from hot demands to cool planning, where her talents were strong.

"Annelise Schmidt," Abigail said. "A vicious and armed teen known for her knife skills. She's the one who found the dog."

Janice looked at Clive in confusion. The blonde girl they'd watched on the television looked like a joyful beauty.

"Marcel Westmoreland," Abigail said. "The black kid. Bill's son knows him. They go to the same high school.

Marcel Westmoreland is a radical and subversive who undermines teachers with sly campaigns of rebellion."

Jared typed in Marcel's bio, as given by the Neddles' paterfamilias.

"Aisha Stewart-Westmoreland. The black pregnant lady with the little girls. An attorney. Some scandal in her background. Bill can't remember it, but will have his people look into it." Abigail frowned. "She must be Marcel's mother. My God. She must have had him when she was in middle school."

A moment later there was another name. "Soo Min Carlevaro," Abigail said. "The television reporter. An Asian."

Abigail said into the phone, "Where is Soo Min from?"

There was a response, and Abigail clarified. "No. Not where she was born. I don't care if she was born in Seattle. I mean, where is she *from*? Korea? Vietnam?"

Abigail's face mirrored her frustration as she gave up trying to learn Soo Min's ancestors' antecedents. To Jared, Abigail said. "Just write down she's almost certainly a screaming liberal."

When Jared raised an eyebrow, Abigail said, "The woman is foreign *and* a reporter!"

Jared nodded and typed.

"Franklin McElroy? Oh. That's interesting. Let me tell Jared." Abigail covered the phone and said, "Franklin McElroy is a property owner in Holiday Valley. Bill says he's a difficult old man, but we shouldn't have any problems with him. Keeps to himself. Put him down as a likely conservative. We may be able to use him. He can't be happy about all these squatters showing up."

Abigail returned to her phone. She listened and said, "Alright." To Jared, she said, "The tall bald man may have been Harold Gibbons, a local actuary. A professional. Bill says he doesn't know the other women in the clip, but he'll work on getting them identified."

To Bill, on the phone, she said, "And the Larry fellow? The Pet-Sitting Service guy? What do you know about him?"

She laughed. "An ex-con? Seriously. Oh, this gets better and better." She tilted her head and said, "I look forward to speaking with you in the morning." She paused and said, "Right. Where do you recommend? The Red Lion? Oh, thanks. Could you book me into their premium suite?" Abigail's eyes fell on Janice and Clive and she added, "And another room on another floor, please, for a couple."

As the limousine cruised past Fort Lewis, Abigail tapped off her phone with a smile. "Neddles is very helpful," she said. "The people who have the dog are definitely squatters. They are a bunch of riffraff and lowlifes."

"There's an actuary?" Janice asked.

"Only one fellow. The Larry guy is a jailbird."

"We're not going out there tonight?" Clive said.

"No." Abigail shook her head. "Neddles said it would not be safe. After hearing about those people, I have to agree. We'll stay at a hotel in Olympia and go out in the morning. He said there is a locked gate at the freeway exit, but he has an override code because he's the realtor for some properties out there."

She sniffed. "He's going to do more research this evening to see if he can identify all the people who are squatting at the Lucky Seven Ranch. Apparently, Olympia is not that big of a place, even if it is a state capital. He'll give me a call in a couple hours."

Abigail moistened her lips and said, "Jared can sleep on a rollaway in my suite. I'll need him close by for our follow-up research later this evening."

Janice started to speak, but Clive put his hand on her knee and gave it a minute squeeze. She sat back into the plush seat. Clive was right. At this particular moment, silence best served the Lord.

"With narrowed eyes, people plot evil"
Proverbs 16:30

CHAPTER FORTY-TWO

"WAKEY, WAKEY."

Jared felt Abigail's hand on his knee. Her hand moved smoothly up his leg to his crotch.

He groaned.

The night before, Abigail leapt on him the moment they'd shut the door to the hotel suite. Jared knew their bonking relieved tensions, but the events of the last few hours seemed to have filled Abigail with a new ferocity. It was as if Abigail was drawing strength, girding her loins, as it were, by demanding the services of his.

The nine-p.m. bonking had been before a quick room service snack, an hour of online research, and a follow up phone call from Bill Neddles. Larry's mother, they learned, was named Marjorie, and she had served a prison sentence for Medicare fraud. The curly-haired woman in the video footage was a vet tech from a westside animal hospital.

Neddles still didn't know who the other two women were. Abigail concluded they were likely just hangers-on. "Look at them," she'd said, freezing a video clip from YouTube. "Odd and old. One round, one skinny. They're nobodies. We don't have to worry about those two."

Jared thought the ten-thirty bonking went well enough. The two-a.m. bonking began when Abigail placed her cleavage over his cock and started a smooth stroking of said cock as it rested between her augmented breasts. He'd been asleep, but his tired Johnson perked up with such an interesting call to action.

A call for a fourth pre-breakfast bonking was too much. Jared pushed her hand away and rolled over with a mumble.

Abigail slapped his naked butt and said, "Come on. Rise and shine!"

He mumbled again. She pinched his butt cheek with some vigor. "Janice and Clive will be along soon," she said. "Time to move. There's been some interesting developments."

Jared sighed, but got up. A shower helped. He finished shaving, and heard Janice and Clive arrive.

Suddenly Jared was wide awake. There was no rollaway bed in the suite. There was, however, ample evidence that two people had enjoyed a romping good time in the one King-sized bed.

Jared cracked open the bathroom door and saw Abigail had everything under control. She was closing the door to the bedroom and talking to Clive and Janice in the sitting area of the suite.

He finished dressing and stopped to pull the bedding up to a smooth finish before he exited to the sitting area. A waiter wheeled in a breakfast spread on a room service trolley and silently accepted Abigail's one-dollar tip.

Jared followed the waiter to the door and discretely handed out a ten-dollar bill, which the waiter smoothly diverted to a vest pocket. Jared returned to the table to take an empty chair and pasted on an innocent smile as he sat down.

Janice blessed him with a smile and a minute nod of approval.

"Sleep well?" Clive asked.

"Oh, yes." Jared ignored the rawness of his tired pecker and said, "Please pass the creamer," as he poured a cup of coffee.

Abigail had the early morning news on. The top report centered on the upcoming Round Two of Rapture, with many gesturing commentators loving or hating the President's all-female Disciples of Discipline. The ecumenical council in Medina, Washington had generated heat and little light as reverends competed to deliver polysyllabic names for not much new.

The "saving Dottie" footage aired, along with a follow-up piece showing lines of broadcasting vehicles waiting outside the Holiday Valley gates. The news anchor said, "Reporters from around the world are flocking to Olympia to learn more about this happy find."

"Neddles will get us through that gate," Abigail said. "But we need to be ready to take action as soon as we are on the property."

"I don't understand," Clive said. "What does "take action" mean?"

"We'll need to convince the rabble out at the ranch that their only way forward is to accept a strong, female-led, Christian path." Abigail curved a finger to Janice who knew to fill Abigail's coffee cup.

Abigail drank her coffee black.

"I spoke to Neddles half an hour ago," Abigail said. "He tells me the boy at the ranch is the grandson of Franklin McElvoy."

"Didn't you say Franklin was a loner?" Jared said.

"Apparently, he's at least willing to let the boy see the dog," Abigail said. "But if the McElvoys have joined in with the squatters, that might work to our advantage. We could always play the 'I'll call Child Protective Services' card."

She looked up and registered the horrified looks of the others at the table. "Just brainstorming," she said lightly. "It can't be a good situation for a child with all those felons running around. Neddles said the blonde girl attacked his son on the school bus. Completely unprovoked."

Jared leaned back in his chair and warily said, "That's unusual. Most of the time it's the girls who get harassed on a bus."

"She must be one of those feminists," Abigail said. She dropped her voice. "Perhaps a poor soul who is sexually different."

Janice pressed her lips into a thin line. Had Abigail always been so hateful? So manipulative? Janice shot a look at Clive. He was sitting very still. His sister was very private and quite possibly a good bit "different."

"The girl isn't that important," Abigail said. "It's the dog and the property we need." She smiled brightly. "And to get those, we need to manage this pet-sitting criminal – Mr. Larry Whats-his-name. I don't know if we'll convince him with prayer, but I'm sure we can come up with something."

*

Warm breath caressed Larry's ear, delivering a moment of seductive joy until Larry woke enough to register it was Dottie next to his face and not Cosmos. As Larry blinked and yawned, he suddenly felt a moist tongue on his.

"Bleah!" Larry woke up completely, spitting as Dottie eagerly continued to wash his face.

He heard a giggle. Cosmos.

Larry shoved Dottie away from his face as he became keenly aware of a crossbar under the chaise lounge that was plowing a rut into his lower back. He rolled over as best he could, slowly registering the challenges of moving while encased in a sleeping bag on the cushions of a chaise lounge. Dottie gave a gigantic wiggle, ecstatic to have Larry awake.

He stroked Dottie's broad head, as he looked around the catio. He'd slept surprisingly well. Then again, he'd had a high-mileage day.

It was hard to believe he'd met Marcel, Frank, Dobbin, and Dottie less than twenty-four hours ago.

And Cosmos.

Larry looked at Cosmos, sitting up on the next lounger.

"Hell of a way to wake up," he croaked. "French-kissing a dog."

Cosmos grinned at him. "You were snoring. I can't blame her." She unzipped her sleeping bag and pulled her knees up, revealing lavender pajamas covered with rainbows and unicorns.

"I love your pajamas," Larry said. He swallowed hard. Where had that come from? Was it okay to talk about a woman's pajamas? Even if you had spent a night next to her?

Cosmos pinked up. "They're kinda juvenile."

"They're perfect for you," Larry said, finding confidence from God knew where. The pajamas were sweet and colorful. However, he couldn't quite get it together to say so – not with Dottie doing her best to climb up on the chaise lounge.

"Dottie, Down!" Larry shoved the dog's feet off the furniture.

"She needs to go out," Cosmos said. "Let me dash to the bathroom, and I'll come help you get her outside."

"We can't just open the door?" Larry waved at the glass door at the end of the catio.

"Nope." Cosmos was firm. "She's too new here. She doesn't even really know her new name. Not yet. And what if Violet got out? Do we know if Dottie likes bacon?"

Larry exhaled. A Violet-Dottie interaction could end badly. They were both big girls.

"We also don't know much about Dottie's temperament," Cosmos said. "She may be sweet with us and aggressive with strangers." Cosmos was pulling on slipper socks as she said this. "Or she may have anxiety issues."

"Well, there's a Roger on the anxieties," Larry said. "Thunder, kittens, toddlers. She's scared of everything."

"She did alright with the kittens and the kids with some encouragement," Cosmos said. "She'll probably be better today. I'll be right back."

Larry scratched Dottie's ears and contemplated relieving himself into one of the potted plants.

"Better be civilized," he told Dottie. "When Cosmos

comes back, I'll go wee in the bathroom like a proper gent, and then it'll be your turn."

Larry looked around the catio. The two ragdoll kittens were curled up on a carpeted shelf of one of the cat-climbing towers. A striped tabby sat on a window ledge, studying birds at an exterior bird feeder.

"Wonder where Lucifer is?" Larry continued to scratch Dottie's ears as he said, "Trust me, there's one cat that it's *wise* to worry about."

A smooth motion from above caught Larry's eye. It was Lucifer, prowling the ceiling rim catwalk through the foliage like a super-model with crisscrossing feet and an air of disdain.

The cat turned his green eyes towards Larry, lasering down beams of spite.

"Good morning to you, too," Larry said.

Lucifer ignored the greeting. He studied Dottie, then continued down the plank, tail jerking in dismissal.

A few minutes later, Larry and Cosmos led Dottie outside, on two leads. The dog pulled like a steam engine as she strained ahead of Larry and Cosmos. Larry was still wearing the sweat pants and flannel shirt he'd slept in, and Cosmos was in her pajamas with added garden boots.

"How long is she gonna be doing this?" Larry gasped as he opened the orchard gate while leaning hard to hold Dottie in check.

"Until we train her otherwise," Cosmos said. "She needs a ton of movement and . . . with that . . . we can start . . . some . . . behavioral modifications." The words came out in spurts as Cosmos dug her boots into the dirt to anchor Dottie to a stop. The dog squatted and peed a river.

Larry closed the gate as Cosmos pulled a brown pellet out of her pajama pocket.

"Sit!" she said, waving the treat above Dottie's nose.

Cosmos nudged the dog's rear with one hand as she continued to show the tiny treat. Dottie was fascinated and . . . completely uncomprehending.

Larry added his hands, one on Dottie's rear, pushing down, the other under her chin.

The light slowly dawned, and Dottie's rear started to sink toward the ground. As soon as there was a facsimile of a sitting dog, Cosmos fed Dottie the treat.

"Let's try, 'Shake hands'," Cosmos said.

Larry knelt down and took Dottie's right foreleg. "Shake hands!" he said.

Dottie washed his face.

Larry set the foot down and laughed.

"Try again," Cosmos said, handing some treats to Larry.

It took a few more tries, but Dottie got into the game. She started lifting her paw for Larry to take.

Larry stood up and said, "That's enough. Go have fun." He unclipped the leads.

One "Good Girl!" later and Dottie was off, racing around the orchard. Larry and Cosmos watched her run, each smiling at the sight of the dog's abundant joy.

"Wow!" Dobbin climbed over the orchard gate and joined them. "Look at her go!"

Dottie came careening back, earned another treat for

something resembling a "sit" and then went bounding off with Dobbin to race to the end of the orchard.

Larry and Cosmos followed.

"Shall we show her the pigs?" Larry asked.

"Sure. We're certainly dressed for it." Cosmos said.

Larry laughed. Somehow life was so very good standing in an orchard early on a May morning with a curly-haired woman in rainbow-unicorn pajamas.

Dottie came to Larry's whistle. Dobbin came too.

"We're going to introduce Dottie to Violet and Nigel," Cosmos said. "Want to come?"

"You bet!" Dobbin's face lit up like it was Christmas morning.

Larry felt the same. How was it that Cosmos made a dog-pig meetup sound like the most fun thing in the universe?

It went well enough. They clipped the double leashes onto Dottie, and she ambled around the bottom of the orchard with them. It was obvious when she first smelled the pigs. Her ears went up, and her entire body alerted to a statue of quivering muscles.

"Yeah. There's pigs," Larry told the dog. "No big deal. We've got your back."

They carefully guided Dottie closer to the pig pen.

Dobbin ran ahead and climbed up on the gate, calling "Pig-pig-piggy!"

Violet and Nigel shambled out of their low shed, and Dottie put on the brakes.

"Don't go getting in there," Larry called to the boy.

"I know," Dobbin said. "Grandpa said he'd show me some pig-herding today, but I'm supposed to wait for him."

"Good idea." Larry looked at Dobbin's bulging jeans pockets that were now nearly to eye level as the boy hung on the metal gate. "Still got that watch?"

Dobbin nodded. "Don't worry. Aisha's really sharp, but I'll get it put back."

Cosmos didn't say a word, but she raised an eyebrow.

"I'm a stupid shit," Larry told her. "I've got no impulse control. I took a watch from the bedroom. Nice watch." He grinned weakly, trying to find the words to explain why the watch had called to him so strongly. "Dobbin's helping me do right. We're putting it back."

Larry licked his lips. He needed to warn Cosmos. It was the right thing to do. "I've got raven eyes," he said. "Something looks nice, and I'll just pick it up."

She smiled. "Pretty things speak to you."

"Oh, yeah. Hell, yeah." He looked down at his feet. "Any cure for that?"

Cosmos shrugged. "Don't go where you know there's bait. Put guardrails in place, like hanging out with friends. That way you can't act on temptation." She looked down at Dottie, who was laser-focused on the pigs and totally unmoving. "Eliminating opportunity is one way to avoid bad behavior. Right now, Dottie can't get to the pigs, so she can't tear into them. They can't get to her either. We're in a controlled environment."

Larry burst out laughing. "We're next to a pig pen with a half-crazy dog, and it's a 'controlled environment'?"

"Yep!" Her curls bounced as she laughed with him.

"Hey, down there!" The call came from Frank, striding through the orchard. He joined them at the gate and looked down at Dottie, who was still rigidly regarding Violet and Nigel.

"How's she doing?" Frank asked.

"Barely under control," Cosmos said cheerfully. "But we're starting in on the socialization and command stuff."

"Well, we got some other 'stuff' that is seriously *not* under control," Frank said. "You guys should hustle back to the house."

"What's up?" Larry said.

"There's about thirty news vans lined up at the security gate." Frank looked down at Dottie. "We've got the only dog on the planet, and now the whole god-damned world is on our doorstep."

"Pigs and children turn out the way you teach them."

Sicilian proverb

CHAPTER FORTY-THREE

"THE WHOLE WORLD wants to see Dottie," Frank said. "I went out this morning to see if I could get some dog kibble from the feed store. I gave up that idea when I saw the traffic jam at the gate. I told them there'd be some information later this morning, but they had to stay out."

Frank said, "I high-tailed back here and checked in with Ilene. She says the internet has exploded with Dottie stuff. Everyone wants to pet her and give her a hug."

"That's not a good idea," Cosmos said. "She's basically just gotten out of prison. She's adjusting, but it will take some time for her to be socialized."

Larry snorted. "I've been out of the hoosegow for fourteen years, and I'm still adjusting." He looked down at Dottie who was still rigidly watching the pigs. "Her normal may not ever be all that normal."

"I'm not saying what's right," Frank said. "I'm saying what *is*. We've got people at the valley entrance gate, and we'd better get a plan in place because I think there's gonna be more."

"First things first," Larry said. "We've got pigs to feed."

"Can I help?" Dobbin said.

"Maybe. Let me see how I do in there first." Larry climbed over the pig pen gate and carefully stood on the inside of the gate. Violet and Nigel came over, tails wiggling.

Larry reached down and scratched heads and necks. "Looking good," he said as Violet snuffled and groaned with pleasure.

Frank watched closely as Dobbin went over the gate and met the pigs. Nigel leaned into Dobbin's shins as scratching commenced. Frank gripped the top slat of the pig pen gate as Dobbin shoved the pig back and Nigel agreeably shifted his bulk away.

Cosmos kept a firm grip on a stone-still Dottie. The dog released a high-pitched whine as she stared at Larry and Dobbin petting the pigs.

"It's okay," Larry called to the dog. "We're giving them a scratch, and now we're going to feed them." He directed Dobbin to refill water bowls as he walked across the pen, with Violet and Nigel trailing him.

The pigs were clearly interested in being fed, but they were well-behaved. Larry leaned over the fence to the blue food bins and shoveled some kibble into the two short feeders.

Violet and Nigel commenced eating with their little piggy tails alert and their large triangular ears swinging down into the food dishes.

This time Dobbin and Larry opened the pig pen gate and slipped outside.

"That went well," Larry said. "They're nice pigs." To Dobbin, he said, "Thanks for the help."

LARRY'S POST-RAPTURE PET-SITTING SERVICE

Dobbin grinned and said, "I could feed them always. Like, my chore."

Larry cocked his head and gave the offer serious thought. He said, "Why don't we do the pigs together for a few more days? Violet's still recovering from ringworm. We need to be keeping an eye on that. We'll get you trained up easy-like."

Dobbin accepted Larry's decree and went skipping down the path toward the house.

"Thanks," Frank said. "For letting Dobbin help."

"No problem." Larry took the second leash end from Cosmos. "I like having a job. Makes sense that Dobbin does too."

Larry and Cosmos pulled Dottie away from her astonished study of Violet and Nigel eating. To Larry's relief, Dottie fell into an easy walk that lasted all the way to the orchard gate.

"Good Girl!" he said.

Dobbin pulled open the gate for the group and asked, "If Dottie starts thinking she's a good girl, is she gonna Rapture up?"

Larry halted, horrified. "I don't know," he said.

His intestines threatened to turn loose. He looked down at Dottie's sweet, wide head. He swallowed. Hard. "I don't want to think about it."

"I think we're okay," Cosmos said. "Harold was saying once the Rapture passed through an area, it seems to be over. It comes in 'waves,' and we're hanging out in a female-owned house. We are going to be okay for this wave."

She spoke with confidence. Larry wasn't so sure, but

he appreciated that her words calmed Dobbin. Her confidence helped him too.

Frank agreed with Cosmos. "The brainaics are saying maybe more waves in years to come, but it'll be different." He shot a wink at Larry and said, "Maybe the next wave will take up all the mosquitos."

Larry managed a snort of doubt as he tightened his hold on Dottie's leash. She was leaning into her collar, once again straining to move.

With a dim inkling of the day to come, Larry let himself be pulled forward.

*

Bill Neddles stalked into the hotel suite with the bearing of an English lord. A beefy fifty-four-year old, he wore creased khaki trousers and an open-necked teal green polo shirt under a loosely structured navy blazer. His close-cut graying hair stood up in an old school flat-top that Jared associated with actors in films portraying soldiers.

An equally beefy teen came slouching in behind Bill, carrying a briefcase. Jared took in the teen's sullen eyes and his expensive rain jacket and concluded this was the Neddles scion with half the IQ and twice the sense of entitlement of the father.

Neddles got down to business quickly. He shook hands, introduced his son, sat down and accepted a cup of coffee, double cream.

"You're interested in buying property in Holiday Valley?" he said.

Abigail leaned forward and said, "I am interested in

relocating the Ross Hour of Prayer empire to this area. I'm envisioning developing a rural spiritual destination for prayer and contemplation. Holiday Valley is my first choice, but, of course, I could look nearer Seattle or Portland."

Jared sat back in his chair, understanding Abigail had just laid down a powerfully interesting card with a side bar of an-opportunity-not-seized-now could easily be lost.

Neddles was no green player in the empire-building business. There was no flash of eagerness or subservience. "Let's look at a map of the area," he said, motioning to his son, who produced a laptop computer from the briefcase.

"You can see the layout here," Neddles said a moment later. "There's a high-quality security gate and significant fencing at the entry. There are three properties currently for sale, and, quite frankly, I think you could get them at three quarters of the asking price, life being as it is at the moment."

"I'll need more," Abigail said. "What about the other properties?"

Jared knew she was only interested in the Lucky Seven Ranch. He was impressed at how she was signaling borderline indifference.

"One nice property is owned by Barton Buckley," Neddles said. "From California."

"I know the Buckleys," Abigail said. "In fact, my daughter, Ruthie, is staying with them."

Jared kept his face very still. According to his memory, Abigail hadn't ever met the Buckleys. She had simply accepted their invitation to take Ruthie from the boarding school. He looked across the table and saw Janice looking at him, intensely.

Janice knew. She knew how little Abigail connected with her daughter's world.

Exhaling slowly, Jared thought about Ruthie. He'd worked for Abigail for two years now and had met Ruthie exactly once.

"Barton gave me a call not too long ago. He might sell," Neddles was saying. "It's a first-class summer home. All the amenities."

"And this?" Abigail touched the computer screen. "This is more the sort of property I had in mind."

Neddles nodded. "The Lucky Seven Ranch. It's not really a working ranch, of course. Six-bedroom house. Fifty-five acres. An apple orchard. The barn is upgraded with solar panels."

He shifted in his chair. "It has some issues. The owners have gone up, and squatters have moved in. And, as you know, this place is massively in the news because they found that dog."

Abigail smiled. "Yes. I've been following the news." She raised an index finger and said, "The Lucky Seven is registered to a woman, correct?"

"Yes'm. Julie Babcock. I did confirm her as being on the county properties listings. She and her husband have both gone up." Neddles adjusted in the seat again. "It would be complicated for you to buy that property right now. The Babcocks surely had a will. We'd have to find the beneficiaries to make an offer. If that's a nonprofit, it won't be fast. And female-owned properties are in high demand."

Abigail's broad smile resembled a shark's open maw

with all teeth gleaming. "I have a source, Bill, in *intelligence*. A good Christian. I had news in the night from this source. We will have a second wave of Rapture sometime in the next few days, but it is almost certain to be limited to communities above the sixtieth parallel."

That got Neddles' attention. "The *Sixtieth* parallel?"

His son looked around the table with confusion on his face.

"That's far north, son," Neddles said. "Way far north."

"Nome, Alaska" Abigail said. "Yellowknife in Canada. That far north."

"Alaska" was familiar. Willie Neddles gave a quick head bob of acknowledgement.

"Our madam President is overreaching," Abigail said. "She's using this tiny second wave of Rapture to install women in power." She shrugged. "I think power should go to those who have earned it."

Jared's stomach squeezed with discomfort. No wonder Abigail had been enthusiastic for a two-a.m. bonking. She'd learned details she could use from her government contacts. Jared swallowed back a bit of bile as he realized that power stoked Abigail's lust more than he did. He was a tool. A really stupid, available tool.

"I need to be on the tip of the spear here," Abigail said. "I need a place to build that platform. Once this mini-Rapture comes to not much, people will be hungry for sane leadership. Like mine."

She tapped the map on the computer. "I need the Lucky Seven, and I need that dog." She smiled. "And I would, of course, always remember those who helped me in this time of need."

Abigail leaned back in her chair. "The limousine should be here soon. How do I get out to the property and past all that crowd at the security gate?"

Neddles said, "Let me do some calls. I've got some contacts in law enforcement."

"Olympia is a state capital," Abigail said. "How about someone from your state attorney general's office? Or a county prosecutor?"

"No." Neddles shook his head. "They're rabble-rousing defenders of the poor. No use at all. The only reason those people didn't get taken up is because they're liberal lawyers – damn goody-two shoes with the bite of an asp. You need some business-oriented minds."

He paused, then said, "Since you're talking about a complex that would have economic benefit to the county, I'm sure I could get a county commissioner in the car. One of them is a big dog fan."

"How is this not carving up the bird?" Janice asked, eyes blazing. She turned on Abigail and said, "You complained about the power shaping at the ecumenical council. How is this different?"

"It's different," Abigail snapped, "Because we are doing the *real* work of the Lord. We'll stop this president from doing a power grab. We'll show those . . . priestly pontificators in Medina just who can *connect with the people.*"

Her color was high. Abigail took a calming breath and said, "We need to get moving. Why don't you and Clive go load your luggage in the limo?"

She turned to Jared. "Be a dear and pack up. I just have a few more details for Bill."

Jared returned to the suite's bedroom, leaving the door

slightly ajar. He silently began packing Abigail's things. He heard her say "McElroy." This was followed by "Child Protective Services."

Then he heard Bill Neddles say, "In my opinion, that Annelise girl should be confined to a mental health facility."

"Where laws are most numerous, there you will find also the greatest injustice."
Arcesilaus (315 - 250 B.C.E.)

CHAPTER FORTY-FOUR

AFTER ESCORTING DOTTIE back to the house, Cosmos left for a quick shower. Marcel joined Larry and the dog in the catio.

"Did you hear about the reporters at the gate?" Marcel said. "Soo Min and Vico went out and filmed. There's a lot of traffic."

"Why can't they leave us alone?" Larry grumbled.

"They don't want you," Marcel said. "They want Dottie." He stroked the big dog's head and said, "Hoc est corpus."

"Hock what?"

"Hoc est corpus. It's dog Latin for 'This is the body.'" Marcel kept rubbing Dottie's head. He said, "It is the root of the magic term, Hocus Pocus."

"Dogs speak Latin?" Larry sat down on a chaise lounge. "Really?"

Marcel grinned. "Dog Latin was a way of making fun of serious people. You know that part in a church service where you get a wafer and some juice or wine?"

"Ah," Larry paused. "The communion-thingy?"

Marcel nodded. "When church leaders started teaching the bread and wine could really be changed into the body of Jesus, there was a lot of snickering. Guys made fun of it with some dog Latin."

"Whoa. You mean the church guys think it *really* is the body of Jesus? Not just, ah . . ." Larry fumbled for the word. He came up with, "a symbol."

Marcel shrugged. "According to many Christian churches, Noah really saved every animal on the planet, Mary was a totally virgin mother, and blessed crackers are really the flesh of Jesus Christ. Transubstantiation – the substance transforms."

"But most churches don't believe in Trans people, right? Man, that doesn't make sense. If the *biscuit* changes, then why can't a person? – and people scream at journalists about fake news." Larry laughed. "Tell me some more Dog Latin."

"I don't know any more." Marcel smiled. "How about some pig Latin?"

"Ix-nay," Larry said. "Even stupid mooks like me know pig Latin."

Marjorie came bustling into the catio, carrying Larry's laundered jeans and uniform shirt. "They're shit-free for now," she said. "Try and be more careful."

Larry stood up and opened his arms wide to hug his mother. "You betcha," he said. "Next dog rescue, no shit, I promise. You can take that to the bank of Not Happening."

Marjorie laughed and hugged her son back. "You know, I'm glad we moved out here. I'm having fun. Me and Odelle and Harold are going to make cornstarch play dough for the girls. That Naomi is so smart! And Esther! What a sweetie!"

"That's good, Mom."

Her eyes softened as she studied Larry. "You better grab

a shower. Frank says there's a world of people out at the gate. You're gonna have your hands full."

"Why me?" Larry protested. "Frank can handle them! I've got cats to feed!"

Marcel snickered. "Cats are already fed. I got up early." He pointed at the cats lounging in different locations around the catio. "They're happy here too."

Larry did a quick survey and smiled when he saw Lucifer tucked into the very top shelf at the back of the catio. The big gray tom had an excellent field-of-view. With his front legs folded under his broad chest and his intense green eyes studying Dottie, Lucifer looked every inch a battlefield commander.

Cosmos came in with wet hair and wearing fresh vet tech scrubs with cartoon dogs prancing on a pink background.

Before Larry could speak words of approval, she spoke. "Harold's making breakfast. He says there's lots of on-line criticism of you for feeding Dottie the chicken pieces yesterday. He's cooking up some grass-fed burgers. He thinks we should broadcast that's what Dottie will be eating today."

Marjorie nodded. "Smart man, our Harold."

Larry handed Dottie's leash to Cosmos. "I'm gonna grab a quick shower. Be right back."

As Cosmos sank down onto the chaise lounge, Marcel shifted to make room for her. Marcel said, "Do you think someone might use the chicken bone feeding as a reason to take Dottie away."

"Oh, man!" Cosmos's eyes went wide.

Marjorie gasped, then said, "Hell, yes! Some people will do anything to get what they want." She clasped her hands to her ample bosom and said, "Me and Larry both have convictions. We get pissed on by authorities all the time."

"Broken tail light isn't just a broken tail light, is it?" Marcel said.

Marjorie nodded. "Anything they can use to give Larry a kick, they'll use." She inhaled. "Marcel, do you think someone could use Dottie to make money?"

"Sure," Marcel agreed quickly. "World's only dog approves . . . I dunno, toothpaste or toilet paper or reverse mortgages. Just having her on YouTube could sell a ton of advertising."

"Then people will be working to take Dottie from Larry," Marjorie said. "We should plan on it."

"Isn't possession like, most of the law?" Cosmos said.

"Not when there's money to be made," Marjorie said. "We need to be thinking on this, and fast."

"I think," Marcel said slowly, "We should talk to Aisha."

*

Jared pushed a hotel luggage carrier to the elevator. He should have called for a bellhop, but when Abigail had reached a hand out to Bill Neddles and then rested her hand on Neddle's fine suit jacket sleeve as she described her wishes, it had triggered a desire in Jared.

It wasn't a desire for Abigail. He felt a need to move, preferably away from the hotel suite.

He'd eased out of the circle of chairs and returned to the bedroom, closing the door with a quiet snick as the metal doorplates connected. He packed his things before opening the suite's second door to the hallway, where he saw the luggage trolley tucked into a niche next to a soda pop machine.

It took just a few minutes to stack his suitcase and most of Abigail's luggage onto the trolley. He didn't pack her enhancements or peignoir. He left her one suitcase sitting open on a gilded luggage stand.

Now he pushed the loaded carrier onto the elevator with some satisfaction. It felt good to be the pusher instead of the push-ee.

A sleek black limousine sat outside the hotel's sparkling glass entry. Jared steered for it. Janice stood next to the passenger front where Clive and the driver were loading Clive's video gear bags into the footwell of the front seat.

As he approached, Janice turned an angry face his way. "Are you happy?" she said.

Jared shrugged. "It's morning. I slept okay." His shoulders tightened with the lie. He hadn't slept well at all.

"I'm not happy," Janice said. "I don't feel we are doing God's work." Her face softened as she said, "When you were hired, didn't you want to serve the Lord?"

Jared managed a wry smile. "Honestly, I'd been looking for a marketing job for over a year. I was tired of serving pizza. I may have been more enthusiastic about service to the Lord in the interviews than I really feel."

He lifted a shoulder in a casual dismissal of his lies. "I grew up in Atlanta. I know what to say."

Janice smiled back at him. "I appreciate the honesty in your answer."

Clive closed the limousine's door and joined them. "It's like this, son. . ."

Jared stiffened. He wasn't Clive's son.

Understanding his misstep, Clive put up a hand. "Jared. I should say Jared. The challenge for Janice and me is that it's really important to us that we truly serve the Lord."

"What are you going to do?" Jared asked.

"I don't know," Janice said. "I saw that young thug in there, and I find I do not believe he is a victim of a girl's unhinged attack."

Jared bobbed his head in acknowledgement. Young Willie Neddles unsettled him too. There was all of his father's dominance and none of his father's talents.

"I'm not liking Abigail's language," Janice continued. "Talking about Child Protective Services – not to protect a child, mind you, but to gain access to an animal with the idea of positioning herself as God's chosen spokeswoman."

Janice plowed on. "We've always known Abigail to be ambitious. We just hadn't seen her be . . . so manipulative."

"The Lucky Seven ranch and this dog are tools to her," Clive said, "And not tools to be used for the glory of God."

"I can see your point," Jared said.

A chime rang out. Jared pulled out his cell phone and read the text message. *Where are you? Abigail*

He typed back, *Loading luggage. Limo here.*

Neddles left. I need you.

Sighing, Jared pocketed the cell phone. "Abigail wants my help."

"We'll see you in twenty minutes then," Janice said.

"Might be twenty-five," Jared said as he slumped back inside the hotel. Under his breath he added, "With my luck, she's wanting it doggy-style."

*

Lucifer surveyed the catio from his upper corner shelf near the rear exit door. The cat walk was his. No other cat dared prowl near him. He approved of most of his catio fellow residents. The two rag-doll kittens were milk-toast personalities. The two striped tabbies appropriately subservient.

He liked the large ceramic casserole litter boxes filled with fresh sand. The water bubbling in the small pond tasted fresh. He approved of the decorative goddess. The statue of Ishtar was an elegant touch, and he liked quiet elegance.

He liked the early breakfast. He'd supervised Marcel serving up two scoops of kibble to a small bowl placed near Lucifer's shelf. The young man had done a reasonable job of it, spilling none and placing the bowl with courtesy.

Lucifer didn't care for the people who had slept on the chaise lounges near the entrance to the kitchen. He also didn't like the little cross-eyed Siamese cat who moved about the catio with confidence.

And he really, really did not care for the presence of that imbecilic dog. The people grouped around the dog finished a discussion and, mercifully, they left, taking the dog with them.

A few minutes later a small blonde boy came skipping into the catio from the back yard. Lucifer watched as the boy flung himself onto one of the chaise lounges and dug into a jeans pocket. The boy pulled out a watch with a fluted bezel and held it up, admiring it as the light played on the handsome watch face.

Lucifer watched and waited.

"All the world's a stage . . ."
William Shakespeare (1564 – 1616)

CHAPTER FORTY-FIVE

LARRY RACED THROUGH a shower and walked into the kitchen, tucking his uniform shirt into his unzipped jeans.

"There's ladies present!" Marjorie's foghorn voice rolled through the kitchen and smacked Larry's eardrums with a crash of outrage.

"What?" Larry said. "Odelle and Ilene have never seen a whitey-tighty waistband?"

The kitchen bustled with bodies. Ilene was flipping pancakes as Annelise opened a can of green beans and dumped them into a big bowl. To Larry's surprise, Marcel sat on the dinette bench, listening to Aisha, who was spooning cereal into a little girl's mouth, opened in a perfect small circle.

Harold sat next to Aisha and offered oatmeal into the second toddler, who was belted in a booster seat in the opposite bench.

Frank was rapidly rinsing dishes and stacking them in a gleaming wide dishwasher as Marjorie made another circle of the kitchen, collecting dirty dishes.

"Get some breakfast, fast," Marjorie told Larry. "There's some stuff you gotta know."

Soo Min and Vico were in the big dining room with Cosmos, who held Dottie in check with a stout leash.

Larry loaded a plate with pancakes, bacon and eggs and went into the dining room.

"No Dobbin?" he said, pulling out the chair next to Cosmos.

"He ate already. I think he's in the catio," Cosmos said.

"Be a great time for him to be out making some deliveries," Larry said quietly.

Cosmos lifted her shoulders and said, "I hope so. I know you're worried."

"Hey, Larry!" Vico boomed. "Can we film you giving Dottie her breakfast?"

"Sure! Give me a minute." Larry shoveled in bacon and eggs and gratefully inhaled a cup of coffee his mother set down beside his plate. He looked at Cosmos, and said, "We should have fed Dottie first, right?"

She shook her head. "Dottie is interested in the food, but she's behaving. It establishes dominance if you eat first."

"Establishes me as a jerk," Larry said, fondling Dottie's ears. "Sorry, girl. I'll do better."

"We need to talk," Cosmos whispered. "Before you do an interview."

"Okay." Larry leaned back in the chair and said to Soo Min, "Where do you want to film?"

Soo Min thought a moment. "The wine room has such beautiful tile and wood. Let's film in there." She smiled. "But, if you don't mind, I'd like a few minutes to get my broadcasting face on."

"Not a problem," Larry said. "Take all the time you like."

Vico and Soo Min left to prepare as Marcel came into the dining room. Marcel knelt down next to Dottie, scratching the dog's ears as he began speaking rapidly to Larry.

"Your mother and I are afraid," Marcel said. "If there's money to be made off Dottie, someone may try to take her from you."

Larry felt a cold chill sweep his body. He swallowed and said, "You're right. Ex-cons don't get the cherries of life." He exhaled. "It stinks."

Dottie whined and shuffled her front feet.

"It's okay, girl," Larry said, even as his heart twisted as he looked at her goofy ears.

"Don't give up without a fight." Marcel said. "We need to show you are a professional." Marcel added, "I just spoke with Aisha, and she said that you don't want anyone to have cause to remove Dottie from you for animal neglect. Be proactive about addressing concerns."

The kid had Larry's full attention. "Shit!" Larry said. "You're right. Okay, I've got the clean uniform shirt on. What else do I need to do?"

Marcel began, and Cosmos contributed. They had just a few minutes to prepare Larry for the world's scrutiny. They made the most of it.

*

Larry, Cosmos and Marcel walked down to the wine room for the filming. Vico filmed Dottie's breakfast arriving in a big mixing bowl, delivered by a smiling Annelise. Larry nodded to Cosmos in approval. She'd been the one to suggest the radiant blonde teen was an asset in a television cameo.

Dottie didn't care that the camera loved her waitress. Dottie shuffled her feet with excitement as the bowl was lowered, then flung herself into the meal.

Soo Min fired questions at Larry.

Yes, he said, it was grass-fed beef. The green beans were canned. The breakfast contained no gluten. Yes, he'd gratefully accept advice from veterinary nutritionists. No, there'd be no more chicken bones for Dottie.

"We'll be scouting for some good quality dog kibble," he said. "We won't feed cat food to Dottie as it doesn't have the correct protein balance." Larry felt good saying this. He wasn't sounding like a complete blockhead.

"What is your background in dog care?" Soo Min said.

Larry was ready. Cosmos had walked him through a few things to say, and, Praise Jesus, the words were popping up in his brain now.

"I've spent my life with dogs," he said. "My dad had a Labrador retriever; my mother had a pug and then a Pekinese. Now I've got my professional pet-sitting service going with zero complaints."

This all skated around the details of the Labrador being given away when Larry's dad died, and left out Marjorie's dogs being spoiled little beasts who had died early from complications of poor diet and virtually no exercise.

"Our animal care team," Larry said, "Consists of me and certified Veterinary Technician Cosmos Ponomarenko and Pet-Sitting Service Technician Dave-Marcel West-moreland. There are three of us on the job. We take our responsibilities very seriously."

By this time Dottie had long finished the bowl of burger and green beans. She pushed the bowl around the expensive rustic floor as she licked the bowl clean. Finally, she belched and looked up at Larry.

Vico knew what a money shot was, and he zoomed in to take this one. The entire watching world saw Dottie's doggy expression of adoration as she kept her eyes on Larry. Her rear end sank down to the floor as she took up a "sit." There was a pause, then Dottie lifted her right front paw to Larry for a shake.

Larry knelt down, took the paw in his hand, and enveloped the big dog in a hug.

"Love you," he said. "Love you a bunch." He could barely speak. A lump in his throat had his words come out in a deep raspy croak.

Dottie's pink tongue emerged to wash Larry's face.

Vico held the camera on the pair, then pulled back to widen the video view. He caught Marcel, Cosmos and the-loved-by-the camera Annelise all wiping their eyes.

"Now that was one breakfast served with love," Soo Min said. "This is Soo Min Carlevaro, reporting, live, from Olympia."

Frank opened the door to the wine room. "We've got incoming!" he said. "There's a big Lincoln Town Car and a limousine coming down the drive."

"And one man in his time plays many parts . . .
William Shakespeare (1564 – 1616)

CHAPTER FORTY-SIX

LARRY GOT TO his feet, vaguely aware that he had not a clue what was happening. Soo Min and Vico looked confused too.

"You'll want to film this arrival," Ilene said. "Whoever this is."

Soo Min and Vico stood up and moved toward the front door.

Everyone else seemed to have a mission. Larry watched through the clear glass of the wine room door as Harold went striding down the hall, pulling on a tan tweed jacket. Aisha handed little Naomi to Odelle and went after Harold. She paused at the edge of the kitchen and picked up a deep blue garment. She slipped the loose piece on, covering her tank top and obscuring her protruding stomach.

Larry blinked. How did he know the kid handed off was Naomi? Somehow, he knew – just as he knew it was Odelle who was holding Naomi, and it was Esther who was finishing her breakfast with the help of Ilene.

Blinking, he watched as Frank and Marcel made a whirlwind trip around the big living room, grabbing up clothing and a sleeping bag and hustling the things into the front office.

Marjorie came into the wine room and said, "Larry, you and me and Dottie are supposed to stay out of sight. We can watch from the front office. Come on!"

"What's going on, Mom?"

She said, "Move your butt. I'll tell you in a minute."

Cosmos and Annelise trailed behind as Larry followed his mother's wide backside down the hall and into the front office. Frank and Marcel stood at the side window, which looked out onto the front portico of the house.

"Sorry about the piles of stuff," Frank said. "We want the front room to be tidy in case they come inside. Harold said he'd work to keep them out though. Come take a look." He paused, then added, "We should keep Dottie away from the window."

Cosmos held out a hand for the leash, and Larry handed her control of Dottie. He joined the others at the window.

"What's going on?" he repeated.

"When you were in the shower, we were talking about how the government or somebody powerful might try and take Dottie," Marjorie said. "Marcel and Cosmos made you an interview plan, but Harold said we needed to use all the tools we have. He said when the first powers show up, we need to look classy. That means my fat ass and your scrawny butt aren't in the picture."

Larry looked out the window, impressed by Vico, who was already filming the arrivals as the big cars came into the circular drive and parked. They watched as the front doors opened and Harold, now tall and stately in his blazer, escorted Aisha down the steps.

"I'm liking the cravat," Marcel said.

Larry lifted an eyebrow in question.

"Harold's neckerchief," Marjorie said. "That's silk, or I'm a size ten."

Larry made his usual food-to-personality comparisons. He couldn't help it. He was nervous.

Tall Harold, with his cream-colored cravat and smooth tweed jacket, looked like a glass of champagne. An expensive brand.

Larry hadn't given much thought to Harold until this moment. Harold was a friend of Odelle's. An egghead. A nice guy. Someone little Naomi respected, which was saying something.

Now it was dawning on Larry that Harold was a Somebody and a good Somebody to have on the Larry and Dottie Team.

Aisha's beaded hair drew the eye away from her protruding belly, which barely showed as the thousand tiny pleats of her royal blue overshirt moved with her descent down the stairs. Her black stirrup pants ended in a cute pair of ankle boots, which made her legs look supermodel long.

With her hand resting lightly on Harold's forearm, Aisha looked like . . . a million bucks. Larry rubbed his eyes. He didn't eat enough upscale food to be describing Aisha.

"Looking good so far," Frank said. "Ilene said we're on the news as a bunch of squatters. Harold and Aisha look like they could own the place."

Two people emerged from the Lincoln Town Car. Annelise hissed.

"Neddles," Annelise said. "That's Willie Neddles and his dad."

"That explains how they got through the security gate," Frank said. "Neddles is the real estate agent for the homes on sale around here. He'd have an override code."

"That the kid you shanked?" Larry asked.

"Do what?" Marjorie gasped. "Annelise! What'd you do?"

"I took care of business," Annelise said. Her face was white as her lips moved into a firm line.

Larry looked at the teen. He knew a thing or two about brave faces and wobbly knees.

"Annelise, help me out," Larry said. "No matter what happens here with these people, you help me out. You stay with Dottie. We'll keep Cosmos or Marcel with you and Dottie. That way you're doing me some good." He didn't add that being an Extra Dog Patrol Person would keep Annelise from being isolated by anyone from the Neddles group.

He said, "The pet-sitting service is a priority, and you can make a difference."

Annelise inhaled and nodded. "You got it," she said.

"Holy Hell," Marcel said. "That's Abigail Ross!" He pointed at the tall blonde emerging from the limousine. "The Ross Hour of Prayer?" Marcel said as the rest of the group in the front office looked confused.

"She's a big deal," Marcel said. "Televangelist. I heard her husband went up, but she didn't. I heard she was going away for a spiritual retreat."

"Did she say to send money?" Marjorie asked. "I'll bet she did."

Marcel grinned. "Probably."

"Know the others?" Larry asked as a handsome young man and an older couple climbed out of the limousine.

Marcel shook his head. "Staff, I guess?"

They watched as Abigail strode forward, blonde hair gleaming in the May morning light. She joined the two Neddles and spoke with Harold and Aisha as Abigail's staff formed up in a half circle a few feet away.

Harold's smile was gracious even as his body remained firmly planted on the first step up to the home's front doors. Harold was tall to begin with. Now the extra five inches of height from standing on the step had him towering over Abigail and Bill Neddles.

Aisha's head tilted as if she was carefully considering whatever it was Neddles senior was saying. She, too, stood square and solid.

"Go get 'em, Soo Min," Marjorie said as the reporter extended a microphone to capture Harold's welcome.

"Are Vico and Soo Min on our side?" Larry asked.

"No," Marjorie shook her head. "We didn't tell them anything. They were out in their vehicle when you were in the shower. Besides, they're reporters. They're not supposed to take sides."

"I think it doesn't hurt for them to be out there filming," Annelise said. "Mr. Neddles can't be too much of a jerk while they've got the camera going."

"Is he an asshole?" Marjorie asked.

"Big time!" Annelise swung her arms up and crossed

them, folding her hands into her armpits in a self-protective hug. "Big ego."

Harold and Aisha carried the moment. Neddles and Abigail smiled and stepped back, young Willie trailing behind them. After a moment, Abigail conferred with her staff. She waved at Harold and Aisha before joining Neddles and son in the town car. Neddles senior took the town car forward, around the gravel loop in front of the house.

The office crowd watched as the town car drove back down the long driveway.

"The limo is staying?" Marjorie said.

"Looks like it," Larry said. "Let's go find out what Harold thinks."

"Wait a minute," Frank said. "Look. That young guy is reconnoitering."

They watched as Jared sauntered away from the limousine and began to look over the exterior of the house. The office crowd all pulled back from the window as Jared came closer.

"Where's Dobbin?" Frank said.

"He was out on the catio a few minutes ago," Marcel said. "You want me to go get him?"

"I'll go," Frank said. "Then I'll check into Mr. Curious there and see what we can learn."

Marjorie waited near the window as the others left the front office. She studied the older couple still standing near the limousine. The driver got back into the vehicle and leaned the seat back as he donned a pair of headphones.

The couple looked around for a moment. The older man started walking toward the broadcast van following in the wake of Vico and Soo Min, leaving the woman looking nervously after him.

Marjorie made up her mind. She would do a little reconnoitering herself. She shoved aside the pile of clothing Frank had piled against the office's exterior door. She could hear Harold speaking to the others in the living room, saying, "Let's go into the kitchen. Odelle will want to hear this."

As badly as Marjorie wanted to know what Harold and Aisha had to say, she decided to continue with her plan.

Marjorie pulled the office door open, went down two steps, followed a row of stepping stones around a large rhododendron and spoke to the woman standing next to the limousine. Marjorie said, "Would you like to come in for a cup of coffee?"

Janice jumped. It was as if this very large woman had materialized out of nowhere. "Um, no. I'm, uh, fine," Janice stammered.

"Well then," Marjorie said, "Do you need to come in for a piss?"

Janice smiled, her sweetness of nature showing with the upcurve of her lips. "Actually," she said. "I rather do."

"Life is really simple. Men make it complicated."
Confucius (551 – 479 B.C.E.)

CHAPTER FORTY-SEVEN

JARED STROLLED DOWN the side of the big house, taking in the fine stone work and mulling over Abigail's hissed instructions to "Find a way in."

Their arrival at Holiday Valley had begun with a rocky start. They'd met a Thurston County commissioner at the security gate, and he'd been all smiles, entering Abigail's limousine for a private consult. The commissioner's interest waned quickly as he correctly divined Abigail's intent to set up "a religious retreat" had more to do with on-line fundraising than providing local employment.

Abigail misplayed her hand there, Jared thought. Aaron Ross would have emphasized the potential for local hires to the commissioner, quite likely inflating the numbers. Instead, Abigail had given a quick report on the how much money she could bring in, broadcasting and taking donations through Paypal and credit cards. Given that Holiday Valley was rural, the commissioner knew a sharp accountant would have any property Abigail purchased put into forest reserve or agricultural categories. As a result, the tax income to the county would be minimal.

Few local hires, little tax revenue, and a media circus

at the security gate had the commissioner wishing Abigail a blessed experience. He emerged from the limo and went around to the media crews, shaking hands, discussing the wonder of a dog discovery and . . . quickly bowing out once Neddles had his town car and Abigail's limo through the security gate.

The only good thing the commissioner had delivered, Jared reflected, was the presence of a state patrolman whose steely eyes kept the media crews and their trucks parked on the side of the road instead of crowding through the gate behind Neddles and the limo.

They wouldn't be so lucky next time they came to Holiday Valley. Abigail's charm hadn't dented the resolve of the tall man in the tweed jacket or the black woman with the remarkable beaded hair and a profile as exquisite as Nefertiti's.

Now Abigail was off with Neddles to "see" the properties for sale in the valley. Jared assumed he had about an hour to "stretch his legs" and come up with some way for Abigail to weasel her way into this big house.

Raised in Georgia, Jared was keenly aware that some homeowners could take armed exception to prowlers. He whistled loudly and kept his hands out of his pockets as he ambled along the perimeter of the house.

He reached the corner and let out an amazed whistle as he took in the long and wide sunroom filled with tall potted plants. He could see three cats lounging on ledges, soaking in the sun as another cat shimmied up a climbing tower embedded in a stand of bamboo.

A blonde boy lay on a chaise lounge, watching the cats.

Jared waved and the kid waved back. Jared pointed to the end door. The kid jumped up and ran to open the door.

"Hey," Jared said, "I'm visiting the area with a friend looking to buy a country place. I'm Jared." He extended his hand, in an adult man-to-man fashion.

"Nice to meet you. I'm Dobbin." The boy had a smooth, firm handshake. Someone had worked with the kid, Jared thought.

"You've got a lot of cats!" Jared put some enthusiasm into the words.

"We sure do! Fifteen of them!" Dobbin frowned in concentration. "But then we have Bella and the two spay girls. That's eighteen."

"Eighteen! Wow!"

"And we've got two pigs." Dobbin smiled, saving the best for last. "And a dog."

"No kidding!" Jared made his eyes go wide. Internally, he found he rather hated himself. This kid was sweet and easy. "Can I see the dog?"

"No!" Dobbin smiled, as if to take away the sting of the refusal. "She's Larry's dog. Everybody's going nuts about her. We gotta keep her safe. There's some bad people in the world." Despite the refusal, Dobbin didn't slack in the hospitality department. He said, "I can show you the pigs."

"I'd like that," Jared said.

*

Janice emerged from the half bath adjacent to the front office. "Thank you," she said.

"It's some bathroom, huh?" Marjorie grinned. "This house has *seven* of them."

"I'm glad I'm not doing the toilets and floors," Janice said. "They must have a professional crew come in."

"You're not rich then," Marjorie said. "Not if you think about who's doing the cleaning."

"I'm not rich," Janice said. "Abigail Ross is. I've seen the size of the crew that cleans for her. Team of six twice a week." Sharing this small insider tidbit didn't feel like a betrayal of her employer. Not anymore.

"It's good to tell the truth," Janice said. "Abigail Ross wants this house, and she wants your dog. She plans to use them to build a new audience, based on the scripture that we're all sinners, only she'll be making money from our shortcomings."

Marjorie's eyebrows lifted. "Had enough of her then?"

"Yes." Janice inhaled. "I know who you are. Marjorie Medicare. Jailed for false billing practices."

Marjorie crossed her thick arms and stared at Janice. "What else do you know?"

"Your son Larry is also an ex-con. He doesn't have a job, and he lives with you."

"You're wrong on that," Marjorie said. "Larry has his own business. He does great with animals, and he's helping a bunch of people, including his momma." She lowered her chin, squashing three layers of skin into broad parentheses around her full cheeks. "And, so what? Didn't you just say we're all sinners?"

"I want you to know what you're up against," Janice said. "Abigail will use public opinion to get what she wants."

"How is she going to do that?"

Janice licked her lips. This was it. If she told Marjorie all she knew, was she a Judas? "Lord, give me strength," she whispered. She looked up, and saw all three hundred forty-five pounds of Marjorie, wearing a cardigan stained with oatmeal over a floral muumuu. Marjorie also wore wool socks and broad box-toed orthopedic shoes with Velcro straps that strained to hold the shoes closed.

If ever there was a casting call for one of God's imperfect lambs, Marjorie could play the part.

Janice said, "Abigail is mesmerizing when she's on camera. She offers people a path to what they think they want. It's not a real path. It leads nowhere but to her bank account. For a long time, she was preaching the prosperity gospel, because people thought they wanted to have nice things."

"Times have changed," Janice said. "People are anxious. We're awash in stuff. Good Lord, so many Christians have storage units! But stuff hasn't helped. People are frightened. So, Abigail tells them to follow Christ, to send in money and, for sure, they will have a place in Heaven."

"Like that'll happen," Marjorie said. "We got babies in cages at the border. We should all burn for that alone." Marjorie crossed her thick arms and said, "I hope all the dogs are in heaven, and you folks get a chance to earn a spot by cleaning toilets for a living."

"That's not the way salvation works," Janice said. "It's not your earthly actions. It's your belief in redemption through Christ."

Marcel spoke from the doorway. "I beg to differ," he said. "Pursuing self-preservation and closing your eyes to suffering of others is the ultimate in selfishness. If there's a Devil, he's in your church and laughing all the way to the bank. He's using the words of the Bible to have evil done to others." His eyes were hard. "It's the sons of Ham all over again."

"I see your point," Janice said. "I've been struggling with this." She said, "It's throughout the Bible. It is the gift of God, *not works*, so that none may boast."

"And yet," Marcel shot back, "James 2:14. *What good is it* if someone says he has faith, but does not have works?"

Janice started to speak, but Marjorie put up a hand.

"Let's get back to Abigail," Marjorie said. "Because you two can talk Bible all year and never get anywhere I need to go. Abigail's white, she's beautiful, she's got money and clout, and she's gonna tell me she speaks for God. How does she get a big, ole dippy dog to be her ticket to more slices of pie?"

Janice closed her eyes. "She goes for Larry," she said, certain in her words. Twenty years of watching Abigail turn life to her benefit, and Janice knew. "Larry will be the key. She'll get Larry on camera. She'll be incredibly charismatic. She'll walk him through some "choices." Janice put air quotes up around "choices." She sighed. "They're not real choices. She's intense. She sucks up all the oxygen in the room, and you can just feel the weight of everyone watching wanting you to make what she's saying is the "right" choice."

Janice exhaled. "It's a rising crescendo that she orchestrates. It's like giving into sex or chocolate, only a thousand times more powerful. You find yourself so *happy* to do what she wants. And you can't wait to make her happy again and again."

Aisha spoke from the doorway. "Fortunately, Larry has a few friends who know a thing or two about facing temptation."

"Shit!" Marjorie said. "Aisha, you're putting money down on our team when you know our track record on taking the bait?"

Aisha nodded. "Yes. I think we put Larry and Dottie up against Abigail. She's a big fish, and she'll have a top game."

Eyes flashing, Aisha said, "But *we* lay out the game board. We go for a win with the world watching. If Larry can take down Abigail and show he's the right person to be keeping this dog, then we shut down other troublemakers."

"Is that why you'd be doing this?" Marcel said. "Because the whole world will be watching?" He scowled. "Just because I asked for your opinion this morning doesn't mean you are part of the pet-sitting service."

Aisha tucked her chin down and leveled a hard stare at Marcel. She said, "I can work for a thousand years and never atone for what I did to you and your mother. We can agree on that." She looked at Marjorie. "Last night I had a good night's sleep. I've had a shower and a chance to eat two meals with some peace. I've had you, Harold, Odelle and Ilene helping me with the girls. I think five adults for two little girls is the right staffing level. Thank you for helping me figure that out."

Marjorie smiled. "Naomi is a bit lively."

"I can go make cornstarch clay with Odelle and the girls," Aisha said, "But I once was a top courtroom attorney." She inhaled deeply and added, "For the first time in in a long time, I feel like that person again."

To Marcel she said, "Courtroom law is all about choreographing drama. I have some skill sets that could be useful to your friend Larry. Bottom line time. Do you want my help with this?"

"The supreme art of war is to subdue the enemy without fighting."

Sun-tzu (544 - 496 B.C.E.)

CHAPTER FORTY-EIGHT

LARRY KNEW ENOUGH to shut up and listen. He was sitting with Cosmos at the kitchen dinette booth with Soo Min and Vico when Marcel, Marjorie, Aisha and a pale gray-haired woman came into the kitchen. Dottie lay on the cool linoleum, head on her paws.

Marjorie said, "We're getting a plan together here. This is Janice, and she wants to help Larry keep Dottie."

A few feet away, Harold had shed his elegant tweed blazer and was wearing a "Romaine calm, Lettuce Carrot On" apron as he and Naomi stirred food coloring into a bowl of cornstarch slurry.

"Keep stirring," he said to the little girl as she stood on a dining room chair at the kitchen island. Odelle was holding Esther, who was mashing a wad of blue dough between her fingers. Ilene sat at the end of the vast granite counter with her laptop open and a cup of coffee nearby.

"We're listening," Harold said. "But aren't you part of Abigail Ross's team?"

"My husband and I serve the Lord," Janice said with a quiet dignity. "I think it's time to pull the curtain back on how Abigail works. She's got a vision of taking this property and your dog and using them to build her next empire."

Harold nodded as he guided Naomi's hand to a better grip on her spoon. "Ilene did some research for us. Ilene, will you please tell them what you found?"

Ilene took a gulp of coffee before saying, "Abigail's between a rock and a hard place. She's a performer. Her husband, Aaron, was the planner. He was taken up, and she's been turned away from the ecumenical council in Medina. The council's P.R. team released a list of those people who they rejected, and her name is on it. Things have been cooling off for the Ross Hour of Prayer. Donations are down, big time."

"Aaron Ross turned into a pile of cinders," Janice corrected. "And Abigail vacuumed up the evidence of his nature," she said.

"Damn!" Marjorie's eyes went wide. "That is stone-cold living!"

"Yes," Janice said.

"Abigail will be back shortly," Aisha said. "We fobbed her off for an hour or so, saying she should examine the valley properties which are for sale, but you are certain this place is her real interest?"

"Yes," Janice said. "It's a luxury place and . . . you've got the dog."

Soo Min spoke up from her seat in the corner. "My producers say the Dottie footage is being viewed by millions. She's a super-star. You're not going to have fewer reporters at the gate. You're going to have many, many more. I think you can expect helicopters overhead later today."

"And what is your role?" Harold asked, his voice easy.

Soo Min grinned and said, "To stay embedded with this news story as long as we can."

Aisha said, "Would you be interested in filming an interview of Abigail and Larry?"

"Yes," Soo Min answered. "Especially if Dottie is present." She exchanged a look with Vico before turning back to Aisha. Soo Min said, "Let's be clear. We report. We tell what is happening."

Aisha nodded. "Got it."

"Abigail's so charismatic," Janice said. "I don't know what she will say, but I do know the cameras love her. She'll be persuasive."

"We gotta do something," Marjorie said. "She can't just swan in here and take Larry's dog!"

"Which the world sees as *their* dog," Aisha said.

Odelle said, "If you're going to set this up, there should be an introduction of some sort that sets the mood our way."

"What is *our* way?" Aisha asked, with a sweeping look over all the people in the kitchen.

Larry appreciated Aisha's question. *She's gathering viewpoints and getting a buy-in*, he thought. *Getting our team together.*

Next to him, Cosmos gave Aisha a "thumbs up." Cosmos said, "Dottie's way! Second chances!"

"That's right," Marjorie said. "It's imperfect people and goof-ball dogs having some second chances." Her triple chins wobbled as she added, "We're Dottie's team. We can keep a dog. We can do some good stuff, even if we have messed up."

Aisha smiled. "The very heart of Christianity, Marjorie. Thank you for that."

Ilene set down her coffee cup and said, "Aisha, you're the showboat talent here. You and Harold. What about the preggers lady you talked about back at Marjorie's place? The woman and the dragon. In Revelations. She's pregnant, and she faces down the dragon. That's dramatic. We could have a fight scene."

Odelle snorted. "You just like dragons."

Ilene shrugged. "Most people do. 'Dragon' is a top-trending password."

Aisha said, "That's not what I was envisioning."

"No fair making yourself the director of everybody," Marcel said to Aisha. "We all want to help. Let's hear Ilene out."

"Aisha, you should do the fight scene," Marjorie said. "You'd be great." She tilted her head and studied Aisha a moment. "More flowing fabric of some sort."

Marjorie opened a kitchen drawer in the service pantry and poked around. "Mrs. Babcock was a teacher, for Christ's sake. She has to have some somewhere." Marjorie opened another drawer and raked through the contents.

"What are you doing?" Aisha asked

"Looking for paper to make stars. We need to make you a crown of stars. The lady with the dragon has a crown of stars." Marjorie gave a glad "Aha!" as she found a flattened band of cardboard.

"That's a Burger King crown," Aisha said. "I am not wearing that. I don't know what you are thinking, but I am not wearing a Burger King crown."

"We'll trim off the top bits and stick some stars on." Marjorie plucked scissors out of a pencil holder.

In the third drawer down, she found colored paper.

Janice looked at the art supplies and said, "We could do some *scherenschnitte* for the dragon."

"Do what?" Marjorie said.

"A silhouette," Janice said, pulling out a black sheet of construction paper. "We put it in front of the right light, and it'll make a big, shadowy dragon."

Soo Min cocked her head. "I *could* do a documentary-style introductory piece," she said. "We could show how costumes and lighting are used to convince people."

Marjorie paged through a booklet of paper samples. She pulled out a gold-embossed page and rapidly cut out squares, which were folded and snipped into stars.

Janice pointed at the stars and said "Add some glitter to the upper edges of the stars. It'll give a glow with a low beam cannister light pointed up. We've got some cannisters in Clive's kit."

"This sounds incredibly cheesy," Aisha said.

"We could read the dragon verse from Revelations," Ilene said. "That sets one hell of a mood."

"Then you enter," Janice said, voice rising. "And we see you facing the dragon."

"Which will look like a grade school production," Aisha said.

"Not with Clive doing the light and filming," Janice responded. "He's a professional. It'll look good."

Marcel said, "And then we say what people believe and how beliefs are guided. I could do that part." He said, "A brief history."

"And you tell them to leave Larry and Dottie alone!" Marjorie said.

Aisha shook her head. "No. We don't tell them what to do. People have free will."

Standing on the chair at the counter, little Naomi dropped the stirring spoon. "Down!" Naomi said.

Harold said, "We just got the color mixed in."

"Down! Down!" Naomi yelled.

Esther joined in. "Down!"

"Here," Odelle said, reaching for Esther. "Let's go see the pigs with Harold. Your mother has things to do, and dragon stories are way more up Ilene's alley than mine."

The little girl turned away with a frown.

"Come on, Esther," Aisha said. "You like pigs. Oink, oink!"

Naomi beamed and oinked and stretched her arms out to Harold. Little Esther was not to be out done. She threw her arms out with a loud oink too. Odelle laughed and picked up Esther. "You are so very silly!"

"Oink!" Esther said.

As Odelle and Harold left with the twins, Larry said, "What do you want me to do?"

"And me!" Cosmos said.

Aisha thought for a moment. "Walk Dottie? She needs to be as mellow as possible."

"More like 'take Dottie for a gallop,' but we can do that." Larry said to Cosmos, "Back to the orchard?"

"Sure."

"I need to touch base with our producers," Soo Min said. "I'll tell them we'll have some new footage soon."

"I'll follow Larry and Dottie," Vico said. "And do some

filming." He stood up, then turned to Aisha. "Where will you be presenting your material?"

"The catio," Marcel said.

Aisha raised an eyebrow. "The catio? Not the big living room?"

"The catio," Marcel said, firmly. "Larry is in the pet-sitting business. Dottie seems fine around the cats, and that can be shown." He grinned. "And we can set Abigail up between two ferns."

Larry didn't get the joke, but Cosmos snickered.

Ilene said, "How can I help?"

"We need a white outfit," Marjorie directed. "See if there's a bathrobe."

"Oh, please!" Aisha said, "I'm not going on television in a bathrobe." She took a deep breath and said, "I appreciate everyone's creative contributions; however, I am not a dress-up doll. I am an attorney, and we need a serious approach to this interview."

"We can do better than a bathrobe," Ilene said. "I spent a summer working in Macy's home décor slipcovers department. I can pleat and tuck like nobody's business. Let's find a bed sheet."

"When I'm good, I'm very good, but when I'm bad, I'm better."

Mae West, Actress (1893 – 1980)

CHAPTER FORTY-NINE

DOBBIN WASN'T IN the catio. Frank opened the back door of the catio and spied his grandson walking toward the orchard gate with the tall young man from the limousine. Frank started to go after them when his cell phone chimed.

"Damn!" It was an alert from the security company, telling him of an unauthorized entry at the front gate of Holiday Valley. The media had lost their patience – or perhaps some dog-mad person from town had pried the gate latch from its concrete pillar.

Whoever it was, he only had a few minutes to get the Lucky Seven secured. Frank ran to the barn and grabbed a tool caddy. He added a bolt cutter, and a loop of wire before yanking open the row of drawers under the work bench. He scooped up some nails and a black marker.

Frank took his load to his ATV and made a second trip into the barn for a two-foot-long board from the lumber scraps. He stopped at the work bench long enough to drill a pair of holes in the board at the mid-point. Moments later he was swinging a long leg over the ATV.

As he turned the key, he had another quick thought about Dobbin. There wasn't time to find the kid.

Ignoring an inner squiggle of disquiet, Frank gunned the ATV and went roaring down the long driveway. He'd lived in the valley forty years, and the drive to the Lucky Seven had always been open, but he had a memory of a faded gate sitting to the side of the wrought iron arch.

He hoped it was still there.

Frank stopped the ATV near the road entrance and hustled to the listing gate, that sat to one side, anchored by a hem of weeds. Frank heaved the gate up and out of its years-long resting place. Huffing slightly, he pulled the long gate up and over the road. A rusty bolt complained, then gave way to shoot home, securing the gate.

He grinned. Step one, complete.

Frank hustled back to the ATV, and began to rapidly sketch in NO TRESPASSING on his lumber scrap as a row of media trucks came around the bend in the road, led by a black extended-cab pickup truck.

The pickup barreled along the valley road at high speed. Frank glanced up occasionally as he furiously colored in the letters on the board. As the pickup slowed to make the turn into the Lucky Seven, Frank could see it held at least four burly white men.

"Four. And a big four," Frank rolled his lips in and let them go with a pop. "Time," he whispered, "for Death by Sugar."

He plastered a big smile on his face and waved as the pickup came to a stop, the grill of the truck inches away from the recently closed gate.

Frank took his time while making it clear he was

moving toward the gate. He kept an eye on the media rigs coming down the road after the truck. He wanted the film crews filming.

Using an immense control that turned his lanky frame into the world's slowest saunter, Frank ambled toward the gate.

A big man stepped out of the pickup and stomped over to the gate.

"Hold on!" Frank called. "That's a sticky bolt! I'm coming!"

The big man paused. He seemed to think Frank was about to open the gate.

Given Frank's pleasant tone of voice, it was a reasonable thought.

Frank stopped and pointed down the road. "Will you look at that!" he called.

The big man turned and saw the dozen media trucks coming down the valley. Frank called, "Wow. You sure brought a party!" He reached into his pocket, pulled out his smart phone and, very slowly, took some pictures.

The big man started to reach over the gate.

"Hold on!" Frank called. "You don't want to be doing that! There's some rust." He made his voice sound as sweet as summer lemonade.

To his great relief, one of the media rigs arrived and pulled up to park behind the pickup. A camera man leaned out and filmed. Frank smiled and waved for the camera.

Frank pocketed his phone and continued his slow walk up to the gate, long board under his arm, hiding the words he'd recently inked in.

He reached the gate and put the board down, the script facing away from the pickup.

"Hi," he said, to the big man.

"We're here for the dog," Burly said.

"Hang on a minute." Frank waved at the camera man at the first media rig. "Come on over. You'll want to film this."

The camera man wasted no time. Within minutes, he and two more media teams were set up and filming Frank.

"We're here for the dog!" Burly repeated.

"Could you introduce yourself?" Frank asked.

"My name doesn't matter."

Frank shook his head. "It does matter." Lifting his voice, he spoke to Burly, the men in the truck and to the media people. "I'm Franklin McElroy. I am a resident of this valley, and I am the head of security for the Lucky Seven Ranch. We are currently closed to visitors."

He swung his recently lettered board up so the camera men could get a good picture. NO TRESPASSING was abundantly clear. Frank was pleased. He always had had a nice hand. His mother had praised him for it.

The other occupants of the truck emptied out onto the road. None of them looked happy.

Frank smiled and waved. "Thank you for your interest," he said. "But we are closed."

"You can't keep that dog to yourself!" one of the men said.

Frank drew himself up to his full six-foot-two and said, "That dog is resting quietly and recovering from some harsh treatment. Visitors will be allowed when the dog is ready to meet the public, but not before. Again,

I am the head of security, and this property is posted *No Trespassing*."

A thin cameraman rotated a cylinder on his lens and Frank sensed the camera focus was on his face. Frank turned to the camera and looked straight in, narrowing his eyes to his best imitation of a steely-eyed movie star. He said, "If you or anyone else comes down this road, it will be over my dead body."

He pulled a hammer out of his waistband and stalked over to a big Douglas fir growing a few feet to the side of the road on the inside of the gate. He propped the board up onto the tree trunk and tapped a nail into the started hole. Then, with a mighty swing, he banged the nail in.

Frank repeated this with a second nail. He'd been nailing boards all his life and knew how to make a driven nail go in square and fast. It was, he felt, kinda dramatic. It ought to make good television footage. Most people couldn't drive a nail in with one big strike. It took some skill.

He had to work to keep his face fierce. He was having a blast.

His wife had always said his ass was his best feature. Now he prayed his old narrow behind wasn't drooping too badly as he stalked back to the ATV. He tossed the hammer into the back bin, and swung a long leg over in a mount up that would make any Harley motorcycle rider proud.

He turned the ATV around and headed back for the house, hoping the film crews and the No Trespassing sign would stop the burly guys from making trouble.

It was time to find Dobbin.

*

Jared followed Dobbin down to meet Violet and Nigel. The May morning grass was as green as any shamrock, and the orchard hummed with bees.

Violet came to the fence and presented her withers for a scratch. Soon Nigel did the same. Dobbin scratched Violet, and Jared scratched Nigel.

"Nice pigs," Jared said.

Dobbin smiled and scratched Violet harder.

A bald eagle soared overhead, white head and tail flashing in the sun.

"Look at that!" Jared marveled.

Dobbin cranked his head back. "An adult. The young ones have a brown head and tail."

"You've seen a bald eagle before?"

Dobbin shrugged. "Sure. They hang out at Mud Bay." He smiled. "In December a bunch of them come in with the salmon run. When they perch in the same tree, they look like big Christmas ornaments."

"Wow." Jared watched as the eagle soared off over the trees. "That's the first bald eagle I've ever seen."

He watched a hummingbird swoop in to hover in front of a honeysuckle vine. Small black spiders the size of pencil erasers scurried through the grass outside the pig pen. A cluster of tan mushrooms peeked out from behind the feed barrel.

Jared breathed deeply. The rank smell of pig soil didn't bother him. It was an honest smell, reminding him of an uncle's place in Georgia.

His cell phone chimed. Jared stopped scratching Nigel and fished the phone out of his pants pocket. "Hello?"

There was no voice. Jared turned his head and repeated, "Hello?"

He looked down at the phone and said, "Damn. The charge is gone. I forgot to plug it in last night." He turned to Dobbin. "Do you have a phone?"

"Nope." Dobbin reached into his pocket. "I can tell you the time. I have a watch."

*"That is the tail of a lion.
Do not play with it."*
Persian proverb

CHAPTER FIFTY

"THAT'S A . . . ROLEX," Jared said. "That's a very expensive watch."

Dobbin smiled. "Yep. That's why Larry took it." He angled the watch face toward Jared. "Little hand between the ten and eleven. Big hand on the six. It's 10:30, right?"

"Right. Where did Larry get the watch?"

"He took it," Dobbin repeated, with some irritation. "It was on Mr. Babcock's nightstand, and Larry took it. Then he felt bad, so he gave it to me to put back."

"Dobbin," Jared's voice came out heavy and tense, making Jared think of his own father, who had so often been disappointed in Jared's choices. No matter. This was serious. "You know that looting has been connected to being incinerated."

"I didn't take it!" Dobbin said. "Larry took it." Dobbin's small blonde eyebrows came down into a straight line of frustration. "Didn't you ever do something you regretted? You know. You're not supposed too, but you think it's fun, and then you do it and it's not so fun?"

Fucking Abigail came to mind, but Jared wasn't about

to share that thought with a boy of Dobbin's age. He came up with, "Sure. Of course."

"So then," Dobbin said, patiently, "You work to make things right. Larry's been really busy with Dottie. It's my job to get this watch back to where it belongs. I just hafta get around Aisha." He smiled. "She's got eyes like a hawk!"

Dobbin stuffed the watch back into his jeans pocket. "Aisha and the little girls are staying in the big green bedroom. I should get back. If she takes the kids for a walk or somethin', then I can run in. I'm fast."

Jared thought furiously. Abigail wanted an in. She wanted something she could use to get control of the property and the dog. Should he say something about Larry taking a Rolex? Using Dobbin as a carrier of stolen goods?

"Come on," Dobbin said. "You can help me."

"You want me to help you put the watch back?"

Dobbin nodded. He pulled the watch out of his pocket again and looked at it. "It's a really nice watch."

"Are you wanting to keep it?"

Dobbin shrugged. Then he grinned. "Yeah. And that might get me incinerated for real."

Jared felt a chill run up his spine as a moment of clarity struck. He didn't particularly care if Abigail got this property, but he sure as hell did not want this cheerful kid turning into a heap of ashes. "Let's go back," he said. "We should do this."

*

Aisha stood her ground. "I am all for an introduction and an historical review of Biblical beliefs, but I am not wearing a Burger King crown or a pleated sheet."

Ilene thought for a moment, then said, "Odelle can do it. With her shape, she always looks pregnant."

Marjorie's eyes went wide. "Let's not be telling her that."

"To quote my boss, Larry, we're burning daylight," Marcel said. To Aisha, he said, "How are you going to set up this interview? How do you know that Larry is going to be okay? He's not the smartest guy."

Marjorie did not object to that comment, which made Marcel even more concerned.

"We count on Abigail acting in a manner consistent with her past actions," Aisha said. "We identify the traits and habits a manipulator uses, and then we show her using them."

"I could set you up with a split screen," said a voice from the door way.

"Clive!" Janice said. "This is my husband, Clive. He's done film and lighting for the Ross Hour of Prayer for years."

He might have looked like a balding man with a soft middle, but he clearly was Janice's hero. Her look of devotion was reassuring.

Clive said, "We often set up a split screen so viewers can see the number of callers coming in, or the number of donations being made. What if we put up a Bingo card of techniques she'll be using?"

Marcel and Aisha made eye contact as the idea registered and each broke into a wide smile.

"Can you give us an example?" Aisha asked.

"Sure. Confident tone of voice or showing an expertise, like a memorized Bible verse." Clive adjusted his glasses and added, "The big one, of course, is offering the audience a vision of something wonderful that is accessible." He sighed. "Which should be, in my opinion, a faith-based life, but that's not always the way it works out."

"Let me understand this," Ilene said. "You're ready to set your boss up for a big face plant?" The grooves on her frown ran deep. "When things went south at Marjorie's office, the smart people looked for someone to leave holding the bag. That ended up being Marjorie. So, I'm kinda interested here, in just why you are helping us."

Clive nodded, "Good question. I've been having some doubts about what I should be doing for a while. Janice has an even better insights because she deals with details for Abigail."

Janice sighed. "It does get confusing. We have been employees of the Ross Hour of Prayer for a long time. We've seen people helped. We've seen some money go to good works. But there's always been a self-serving part of Abigail. Always. We turned a blind eye to it." She took a breath and said, "The Ross Hour of Prayer has nearly two billion dollars banked. Abigail has abundant luxuries and a daughter she rarely sees. It's become clear to me that we are not in the service of the Lord."

"Two billion banked?" Marjorie gasped. "Why the hell is she bothering us?"

"Because your dog is the path to her building a new empire," Janice said. "She wants a bigger, better empire."

"Hence my willingness to do a split-screen Bingo card," Clive said. He looked across at Marcel and Aisha, "I met your friend, Frank, who tells me he shut the front gate on the ranch road. He said there are media trucks and some rough men gathered there. He put up a *No Trespassing* sign."

Clive went on. "I also just got a call from Abigail. She and the realtor are on their way back. She says the other properties won't do."

"No surprise there," Marjorie said.

"She said they'll have the limo meet them at the ranch gate," Clive said. "Whatever you're planning to do, there isn't much time."

*

Frank found Larry, Cosmos and Annelise working with Dottie on a grassy lawn in front of the barn. Vico was filming.

"Have you seen Dobbin?" Frank asked.

"No," Cosmos said. "He was in the catio a while ago, but we didn't seem him when we came out."

"I'll bet he's down with the pigs," Larry said.

"I don't like him going down there by himself," Frank grumbled. He went stalking around the barn and past the vegetable garden, where he found Ilene on her way to find Harold and Odelle.

"We need Odelle for our show," Ilene said. "She's gonna be the pregnant woman facing the dragon."

Frank said, "Is Dobbin inside?"

"No. I don't think so. It was me, Marjorie and Aisha. We're working with those two folks from the limo. Janice and Clive. They seem real nice. They're helping us put together a show to help Larry keep Dottie."

They found Odelle with Harold in the vegetable garden, pulling up carrots with Naomi and Esther. Ilene said "Odelle, come quick. We need you for a show part."

Odelle got up from the ground and gave little Esther a pat on the shoulder. "Be back in a bit." She left with Ilene.

"Have you seen Dobbin?" Frank asked.

Harold rocked back on his heels and said, "Nope. We were on our way to see the pigs, but we got sidetracked. Want us to go down there now?"

"Nah. I'll go. Looks like you're cooking carrots for dinner."

Naomi heard Frank. She frowned and tried to shove a carrot back into the earth. "It's okay," Harold told her. "I'll eat them."

Naomi yanked the carrot back out and dropped it into Harold's hand.

Frank laughed, then moved on, yelling, "Dobbin!" through cupped hands as he neared the orchard gate.

"Over here!" Dobbin yelled back.

His grandfather sped-walked through the orchard and joined Dobbin and Jared, who were leaving the pig pen.

"I thought we agreed you'd stay at the house," Frank said.

"My fault!" Jared said. "I wanted to see the dog, but Dobbin said only a tour of the pigs was available. I took him up on the offer."

Frank put an angry eye on his grandson, then relented. Getting strangers away from the house was a good idea. He just wished it wasn't his young grandson doing the job. "Okay," he said. His brain flashed with a memory of both his wife and his daughter saying he should be more positive and much more expressive.

"Good job," he added.

Dobbin grinned.

"Now," said Frank, "We need to skeddale back up to the barn and make some more *No Trespassing* signs."

"I imagine my employer will be looking for me," Jared said.

"Good." Frank knew he sounded a bit unhospitable and decided he didn't care.

They started back up toward the house and barn, weaving between the orchard trees as Frank told them about the media crowd and the pickup full of men at the front gate. "We got our work cut out for us," he said. "Keeping all that lot off the property."

They stopped for a moment to watch when Larry arrived at the orchard gate and released Dottie for a run. The dog became a dark streak of happiness as she rocketed around the trees. Vico kept filming.

She stopped to greet Dobbin with a face wash. Vico grinned as he captured the very happy dog and the laughing boy.

"Wow," Jared said. "She's big."

"She's awesome," Dobbin said.

The dog dashed off. Dobbin, Frank and Jared continued their trek back to the house.

"I'm gonna run inside the house a minute," Dobbin said to his grandfather.

"Oh, hell no. I don't want to lose track of you again," Frank said. "If you need to take a leak, find a tree. The rest of this morning you stick with me. We've got too much going on."

Dobbin threw a panicked look at Jared, who surprised himself by saying, "Frank, until my boss shows up, I've got time on my hands. Let me know what I can do to help."

"When the dragon saw it had been thrown to the earth, it pursued the woman."

Revelations 12:13

CHAPTER FIFTY-ONE

"Today we will look at the story of the woman and the dragon," Marcel said. He held a Bible and stood in front of the pale brick wall of the catio with his "Dave" shirt neatly tucked into his jeans. "The story is told in the book of Revelations. The woman is clothed with the sun and wears a crown of stars. She is pregnant with a son."

Odelle stepped into the spotlight on Marcel's right. Clive crooked a finger and Odelle took one further step.

Vico filmed, running a big camera set on a sturdy tripod.

Odelle held her chin up, hoping her old lady jowls weren't too evident. She cupped a hand under her protruding stomach, the way a pregnant woman would. Ilene's well-pleated and quickly stitched sheet held up. The glitter-rimmed stars on the paper crown stayed in place.

Clive gave her a thumbs-up.

"The woman delivers a son, but danger is near," Marcel said.

Janice, crouched on the floor a few feet away from Clive, brought her silhouette of a dragon near to a small cannister light.

She slid the paper in front of the light as Marcel continued. "A great dragon appears."

Janice's cutout worked beautifully. An eight-foot shadow dragon appeared on the wall next to Odelle.

Marcel said, "The dragon prepared to devour the woman and her baby. God snatched the child up and the woman fled into the wilderness."

Odelle stepped back out of the spotlight. She turned quickly and disappeared through a wall of potted palms.

"What follows," Marcel said, "Is a war between the angels of God and the forces of Satan." He paused, then said, "Is this what *did* happen or is it what *will* happen? Is this Biblical passage from the dreams and visions of a man named John or is it a road map to our future? Perhaps it is all just an allegory for the struggles within our hearts, that fight between good and evil."

Larry, sitting quietly with Cosmos, Annelise and Dottie at the back of the catio liked Marcel's voice. It was dignified. It carried.

And Marcel wasn't finished. He said, "The one thing we can know *with absolute certainty,* is that people will use these dramatic words to lead others. Some of the leaders will be good-hearted people who are trying hard to do right." He shook his head, "And others are predators looking for opportunities to accumulate wealth and power."

"How are you going to know?" Marcel asked. "How are you going to evaluate the people who are positioning themselves to lead our nation and the peoples of our planet? Let us review a few tools you have to make a strong evaluation. But before we discuss the tools you have, let's meet some of my friends."

He smiled, motioning Odelle forward. "Today's woman wearing a crown of stars was played by my friend Odelle. The dragon is a paper puppet produced and manipulated by our friend Janice."

Marcel paused. "And now I am going to introduce you to a regular guy. My boss, Larry, of Larry's Pet-sitting Services. Larry has a dog named Dottie. Later today you will see a powerful and persuasive woman do her best to convince Larry to give up a dog he loves. Her plan is to build an empire based on this dog, who may be the only dog left on our planet."

He took a breath. "And our plan is to show you the techniques a charismatic person uses. These techniques are used by religious leaders, politicians and others to inspire and to manipulate."

Soo Min stood to one side, watching the taping.

*

In the dining room, Naomi and Esther played toddler games on computer tablets. Naomi sat in Harold's lap at the dining room table. Ilene held Esther. The girls had different games going, with Harold and Ilene both making noises of approval and engagement.

Aisha sat nearby, scribbling notes on a legal pad. She sat back and said, "I have the backbone of a plan."

"Good," said Harold. "Let's hear it!"

"Abigail will arrive shortly. She has seen the media at the gate. When she gets here, we'll offer her a televised sit down one-on-one with Larry. We promise exclusivity for one afternoon session only. She won't like being rushed, but she'll take the offer. We've got too many options out there for other interviews."

Aisha tapped a finger on the table. "We set them up in the catio. Marcel's 'between two ferns' idea is brilliant."

Ilene shifted as she continued to support Esther. "Larry's going one-on-one against this lady preacher? *Our* Larry?"

"It'll be Larry with Dottie," Aisha said. "Vico will do the filming. Clive will do lights and sound. Annelise and Marcel will run the laptop that provides the split-screen graphic."

"Uh," Ilene said. "Larry gets kinda shifty-eyed when he's crowded. His mind freezes up too."

Aisha's cell phone warbled. She answered. "Hi, Charles. Busy here."

She listened, face frowning.

"I'm so sorry," she said, "But I'm not surprised. You don't have much clout with that crowd. You'd have to have a church of twenty thousand to be heard."

She listened again, then said, "Did you hear Larry and Marcel found a dog?" She didn't give her husband a chance to answer. She said, "We're working on a broadcast that may change the world here, and I am a chief architect of the programming. You could come home and do childcare while I build a legal practice protecting property rights for the poor. Try that idea on. Bye."

She stabbed off the phone. She sighed and looked at Harold. "I should ask. Are you okay taking care of the girls while I see this Abigail interview to completion?"

"Glad to," Harold said. "You okay?"

"No," Aisha said. "I am frustrated and trying to find my way forward."

There was a pause as they heard the catio door open. They could see Odelle coming into the kitchen, holding her pleated sheet up as she walked.

"Odelle," Harold called. "Could you please come over here?"

Her face lit up with a smile as she made her way to the dining room. "My starring role is done," Odelle said, pointing to her crown.

"Very punny," Harold's eyes were soft as he looked at Odelle. He turned to Aisha and said, "I spent thirty years married to an angry and bitter woman. I did my best, but I never could make her happy."

Aisha shifted in her chair. "Is this where you tell me a person makes her own happiness?"

"I don't think you need advice from me." Harold eyes were kind. "I failed miserably. I tried. She tried too. Her anger grew, and I buried myself in work."

Aisha closed her eyes and said, "I know bitterness is a weed. With constant watering, it becomes a tree that shades out everything – including love and friendships."

She opened her eyes and looked at the twins. "The girls are so much better behaved here. Or maybe they're the same as always, but my last nerve isn't being shredded every second of every day."

Aisha took a deep breath. "No matter what happens next, I am getting more help. I am not going back to doing everything by myself. I wasn't recognizing the price I was paying."

Odelle said, "You should hire Harold as your nanny."

"Would you do it?" Aisha said to Harold.

Harold smiled. "It's worth discussing. After decades of forecasting, I'm very much enjoying living in the moment with Naomi and Esther – but it would have to work in with my two immediate goals."

He shifted the little girl on his lap and said, "First, I want us all to survive in good order, including Larry and that ditzy dog."

He stopped and adjusted Naomi again on his lap. She paused in her swiping at the tablet and looked up at him. "You can do some more," he told the little girl. "I'll wait."

"What's the other goal?" Aisha asked.

Harold grinned. "I have to convince Odelle to marry me." His eyes danced. "But after that, if it's okay with her, then I'd love to help with Naomi and Esther."

Ilene whooped as Odelle gasped.

"Was that a proposal?" Odelle finally said.

"Not yet," Harold said cheerfully. "We have to survive this next round of Rapture, and I want to find a ring and a nice place to pop the question."

Odelle rocked side-to-side, a wide smile on her face. Then she rushed around the table to give Harold a hug, a task complicated by her outfit and Harold's lap of Naomi.

"I adore you," Odelle said. "And you'll be coming with babies! I always wanted babies! How perfect is this?"

Aisha started to say the babies were *her* babies, but as she opened her mouth to speak, Esther pulled a booger from her nose and stared at the glob on her finger. She wiped the glob on the tablet, fascinated as streaks appeared on the screen.

Ilene reached for a paper towel, and Aisha decided she would be firm about family boundaries another time.

The door from the catio opened. Soo Min came into the kitchen. She saw the dining room group and came to them, moving briskly.

"We have some issues," she said. "While I can report on techniques used by public speakers and religious leaders, I can't support an on-camera sand-bagging."

*"An investment in knowledge
always pays the best interest."*
Benjamin Franklin (1706- 1790)

CHAPTER FIFTY-TWO

AISHA BROUGHT HER chin up and raised an eyebrow. Her heart was thumping with the all-but-forgotten joy of a real mental challenge. This was terrain she recognized. Soo Min was handing her a "reverse your course now" problem. As an attorney, Aisha's next move would be a step-to-the-side followed, hopefully, by rapid moves forward.

She was out of practice, and yet the call-to-action adrenaline coursed through her veins with a familiar pull. Presentation was pivotal. She never had been able to pull off the "I'm just a country bumpkin" presentation made famous by television's Columbo and Matlock characters. She did better as a concerned problem-solver.

She said, "It's still current news to report on Larry and Dottie. And the arrival of Abigail Ross certainly will be interesting to many. How would you like to proceed?"

Soo Min came to the table and took a seat, caressing her large abdomen. "I'm not going to broadcast the Bingo card the kids put together. It's hilarious and spot on, but it's too brutal. At the very least the Ross team needs to have a true understanding of the nature of the interview."

The reporter took a breath and added, "Abigail Ross needs a fair playing field to make her case."

"Understood," Aisha said. "I respect your professionalism." She paused. "The cameras are set up in the catio. It does seem like a good space for an interview. It's a familiar space now for Dottie, and the cats don't seem to be a problem. Can we agree on the catio as a setting?" She wanted to keep Marcel's between-two-ferns going if she could.

Soo Min easily agreed to location.

Harold arched an eyebrow. Aisha suspected little slipped by Harold. He was her ally today. He said, "We should give you two a few minutes to finalize details. Hey kids, time to stretch our legs. Let's go look at the kittens in the barn."

The girls were agreeable, with Naomi shrieking, "Down! Down!"

Aisha stilled her daughter with a "Shush!"

It took a few moments for Odelle to be unpinned from her sheet and to put the tablets away. Aisha insisted the toddler nose boogers were cleaned from the tablet screens.

Ilene said, "Odelle, why don't you go with Harold on the kitten tour and I'll check in with Marjorie? She and I can get the catio tidied before this big broadcast."

Her sister beamed, happy to have Harold and the little girls to herself.

As they steered the twins away, Harold said, "Maybe Marcel and Annelise could put their video and Bingo card up on YouTube."

Soo Min smiled. "That is, of course, a choice they could make. Vico has footage from this morning of Dottie. I'll see if they want to use some of it as part of an intro. I'm also glad to walk them through some of the video-editing tools we have in the broadcast truck."

Aisha's heart rejoiced. Harold had just handed her team a giant step forward. Teens posting cheeky stuff on YouTube would actually be more widely distributed than a reporter's documentary. Some of Vico's fresh footage of Dottie would carry the clip to the top of the day's viewing lists. She could trust Marcel and Annelise to be on top of that detail.

"What are your other concerns?" she asked Soo Min.

Soo Min thought for a moment, then smiled. "Odelle was marvelous. I am concerned that my viewers will think this is a compound of pregnant women." Her smile broadened. "Actually, I don't have to worry about that. Vico keeps focusing on Annelise. The camera loves that girl."

"Good, I guess?" Aisha said.

"It is good. Viewers respond well to certain faces. Annelise has a great face for filmwork." Soo Min paused, then said, "Larry, not so much. I am assuming the camera likes Abigail Ross very well, or she wouldn't be such an effective televangelist."

"Is there anything we can do to help Larry look his best?" Aisha asked.

"Add another person," Soo Min said instantly. "Not Annelise. She draws the eye so much she overpowers."

Aisha thought of Marcel, then rejected the idea. A young black man would turn off some viewers. That was simple reality. Unfortunately, Larry's mother, Marjorie, wasn't photogenic – at all. Aisha thought rapidly.

"Cosmos might be willing to help out," Aisha said.

Janice came into the dining room and said, "The limo

driver just left to fetch Abigail from the front gate. My colleague Jared hasn't been answering his phone. Have you seen him?"

*

Jared was in the barn with Frank and Dobbin, inking in more *No Trespassing* signs. His cell phone vibrated, then died.

"I'll bet my boss is on her way," he said.

"Thanks for your help," Frank said. "Dobbin and I will put these up and then we're headed home for a bit. We need to feed the chickens."

Dobbin's face crinkled in distress. He turned his worried face to Jared.

"Jared, there you are!" Clive walked into the barn. "Abigail will be here in just a minute or two. There's a plan for her to have a televised meeting with Larry and the dog."

"Got it," Jared said. "I'm coming."

"We should go meet the limousine," Frank said to Dobbin. "The driver can tell us if those guys at the front gate are behaving."

Jared made a small hand signal to Dobbin, who fell back as Clive and Frank left the barn.

"Give me the watch," Jared whispered.

"Huh?"

"Give me the watch. I'll put it on and act like its mine. I'll look for a chance to put it back." Jared extended his hand, insistent.

Dobbin dug into his pocket and pulled out the Rolex.

He passed it to Jared, saying, "It goes in the nightstand drawer in the big green bedroom where Aisha and kids are staying. On the window side."

"Got it." Jared slipped on the watch, enjoying its balance and heft. It was definitely a gorgeous watch.

They followed Clive and Frank around to the front of the house and watched as the limousine glided up. The big car came to a halt. Moments later, the driver was holding the rear door open for Abigail. She emerged, her eyebrows down in irritation.

As Bill Neddles and his son stepped out from the opposite side of the vehicle, Abigail snapped at Clive. "Where's Janice?"

"Inside," Clive said calmly. "She's been meeting people."

"I need to talk to her." Abigail turned to Jared. "You haven't been answering my messages!"

Jared pulled his cell phone out of his rear pocket and held it up. "Forgot to charge it."

Abigail's eyes went wide. "Where did you get that watch?"

"This watch?" Jared shrugged. "I've had it awhile."

Dobbin was standing next to his grandfather, and now reached out to grasp Frank's hand. Frank looked down at his grandson's worried face and then looked back at Jared, not comprehending, but on alert.

"Don't lie!" Abigail barked. "You have never worn a watch! And certainly not a Rolex! Don't you know that looting can get you incinerated?"

"It's not Jared's watch," Dobbin shouted. "Larry took it. We're helping Larry. We're putting it back."

Frank's face turned deep shades of red and purple as

he looked down at Dobbin. "You had this watch? Larry gave it to you after he took it? You've been receiving stolen goods?"

It was a very good thing that Larry was away, far down in the orchard exercising Dottie because Frank surely would have throttled the "stupid, thieving lowlife" if Larry had been within grabbing distance.

Frank made do by yelling, "You could have become ashes!" to a white-faced boy. Frank grabbed Dobbin's hand and yanked his grandson along as he headed for the ATV and home.

Aisha opened the front door and descended the steps. She hadn't heard Frank. In ignorance of the purloined watch, Aisha spoke to Abigail, saying, "You've seen the media at the front gate. We are prepared to offer you a one-time televised opportunity to speak with Larry about his dog."

Abigail looked at the retreating forms of Frank and Dobbin. She smiled softly and said, "Thank you. I'd love to speak with Larry."

Clive, standing nearby, whispered, "I trust in the Lord. Dear God, please show us what to do."

"Fall down six times, stand up seven."
Japanese Proverb

CHAPTER FIFTY-THREE

"SHE'S GETTING CALMER," Larry said as he and Cosmos watched Dottie trot around the orchard.

The big dog jogged to the next tree, sniffed the base, squatted to urinate, then looked back, checking on Larry's presence.

"She's still got some anxieties," Cosmos said.

"Who doesn't?"

Cosmos laughed. "You're right there."

They strolled down to the pig pens where Larry leaned over the fence to give Violet a great head scratching. Violet leaned into the fence, sighing with piggy delight.

Cosmos scratched Nigel's hairy back while Dottie kept an earnest watch.

When Larry's arm brushed against Cosmos, both jolted, then smiled and went back to pig scratching.

"We should get back," Larry said. "The preacher lady will be showing up soon, and it'll be showtime."

"Nervous?"

"Hell, yeah." Larry sighed. "Cosmos, I'm kinda a loser. I can hold things together for a little bit, but the wheels always come off. I'm used to it. But I don't want to let

everybody down." He reached down and scratched Dottie's ears. "Especially not you and Dottie."

Cosmos put her arm through Larry's. "I feel like you
saved me," she said. "Right when my life was falling apart,
you showed up with a job and a direction. You even gave
me gas money. Then you saved Dottie. I don't see how
that's being a loser. There's eighteen cats eating a breakfast
of kibble this morning because of you."

"That was Marcel, because I slept in," Larry corrected.

"You're being difficult."

"Yeah. Wait until you see me being disastrous." He
sighed. "Come on. Let's go."

They strolled back up through the orchard. Cosmos
left her hand threaded through Larry's arm as Dottie trotted alongside.

They saw Harold and a beaming Odelle coming
through the gate, each holding a little girl by the hand.

Larry chirped to Dottie. The dog plopped her rear end
down and offered a paw.

Larry shook Dottie's paw and snapped on a leash. So
far, the dog had been fine around the cats and the kids,
but this was no time to have a child knocked over.

"We're off to see the pigs again," Harold said. "And
we have big news."

"Yeah?" Larry said.

"We're engaged to be engaged," Odelle said. "Harold
is going to pop the question just as soon as things
settle down."

"Congratulations!" Larry leaned in to give Odelle a
kiss on the cheek. "Harold's a lucky man."

Naomi tugged on Harold's hand and the pig-visitors continued on their way.

Larry and Cosmos stood together and watched them go. The May sunshine lit up the young green leaves of the trees. It was a beautiful morning.

"Clouds coming in," Larry said. "Might rain."

"That's the challenge here," Cosmos agreed. "The sunshine never lasts."

*

Inside the catio, Lucifer tucked his legs under his body and beamed hate-rays of disapproval down on the people below.

Marcel and Annelise sat hunched over a laptop computer, talking rapidly. Their excited voices irritated Lucifer.

Marjorie and Ilene were pulling potted plants around. They moved furniture, discussed things at high volume and then moved more things. Marjorie's booming voice was also irritating. Ilene's high cackle was worse.

Vico and Clive moved in and out of the catio, stringing cables and lights. Finally, some coherence began to emerge. The chaise lounges were now out of the way in the far end of the catio. A mammoth video camera on a thick spoked tripod faced two wicker loveseats arranged in a V formation.

Ceiling high swaths of potted bamboo formed a backdrop for the loveseats. Two large pots of ferns flanked the seating.

Marjorie and Ilene discussed the rag doll kittens at length and in full volume.

"Let's make it real nice," Marjorie said. "We can hot-glue some wisteria vines onto the cat tower shelves. It'll look like a waterfall of green stuff."

"You think there's time?" Ilene said.

"Let's get the bones in place, and we'll see."

Ilene pulled a cat tower over and snuggled it into the bamboo behind one of the loveseats. Marjorie carried two drowsy kittens over to the tower and placed them on a middle shelf in a close muddle. The kittens yawned and were adorable.

"Vines would be extra nice," Ilene said.

"Let me see if I can find a glue gun," Marjorie said. "Can you scoot that fern to the left a foot or so?"

Ilene managed to shove the fern pot, producing an ear-splitting squeal as the heavy pot slid across the hard tile.

Lucifer hated the women and his co-species catio inhabitants. He liked this new kingdom of his – but this interference, this kitten cuteness and this human cacophony had to stop.

*

Aisha checked in on Marcel and Annelise. They were working on the "Recognize a Charismatic Manipulator" Bingo card. The first line read: wears bright colors or dramatic clothing; speaks with confidence; displays an in-depth knowledge of a topic; identifies something you want; and offers you inclusion.

Annelise said, "We know we need more about the language of seduction - all the stuff that makes a person believe and hope things are about to be wonderful."

"Put in promises," Aisha said. "Promises of transformation. Promises of an inspired and worthwhile future."

"Okay," Annelise said.

Aisha frowned. "Everyone is getting the same card?"

"No. That wouldn't be any fun. I've got a sorting function going so the square contents will load differently from our list of options," Marcel said."

"I'm supposed to fetch Larry and Dottie soon," Annelise said. "Vico wants some more footage."

"I'll go with you," Aisha said. "I need to go over some things with Larry."

They left Marcel hunched over the laptop. Neither woman saw Willie Neddles, studying them from the shadows of the barn.

Willie's heart leapt when he saw Annelise emerge from the back door of the catio. He pulled back into the barn when he saw Aisha join Annelise.

He watched as the two women walked through the vegetable garden, headed for the orchard.

Now was not the time to settle scores with Annelise. He needed to be patient.

*

"We need to go over a few things," Aisha said when they reached Larry and Cosmos in the orchard.

"And Vico wants more footage of Dottie," Annelise said.

"Let me take Dottie," Cosmos said. "We can use the lawn in back of the house and practice some sits and stays. A black dog on the green grass should show up well." She turned to Annelise. "Want to help me with that?"

"Sure!" Annelise's smile lit up the day like deli lights on a bank of cheese trays. Larry smiled back at the teen. It felt good to be around such enthusiasm.

A moment later, the dog and the two young women were on their way out of the orchard. Aisha looked at Larry and said, "The interview is on for one o'clock. You and Dottie will be interviewed along with Abigail Ross. The broadcast will be live. The discussion topics will be the Rapture, and what Dottie represents."

She took a breath, and said, "I'm assuming you have a bit of a checkered past."

Larry winced. He tried a grin. "My past is so checkered I could work as a NASCAR finish line flag."

Aisha frowned.

Larry cleared his throat. "That's nothing to brag about. I know."

"Have you killed anyone?"

"Oh, hell no!" Larry stared at Aisha. "I'm a weenie. I'm a stupid shit with no impulse control." He swallowed and licked his lips. "Is that what the preacher lady is goin' to be sayin'? That I'm dangerous?"

"We never know exactly what the opposition will say," Aisha said. "But we do get broad hints from her past behavior. She's going to come after you to repent and to yield to her leadership. That's what televangelists do."

Aisha said, "Here's the thing. If she comes after you with some detail from your past that is unpleasant, and *it is true*, then don't lie. Trust me on this. You're going to want to equivocate."

Larry raised an eyebrow in question.

Aisha smiled. "You're going to want to evade the truth.

This is human nature. I'm asking you to fight that feeling. I want you to *own* your history."

"Ah, given my history, how is this a good thing?"

"It says you're already on the path to redemption. You don't need her help. You know who you were. You know who you are today. You are a changed person now, and you have a job you are doing. You are taking care of cats and a dog."

Larry rubbed the scratches on his forehead. When the orange tiger cat had tried to use him as an escape tower, she had gouged him good. The slices were healing over, leaving an itchy pair of parallel tracks. He tried to stop rubbing.

He thought of Dobbin. He sure hoped the Rolex was back in its drawer.

Aisha reached out and put a hand on his arm. "We are each imperfect, but worthwhile. That reminder is your mother's gift to our team," Aisha said. "Normally I'd make a careful review of your entire history, and we'd practice what to say on each and every sticking point. We don't have time to do that today, so we'll go with a broader, less specific plan. It is still a plan, and it's a good one."

"Ah, I don't know." Larry clenched and unclenched his hands. "Are you sure we wouldn't do better with you or Annelise doing the show?"

"You are the YouTube star," Aisha countered. "People have seen you with kittens. They've watched you rescue Dottie. They've heard you tell Annelise about how predators work. You've already demonstrated a good side that cares about others. You're the one they want to see."

"If I screw this up, do we lose Dottie?"

"No." Aisha shook her head, sending her beaded braids into a ripple of color. "We're not in a court of law. We're in the court of public opinion. You mother and Ilene are working to make the catio look homey. Soo Min will do the interviewing. We've got home court advantage."

She inhaled and said, "I'm wanting you to do this today because I think it can shut down others who will be wanting Dottie. If today goes sideways, we re-group and think of our next move."

Larry nodded. He pulled out his wallet. "I think I'm supposed to give you a buck to make it official, right? You're my lawyer?"

Aisha's smile went wide, bright and kind. "It's not necessary if you and I are in agreement that you are my client."

Larry fished two twenty-dollar bills out of his wallet. "When the chips are down is no time for me to be confused about who my legal eagle might be. I need the best my money can get." He handed the money to Aisha.

She took the folded bills with a dignified nod. "Please take the advice you just paid for. Acknowledge past mistakes, and then move on, quickly, to talk about the work you are doing now."

"Why is it I feel like I'm getting on a roller coaster?"

Aisha smiled. "A reasonable feeling for the situation."

"Thanks," Larry said. "I think."

*"The will is commendable,
though the ability may be wanting."*
Ovid (43B.C.E - 18 C.E.)

CHAPTER FIFTY-FOUR

ABIGAIL WANTED. SHE wanted Jared brought to heel. He'd been doing God-knew-what while she'd been trudging through three small summer homes, fulfilling her promise to look at the other Holiday Valley properties.

She wanted the Lucky Seven Ranch.

The Lucky Seven was beautiful. It was spacious. It had such a lovely vegetable garden and greenhouse.

As she stood on the curve of the drive and took in the plate-sized rhododendron flowers, she could see herself here for years to come. With six bedrooms, she could have Ruthie here and still have room to breathe. It was a serene and special place. She had to have this place. It was the place to start her next empire. A new place for a new path to fame and fortune.

Which meant she needed to calm down and concentrate. To get what she wanted, she needed to focus and execute. To Jared she said, "What have we learned?"

"The dog is large and closely monitored," Jared said. "You'd want someone with dog-handling skills if you took her on."

Abigail shrugged. People could be hired. "What about getting into the house?"

"I haven't been inside. I think I saw Janice go in." Jared paused. "How was the crowd at the gate?"

"More media trucks have arrived. It's insane."

Abigail looked at Vico's broadcasting truck with the station's logo emblazoned across all sides. "That's a Seattle channel. We should assume it's liberal." She said the word "liberal" in stretched-out, disdainful syllables as one might say "syphilitic."

She sniffed. "Make yourself useful. Go down to the gate and bring someone from a station that we can trust." She frowned, which brought out the fine lines around the top of her lips. "I'll tell the attorney we need a fair-and-balanced interview."

Abigail looked at Jared with a steely eye. "Get the biggest name you can find. Make sure they know I'll remember in the future anyone who is fair to me today."

*

Frank was not done blistering Dobbin's ears. He told his grandson what a truly, colossally stupid thing it was to take on stolen goods. Dobbin's tears didn't stop the lecture.

They walked to the fence line near the barn. Frank hung another No Trespassing sign on the box wire. He lifted Dobbin over the fence, and then climbed over.

It was a long walk across a grassy field from the fence line to Frank's place. Dobbin fell behind, sniffling. Frank kept walking, stony-faced and furious with Larry, the preacher lady, Dobbin and even the damn dog.

He missed his wife. He missed his daughter. He didn't particularly miss his son-in-law, but he sure missed his old life. Keeping up with Dobbin 24/7 was a chore. He was too old for this.

Frank finally slowed when he reached the gravel drive near his house. His wife and his daughter would say he'd been too hard on Dobbin.

Dammit. The kid could have been incinerated. Life without Dobbin was not to be contemplated.

He looked back at Dobbin, stumbling over the rough ground, head down, hands wiping his face as he cried. He looked the very epitome of a kid who was having a miserable day.

Frank waited until Dobbin got to the driveway of his house to say, "I think we should start this conversation over."

Dobbin drug a hand under his nose, sniffed, then nodded.

"It scared me," Frank said. "I don't want to lose you too."

Dobbin wiped his face. "I wasn't doing bad stuff. I was doing good stuff. I was making things right." He sniffed again. "I was trying, at least. And when I got stuck, I asked for help. That's what you tell me to do. And Jared was helping me."

"Why didn't you ask me? Why did you get help from that fancy-pants preacher's pet?"

Dobbin shrugged. "Because you said Larry was a low-life. I like Larry."

With a sigh, Frank clapped a hand on Dobbin's shoulder. "I like him too."

"Can we go back?"

"Let's feed the chickens," Frank said. "I want to grab a shower and check a few things."

"Then we can go back?"

"Sure. I think we'd better. Something tells me Larry is going to need all the help he can get."

*

Jared spoke to Bill Neddles. The realtor was leaning on his car, scrolling on an iphone.

"Could you give me a lift out to the gate?" Jared said. "Abigail wants me to invite another press team in."

"Sure. Let me text my son." Neddles took a moment, then said, "The interview is still on?"

"Yes. One o'clock."

Willie Neddles slouched out from the corner of the house. Jared tried on a smile, which Willie ignored.

"We're giving Jared a lift out to the gate," Neddles senior said. "Get in."

The surly teen threw himself into the back seat of the luxury car, saying, "This is such a stupid place. All they have is a barn full of cats."

Jared noticed Bill's eyes moving rapidly to the rearview mirror. Neddles said, "You left them alone, right, son?"

Willie shrugged. "Mostly."

A tremor went up Jared's spine. He was not liking Abigail's realtor and son.

Neddles eased the big car down the long drive. "Get the right media in and Abigail's life is going to be a lot easier."

"Yes, sir," Jared said. "Any outlet to recommend?"

"Just the usual. I saw a Prayer Daily truck, and Channel 15 from Seattle is a nice conservative station. Law and order sorts. They'll help you shift those squatters right out of that nice house."

"You need some muscle to move those losers out, I'm here to help," Willie said from the back seat.

Jared thought of Dobbin, scratching Violet in the sunshine.

"Now look at that," Neddles said, bringing the car to a stop near the Lucky Seven's front gate. "The big talent has rolled in.'"

*

Larry tried to calm his nerves. Aisha walked him through what was going to happen. He'd sit on a wicker loveseat in the catio with Dottie and Cosmos. Abigail Ross would be on a facing settee. Soo-Min would lead them through a discussion of the Rapture and the discovery of Dottie.

It sounded so simple. He was supposed to show, again, that he cared about Dottie, and that he could do a good job of taking care of the dog and the cats.

But he wasn't a complete idiot. There was more at stake. His mother and Aisha had made that clear. Facing down Abigail Ross meant showing the world he could handle this shit.

Of course, if it came down to government thugs with jack boots and smart bombs wanting Dottie, his goose was cooked. Except that it wasn't just him. It was his mother, Odelle, Ilene, Marcel, Annelise, Cosmos, Aisha, the twins and Harold. Everybody's goose-s would be cooked. Geese. Goose. Larry couldn't focus enough to decide.

He hated the feel of his dry mouth. If he drank a bunch of water right now, he'd have to go pee in the middle of the interview.

Janice and Marcel came in. Janice had a make-up kit and quickly dabbed powder over Larry's face.

"This will keep the shine down," she said.

He tried to hold still, but when Marcel said, "Are you saved?" Larry couldn't still a jerk of recoil.

"What the hell?" he said.

"Be still!" Janice said. "I've got just a few minutes, and I need to do Cosmos too."

Larry sat still, eyes on Marcel until Janice finished and left to find Cosmos.

"I asked," Marcel said, "Because it's a question that Abigail Ross is sure to work in. She'll try and pin you down as an outsider."

"Well, screw that." Larry frowned. "I get what you're saying. If I say, 'yes,' then she works the whole God angle. If I say, 'no,' then her team wins, I dunno, righteousness points or somethin'."

"You got it. What are you going to say?"

Larry grunted. "I guess I better think of some thin'."

"Look!" Marcel pointed to outside the catio windows. "That's Declan Hoopler!"

The nation's handsomest television news anchor paraded by, accompanied by Bill Neddles, his son Willie, Jared and a mild-looking man wearing glasses and a beige knit cardigan.

Larry took Dottie over to the settee. There was nothing

more he could do. His shirt was tucked in. His face was powdered. He had a sinking feeling that the interviewer was about to be Declan Hoopler instead of Soo Min.

He sat down on the right-side cushion, pulling Dottie into a "sit." The dog panted heavily and rested her head on Larry's knee. He commenced scratching her ears. If he blew this interview to hell, at least Dottie would have a good time.

Cosmos came in with Aisha and Marjorie. Cosmos offered a weak smile. Larry could see she'd been powdered, and her lips were a bright pink.

"You look great," he said.

Cosmos generated a slightly more confident smile. She sat down on the left-side cushion of the wicker loveseat, giving Larry plenty of room.

Aisha and Marjorie put their heads together. They conferred quietly and cast concerned looks at Larry and Cosmos.

Larry heard, "Sad-looking peckerwood," from his mother. Her tugboat-worthy voice carried, no matter what.

"Not well-balanced," Aisha agreed

Finally, Aisha came over and said, "We'd like to put a cat with Cosmos."

"Oh! One of the kittens!" Cosmos smiled.

"No. The Siamese," Aisha said.

Marjorie came forward carrying Bella, who fell into a purr once in Cosmos' lap.

Aisha stood back and studied the group. Larry, in his name-labeled uniform shirt and jeans, looked like any working man anywhere. Dottie looked like a working man's dog. Cosmos, colorful, pretty and plump, did not look like a television star, but she looked nice. Bella was the crowning touch. The cross-eyed cat turned toward the cameras and meowed, her bizarre eyes radiating sweetness.

"Good," Aisha said. "We've got the 'underdog look' nailed."

Larry suspected he wasn't supposed to have heard that. He sure hoped Cosmos hadn't.

Abigail Ross came into the catio, striding in with a strong, floating walk.

Larry watched her. He tried to calm his mind by thinking of Abigail as a food. She was a tall, trim woman with an air of confidence and substance. Her royal blue dress flowed from the shoulders down to a tucked waist and then flared out in a wide skirt. She wore a short, tailored eyelet jacket over the dress. It was a smooth dark periwinkle with a royal blue trim. She sat down on the opposing settee and crossed her elegant long legs at the ankle. A large gold cross necklace hung like a traffic sign pointing down to beautifully supported breasts. She smiled a smile of white teeth and smooth, red lips.

She's a French dip sandwich, Larry decided. *Nicely sliced roast brisket on a fresh-baked, sourdough roll with a side of fresh horseradish sauce and some salad made of the little green oak-leaf looking stuff. Not iceberg lettuce. Argula.*

The analysis made Larry nervous. He was more of a Junior Bacon-cheeseburger-off-the-Value Menu kind of guy.

He stroked Dottie's head and tried to suck in his gut.

"You must be Larry," Abigail said. She stretched out in a long lean forward, offering her hand.

"Yeah." Larry leaned forward and shook her hand,

hoping his own hand wasn't too gross with sweat and dog smell. "This is my friend Cosmos," he said.

Abigail turned a full watt smile on Cosmos, who stood up with Bella and stepped closer to shake Abigail's hand.

The televangelist said, "And the famous Dottie! Does she shake hands too?"

"Ah, sometimes. We're working on that." Larry threw a look at Cosmos, who raised her eyebrows. The video of Dottie shaking hands had gone, in Marcel's words, "super, duper, amazing hyper-viral." But Abigail hadn't seen it?

Cosmos lifted her shoulders, showing her uncertainty. Larry suddenly felt a smidge better. Dottie had fans. Serious fans. Lots of them.

Soo Min came in, with Clive and Vico. "There's been a change in plans," the reporter said. "Declan Hoopler is here, and Adam Roberts. Declan would like to do the interview, and Adam wants to do a radio broadcast."

Abigail raised an eyebrow. "CNN and NPR? You invited them in without consulting me?"

Larry eyed Aisha, who stood behind Vico at the big camera. Aisha looked aloof as always, but Larry thought he saw a hint of a smile tugging at her lips.

Jared stepped forward. "I invited them in, Abigail." He smiled like an eager puppy. "You said to bring in big names." His smile went to full grin. "We can't get any bigger than Declan Hoopler!"

"Science is nothing but perception."
Plato (428 - 348 B.C.E.)

CHAPTER FIFTY-FIVE

LARRY HAD TO hand it to Aisha. She stood her ground. Declan Hoopler wanted to bring in his own sound and film crew. Aisha said "No. Vico Carlevaro is our cameraman. Clive Trygstad is our lighting and sound person." She turned to Soo Min. "We arranged for you to do the interview. I'd like you to continue in that role."

Soo Min shook her head. "I've received directions from my station. I'm to support Mr. Hoopler."

"Very well," Aisha briskly agreed to the inevitable on the interviewer, but she held firm on Vico and Clive. "We are set up for a 1 p.m. broadcast. We don't have time to bring in more people." She added, "You've seen the crowd at the front gate. If we open that gate, we'll have a circus on our doorstep."

Adam Roberts went three shades of puce as Aisha briskly dealt with his radio broadcasting options. He wanted a separate interview with Larry. Aisha said he could broadcast the one p.m. conversation, but all other opportunities might be days away, if ever. Hoopler jumped in with objections of sharing the interview. In the end, Aisha said, "Our colleague Marcel's YouTube video is receiving millions of views as we speak. If we cannot come briskly to a conclusion here, we'll just ask Marcel to continue uploading new content."

Hoopler and Roberts took the deal.

Abigail Ross listened intently. She wanted to keep Clive on the set. She refrained from entering into the discussion, but she motioned Jared over. "What were you thinking?" she hissed in a whisper.

"Big names, big opportunity," Jared said. "You do well here, and you're gold." He winked at her even as his stomach boiled with acid. He wasn't really sure why he had come back with NPR and CNN representatives. It had seemed right at the moment.

Abigail could do little. "Get Bill and his son some chairs," she directed. "I need an audience."

"I" Jared noted. Not "We." He moved to obey.

Battling egos managed, Aisha stepped back and motioned to Vico and Clive.

Clive set Abigail up with a Lav lapel mike, gently tucking the transmitter into an inside jacket pocket. Abigail's clothes were tailored with smooth lines for television in mind. There would be no rasp from a stiff fabric or disconcerting glare off a white trim or checked shirt front.

Vico set up Larry and Cosmos. Larry's mic went on his shirt collar with the wire to the transmitter being snugged under the collar. Vico shoved the transmitter into Larry's rear waistband with a grin. "This system can pick up small noises. Sit still," Vico said. "And try not to fart."

He was gentler with Cosmos, then turned to coordinate the set up with Clive.

"Welcome," Soo Min said into the camera. "This is

Soo Min Carlevaro coming to you live from Olympia, Washington. This afternoon we are sharing a conversation about the Rapture and the appearance of a dog in western Washington. Our guests today are Abigail Ross of the Ross Hour of Prayer and Larry Dinkelman and Cosmos Ponomarenko of Larry's Post-Rapture Pet-sitting Services. We also have Dottie, the dog, and Bella, the cat, with us. Our moderator this afternoon is Declan Hoopler. This interview is being simultaneously broadcast on NPR stations."

The camera view shifted to Declan Hoopler. Behind him, Larry nervously licked his lips and cast his eyes about. Marjorie, Marcel, Annelise, and Ilene were standing at the back of the catio watching and all four put a hand to mouth in worry. Larry looked shifty as hell.

Hoopler began easily enough with a hello, but Abigail moved to take control of the interview. "We should open in prayer," she said. "You don't mind, do you, Larry?"

"Ahhh," Larry said.

"Lord!" Abigail shouted, holding her arms aloft. "Lord! Give us relief and comfort in these challenging times. Guide us, Lord, to a place of peace."

Around the globe, millions of people marked off "words of inclusion" on their Bingo card. They also marked off "speaks with confidence" and "identifies something you want." In a number of homes there was spirited discussion as to whether Abigail's royal blue dress was a "bright" color.

Abigail said, "We know, Lord, from Deuteronomy 8:2 that You led the faithful through the wilderness for forty years, testing and humbling Your followers so the contents of their hearts would be clear. It was shown who kept Your commandments."

Abigail took a breath to continue.

Marcel quietly slid out of the back door of the catio. He held up his smart phone and hit the Instagram app. Holding the smart phone at arm's length he said, "Those of you playing the B5 Rapture Bingo card are close to filling a full line on the card already. I invite you to play a "black-out" version. Keep watching and see if you can check off every square on the cards."

He repeated his message on Twitter, then eased back into the catio just in time to hear Abigail pronounce an "Amen."

*

Up in his house, Frank came out of the shower and turned on the radio, permanently set to NPR. He caught the opening introductions and now heard Abigail's prayer.

"Lord love a duck," Frank said. "NPR is actually broadcasting that Christ-jacking bible-up-my-ass-ology?" He took a breath and added, "How do you show animal-handling skills on a radio show?"

Grabbing his jeans and hopping to the living room as he tried to move and insert a foot into a pants leg, he yelled for Dobbin.

"We gotta get down there," Frank said, as Dobbin came out of the kitchen. "Larry needs our help."

*

Declan Hoopler moved in with his first question. To Larry, he said, "What do you think about the Rapture?"

"Ahhh." Larry took a breath. "My friend Marcel, is a

smart guy. He thinks there's a mechanism to it. We don't understand it just yet, but it may something to do with a person's biochemistry. Who we are could give us a certain biochemistry, and that may be firing off sump-thin'."

"Interesting." Declan Hoopler leaned forward in his chair. "I haven't heard this theory. Is Marcel a scientist?"

Larry thought of the Moscow Mule he'd once had at Odelle's place. It'd been a fizzy and smooth cocktail with a ton of kick. Declan Hoopler was a walking, talking Moscow Mule.

"Not yet," Larry said. "Marcel sure is smart, though." Larry knew this was a weak answer.

Hoopler confirmed Larry's person-to-food analysis with his next question. "Larry, are you Saved? Have you taken Jesus Christ as your personal savior?"

Larry blinked. He thought that question would be coming from Abigail. He looked over to the televangelist and saw she had a raised eyebrow and a small, frozen smile. The question seemed to be a surprise to her too.

"Sure!" Larry said. "I call on Jesus H. Christ all the time." He reached out a hand to stroke Dottie's head. His large knuckles, undusted by makeup powder, had a shine in the lights. "I'm kinda dyslexic, so Dog is my co-pilot."

Hoopler burst out in laughter. Abigail frowned, her eyebrows slashing together in a furious V.

The news anchor said, "Is that why you're the one who found Dottie?"

Larry shook his head. "I didn't find her. Our friend Annelise found her and came and told me. Then the Larry Pet-Sitting Services team went out together."

"Right. I remember seeing that." Hoopler turned to Abigail. He said, "And, Ms. Ross . . ."

"Abigail, please." If Larry was going to play the "I'm just a regular guy" card, Abigail wasn't going to insist on formalities.

"Alright. Abigail, why do you think we've had this Rapture?" Hoopler said.

"Obviously this is the will of God. We are seeing God's discontent with our wicked ways, and God's blessings coming to those who are pure in heart. Those of us remaining are called to follow Christ. We must pay attention to the signs that those in female-led households will be protected. We must embrace the sweet beauty of honorable women. In the Bible, Proverbs 31:10 tells us the virtuous woman is more valuable than rubies, and she is worthy of trust."

Abigail took a breath and plunged on. "Which is why I am here today. I am ready to take up the work of planting fresh vineyards. I am ready to reach hands out to embrace the poor and the afflicted."

She straightened up another inch.

Larry was impressed. Abigail had excellent posture.

Abigail said, "We must all work to be like the woman of Proverbs 31. 'Strength and honor are her clothing; she shall rejoice in the time to come. She opens her mouth with wisdom, and her tongue is the law of kindness."

*

A group of men in a tavern in Dubuque were watching the interview over early afternoon beers. When Abigail said, "Her tongue is the law of kindness," the men moved in unison to mark "promises words of relief" on their bingo cards.

*

Abigail lectured on with "Favor is deceitful, beauty is vain; but the woman who fears the Lord, she shall be praised! Give her the reward she has earned! What we need, Declan, is a new world order. Not of women taking control, like our President is trying to do with her diabolical Disciples of Discipline."

She said, "Nor do we need women ignored, as the ministers in the Medina council are doing. We need women working the earth, reaping its goodness and managing our homes and lives with a fresh commitment to Christ. That is what this Rapture is telling us."

"And you think you are the right person to lead everyone?" Hoopler's tone was polite.

"I am one of many. I am here, with Dottie, and I am ready to serve."

Vico, eye to the television camera's rear viewer, marveled. The camera loved Abigail. He knew some of the things that cameras loved. Wide set eyes, strong features, full lips, and a small chin all helped, but Abigail had something extra. Her personality seemed to shine through, giving an aura of earnestness and light.

Above the interview, crouched on the upper catwalk of the catio, sat a gray cat with lime-green eyes. He looked down at Dottie and lashed his tail.

"All cats are gray at night."
A Russian Proverb

CHAPTER FIFTY-SIX

"LARRY, WHAT ARE your plans for Dottie?" Declan Hoopler's voice was smooth and matter-of-fact.

"We're going to keep working with her," Larry said. "Good food. Exercise. Some training. Cosmos here has been our lead on the training part."

Hoopler didn't take the re-direct. He stayed focused on Larry. "And you think you're qualified to take care of the world's only dog?"

"Ahh," Larry said. He couldn't help it. He looked around the room, seeing Aisha, Marjorie and Ilene standing at the back behind Vico. Marcel stood further back in the catio. Marcel flashed a thumbs up. "Yeah," Larry managed, knowing he looked shifty-eyed. "I think we'll do alright."

"But you're a convicted felon," Abigail interrupted. "And you've been handing stolen goods to a minor, haven't you?"

There was a giant moment of silence as Larry struggled to breathe.

"Let's pause for a commercial break," Declan Hoopler said. "We'll be right back."

Hoopler knew his business. For the next five minutes, the millions of people watching would sit through whatever combination of ads his producers wanted to insert. No one would want to miss Larry's response to Abigail's charge.

Janice, standing behind Vico, closed her eyes. She couldn't watch any more of this. Abigail looked and sounded fabulous. Janice edged away. She found the back-exit door and gently opened it. She stepped into the May sunshine and eased the door shut.

Janice turned away from the house, bowed her head and said a prayer. "Lord, guide us. Be with us. Help us find a way forward that is truly in Your service."

An old pickup came bouncing over the field to her left. Janice watched as Frank drove the truck up to the fence. He and his grandson climbed out. Frank lifted Dobbin over the fence, then clambered over himself.

They jogged over to her.

"How's Larry holding up?" Frank demanded.

"Not so good," Janice said. "Abigail is sounding marvelous, and Larry looks . . ."

"Like a shifty lowlife?" Frank said.

"I was going to say 'uncertain.' Overall he's not doing well."

"Come on, Dobbin. The world needs to know Larry's good side," Frank said. "I've got an idea."

*

Janice wasn't the only one convinced Abigail was already the winner of the day. Bill Neddles nudged his son. The two stood up, then eased along to the back door. Neddles motioned to Jared, who stood up and followed.

Outside on the lawn, Neddles said, "Willie and I are going back to the front gate. Abigail's going to own this place by evening. She'll have the dog and a following of thousands. Maybe millions. I'll bet we can get a news organization like the Prayer Daily group to buy one these valley cabins. Full price."

"I understand," Jared said, shaking hands. He added a smile and disciplined himself not to wipe his hand on his trousers after gripping Willie's sweaty palm.

"That was a brilliant piece of work," Neddles said. "Inviting CNN and NPR in. I thought you'd lost your mind, but Abigail is doing so well in there. You are one hell of a PR man."

"Thanks." Jared put on another bright smile and said, "Got to get back in there. Have a nice day." His face fell into a scowl as he turned away. Now, more than ever, he was ready for a change.

*

Thirty yards away, Janice walked down to the vegetable garden. She saw Harold and Odelle resting under a tree, with the two little girls asleep on a blanket laid on a swath of grass.

Janice approached quietly.

"How's it going?" Harold said.

"Not well." Janice sighed. "Abigail is so very good on television."

"And Larry's not," Odelle said.

"Not so far." Janice looked out over the blooming orchard, her heart heavy with confusion and no small amount of grief.

"How are you holding up?" Harold said.

Janice laughed, a short, bitter bark. "Also, not so very well." She looked down at the sleeping toddlers. "They are so sweet and innocent."

She knelt down beside the sleeping girls, tears flowing. "I spent so many, many years on the wrong path. I'd like to say we were innocents, but we just closed our eyes to what Abigail was doing. She is so very good, but I should have seen. I am an idiot."

Harold shook his head. "I don't think you are stupid. I'll bet there were good actions and important moments in those years."

Janice wiped her face and sniffed. "You're right. We did do some good."

Odelle reached out and patted Janice's shoulder. "What can we do to help?"

"Join me in prayer?" Janice reached out her hands.

Harold and Odelle formed a circle with Janice, who said, "Lord, please send your love and guidance. Larry needs some help right now. Give us an instrument to serve Your will. Please help us to act with courage and kindness. Amen."

"Amen," Odelle repeated. She gently let go of Janice's hand and said, "What would make *you* happiest?"

Janice thought for a moment. "I've always wanted to play piano," she said. "I had some lessons when I was a kid, but I froze during the fall recital. My mother said the embarrassment wasn't worth the lesson fees."

Harold grinned. "There's a baby grand at my house. It came with the music room. Neither my late wife or I knew how to play. It's been untouched for years. If you want a piano, you can have it."

Janice smiled. "A baby grand? No, thank you. I'm not sure what Clive wants to do next. Wherever we end up, it'll be a small place, but thank you." Janice wiped her face again.

She said, "We might go somewhere and teach. Or maybe Clive will work in sound, and I'll do some volunteering." She smiled again. "Your good cheer is very kind. I do feel better."

Clasping her hands together, Janice looked down with a worried expression. "Clive tells me to be open to new things, and not to pray for a specific action. Our horizons can be too small, and it's best to not be locked into one way or one set of tools. I am going to trust that a path will become clear, even if I am not seeing the way forward just yet. There are instruments God can use that I cannot see."

Janice looked up from studying her clasped hands. She frowned, and said, "Good heavens, what is Frank up to?"

*

The commercial break didn't help Larry any. His brain stayed frozen. Abigail knew about the Rolex. She knew about Dobbin.

Aisha could not advise him. Declan Hoopler was sitting at the front of the interview space, going nowhere. It would not look good to receive coaching from the sidelines. Aisha remained behind the video cameras, leaning in, with her thumbs up.

Everyone else was crowded back against the catio wall of windows. Marjorie looked pale and worried. Marcel was frowning and whispering to Annelise. Soo Min's face was still and unsmiling.

Larry swallowed and rubbed the scratches on his forehead. "Think," he muttered.

Ilene did manage a word of support. She walked up briskly carrying bottles of water. She handed one to Abigail, then one to Cosmos. As she handed a bottle to Larry, she side-whispered, "Fight, dammit!"

The commercial break was over all too soon. Ilene collected the bottles, and Declan Hoopler asked. "Are you a thief, Larry?"

"Ahh," Larry said. He couldn't help it. His eyes flew around the catio. Dottie, still sitting at his feet, shifted her front paws and whined.

Did he deny what Abigail said? What proof did she have? Would they put Dobbin on television?

Would Frank use his guts for garters? That was a given, he decided.

"Ahh," he said. Shit. He might as well say "Guilty, your Honor."

He could see Aisha looking at him, intensely focused. Cosmos put her hand on his elbow.

Aisha had told him to own his sins. He'd already told Annelise about going to prison for kiting checks. The whole world had watched that conversation. And Cosmos already knew what a screw up he could be. Cosmos even knew about the watch.

Suddenly Larry knew what he had to say. He cleared his throat and looked at Abigail.

"First," he said, "I did screw up recently. I picked up a Rolex that wasn't mine and put it in my pocket. I'm damn lucky I didn't vaporize on the spot."

Abigail looked triumphant.

But Larry wasn't finished. He said, "Number Two, I'm working to fix my mistake."

Cosmos smiled. He could see Aisha nodding her head.

Larry scratched Dottie's ears. The dog panted and leaned into Larry's legs. "And Number Three," Larry said, "I'm not ashes yet, so the Good Lord must be fine with me, even if you're not."

*

In Moscow, men holding down bar stools cheered. "*Molod'yets, Larry!*" one yelled. Moments later #Attaboy-Larry was trending in fourteen languages.

*

Declan Hoopler now spoke to Cosmos and said, "What is your take on choosing our next leaders?"

Cosmos lifted her chin; a move Janice had suggested with a whisper into her ear an hour earlier. With some considerable dignity, Cosmos said, "We want to believe what we are told. But I am in the veterinary care industry, and I know people's loyalties can stop up the information they can take in."

Her sweet, round face fell into a frown as she said, "People don't want to hear about their loved one dying.

They don't want to hear there is no cure. We all love the idea of miracles because miracles could make our lives easier."

She looked at Abigail and said, "People really hope you are right, and a new world order is going to fix things." Cosmos shook her head. "But predators are going to feed on that hope. We can't believe any words an entertainer or politician or pastor says."

Declan Hoopler leaned in. "That sounds terribly grim. We can't believe *any* words?"

"No. We can't believe words." Cosmos said. "We have to watch behaviors. When we study an animal or a person and really get to know them, then we can predict how they will act next."

She fondled Bella's ears, and the cross-eyed cat purred. Vico brought the camera focus in close as Cosmos said, "Larry has a talent with animals. I have seen this consistently. I think he accepts animals as they are." She gave a half smile as she glanced at Abigail, "Well, most animals."

Aisha's smile widened.

Cosmos shifted on the loveseat. "I think it may take years of study to understand this Rapture stuff – meanwhile there will be people being predators. They'll be doing their best to get ahead, and they will use our feelings. They'll make big promises to benefit themselves."

"Why do you think Dottie wasn't taken up with the other dogs?" Hoopler asked.

Cosmos shrugged. "Different biochemistry? Different mental state? We don't know."

"Do you think Larry is the best person to take care of Dottie?" Hoopler casually crossed his legs, "Given Larry's criminal past and lack of formal education in dog care?"

"The best person?" Cosmos grinned. "Try that on any parent! What if only the best people got to have a kid? Sometimes 'not being the best' is where we start, and a chance to prove ourselves is a path to improvement!"

At the back of the room, Aisha flashed a double thumbs up. Cosmos was nailing it.

Declan Hoopler turned to Abigail. "What do you think of that? Larry as an imperfect person having a second chance?"

"Of course, I believe in second chances," Abigail said. "I preach redemption every day. I am not seeking perfection, but a path forward for all people. I want to build a movement of love and acceptance. However, we also need to be wise with God's gifts and alert to God's instructions."

She pointed at Larry. "You wear the mark of the Beast," Abigail said. "On your forehead."

"Huh?" Larry stared at her.

Declan Hoopler said, "The mark of the Beast is from the book of Revelations in the Bible. It's a mark on the forehead or right hand. It's said the beast is the anti-Christ, who arises from the sea and marks his followers."

"Huh." Larry reached up and rubbed the twin scratches on his forehead. "I got this from an orange tiger kitty who didn't want to go into a transport box. She used me as an escape route." He smiled. "We were able to get her moved, and she's doing fine."

"So, your scratches are not the Mark of the Beast," Declan Hoopler said.

"She's definitely a beast," Larry corrected. "But she's not from the sea or even from a lake. We picked her up from Little Rock, south of Tumwater."

At that moment a large gray cat stalked onto the impromptu studio set, his movements smooth and stately. With an immense regal air, the cat stalked by Dottie, Larry, Cosmos and Bella with no acknowledgement of any sort. The cat went directly to Abigail. He paused for a moment before leaping up gracefully to the cushion space on her right.

With an aplomb worthy of any media star, the cat turned to the camera, giving Vico a money shot of intense green eyes.

"Oh," Abigail smiled. She reached out and stroked the cat's head.

Larry could feel his own eyes bugging out. "Be careful," he said, "That guy's not always friendly."

A deep booming purr emanated from under Abigail's hand. "Looks like Larry's not the only one who can connect with animals," she said. "What's this kitty's name?"

"Well," said Larry. "His name is Lucifer."

The verdict of the world is conclusive.

St. Augustine (354 - 430)

CHAPTER FIFTY-SEVEN

TWO THINGS HAPPENED simultaneously. Abigail's hands tightened on the cat as she processed the name 'Lucifer,' and Dobbin opened the back door of the catio. Frank brought in Violet, using the catch pole to steer the pig.

Lucifer wasn't a cat accustomed to being handled. Abigail's shock grasp didn't just irritate. It was intolerable. Lucifer twisted with a hiss and raked the back of Abigail's right hand.

"Sonnaofabitch!" Abigail shouted.

Lucifer swarmed up Abigail's front, intent on the cat tower behind her. His claws dug into her dress front and jacket as the televangelist swatted at the cat. He gouged her cheek with a front claw as he journeyed up, then raked her forehead with a hind foot as he made it to the top of her head.

Abigail howled and swatted at the cat as he launched from her head to the cat-resting platform holding the two sleeping kittens. Abigail pivoted and sprang out of the loveseat, lunging after Lucifer. Her hands collided with one of the waking kittens.

A horrific gasp united millions of viewers as they saw Abigail grab the kitten and pitch it out of her way. The kitten sailed through the air, rotating as it dropped. The little cat landed on its feet, but it was a near thing.

Viewers saw Cosmos's face, a study in shocked horror, as the kitten arced through the air. Cosmos scooped up the stunned kitten one-handed as she cradled the cross-eyed Bella in her other arm.

Lucifer's tail stood erect as a cell phone tower, giving Vico a clear camera view of the cat's tight anus and rear legs as the cat's muscles contracted to support a steady stream of urine shot in a straight line to Abigail's right shoulder.

Abigail roared a "Fuck you!" as she lunged after Lucifer.

Frank pulled the release on the catch pole. Violet came rocketing forward to greet Larry.

Dottie saw the incoming pig and immediately leapt up into Larry's lap, doing her best imitation of a terrified Chihuahua.

Violet charged past Abigail, the pig's mass pushing against the back of Abigail's legs, sending her crashing into the settee and setting off a new round of ripe profanity.

Larry found himself doing three things at once. His left arm encircled Dottie as he said, "You're okay," while his right hand reached down to scratch Violet's ears. His stomach, however, shook with laughter. His round belly jiggled and millions of viewers howled along, enjoying the melee.

Lucifer swarmed up the cat tower to the cat walk and quickly disappeared into the patio's upper foliage.

Abigail whirled around and shouted at Larry. "This is not funny!"

Larry was laughing too hard to respond. Violet leaned against his legs, grunting. Dottie shifted in his lap and licked his face.

Cosmos, however, had plenty to say. "Don't you EVER throw a kitten like that again!"

"Oh, fuck you sideways, you fat little turd!" Abigail stomped off toward the back door, stopping to scream at Jared. "I said 'fair and balanced' and you brought in CNN and NPR!"

"I take complete responsibility," Jared said. "And offer my resignation."

"You can't resign!"

"Okay. I quit."

"Jared, we've been fucking like rabbits. You owe me. You can't quit!"

"I just did."

"You want me to leave you out here in this cluster-fuck of a zoo?"

Jared shrugged. "Actually, I think Larry could use a good PR man. If he'll take me, I'll volunteer to help."

"You snake!" Abigail hissed. "God is going to turn you into a pile of cinders. And when he does, I will, by God, vacuum your ashes up in a sweeper, just like I did that pile of charcoal that was Aaron!"

"Ah, Abigail?" Jared pointed to her jacket front. "I believe that lapel mic is still transmitting."

Abigail tore the jacket off. She flung it and the transmitter to the ground. She stormed out of the catio, slamming the door as she went.

"I believe this brings us to the end of our interview with Abigail Ross," Declan Hoopler said. "It looks like

Larry has a future here caring for Dottie and the Lucky Seven Ranch."

A scattering of raindrops hit the windows of the catio, followed by a bright May sunbeam which created a rainbow on the wall behind Larry, Dottie and Cosmos.

Aisha looked at Marcel and smiled. She said, "I do set my bow in the clouds."

Marcel said, "as the everlasting covenant between God and every living creature."

"Amen to that," Marjorie said. "Anybody else need a beer?"

*

Dottie's Tails Blog – June 16

Hey, Dottie Fans! Today was a big day at the Lucky Seven Ranch. Our friends Odelle and Harold were married in the orchard under the apple trees. Reverend Charles Westmoreland officiated. Naomi and Esther Westmoreland were Brides-toddlers in matching dresses of light pink.

Dottie wore a smashing bowtie adorned with pink rhinestones.

Harold's assistant, Janice, played "Chopsticks" on a portable electric keyboard and the bridal bouquet was caught by our very own Cosmos!

After a honeymoon weekend in Tenino, Harold and Odelle will resume their work as nannies and non-profit organizers.

Check back tomorrow for Marcel's report on Larry's Pet-sitting Services T-shirt sales. We're launching a new

shirt soon with a big picture of Lucifer. Get your devil on and pre-order! Remember, all proceeds go to support the Lucky Seven Ranch and nationwide cat-spaying programs! Ciao,
Annelise.

Emails – June 17

Dear Ms. Stewart-Westmoreland,

My son Willie has been incarcerated on attempted rape and assault charges. He needs a good attorney. I am prepared to offer you a discount on commercial office space in return for your work representing Willie.

Sincerely,
Bill Neddles

Dear Mr. Neddles,

Currently Ms. Stewart-Westmoreland is limiting her services to low-income clients. She is focusing on sentence mitigation and parole-reduction actions. This work has been generously supported by a local donor and the Church of the Evergreen Life, where our offices are currently located. We are filing for non-profit status, but we will continue to have a limited scope of services. As a result, we are not the proper office to fit the needs of your son at this time.

Thank you for your interest in the Second Chance Post-Rapture Legal Services office.

Sincerely,
Marjorie Dinkelman
Special Assistant to Ms. Stewart-Westmoreland

*

A tired musician slid her harp into its hard case and snapped the case lid shut. She began the tricky job of wheeling the large case out to her car. Three hours of performing background music for tourists enjoying high tea did not pay well. It was also hell on her body. Everything hurt. She should take some paracetamol. Screw that. It was too exhausting to dig through her bag for a vial that was almost certainly empty.

She trudged on, head down, gathering an eyeful of undusted baseboards lining the hallway leading to the hotel's kitchen. She trundled the harp case to the back door. She'd have to cross the ankle-twisting cobblestone alley to reach the grungy staff parking lot. And she'd have to hold her hemline high. Harpists played in beautiful long gowns not made for crossing muddy lanes.

She tried not to think about lifting the harp and fitting it into the back of her tiny economy car. Thinking about the finger-pinching, muscle-straining struggle might trigger a bout of tears.

The week ahead looked grim. Rain forecast. No bookings. Rent due. It was all a bit too much. Harpists were glamour girls except when they weren't on stage – which was most of the time. Practicing harps and moving harps called for the skills of both a fruit-picker and a stevedore.

She opened the heavy metal exit door and gave a great cry of surprise, causing two waiters and a bartender on break to come rushing through the kitchen to render aid.

All four people watched a shower of feathers falling from the sky. As the feather-fall intensified, a figure coalesced at ground level. A lanky, tall dog emerged, feathers resting on his tawny curls as he ambled out of the feather storm.

The harpist fell to her knees, her harp and harp case crashing to the asphalt, as the Irish wolfhound came to her and accepted her shower of tears and a warm welcome to the city of Cork.

At the same time, a beagle showed up in Milwaukee, and a toy poodle appeared on a beach in Uruguay. An outback bar in Australia acquired a small, scruffy Affenpinscher, who was promptly named "Foster" by the cheering patrons.

In the space of ten minutes, two hundred and forty-five dogs returned to the planet.

The End for Now

ON THE ORIGINS OF LARRY

In 2011 a man named Bart Centre offered an online-sub-scription service for Post-Rapture pet care. Any one taken up to Heaven and subsequently unavailable for Fido's "walkies" would know their pet was registered for guardianship services. Bart charged one hundred and thirty-five dollars to enroll a cat or dog.

Bart's business, Eternal Earth-Bound Pets, ran into trouble with the New Hampshire Insurance Department, resulting in Bart stating his service was an attempt at satirical humor. He had not acquired any paying clients.

However, as Bart retired from the post-Rapture Pet Ser-vices industry, a woman professing an ardent Christian faith set up the After the Rapture Pet Care website. This registry promises "Biblically appropriate" pet care. The registration fee is ten dollars. The unnamed organizer promises non-Christian volunteers are standing by to access a database of the registered pets and will coordinate post-Rapture services. There is no mention of who will be paying for post-Rapture kibble or veterinary bills.

I was driving home late one evening in 2019, clicking through radio channels, when I heard two DJ's discussing the psychological illness of "Left Behind" anxieties. Anxieties are real and can be formidable, but DJ's are consistently cheeky sorts. I wasn't sure how much of what was being said was in jest.

One DJ described the pet care registry as an example of the anti-anxiety post-Rapture industry. He said the website had to be a scam as no one could ensure this pet-sitting service worked in the chaos which would follow the Rapture. His talk show partner joked a fictional "Larry" designated to activate a database of pet care volunteers would not do so because "Larry" would be thinking about other things.

When I arrived home, I checked online. After the Rapture Pet Care still has an active website with T-shirts, coffee mugs, and tote bags available for purchase.

I couldn't get Larry out of my mind. I could picture him, imperfect, worried, agnostic and contemplating a list of cats . . . It was, I thought, time to tell Larry's story. Now, in the summer of 2020, protests of great injustices and a pandemic roil America. I hope all the imperfect Larrys will keep going, despite knowing society has stacked the deck against them. Please move forward, with a beer, a cigarette, a dog or a pickle to meet the challenges of the times.

"Onward" is the only way out of the darkness.

FRIENDS ON THE JOURNEY

Larry's adventure began on a drive home from an open-mic night at the Arbutus Folk School in Olympia, Washington. I am grateful to Stacey Waterman-Hoey and Mark Iler for hosting the Arbutus open-mic and to all the musicians who enrich my life, especially my husband and editorial advisor, Cliff.

I also appreciate the Tuesday Rebels, Connie Jasperson, Lee French, Melissa Carpenter, Johanna Flynn and Jane Martin, who chose to love Larry. Judy Kiehart, Diana Reale and Sheila Rodriguez of the Olympia Writer's Group are delightful and powerful editors who kept me from many, but not all, of the mistakes that writers can make. Steve King offered early words of encouragement, which were particularly appreciated as I know him as an avid bibliophile.

I'm also deeply indebted to Sally and Gregg Bennett. Sally keeps me sane and healthy as a partner in documenting the neighborhood fungi, and Gregg cast an educated eye on my make-believe congregation of animals.

Jim Dempsey of Novel Gazing and Leighann Brownwood of ohleighann gave critical feedback that helped

Larry's story significantly. Finally, the talented team at Damonza.com designed the cover and rescued me from the nightmares of book formatting. I most truly could not have done this without your support.

Sooner or later I'll realize that I've left a name off this section. I'll be horrified as I recall what a good egg that friend or family member is, and I'll be truly contrite. Know you are loved and valued even as my brain temporarily parked you in a spot obscured with a thick mental fog.

Thank you, everyone! You are so appreciated and loved.